Other Sorrows,
Other Joys

Also by Janet Warner

Blake and the Language of Art

Other Sorrows, Other Joys

THE MARRIAGE OF
CATHERINE SOPHIA BOUCHER
AND WILLIAM BLAKE

Janet Warner

St. Martin's Press ≈ New York

For J. P. W.

www.stmartins.com

Design by Phil Mazzone

Library of Congress Cataloging-in-Publication Data

Warner, Janet A. (Janet Adele), 1931–
    Other sorrows, other joys : the marriage of Catherine Sophia Boucher and William Blake
/ Janet Warner.—1st ed.
        p. cm.
    ISBN 0-312-31440-X
        1. Blake, Catherine Boucher—Fiction. 2. Blake, William, 1757–1827—Fiction.
    3. Authors' spouses—Fiction. 4. Married people—Fiction. 5. England—Fiction.
    6. Artists—Fiction. 7. Poets—Fiction. I. Title.

PR9199.4.W36O74 2003
813'.6—dc21

                                                                        2003046836

First Edition: December 2003

10 9 8 7 6 5 4 3 2 1

$\mathcal{L}$ist of $\mathcal{I}$llustrations

Original works are by William Blake (1757–1827), and on paper, unless otherwise noted.

This is the imagined life of a woman who really lived in the late eighteenth century—Catherine Sophia Boucher, called Kate—wife of the English poet and artist, William Blake. If you read between the lines of his poetry and letters, this is a story you might find . . .

What is the price of Experience? do men buy it for a Song?
Or wisdom for a dance in the street? No, it is bought with the price
Of all that a man hath, his house, his wife, his children.
Wisdom is sold in the desolate market where none come to buy,
And in the wither'd field where the farmer ploughs for bread in vain.

Mutual Forgiveness of each Vice
Such are the Gates of Paradise

Ah, are there other wars, beside the wars of sword and fire!
And are there other sorrows, beside the sorrows of poverty!
And are there other joys, beside the joys of riches and ease?

—WILLIAM BLAKE

Part One

LONDON 1829

Blake, *Eve Naming the Birds* (c. 1810), pen and tempera on fine linen (73.5 × 62 cm). Courtesy of Glasgow Museums: The Stirling Maxwell Collection, Pollok House

1

In Which I, Catherine Blake, Decide To Tell My Story To Mr. Tatham, and Recollect My Early Years

From the Journal of Mr. Frederick Tatham, age 24, Sculptor, and Biographer of William Blake, Artist, Poet, and Visionary. April 12, 1829. 20 Lisson Grove, London.

*A*lthough almost two years have passed since the death of my friend the Inspired Engraver and Poet, William Blake, for whom I had the Honour of being Executor, it has never occurred to me till now that I might record for Posterity the recollections of his Beloved Wife, Catherine, who is now my Housekeeper.

It is my Desire to compile a Life of this extraordinary Man, whose Art is as Sublime as his Poetry Obscure, and how better to Understand his Nature than through the words of his devoted Companion in Life?

Indeed Catherine herself is worthy of a Memoir, as she is to my Wife and myself a dear friend, as kind as a Mother or affectionate Sister. We call her Kate, as her husband did. She toils for us harder than she should, for she is past sixty years, and since Mr. Blake's death, increasingly frail. Though careworn, her Visage still shows the traces of a face which must have been lovely in youth, and her Eyes are black and lit with an inner fire, much like Mr. Blake's, and she certainly has a Will of her own.

And what Obedience and Devotion her dear soul showed to her William! Because she had never been a mother, Blake was at once her lover, husband, child.

She would get up in the night, when he was under his very fierce Inspirations, which were as if they would tear him asunder, while he was yielding himself to the Muse, or whatever else it could be called, sketching and writing. And so terrible a task did this seem to be, that she had to sit motionless and silent, only to stay him mentally, without moving hand or foot: this for hours, and night after night!

I will entreat her to tell me her story.

From Kate's Notebook.
April 12, 1829.

Now that the supper plates are all put away, and the hearths cleaned and ready for the morning fires for Mr. Tatham, I climb the stairs to my little white-washed room at the top of the house and wait for William. He always comes. First the sound of his voice: "Kate, beloved," he says. Then the room lights up even though I have only one candle. And there he is.

He looks as he did when he was well: broad and strong, with his grey eyes bright and smiling, his brow clear. He sits in the chair by my bed, and he tells me what to do. Today he says I should let Mr. Percy buy his books, so tomorrow I will tell Mr. Tatham, who will be pleased I agree with him for once.

When William sees that all is well with me, he will sing me a song before he goes. It will be even lovelier than the ones he wrote when he was alive, though my favourite is still *Infant Joy*, the poem for the baby we lost so long ago.

Tonight I say to him, "Mr. Blake, is our baby with you? Is she happy now that you are with her?"

"My beloved Kate," he says, "she is happy. Who cannot be happy in these fields of light? When you come, I will show you."

And so I am content, and go to bed.

. . .

I have not always been content with William, in spite of so many years when I was happy to be his wife, and help with his Art. Now that I am old and have time to remember, I still resent poor Mary Wollstonecraft and all her brilliance. Nor do I forget beautiful Elizabeth Billington, who sang her way into William's heart and nearly broke mine. Yes, a Marriage is made up of many more people than the two who are in it!

All my life I knew I was considered the perfect wife for William Blake. I was helpmate to a talented artist—some even thought him a Genius. Or a Madman. I, on the other hand, was perfect—which meant I always did what was expected of me. And so I did, most of the time. Some Secrets, however, I kept to myself.

Mr. Tatham is trying to help me sell some of William's work.

Excerpts from a Letter to a Gentleman which Mr. Tatham wrote for me yesterday.
April 11, 1829. Regent's Park, London.

Sir,

In behalf of the widow of the late William Blake, I have to inform you that her circumstances render her glad to embrace your Kind offer for the purchase of some of the works of her departed husband...

The artists of the fourteenth and fifteenth centuries have done much, but they had friends, pupils, and every assistance; but this man had to struggle with poverty in a Commercial Country, and has produced these *mountains of labour*, with the assistance only of a fascinated and devoted wife, who, as a beautiful damsel, loved, as a woman, cherished, as a wife, obeyed—as a willing slave incessantly laboured, and as an aged nurse, attended, and alleviated his last sickness; and now, as bereaved, deplores but patiently acquiesces.

...I can only add, that, should you, Sir, be inclined to possess, for the embellishment of your own collection and the benefit of the widow, any of the enumerated works, they shall be carefully sent to you upon your remitting payment.

And communicating either with myself or Mrs. Blake, you will Receive her ample thanks and the acknowledgements

of your obedient and humble Servant
Frederick Tatham

Yes, I was a fascinated and devoted wife . . . but a willing slave? I was his partner! An aged nurse? Strange, but I have never thought of myself as old.

April 15, 1829.

When William visited me last evening, he said it was a good idea for me to tell Mr. Tatham about our life together, about our early successes, about the quarrels, about that awful Trial, and our descent into Poverty, though rich in Vision always. But shall I tell him about my true struggle, about my Jealousy of William, about my temptations and deceptions? Perhaps it will help me see my life better—to expiate my Guilt—if I now speak of my life, and pray the Good Lord will inspire my thoughts and guide me through the terrors of Memory.

We sit in the Morning Room at Lisson Grove. While Mr. Tatham takes a dish of tea, I clasp my hands carefully on my white linen over-skirt, and begin . . .

It was a cool English summer that year, the year I met William Blake. The cottage was dark, but the morning fire kept it cheerful and warm as I sat by the hearth, a girl of nineteen, peering at myself in a bit of polished brass, trying to see if I looked ready to go to Church. I saw a tangle of curly black hair, black eyes, a pale complexion—considering how much time I spent outside in the market garden—and good teeth. I laughed at myself, mostly because I, Catherine Sophia Boucher of Battersea, felt good to be alive in the year of Our Lord 1781. I expected to see William at St. Mary's Church, since we had spoken recently in the Churchyard when he was drawing the tombstones.

I knew I was going to marry William. My Voices told me I would meet my future husband under my own roof—and so it had happened. My Voices are never wrong. They have spoken to me all my life, even before I met William, who had his own Voices and Visions. Later I came to see his Visions, too—but I always had my own. I had girlish dreams as well, of a husband who would look after me, and love me above all other women as the *Song of Solomon* tells. *I am my beloved's, and his desire is toward me.* And so it came about.

Not long before, my mother told me we were going to have a lodger for a short time, a young man who was feeling poorly because his heart had been broken by a girl named Polly Wood. I was not prepared for what happened when I first saw him.

When I came into the room, a white light pierced my heart. *It is he,* my Voices said. As he looked directly at me, a wave of Faintness came over me. I ran into the garden to recover. My heartbeat finally stilled, and composing myself, I went back inside.

He was looking into the fire pensively, his fair hair curling about his ears; a rather large head he had, and keen grey eyes. He was not above medium height, but taller than I, and his shoulders were broad. He looked at me and smiled.

I said, "I understand your spirits are low, Mr. Blake." Then he spoke quite openly about his injured feelings, with which I sympathized.

"Do you pity me?" he asked, with a sudden, direct gaze.

"Indeed I do," I said.

"Then I love you," he said.

It happened so quickly.

I believed him. We were already spiritually connected, though at the time I did not have the words to express it, as I have now. To our minds, Pity was a Divine quality, as important as Love, and necessary for love to begin. *Mercy, Pity, Peace and Love is God . . .* are not those William's very words? *The Divine Image.* That is what we were to each other.

I knew instinctively not to play Courtship games with William. I let him see me naked that summer, standing in a corner of the sunny hayloft, with my long black hair hanging over my shoulders. Of course, I saw him naked, too.

The Nakedness of Woman is the work of God, said William.

The Nakedness of Man is quite fetching, too, said I.

. . .

We began to meet in the Churchyard and walk out together. We rambled the green Surrey fields to the edge of London, or I accompanied William while he sketched. There was a day in late summer when I told him about my Voices, and he told me about his Visions.

The first vision he remembered occurred when he was four years old and God put his head in at the window and set him screaming. Then when he was about eight, walking by Dulwich Hill, he looked up and saw a tree filled with Angels, bright angelic wings bespangling every bough like stars.

"What happened then?" I asked.

"I ran home to tell my parents. My father said I was lying and would have thrashed me—but my mother stopped him." William smiled at the recollection. "Now they believe me," he said.

I felt a little shiver. "Do you see things often?"

"All the time."

"Are you not afraid?"

"Very much afraid. Sometimes I shake with Fear. But then the Vision will speak to me, and tell me to draw its picture. Then I know that I can control it, and even tell it to go away."

"But what if it is an Evil Spirit?"

William put his arm around me.

"There are no Evil Spirits, Kate. There are only Human Spirits. Some might wish to do harm, but one can overcome them with good thoughts. *You* have the power to overcome any evil—I could tell that about you right away."

I fervently hoped William was right to have such confidence in me.

I did already know I could dispel Evil, but had never told anyone about it. I had been too afraid of what I had seen and done. But now I confessed to William that I could, for lack of better words, stand outside myself and see things as if I were somewhere else.

He was much interested.

"How do you get there?" he asked, clasping my hands tightly.

"I merely lie quiet, close my eyes, and tell myself to leave. A shudder comes over me and I leave my body," I told him.

"Where do you go? What have you seen?" He was agitated.

In truth, I had only experienced this travel twice, for it had frightened me. It had happened in my sixteenth year. The first time, half asleep, I had left myself in my little bed shared with my sister Sarah, and looking down, had seen myself lying next to her. I had no idea how I accomplished this. I felt an infinite freedom and exhilaration. I had only thought a moment about going outside, when immediately I was out in the cow yard, but my feet were not touching the ground. I did not feel cold in the least, though it was winter. I thought I must be dreaming, but I was sensible of a different atmosphere than dream.

I noticed suddenly a grey shape near the barn door. From it emanated a horrible energy. I knew it wanted to draw me in. I experienced terror for the first time in my life.

"Leave me!" I cried in my mind to the shape. And then I prayed.

"Dear Jesus, keep me safe."

I made the sign of the Cross with my two index fingers, and held my arms out in front of me. The evil thing faded away.

I wanted then only to get back to my sleeping self. I was afraid I could not do it. How could I find my way back? Into my mind came the image of my physical self, and I slipped back into my body.

In the morning, I was not sure I had not dreamed. Yet the remembrance of two things, the freedom and the terror, stayed with me for many days.

William seemed to understand everything. Silently, he took me in his arms and held me close for a long time.

We were not always so serious. One day on our walk we came upon a garden at the edge of a field, and I saw the most beautiful thing. It was a Rose, but it had been made to grow tall and leafless for about three feet, until it burst into a bouquet of pink blooms.

"Oh, how lovely," I said. "I have never seen a Rose-tree before!"

William looked at me and smiled.

"It is like you," he said, "my pretty Rose-Tree."

My mother used to call me by a flower name, too. *Rosebud*, she called me. I was her last baby, the youngest of nine alive. My brothers James and Richard were twins, and played with me all the time. They were only a year or two older than I was. My sister Sarah told me when I was five (and she was ten) that there had been twin babies, Charlotte and Juliet, born before Richard and James, but they had died after only a month. We used to play a game of dolls, called Funerals: we'd wrap up our little cloth dolls and pick flowers to cover them, and bury them in the field with stones at their heads. Sister Jane, who was twelve, scolded us and forbade us to play that game ever again, and not to tell Mother.

I thought my mother, Mary, very beautiful. She had large black eyes over which arched dark eyebrows. Her cheeks were plump, so her face seemed all curves. Her hair was curly and dark brown, tied up in a kerchief to keep it out of the way. In spite of all her childbearing, she was not heavy, and moved lightly and quickly, having little patience with any of us who were lazy. She worked very hard herself, which was a pity because she and my father had not always been poor, and could remember better days before I was born, when they owned several acres of land and had a respectable farm.

In those days, my father was a dark, wiry man who had much energy and a good singing voice. His name was Will, and he could remember stories told by his old grandfather, Jean-Bernard. It is said our surname used to be Bourchier, not Boucher, as we came to be called, because Jean-Bernard was a Huguenot and came to England from France to escape the persecution of Protestants in 1686.

Jean-Bernard was just twenty-three years old and wanted to marry, but refused to give up his faith and convert to Catholicism. He was in danger of being tortured, so he fled with his new wife, and they settled near Ely, where there is a great Cathedral. Since he was a carpenter, he soon found work there. His son Richard became a farmer on the edge of the marshes, and that is where Richard's boy, my father Will, grew up.

My father used to tell us stories about the great Cathedral that could be seen everywhere from the surrounding countryside. He used to see it in his dreams, he said, a guardian of the land, standing against the horizon. Sometimes the River Great Ouse would overflow its banks and the Cathedral would look like a great ship, or the island that Ely once was, before the fens were drained, and water surrounded it. He had been told that the whole of England was searched in Medieval times to find oak trees large enough to build the corner posts for the Cathedral's great wooden lantern tower. He told us that when he was a boy, rich and poor would go to services together in the vast nave, and that is where he learned to love music. When he grew up and married my mother, she used to play a little tin whistle and he would sing for us. My favourite song was "Barbara Allen." The tune haunted me.

Our life on the farm in Battersea was always busy. I remember following my father as he walked down the long lines of a plowed field, sowing seed for carrots. He had a bag over his shoulder, and would let the seed slip through his fingers evenly. I was about ten years old then, and he said, "you can do this!"

And so I was given a little leather bag of my own, and I sowed the seeds far and wide, not always in the furrow. When the little feathery green tops began to show, I had to thin my furrows so they were neat. I used to eat the tiny carrots right out of the ground. Nothing tasted as sweet, unless it was the little green peas fresh out of their pods that we sometimes ate as we picked them.

"Kate, come quick, Blossom's dropping her calf!"

I remember my sister Sarah calling me from my cross-stitch one March morning.

Blossom was our black cow. We all helped look after her and learned to milk her. Each year she had a calf, which my father usually sold, or sometimes we kept it and had two cows that year. This time he said we could keep Blossom's calf and look after it ourselves, so we children were all excited.

Blossom was standing completely silent under the oak tree at the edge of the field, not far from the house. The calf was halfway out. I had seen cows give birth before, but it always surprised me how they did it. The calf just dropped out the back end.

Suddenly there it was on the ground, a dark brown bundle with impossibly long legs. Blossom began to lick it all over.

"Now watch," said Sarah, "the calf will try to stand up."

But, strangely, it did not. The little bundle barely moved. It did not struggle to its wobbly long legs as I had seen before; it did not reach for its mother's teats. Blossom stood by silently, licking.

But nothing happened.

"Go and get Papa!" commanded Sarah, her dark eyes fearful.

So I ran as fast as I could to behind the barn, where Papa was mending a plow.

"Something is wrong with the calf!" I cried.

When we reached the field again, Blossom was standing mutely beside her calf, looking at us. The calf was motionless.

"Can you help it, Papa?" I cried.

"No, Kate."

I began to weep, and so did Sarah.

Blossom just stood there without a sound. We went back to the house, crying.

"What will you do with the baby cow?" I wept.

"I'll bury it soon," said my father, "but we'll let Blossom grieve over her calf a little longer."

For the rest of the day, Blossom stood silently guarding the body of her dead calf. And then my father led her back to the barn, alone.

I have always had an interest in the world of spirits. I listen to my voices, and I sometimes know what is in a person's mind. I believe this ability came from my father, who told me of a strange thing that happened to him one day when he was only ten years old.

He was hurrying along the edge of the marshes on a grey October day when the wind blew cold off the sea, for he was late for supper. He had been searching for treasure. The old folk used to say that there was a great silver hoard buried somewhere on the fens, left there by the Romans. In the light of late afternoon, he saw a figure seated on a rock near the shore. It was a young woman, whose long hair glimmered over a dark cloak. At first a great fear overcame him, but he could not refrain from drawing nearer, for she was extraordinarily beautiful.

She asked him to take a message to Mr. Ellis, the Blacksmith, and she made Will a strange promise. She said if he did as she asked, he would be able to read the thoughts of others.

Will ran all the way to the blacksmith's yard.

Ellis was busy at the forge, sparks flying.

"Well, boy," he looked up, "cat got your tongue?" He was a big, powerful man with a dark beard and black eyes.

"I have a message for you," said Will, and swallowed hard.

"Well, say it then, boy."

"It is from a lady on the shore. She asks you to come there this evening."

Ellis blanched.

Will realized with a shock that he knew what Ellis was thinking. *Not her, how can it be?* Then the blacksmith tried to appear calm, but his thoughts became jumbled. Will could not really make them out, though he said later they were mixed with fear and longing both. Will ran home to dinner and never knew if Ellis went to the shore. But from then on, Will could read people's minds if he wanted to.

Perhaps because of this gift, he became a taciturn young man, almost withdrawn, to remember what my mother said of him. He did not marry till he was twenty-seven, and then he chose her, a vivacious girl of eighteen. I have noticed that quiet men almost always choose talkative wives.

I suppose my mother and father were happy together, because there were so many babies, but it is sad to think that Mother became so worn out with childbearing that she banished Father from her bed after I was born. She was thirty-seven years old then, and had twenty years of life left to her—enough to raise me and see me married to William. She died just two weeks after our wedding, never having told anyone she was sick, so as not to spoil our celebrations.

There are some things I cannot tell Mr. Tatham, things I did not tell even William. I was not a Virgin when we met. I do not think William would have cared. Because I was so small down there, Jeremy Adam had not really penetrated me. I passed for a Virgin.

It had happened when I was thirteen, and only just come to Womanhood. About two miles away from our Farm was a fine Manse, where lived the Reverend Jeremy Adam and his wife and four young children. My Mother told me that Mistress Adam was looking for a Maidservant to help with the children and do some cooking.

"You could earn a little money there," she said to me, "and you need not live there. You can stay at home and go out each morning to look after the children. Would you like that?"

I knew money was scarce at home, and I could tell that Mother wanted me to take the work. So I pretended that I would be happy to go, though inwardly I did not want to spend the day among strangers.

On my first day, in October of 1775, I put up my hair, put on my best white collar, grey dress, and bonnet, and at the break of dawn walked the two miles to the Manse. I saw the Dawn come up with purple streaks in the pink sky, and heard the hedgerows come alive with squeaks and twitters. I turned over in my mind my Mother's admonitions to be always polite, to curtsey when introduced, to say "Yes, Ma'am" and "No Ma'am" to Mistress Adam, and to stay below stairs when not needed. When Mrs. Adam first interviewed me, I had received the impression of a pleasant but distracted young woman with unruly, curly fair hair, again big with Child. I had not yet met her husband, the Rev. Jeremy Adam.

The children were beautiful: a set of twin boys about a year old, and two girls under six, all with fair curls. On the first morning, I was in the Nursery with them, beginning to play a game on the floor with their wooden blocks, when their father entered.

He was of medium height, broad shouldered, with blue eyes and black brows and lashes.

"So you are the new Girl," he said, "name of Kate, I hear."

"Yes, Sir."

"Stand up, Miss, when I speak to you."

I stood up, brushing my skirt, and looked at him. There was something about him I did not like. He looked me up and down; no one had ever looked at me like that before, and it made me shiver.

"Look down when I am speaking to you, Miss," he said. Then, "you'll do."

And he left the room. I was left puzzled and uneasy.

For three weeks, I did my work at the Manse, and seldom saw Jeremy Adam. I was even beginning to enjoy my days with the children, the good hot meal I was given in the afternoon, and my walks home along the country road at six, when the moon was out. Most evenings my Father would come to get me, and we would chat companionably all the way home.

But then it all ended. One day in late November, I was out behind the house hanging some newly washed children's clothes on a line. The family did not wash their Laundry very often, but I liked to keep the children in clean gowns, so I would boil up a small pot of water on the kitchen fire just for them. On this occasion, I had just finished hanging the last bit of laundry with a wooden peg, when I turned to find Mr. Adam close behind me.

"What a fetching picture you are, Miss," he said, moving even closer. I could smell spirits on his breath. I backed away, but he caught my arm.

"Come here," he said, pushing me into the stone wall which ran along the side of the house. There were tall rose bushes growing there, some still with pink blossoms, even in November. The thorns scratched my face as he pushed me forward. My heart beat furiously and a horrible Fear took away all my power of speech, though his rough hand over my mouth kept a scream echoing in my head.

"Don't make a sound," he rasped, as I felt his hand go under my skirts and up to that secret place where I had only recently discovered mysterious Sensations by myself.

I could hardly believe what he was doing. He was behind me; surely that was not his hand thrusting against me? Something was hard, and he pinched my buttocks with one hand as he held me imprisoned against him. That hard thing pressed and pressed against me as if it would break into me. Growing up on a Farm, I knew how animals mated, but I did not think Human Beings mated that way, too.

I began to weep, and I felt something wet and sticky between my legs.

"You're damned small, Miss, but that means you're safe! Now it wasn't all that bad, was it?" The Reverend Adam did up his trousers and chucked me under the chin.

"Now, not a word about this or you'll lose your position here. No one will believe you and you will be Ruined. You'll even like it next time! I'll get that Maidenhead!"

Next time. I could hardly breathe. He left me abruptly.

I do not know how I finished my day at the Manse. My mind was whirling. What had I done that Rev. Adam should single me out? Had I smiled at him in a flirtatious manner?

Was it my fault? And he a Clergyman! It seemed to me a cruel thing he had done to me, who had till that time experienced only Kindness at the hands of others.

And what was I to do? I determined I would never return to the Manse. I did not care what anyone thought; I would never go back.

But I would not tell the reason, for I was too ashamed. I felt dirty, somehow, guilty of some vague Sin attached to my person.

I thought of a plan, and indeed it worked. I pretended to be sick, and threw up my food purposely for several days, by sticking a finger down my throat. I grew alarmingly thin. My Mother kept me at home and looked sharply at me. When my courses came in December, she seemed relieved and brewed me a Herbal tea. I told her I did not like looking after the Adams children and would not go back. She did not argue with me.

From Kate's Notebook.
Monday, April 20, 1829. Lisson Grove, London.

I see that young Fred Tatham is in his study busily making notes for his book about William and me. He has copied my recollections down almost word for word and wants me to write them out for him to read at leisure. I will tell him most things frankly, but he will not know about this, my secret Journal, where I have written down my private thoughts for so many years.

I will, however, provide Fred with William's treasured Notebook, which contains the drafts of so many poems. There is also a collection of notes and many copies of letters among William's things which I will give him.

I know that Fred would like to be an artist like William, but he is not very talented. All his best friends are artists—they were a group of young men who called themselves The Ancients. They used to come calling, and sat at William's feet in the last few years. They made William happy by their devotion to him. It was our patron Mr. John Linnell who introduced them to us. I suppose I must be grateful to him for that, at least.

They were all young men five years ago. Frederick was nineteen, the same age as Samuel Palmer, and George Richmond only fifteen. Then there was Edward Calvert, who used to call William "that blessed man," and John Giles, who called him "Divine Blake." Samuel Palmer was especially fond of William. They say that he used to kiss the bell handle of our door before he pulled it.

Mr. Tatham lately came into the parlour where I was dusting and asked me a question. He reminds me of a brown bird, with his dark hair and bright brown eyes.

"Do you know what happened to Ellis?" he asked, reminding me of the tale my father told.

"Well, it was very strange," I said, brandishing a feather duster. "It seems that just after that, Ellis disappeared. And then a week later, his drowned body washed up on the shore. Everyone thought it was an accident. But my father had an uneasy feeling, of course! It is dangerous for mortals to enter the fairy world."

I like looking after the Tathams. I came in March of last year, when they had been married only ten months, and took over their household. I had lived for a short time after William's death with John Linnell, but I prefer Frederick and Maria. I am suspicious of John Linnell, even though he did commission so much work for us. William spent entirely too much time with him.

I get along much better with Frederick, even though we had a terrible row before I came to live here. I suppose I objected too often to his well-meaning advice about William's Will. I do resent advice. Finally, exasperated with my objections, Fred lost his temper completely and threw the Will into the fire, saying, "There now, you can do as you like—the Will no longer exists!" And he turned on his heel and left the room.

Early the following morning, I called on him. I told him that William had been with me all night and required me to come to him and renew the Will. I apologized as best I could, and since that day I always do as he advises, though I might hesitate and sigh, "there's no help for it." In all business matters, I really like best to consult William's spirit.

I am not sure that Fred believes in William's appearances to me. That is strange considering that Fred wants to be a Visionary himself. What does Fred see? He does behave oddly sometimes.

Only last year in Regent Square Church, at a sermon of the celebrated Scots Presbyterian preacher Edward Irving, Frederick became completely overcome with enthusiasm and cried out to the Lord for direction. Everyone had turned to look at him, though not only he had been astounded at the sermon. Frederick had fallen to his knees at his pew, praying aloud.

This was not the first time Frederick had seen Edward Irving, whose dark-haired presence, tall and commanding, reminded me of an Old Testament Prophet. Frederick had been only eighteen when we all heard Irving preach in the little Caledonian Chapel on Cross Street, which had once been the Swedenborgian Church William and I had joined.

Irving was fond of the text of his first sermon, Acts 10:29: "Therefore I came unto you without gainsaying, as soon as I was sent for: I ask therefore for what intent ye have sent for me?" William had been impressed with the fire of the young preacher, but had seen something uncontrolled in him. He told the Ancients: "Irving is a highly gifted man—he is a *sent* man. But they who are sent sometimes go further than they ought."

I know that Frederick, in his secret heart, wishes he too were a *sent* man. He would like to go far . . . he just is not sure where, exactly.

Tuesday, April 21, 1829.

Mr. Tatham likes me to tell him my stories while he takes tea.

Isn't it strange how no matter how old you are, inside yourself you are always about twenty? I remember as if it were yesterday how nervous I was when, one day in September, in 1781, William took me to meet his family. I had dressed carefully, pinning up my unruly black hair under a lace cap. Today I told Fred about it.

It was raining, and I was cold. Cold from nerves, as well. There was much to be worried about, for I was only the daughter of a market gardener, and William's father was a hosier and haberdasher in London. His house was on Broad Street, Golden Square; it was, to my eyes, large and gloomy. The living quarters were above the shop. The bare, polished floor reflected the meagre light of the coal fire in the room where we waited to meet William's father, James, and his mother, named like me, Catherine.

It was a formal room, with an oak table in the centre, and straight-back chairs clustered near the fire. Along one wall was a shelf of books with coloured bindings, and on the walls were drawings—some I recognized by William's hand. One especially caught my eye: the drawing of a young naked man, with one foot on earth, his arms out-spread in a dance of joy.

Mr. and Mrs. Blake came into the room with grave faces. I lowered my eyes.

"Look up, child," said Mr. Blake. Then, "A pretty maid," he said to William, as if I were not there. He was a tall, stern man, with steely eyes.

"This is Catherine Boucher, Mother," said William, turning to Mrs. Blake. I curtsied to her. She was kindly looking, at least, with a rosy complexion.

"Are you a believer, child?" she asked.

"Yes, ma'am," I said. I knew that the Blakes were Dissenters, and very pious.

There was an awkward silence. Mr. Blake motioned us to sit down.

"I must be honest," he said, looking at me gravely, "this is not the marriage we would choose for our son. He has attended the Royal Academy Schools—he is an Engraver now, and he has many impor-tant friends . . ."

"Father!" broke in William, his colour rising.

"I must be honest," repeated Mr. Blake, "with a good marriage, even *you* might rise in the world."

I did not understand his dry tone. I began to feel humiliated. Who were these people that they could sit in judgement of me, and deem me unworthy or unsuitable, because I was not born to wealth or achievement? They knew nothing of me, whether I was honest or deceitful, whether I loved their son truly. I do not think they cared about my feelings at all, and I was fighting inwardly to be composed under their scrutiny.

"You are a comely girl, my dear," said Mrs. Blake. "Tell me, what are your favourite pastimes?"

"Sewing, ma'am," I said, "and cross-stitch." I could have said that I could sing well, but I was afraid she would ask me to perform then and there.

"Do you read?" she asked.

I caught my breath. I felt my cheeks go hot. William interrupted.

"Enough, Mother! You will soon learn what talents Kate pos-sesses. It is time she met the rest of the family. Where is Robert?"

Mrs. Blake said no more and motioned us into the next room. It was a dining room, with a large table in the centre, set for the midday meal. Standing near the leaded windows were three young men and a girl. There was a family likeness among them: grey eyes and a breadth of forehead, but their expressions differed greatly. The eldest brother, James, named for his father, had a shrewd look I did not like. He was almost two years older than William, and in business with his father. The middle brother, John, a Baker, I was told, looked at me boldly. I looked back. The youngest brother, Robert, about fourteen years old, was charming and friendly. Their sister was just seventeen, pleasant and smiling then, so unlike the scold she was to become. Her name, like her mother's and mine, was Catherine, though they called her Cathy. Too bad she is not prettier, I thought.

Soon we sat down to what was for me a fine meal, a joint of beef with plenty of vegetables, followed by a sweet pudding.

Suddenly there was a strange thud, and Robert slid from his chair to the floor.

"Another fit!" cried Mrs. Blake, pushing back her chair and running to Robert.

William reached him first. Robert looked dreadful, his limbs rigid and his mouth gasping. He began to thrash. William held him firmly till the spasm passed.

"There, there, Bob," he said repeatedly to Robert, who was soon quiet. "It is the falling sickness," he said to me. Then he turned back to Robert, who was coming to himself. I never saw William so gentle.

"My God," said brother James, "will it never end?" He left the room.

Mrs. Blake looked distracted. Cathy had tears in her eyes. I sensed that Robert was the favourite of them all, and that this illness was a cloud that hung over them. After Robert was taken to his bed to rest, William and I sat by the fire.

"Kate," he said, taking my hand, "if you love me, you must love Bob."

I promised I would.

William taught me to read and write. He began shortly after I met him, when we would sit in the apple orchard with his drawing paper and pencils all around, and he drew me pictures of the letters. *A is for*

Apple. He made me laugh by drawing little people and flowers among the strokes. *B is for Blake*. Once he drew me the whole alphabet made out of little bodies in the shape of letters. *K is for Kate. L is for Love. W is for William.* He said I was a good student.

After I met Robert, he too would help me. We read the Bible together. I already knew the stories, but I loved the rhythm of the words. All the Blakes knew the Bible, almost by heart.

I never learned to spell all that well, but I could read and write, though not easily, after a few months. Then I learned that William was not only an Artist, but a Writer as well. It seems he had been writing poems since he was twelve years old, and he had pages and pages of them! Robert recited William's verse to me, and later William read them to me and helped me read with him. The poems were musical to my ear, but I did not always understand them. I did like the one he wrote for me in which he called me his "black-ey'd maid" and compared me to an Angel:

> So when she speaks, the voice of Heaven I hear
> So when we walk, nothing impure comes near
> Each field seems Eden, and each calm retreat
> Each village seems the haunt of holy feet.

One day that first summer of our Courtship, William asked me, out of the blue, what had been my second experience of travelling out of my body? I thought he had forgotten my confession, but I wanted all to be honest between us, so I told him.

A few weeks after my first experience, I had decided to try again. I tried to recall how it happened, the relaxation and then the shudder, followed by floating out of myself. Again, I saw myself sleeping next to my sister, and then I was outside in the apple orchard, which was in bloom, though I could not tell what time it was.

I was enjoying the sensation of freedom, when I saw coming toward me a child, a little girl. She was in tears.

I spoke to her, not in words, but in my mind.

"What is the matter?" I asked.

"I am lost," she said, "I want my Mother."

Then into my mind came the image of a sickroom, and a small bed with the little girl lying pale in it, and a young woman sobbing beside her.

"I am afraid you must leave your mother for a while," I said gently. I took her hand.

"But who will look after me?" she asked.

I became aware of the same awful Grey Presence hovering near I had sensed before.

Go Away, I willed it. And I thought, *surely this child must have a Guardian Angel. Where is it?*

The Grey Presence came nearer. I summoned all my courage and once again prayed, *Please, Jesus, help us.*

And then it happened. A light came all around us, and the child was taken up into it, leaving me behind, but with a great feeling of Peace. I went back to myself in happiness.

When I finished my story, William looked shaken.

"I would not have you practise this Art again," he said.

He made me promise never, ever to do it more, and except for one other time, some years later, I never did.

My parents liked William and were happy that he was courting me. He had decided he needed a year to save enough money for us to begin our life together, and so spent much time back in London. My father approved of William's practicality; my mother was more concerned about his Character. She detected a nervous energy about him, and said one day, "Are you sure about William, Kate? Wouldn't you have preferred Ian, that amiable Stonemason from the village who used to come around?"

I think she did not really know what an Engraver did for a living. I did not know myself until William showed me his work, how he painstakingly transferred drawings or paintings to a copper plate with a special tool called a burin, and how the images were printed onto paper in a heavy press with odd-smelling inks. He had apprenticed seven years with a distinguished engraver, James Basire, near Covent Garden in London.

I had much to learn about William's way of life, which was much grander than my own. His father had paid over Fifty Pounds to Basire for the apprenticeship. This was more money than my father would see in a single year. William had lived in a large house with Basire, and gone out every day to draw statues in Westminster Abbey. Then he would come home and learn to engrave the drawings. Strange work or not, after I met William, no other man interested me.

He was so changeable, for one thing. One moment he would be full of high spirits and make me run after him through the orchard, climbing the old trees and shaking apples down on me. The next he would be withdrawn and pensive, and I would have to coax him out of a melancholy mood with kisses. There were times, too, when I was almost afraid of him, when he flew into a rage over some trifle, some thoughtless remark by one of my brothers, perhaps a disagreement over politics, about which he was vehement. I had never known anyone with so much energy—it seemed to flame out of the curls of his hair.

He had so many ideas I had never before considered. One June day, we were sitting at the edge of Mother's flower garden, admiring the red hollyhocks.

William said, "Here's a poem for you:

> He who binds to himself a joy
> Doth the winged life destroy
> But he who kisses the joy as it flies
> Lives in Eternity's sun rise."

"That's beautiful," I said. "What does it mean?"

I picked a hollyhock blossom and put it behind my ear.

"It means we cannot be devoted only to each other, Kate. Our love is deep enough to include others. We will never be jealous of each other."

I was puzzled.

"I don't know if that is really possible," I said. "I can imagine being jealous if you paid attention to another girl. It seems only Human Nature to be jealous."

"Nature!" William scoffed. "Nature is fallen. I want us to be Imaginative, to be Visionary." He plucked the flower out of my ear, and put it in my bosom.

"I want our desires to be free," he continued, "and then we will never tire of each other." He kissed me lightly.

"Of course, I will try," I said. I would have promised him the moon. In my heart, however, I hoped never to be put to the test.

The year after I met William, my life changed. I learned to read and write, and his family came to accept me if not to love me. I knew they thought William was marrying below his station. I was well aware of this difference in class and apprehensive at the thought of living in London as the wife of a young man with good prospects. I was determined to be a credit to William.

William and I had a magic between us; we were in the centre of a circle which enclosed a private world. I knew there was another world just beyond the circle—I could sometimes see its shape and the shadows that would come close to us—but in that first year of our courtship there was much laughter and delight.

Our Wedding Day was set for Sunday, August 18, 1782.

2

In Which I Marry Mr. Blake And Go To London

*S*t. Mary's Church in Battersea had been recently rebuilt and stood alongside the river. The light shone through the red and gold eastern window as we said our marriage vows, and I remember a gold tassel gleaming on crimson curtains. I made my wedding dress of blue silk, a lovely material which William's father had given me, fit for a lady, he said, and I wore a wreath of daisies and blue ribbon for my hair. William picked me a bouquet of blue corn-flowers.

We signed the register: William wrote his name, but I, being too shy to practise my newly learned handwriting, merely placed an X on the book. Then James, William's father, signed the book, as did the parish clerk. At last we were truly and legally married, and I ceased to tremble.

I was happy that William's mother and father came to the wedding, along with Robert and Cathy. We had a merry wedding meal in the house of James's elder cousin Henry, who lived in Battersea. My smiles at the party concealed only the slightest misgiving. Although my voices had always said *Marry him*, my mother had said to me that morning, "Remember, Kate, there is something odd about the Blakes.

You may be marrying above your station, but all those people are too nervous for my liking. Keep that husband of yours calm, or there's no telling what may break loose!"

Yet now she, too, was smiling, and even my father, who had been melancholy of late because of poor crops, smiled and toasted our happiness.

"To the happy couple!"

"To my pretty Rose-Tree," whispered William to me, raising his glass, and calling me his private name.

In the long evening light we drove to London with Robert in a hired carriage and spent our first night alone as man and wife in our new lodgings at 23 Green Street. William had rented rooms for us in the house of a Mr. Taylor, and here we would live for two years with the world all before us.

I loved William's broad shoulders and sturdy legs. I loved his capable hands. Best of all, I loved his curly bronze hair and his grey eyes. His eyes, which seemed to see more than was there. When he looked at me, I seemed to grow in my own regard. I filled with light, just for him. I hope Frederick Tatham can divine this without my saying.

Can you imagine what it was like for me to live in London in 1782? I was twenty-one years old, full of life, and I had seldom ventured out of the green fields of Surrey. I had been to see the timber bridge over the Thames at Chelsea, and watched the young men fishing from it, but except for the visit to meet William's parents, I had hardly ever been to London.

Green Street was around the corner from Leicester Fields, where William told me the famous painter Sir Joshua Reynolds lived, and the Engraver William Woollett lived near us, too. We had three rooms one floor above the street and I could use the fire in the Kitchen downstairs to cook. William immediately set up one room as a Workroom. We put our bed and clothes cupboard in the smallest, but brightest room, and used the other as a Sitting Room. It was peaceful and open there; we could hear the Cock crow and see hens and chickens strutting about the street.

What a difference a few turns made when you walked in the City! Oh, the dirt and the noise—and the streets winding and narrow with sharp stones underfoot and other things stinking and horrible to step in! And you had to be careful not to bump into Hackney Chair men, or horses and carriages, or boys who would rather steal your Purse than help you up if you fell in a puddle. At Charing Cross, the drunken young whores even offered their favours to me, and then called us filthy names as William brushed them aside. If the sun was shining, and the blue sky above the tiled roofs looked freshly washed, and there was a young girl selling flowers on the corner, then the cries of the street vendors seemed like singing, and I knew why William spoke of "Infinite London."

Each day I awakened with the morning light, William's hand resting on my breast. I turned to him, and he came to me and we found ourselves moving to a music which seemed to emanate from the sunlight filling our small bedroom. Content, I would smile, warm under the cover, as he rose to start the fire. He would bring me a dish of tea, and we talked about the day ahead.

William was busy with engraving jobs from paintings by his good friend Tom Stothard. Tom was the most amiable of William's friends—all of whom I met that first year. Tom and William used to go drawing together and were once taken for French Spies by some English soldiers when they had sailed up the River Medway to sketch. They had not known it was an important Naval Base. William still was not at all happy when he told me about it two years after the event. I think it frightened him to be apprehended by Authorities, but then, who wouldn't be?

William hated the American War, but it was dangerous to say so, and though that war ended the year before we were married, everyone was afraid that Revolution would spread. I was confused, because I think William wanted Revolution to spread. He would look up from his work and exclaim, "There are too many laws, Kate! We are chained before we know it . . . customs and ideas . . . customs and ideas . . . and tyrants in Government!"

"But Mr. Blake," I would say, speaking formally as I had heard married ladies addressing their husbands, so he would know I was serious, "surely it is best to do things the way they have always been done. As for the Government, what can folk such as we ever do about it?"

"I have seen Fires," he said. "I have seen Riots last year . . . I was there at Newgate when the prisoners were set free to protest the American War. There was an Energy there, but it was horrific. There has to be another way for that energy to be used—I think about it all the time. I believe we have to imagine first what world we want, then it will come about."

"That doesn't seem all that practical to me," I said. "Dreamers can dream all they want, but unless other people know what they are dreaming, what good is it?"

"But that's it, Kate!" he said vehemently. "It is through Art and Poetry that people will change. Flaxman, Stothard, Cumberland and I . . . we all think this way."

I wanted to think about this for a while. I liked John Flaxman and Tom Stothard. William knew Tom from student days at the Royal Academy Schools; he had a long, thoughtful face and good brown eyes. He and William were best of friends, especially since the River Medway incident, and it was Tom who introduced William to Flaxman, all before I met William, of course.

John became a very famous sculptor, but in those days he was merely a thin, stooped, young man with talent, and he was always kind to me, when others were cool or snobbish. George Cumberland, too, has ever been a friend to William and used to spend many an evening sketching in the company of William and Tom and John in our lodgings. We had but little furniture, yet the walls were covered cheerfully with engravings and water colours that William liked to collect.

Sometimes Nancy Flaxman, John's pretty green-eyed wife, would accompany her husband to our place, and she and I would drink tea and gossip. Nancy was my first friend in London. She and John had been married just two months earlier than William and I.

William liked Nancy's company, too. I could tell, because if he did not like a woman, he simply ignored her. But he never ignored Nancy. He always had a smile and a jest for her, or he would ask her opinion of a drawing he was working on. I was happy that John Flaxman seemed to like me, too, so that the four of us spent many a companionable evening together. They were destined to be our friends all our lives, except for those few years when William fought with everybody, though eventually we did reconcile. Of course, John never knew the terrible thing I did in his name, out of desperation.

John's personality was a contrast to William's. He was so reserved and austere that William nick-named him "The Law-giver." Yet he was kindly; you could see that in his large blue eyes and the high brow covered by a fringe of brown hair. His stoop was rather obvious, and he tended to delicate health, so Nancy was always hovering over him with a shawl to keep off draughts.

John and William had many common interests. They both loved the poetry of Thomas Chatterton, the tragic boy who poisoned himself at the age of seventeen, only thirteen years before. He had pretended to discover the poems of Thomas Rowley, a fifteenth century monk—but in reality, he had written the poems himself. John and William admired the ancient style, just as they admired the architecture of the old Gothic churches.

"Chatterton never wrote those poems," declared William one morning when we were walking along the Thames Embankment with the Flaxmans, deep in conversation.

"Do you mean Rowley really existed?" asked John, surprised.

"Of course!" said William. "In his mind, the spirit of Rowley dictated the poems. It is obvious."

"I grant you that spirits exist," said John. "I am a follower of Emmanuel Swedenborg, as you know, and he lived in the company of Spirits—even as you do, William."

"Yes, Rowley was real. I have seen him myself."

"And I suppose you have heard him recite?" asked Nancy with a smile. She was not afraid to tease William.

In those early days, I became very upset with William because of Nancy, over whom we had our first quarrel.

"Nancy is full of life," William observed to me one evening just after the Flaxmans had left for home. "I would like to take her to bed."

I could not believe my ears. I well knew William had a good appetite for the love of women, but since we had been married, he had never spoken to me of lust for another. I suppose my speechlessness gave my shock away. I had been undressing for bed, and my hair was loose about my shoulders. I began to brush my hair. I felt horribly hot and faint.

"You would not mind, would you, Kate? You know how we have spoken of a marriage without Jealousy!" William took the brush and stroked my hair slowly.

"That is all very well," I said quickly, "but our marriage is not theirs. Poor John would hate to hear you speak like this! Nancy would never even think such things!"

"That is so. But Kate, tell me now—do you not agree with me? You used to agree we should not bind our joys, and then our love would always be free."

I moved away from him slightly. I could feel my heart beating.

"I said it once, but that was before I knew what it meant."

"You can't mean that you will allow Jealousy to enter our house!" William turned me to him.

"How can I help it?" I cried. "I don't want to share you with some-one else! I am not as selfless as I thought!"

"But it is not a question of *sharing*," said William, as if he were speaking to a child, "it is *expanding*. There is enough love to encom-pass everyone. We must love one another, Kate. Jesus Christ said it, you know that."

"And I know the Bible says 'Thou shalt not commit Adultery.' That you should not even lust after a woman in your heart! And now you do! It is a sin!"

"Those commandments are made to be broken!" He was almost shouting at me. "I will not be chained by them!"

I began to weep. William could never bear to see me weep. He took me in his arms.

"Come, now," he said gently, "I love you, Kate. I would not hurt you deliberately. If you are not ready yet for these ideas, well—they can wait."

I thought, why would I want to be ready for these ideas? What posi-tion would they put me in? I was no adventuress. I wanted to be faith-ful to William unto Death. I had never told him about Jeremy Adam, so he had never a reason to be jealous of me. Not that William would suffer jealousy, if I were to believe his professions of Unposessive Love. I did not quite trust those ideas.

"Let us love one another as well as we can," said William. "We must be kind to each other and not quarrel."

"And you won't speak to Nancy about this?" I was still tearful. I seemed to be shaking from some deep source inside me.

William promised he would not.

In those days, I made it the Object of my Life to please William. Any good Woman would do the same, but I knew William was not an ordinary man, so I wanted to be the perfect Wife for him. I comprehended very soon that Peace and Quiet were Necessities when he was working, so I cultivated the Art of being Still, though it was against my Nature. Neither did he like to argue with me, though he relished disputing with others, I noticed. To my surprise, I observed he liked Women to show Respect for their Husbands when in Company, and to defer to them in matters of Opinion. I wondered why I should have to agree with everything William said. Silently, I watched and waited and behaved as well as I could, at least for a time.

"John thinks William has a fine poetical talent," said Nancy to me one evening later that winter when we were sitting close to the little fire. This made me feel proud, because William was always writing when he was not drawing, and I really had no idea whether his poems were of any value. I always thought they were beautiful, but I knew I was untutored.

"John wants to help William publish his poems," Nancy went on, her green eyes brightening, "and he has a friend, The Reverend Mathew, who will undertake the expenses." And that is how we came to meet Anthony Stephen Mathew and his wife, Harriet.

The Mathews lived in Rathbone Place, near Charlotte Street, where Anthony Mathew was minister of Percy Chapel. I was amazed the first time I saw their house. I knew that John Flaxman had designed the interior for them, but I had never seen anything like it. I don't think William had either, but he would never admit it.

The windows seemed made of multicolored glass, but in reality were painted. In the salon, where we always gathered, the walls were coloured pale green, and around the ceiling were human figures of sculptured sand in flowing costumes—Greek, I think. Around the walls were placed chairs of plain design, but light in appearance, and they were upholstered in a striped green satiny fabric. On the walls, candles flickered from brass holders, and over the carved mantel of the fireplace was a delicate gilt-framed mirror, quite a rarity among people we knew. In one corner stood a small inlaid harpsichord, which Harriet Mathew liked to play. We usually drank tea or lemonade, and ate small sugary cakes.

I always wore my blue silk wedding dress to the Mathews' parties. I held myself very straight and tried to appear composed when William was asked to sing one of his poems. As other guests would always remark, he had a fine tenor voice.

I remember especially one evening when he sang one of his haunting and melancholy poems about the orphan children in church on Thursdays. It ended with the line: "Then cherish pity lest you drive an angel from your door."

When he finished, people were so moved that no one said anything for a long time. The trouble was, when he was not singing or reciting, William expressed his opinions in no uncertain terms. I never knew what to say to anybody about anything. I hated my ignorance and hated always feeling inferior in birth and education.

"What do you think of the state of Poetry, Mrs. Blake?" said Mrs. Mathew to me one evening. Harriet Mathew was a pretty woman with short brown curls around her face. I knew she was being kind, trying to include me in conversation, but I had not the slightest idea how to reply. *The state of Poetry? Whose Poetry?* I had only read William's, and a little Shakespeare, and of course, the *Song of Solomon.*

"Poetry is a fine occupation, I am sure," I whispered, "if one has a good musical sense."

"Why, that is an excellent observation," said she, in some surprise.

Then I thought of what William had said.

"Do you think," I asked Harriet Mathew, "that Poetry can change people?"

By this time a Mrs. Montague had joined us, a witty, fashionable woman, who had hitherto ignored me.

"I think it can," she said. "Indeed, Art and Poetry together can have a powerful effect for Good. I truly believe that."

"I would like to believe that were so," I said, "but is there any proof that Poetry or Art ever stopped a War, or prevented a Revolution?"

They were silent a moment.

"Perhaps not," said Harriet Mathew, "but a Novel can have a powerful effect on Morality. Just think of *Pamela*."

"How pertinent!" laughed Mrs. Montague, looking at me directly, "especially in your company, Mrs. Blake." I did not know then that *Pamela* was a novel about a serving maid risen above her station, because she refused to give her favours outside of marriage. I smiled to cover my confusion. Mrs. Mathew rescued me from the wit of Mrs. Montague by changing the subject. She told Mrs. Montague that she and her husband were helping to publish William's book of poems, called *Poetical Sketches*.

Everyone was so Learned at these evenings! There were several Women who were Authors, namely Mrs. Barbauld and Mrs. Hannah More. They talked to the Gentlemen as if they were Equals! It made me uneasy, because I realized I wanted to do the same, and indeed I resolved to learn all I could about Literature and Art.

Politics, too, was a favourite topic of conversation at the Mathews' parties. I remember one visit when William and a Gentleman were arguing vigorously about the American Rebellion and the War just past, and the effort King George had made to ruin Trade with the Colonies to keep them Subservient.

"England treated the Americans as if they were Children," said William, "and so like Children, they threw off the Yoke of Authority. Good for them!"

"It is a dangerous Path," said the Gentleman, who seemed taken aback at William's enthusiasm.

I told William I did not enjoy going to the Mathews' evenings, but he brushed aside my objections as nerves, and told me he enjoyed a bit of company and conversation. After all, he was getting work from the people he met there and attention when he spoke frankly of religion or politics. After a while I detected in him an impatience or boredom with the conversation, which sometimes seemed silly and pointless.

"The place is like an island in the moon," he said one day, "quite lovely and sometimes amusing . . . but neither of this world nor the next! Where's the meaning?"

I noticed after that William was more pointed in his conversation, sometimes offending the group.

"It would not be prudent to support the abdication of King George," said John Flaxman, rather mildly, during a conversation with several others, including William.

"Prudence is an ugly old maid, courted by incapacity," responded William, who was so pleased with that utterance that he later wrote it down. In the end, he offended guests at the Mathews', because he was so outspoken.

He was considered odd because he railed against the cruel practice of having little boys clean our chimneys. We had recently seen a little troop of Chimney Sweeps on the street, black as soot, carrying their brushes and rags and pails. I had never thought much about it, because everyone in London had to have chimneys cleaned, but suddenly William could talk of little else. It made people uncomfortable in the Mathews' drawing room to be reminded of such things.

And then, unknown to William, a dismaying event took place.

A new guest appeared one evening. He looked vaguely familiar, and in a flash, I knew him. It was the Rev. Jeremy Adam. He bent over my hand, not recognizing me. It had been, after all eight years, and I but a girl. Why did my heart nearly stop? He was the guilty one. As I left the room, I could feel his eyes following me, puzzled.

To escape Mr. Adam, I had stepped through French Doors into the Flaxman's little walled garden. There I sat on a stone bench, my heart beating furiously. It was an early Spring evening, with the scent of blossoms in the air.

To my dismay, I realized that Jeremy Adam had followed me. He came to the bench and bowed.

"Mrs. Blake, I would be honoured to become better acquainted."

"Indeed, Mr. Adam. May I ask why?"

"There is something about you. I cannot explain. It is as if I know you. Do you not feel it?"

Oh, he is flirting with me, I thought. My feelings were confused, but Fear was uppermost in my heart. Above all else, I did not want to be recognized by him.

"I cannot think where we could have met," I said, "I do not come from these parts."

"It is really of no matter whether we have met before—only that we have met now."

His smile repulsed me. He was a horrible man who preyed upon women. Like a bird in a net, I was paralysed.

Just then, a familiar broad-shouldered figure came through the French Doors.

"Oh, Kate! Come and hear Mrs. Mathew play the harpsichord," said William. He glanced at Rev. Adam curiously. "And you, too, Sir."

"This is my husband, William Blake," I murmured.

Jeremy Adam was not one to waste his time on husbands. He took his leave, bending over my hand, and looking into my eyes. And then, I am certain, I saw a look of dawning recognition pass across his sharp features.

I rose and hurriedly followed William into the house, where I feigned a headache and caused us to leave soon after.

The invitations to the Mathews' evenings tapered off. I avoided attending, even when we were invited, to avoid Jeremy Adam. The little pile of *Poetical Sketches*, newly printed, never seemed to get sent to any bookseller. We had them around for years. William lost interest in those first poems of his, because he had so many other ideas.

I began to realize that William was prey to nervous anxieties, as my mother had divined. He would often complain of pain in his abdomen—this happened often after he had seen a vision. I would bring him warm milk and put my arms around him for comfort. Some nights he would awake in terror from a bad dream. Then he would take up his drawing materials, and I would sit by him, shivering with my shawl over my shoulders, while he captured the vision. This would give him power over it. It would calm him to have me by him, he said. I learned to stay very still and focus my thoughts on peacefulness.

Sometimes William would work late into the night, and I would go to bed alone. Half awake, half asleep, I would hear his voice in conversation with others. The tones were sometimes low, sometimes strident. Never once did I think we had human visitors. I knew from my own voices, the same sound of his. And I saw a light through the door—not the light of a candle, something bluer, more luminous. Sometimes he would tell me who his visitor had been: an ancient

King, a dead poet, the ghost of someone nobody knew. Visitors from the world of spirits with desperate eyes and stories to tell.

There were other spirits, too. I could hardly believe it at first, because it frightened me so much. Visitors with wings and auras that even I could see, when I crept to the door and opened it a crack, because the light from underneath had been so bright, like lightning. Magnificent creatures, with long hair like flames, neither male nor female, carrying spears, or bows, or musical instruments. And then I would prostrate myself upon the floor and pray to God to make me worthy of these visions, because I knew it was my destiny in life to help William understand what to do with them. And I knew William would not always know what I saw, that it would also be my destiny to watch over him. I knew, too, that I resented this, my role in life.

From Kate's Notebook.
Tuesday, April 28, 1829.

I know that young Mr. Tatham has a great desire to be a Good Man. He is so prim and proper sometimes it annoys me, but then I remember how his Father has been a close friend and Patron of ours, and I forgive Fred his pompous ways.

"Mrs. Blake!" Fred called to me this morning from the breakfast room, "Mr. Linnell is to call today, and I have written the Earl of Egremont in Petworth. I think he is interested in the *Faerie Queene.*"

"Sir George?" I responded, emerging from the kitchen with my hair tied back in a white kerchief and flour on my apron. "He was formerly a patron of William's—he owns the *Vision of the Last Judgement* and something else as I recall. But of course, I remember him from Felpham. He was one of the Justices of the Peace at William's trial."

Frederick, who had not even been born in 1804, the year of William's trial for sedition, is always interested in my remembrances of our three years in Sussex.

"I believe he always liked us," I said. "William tutored his children in drawing. But what do you think we should ask for the *Faerie Queene?*"

The painting is a large watercolour which shows a procession of all the characters from Spenser's poem, most on horseback. There are

Blake, *The Whirlwind: Ezekiel's Vision of the Cherubim and Eyed Wheels* (Illustration to the Old Testament, Ezekiel 1:4–28) (c. 1803–1805). Pen and water-color over graphite on paper. Reproduced with permission. Copyright © 2002 Museum of Fine Arts, Boston. Gift by subscription, 90.95. Courtesy of Museum of Fine Arts, Boston

spirits in the sky above. It had been painted as a companion picture to the similar procession William had done of Chaucer's *Canterbury Pilgrims*.

"I think you might ask a great deal," Frederick said, "the Earl of Egremont is a wealthy man. Perhaps eighty pounds."

I gasped, "That is a fortune! I would never be needy again!"

"That is what I hope," said Frederick, smiling.

"I don't think I need to talk this over with William," I said, "you go ahead and see what you can arrange!"

And I thought, Now if he could only wheedle the *Job* engravings out of John Linnell.

I can see them together now, William and Mr. Linnell. They liked to go out together, to plays, or to the opera. Both were short, powerfully built men, sandy-haired, William old enough to be Linnell's father. They were both artists and so had much in common despite the thirty-five years difference in their ages. I have to admit that Linnell, now at thirty-seven years, is an outstanding engraver too.

I could see that Mr. Linnell had great respect for William, not only as deference by a young man for an older mentor, but because he genuinely admired his conversation. He saw that we had commissions in our poverty, introduced us to patrons, and even paid us in advance for making engravings from watercolours of the *Job* designs.

Yet I do not like Mr. Linnell all that much. He looks angelic with his high brow and wide-set eyes, but he thinks he owns everything William painted!

Oh, I know he gave us fine Dutch paper to use for the *Dante* watercolour designs. William had made one hundred and two compositions, not all finished, of course. And then there were the twenty-nine watercolours illustrating *The Pilgrim's Progress* that William left uncompleted. I had coloured some of those myself, lightly washing the outlines with green or blue.

Mr. Linnell had paid William by the week for the Dante designs, and so he had taken them all away after William's death.

"When Mr. Linnell comes today," I said, "I want you to remind him that he still owes me money for the Dantes!"

3

In Which I Become Acquainted with the Blake Family

Friday, May 1, 1829.

I began today to tell Mr. Tatham about William's family. I tried so hard to like them, I really did. But I only succeeded in being fond of Robert, who used to come often to visit us in Green Street. He was fifteen then, rather delicate looking because of his falling sickness, and there was the sweetness of his expression! He looked like a younger version of William, with straighter hair. He would spend hours drawing in his Notebook with William, for he was attending the Royal Academy Schools, as William had.

Sometimes Robert would come with us on our long walks beyond London, where the fields lie green and pleasant. After a day's walking, we would come home and have bread and cheese and porter, and talk into the early hours. Or at least William and Robert would talk. I would often fall asleep in my chair, waiting for them to go to bed. Robert spent so much time with us that sometimes I resented it. I never seemed to be alone with William.

One night I said to Robert, somewhat testily, "Don't you think it is time you went home, Bob?"

Well! You would have thought I had uttered the most terrible blasphemy. William stood up in a rage.

"Kneel down and beg Robert's pardon directly," he commanded, "or you'll never see my face again!"

I was astonished, but I recognized that one of William's rages was coming on, so I swallowed my pride, though I thought it very hard, and knelt down in front of young Robert.

"Robert, I beg your pardon. I am in the wrong to speak to you in that way."

Then Robert said something which endeared him to me forever.

"Young woman, you lie," he said, "*I* am in the wrong." And he took himself home. We always got along after that. I was never again jealous of William's love for him. Which was just as well, because I never got along with the rest of William's family.

His father and mother, though resigned to our marriage, were never really pleased to have me for a daughter-in-law. They would have preferred someone who brought money into their Haberdashery business. Mrs. Blake loved to be in the shop on the ground floor of their house, arranging ribbons, gloves and stockings on the long wooden tables. I much preferred the materials of William's trade, the papers, pens, inks and engraving tools.

William's mother, after seeming friendly to me, had begun to be quite critical. She would say, "You really are too thin, dear," or "Don't you think William should visit his Father more often?" or, pointedly, "Time for babies, isn't it?" I felt she was watching everything we did. She seemed to know every time we went to see Mrs. Mathew, or had dinner with the Flaxmans, or what Engravings William had in hand.

She always seemed to be whispering to Cathy, William's sister, about things that excluded me, or she drew unfavourable comparisons between us.

"Why can't you set a table properly like Cathy?" she complained to me. She never appreciated anything I did do well, like Embroidery. I made her a cushion cover with a bouquet of daisies worked in cross-stitch. She accepted it politely enough, but never used it, I noticed.

Mrs. Blake had always been possessive of William. She was convinced he was a Genius, and had always encouraged his drawing and writing. She was very ambitious for him, and he certainly enjoyed his mother's encouragement and attention when it suited him. Then when he wanted to do something she disapproved of, he would blithely go his own way, knowing she would always come around. After he married me, William seemed to think I could handle his mother's attentions and interferences in our daily lives as he did not want to be troubled by such details.

It used to drive me to distraction. Every thing I did was commented upon.

"I am going to make a Baked Custard for William," I told her one day, as she watched me take little packets of Mace and Cinnamon out of my cupboard.

"He much prefers it with Almond Milk instead of Cinnamon," she said, peering over my shoulder. Then she spent twenty minutes instructing me how to pound Almonds and add them to Barley water, as if I did not already know. I had my own copy of *The Art of Cookery made Plain and Easy*, which my sister Sarah had given me as a wedding present.

I started a little garden out behind the house on Green Street. It was only a small patch between the brick houses, but it was sunny. There I grew carrots and peas from seeds my father gave me. I planted huge sunflowers down one side, and even managed blue forget-me-nots and a rose bush which bloomed pale pink. William's mother found me there one day about a year after we married, and decided to have a little talk.

"My friend Mrs. Grant has a beautiful new Baby Granddaughter," she began. "James and I are so looking forward to Grandchildren. Do you like children, Kate?"

"Of course."

"Well, then, are you and William going to have a family soon?"

She did not say *if not, why not*, but she might as well have. I was upset by this visit. I wanted to have a baby very much, but nothing had happened. I had always imagined it would be easy for me to conceive, given the fertility of my mother. But no baby had yet appeared. William wanted a child too, and we fully expected to have more than one. I was not seriously worried that I had not become pregnant in the first year of marriage, but there was a little nagging fear some-where in the back of my mind that Mrs. Blake's words stirred. I cut two big sunflower heads to put in a jar on my dining table, and said truthfully, "I, too, hope we have a baby soon, but it is in the hands of God." Here was just one more way that Mrs. Blake made me feel inad-equate.

"You seem melancholy, my little Rose-Tree," said William to me not long after my conversation with his mother. I told him, and he kissed me tenderly and said I was all he needed: children could come or not.

(There is something that I cannot tell. William was an unconven-tional lover. The Act of Love was magic. It took us to places inde-scribable, and William knew ways to get there, secret places to touch with fingers and tongue; incense to smell and fragrant oils to massage. It was a way to worship the Body.)

I was beautiful in those days, and so was William. So many around us were not: poor Flaxman had a curved back; several other friends had pock-marked faces from childhood diseases. Robert Blake, look-ing thin, still had falling fits and had begun to cough rather too much. William, however, was broad, straight and full of energy, and I was full-breasted and small of waist. Men turned to look at me when I passed by. The memory of our nights in the candle-lit bedroom haunted my days, giving me confidence to stand up to William's mother.

I perceived that William's sister, Cathy, wanted to be my friend. She was a plain girl, but she had the fine grey eyes of all the Blakes, and a ladylike manner, which she keeps to this very day, though we are not friends anymore. In those days, she often engaged me in conversa-tion, or paid a visit to us in Green Street. She and I would sit and sew together; sometimes she came with William and me when we went to the stationers to buy drawing paper and quill pens. But Mrs. Blake did not like to see us becoming close.

Mrs. Blake had a round face, cold blue eyes, and an imperious manner. She could be vivacious and charming, in which case everyone around her was cheerful, or she could be shrewish and cruel, and then there was a dark mood in the house that you could almost feel. I could even see its blue colour. Everything in the household revolved around her, and if she was not the centre of attention, she soon brought the conversation around to where she was. Thus if Cathy and I were whispering about some inconsequential matter as young women will, Mrs. Blake had to take over.

William's father, James, seemed oblivious to family relations. He was a tall, taciturn man, especially when his wife was near. He liked to wear dark clothes and a broad beaver hat. He was very much a man of business, always carrying with him his Account Books. He was ambitious for William, whom he recognized had a special talent, and he gave us money for art supplies without being asked. Yet there was always irritation in his attitude to William. Though he never accepted my marriage to William, he was always civil to me, once it had taken place. He seemed to be short of breath quite often, and I noticed he did not walk out in the City as frequently as he did when I first met him.

On an evening shortly after my conversation with Mrs. Blake in the garden, I had gone alone to the Blakes' house on Broad Street to visit Cathy. William was working at home. Cathy and I were sitting by the fire doing needlework, and William's brother John, the Baker, was helping his father do some accounting at the big oak table behind us. All was peaceful until Mrs. Blake entered the room.

"I have lost my cameo brooch," she complained. "It is my favourite piece of jewellery, given me by my mother. Cathy, have you seen it?"

"No, Mother," replied Cathy, "and I have not seen you wear it recently."

"But I know it was in my box," complained her mother, "and the box was on my bedside table. Someone must have stolen it!"

"Mother, you always are hasty," observed John. "Why would any-one steal only your cameo and nothing else?"

"Because that would be the one thing they wanted," said Mrs. Blake. "It was always much admired. You have always liked it, haven't you, Kate?"

I felt my cheeks go hot. The implication was unbelievable to me. I did not know what response to make, and I was angrier than I have ever been in my life, and could not show it.

"Yes," I replied in as quiet a tone as I could manage, "it is very beautiful." And indeed it was a lovely oval cameo with a silver surrounding edge, and a delicate white profile on the amber background.

"Cathy, come and help me look for it," ordered Mrs. Blake.

As Cathy followed her out of the room, John Blake smiled at me pointedly. I had never liked him, especially since he was so familiar with me. He reminded me of Jeremy Adam. Ever since we first met, he took liberties that no man should with his brother's wife.

On one occasion, not long before, he had come upon me alone in Mrs. Blake's kitchen.

"Aha, the fetching Mrs. William Blake," he said, coming close. I was backed up against the oak table. John boldly put his hand in my Bosom, tearing my muslin collar. My stomach lurched. I gasped, but he had already another hand up my skirt, pinching my Buttocks.

"Stop this!" I cried. "How dare you handle me so!"

"You are too tempting Kate," he smiled, slowly backing off, but with a lingering finger on my nipple, "You'd do better to hide your Charms."

He made my skin crawl, and a horrible wave of Shame passed over me. What was there about me that made this happen? Was it really my fault? After that, I always kept my distance from John. I never told William, for it would only have made trouble in the family. From then on, John disliked me as much as I him.

Mrs. Blake and Cathy were still out of the room, looking for the Cameo.

John said, "You could get a pretty penny for that brooch at a pawn shop."

"I am sure it is only mislaid," I replied.

"Why don't you ask Brother William to go into a Trance and find it?" John laughed unpleasantly. He never lost a chance to sneer at William. I could never understand why James Blake seemed so much fonder of John than his other sons. He had a recklessness about him. Later, when he joined the Army and was killed fighting Napoleon's army in Holland, I was not grieved.

No more was said about the cameo, though Mrs. Blake did not find it. I returned home, quite depressed, to find William in a Trance. He was seated at his drawing table and staring intently at the corner of the room, from whence emanated a shifting light. I felt annoyed, as I really had wanted to speak to him about what happened. Once William was in one of his Visions, I had to wait till it was over. I sighed.

"What do you see?" I asked in a whisper.

"It is Joseph," he said, not moving his gaze, "son of Jacob, whose brothers sold him into Egypt, who interpreted the dreams of the Pharaoh! He is telling me to put him in a picture." I was glad William had a new inspiration for his watercolours, as he was planning to exhibit next year at the Royal Academy, though I wished he had a little more time for my concerns.

"Tell Joseph you are going to bed," I said.

Mrs. Sarah Goodhouse, the Midwife, answered our knock herself. She lived not far from the Blakes' near Golden Square, and had a reputation for delivering healthy babies.

Her red hair was tucked into a frilly cap, and she wore a long white apron. She was tall, with graceful movements. She smiled, beckoning Cathy and me to sit with her at a scrubbed wooden table. A girl of about ten years was sweeping the hearth and soon took the ashes outside. The clean room smelled of lavender. Dried flowers and twigs hung in bundles from the low ceiling, and along one wall was a shelf of glass vials and jars, all labelled with strange names which I carefully sounded out, *valerian, feverfew, elecampane, mandrake.*

"Which one of you needs my help?" the Midwife asked. Cathy giggled nervously. I told my problem briefly.

"It is early yet," said Mrs. Goodhouse, "but come, and let me examine you." There was a small bed at one end of the room in an alcove. Mrs. Goodhouse indicated that I should lie on it, and she drew a curtain for privacy. She pushed my skirt up around my waist and felt my waist and stomach firmly. Then she did something that shocked me, though she did warn me.

"I will feel inside you," she said, "to be sure all is well there." It was an odd feeling, not exactly painful, but uncomfortable, and I gasped.

"You are normal there, Mrs. Blake," she said. "Do you bleed every month?"

"Well, almost," I told her truthfully, "but I cannot count on the same day every month. Some months I wait one week or more, and then I feel much pain."

"And do you bleed heavy?" she asked.

I told her I did not.

"Well, then, I will give you something to help you bleed properly every month. That would be a good beginning. You are young and strong, and I do not think you need worry just yet that a child does not come. Do you love your husband?"

I assured her that I did.

"And does he give you pleasure?"

I was embarrassed that Cathy could hear, she being eighteen and unmarried still, but I replied that he did. I thought, it was more than pleasure: I could not express it.

Mrs. Goodhouse busied herself preparing a potion for me as I straightened my clothing.

"This is Angelica syrup," she said, "add a teaspoon to a cup of hot water and drink it once a day. It is pleasant tasting, do not fear. And come and see me again if it does not work. And keep yourself calm, my dear, and free from worry."

As I paid Mrs. Goodhouse a few pennies, I felt happy and confident that things were going to work out. Well, that is what youth is for, isn't it? We are all hopeful then and sure that fortune is going to smile on us. And it always does, for a while.

Cathy, who did not get about very much, was fascinated by Mrs. Goodhouse's herb cupboard and glass jars and bowls, the copper pots hanging over the cooker, the dried flowers. I think that's what inspired her to study herbal lore.

She was too excited to want to go home right away, and so we wandered about the streets in the late afternoon. It was a day in mid-September, clear and blue, with a trace of the heavy heat of summer still in the air. We jostled our way along the roads, keeping close to the wall and dodging Chair-men and little boys who might pick our pockets.

Then something strange happened. It had been a long time since I had heard a voice of my own, instructing me to do something. But now, out of the blue, came a voice in my head, saying "Turn down this street."

"Let us see what is down here," I proposed to Cathy, and we headed off to our right. At the end of the street I saw a house with a trade sign of three golden balls. "That is the house of a pawnbroker," said the voice. I could hear my own heartbeat as we approached. What was I to find? I could not possibly go into the house, as it was hardly respectable to do so, but as it happened the old Jewish Merchant was sitting outside behind a little table. On the table were several gleaming objects.

"Good afternoon, dear Ladies," said the Jew to us, his dark eyes observant, "won't you stop and look at some pretty baubles?"

"Look," said my voice.

I looked. On the table was a small silver box with a hinged lid, a man's round gold watch, a necklace of coloured glass beads all inlaid, and Mrs. Blake's silver-rimmed cameo brooch.

We ran all the way home. Cathy was mystified, but I was not, remembering John Blake's words to me about the brooch being able to fetch a pretty penny at a pawnshop.

"We must not tell your mother," I warned her, "for she could not afford to buy the brooch back from the Merchant, and she would move heaven and earth to find out who pawned it. Everyone would be in turmoil—it would be very unpleasant!"

"But who could have pawned it?" Cathy asked, her grey eyes troubled. "Only our family members knew where it was kept."

That evening at supper at the Blakes', I had occasion to observe John. He seemed cheerful.

"I passed a Pawnshop today," I could not resist saying, "and I was surprised at the lovely jewellery for sale."

Cathy looked up at me, surprised. John looked at me with interest. The others went on with their meal, oblivious.

"Probably most of that jewellery was stolen," observed William, "I have heard there are bands of children who steal together."

"Is there not a terrible Retribution for those who steal?" asked Mrs. Blake. "I believe it is Hanging."

"What kind of jewellery did you see?" asked Cathy, surmising my intent.

"Oh, necklaces, brooches, little things like that."

John said nothing, but toyed with his fork.

"I wish you had seen my Cameo," said Mrs. Blake.

Cathy began a little fit of coughing, almost drowning out John's words.

"But that would mean it was stolen, Mother, and you know it is only misplaced," he said.

I looked squarely at John, whose mouth twitched slightly.

"Then let us hope Mrs. Blake soon finds her Cameo," I said. "It would be horrible to think that thieves can be at work so close to us."

"Yes, indeed," said John. And he smiled at me, bold as brass.

Cathy and I never spoke of this again, even when Mrs. Blake repeatedly bewailed her loss. Cathy, no doubt, believed John had pawned the cameo, but as I warned her, tacitly agreed not to stir up trouble in the family. Nor did I ever tell William. It would only have inflamed his dislike of John and brought on a Rage. If Mrs. Blake really disliked me so much that she thought I was capable of stealing from her, then John's action had played into her hands. Yet she did not pursue the issue.

Two months went by, and I took my Angelica syrup faithfully, but to no avail.

At this time William was always busy engraving book illustrations of Tom Stothard's pictures for novels. Tom had commissions from Harrison's *Novelist's Magazine,* which reprinted popular novels, one part every week, and sold them for sixpence. Tom was working on *Clarissa* by Samuel Richardson, who, I learned, had written the story about Pamela, the serving maid to whom Mrs. Montague had compared me.

"Do you have to make so much noise?" I complained one day, as William banged away with hammer and chisel on the Anvil in his workroom. He had just been to the Brazier to purchase sheets of Copper.

William at the Anvil was an impressive sight. The strength of his arms was channelled to his Task, his Energy seemed to fly out the ends of his fair hair. He carefully squared the cut edges of the copper plate with hammer and chisel, and then began to polish it with a piece of willow charcoal and water. He ignored my complaint.

"Kate, will you pass me that dish of Olive Oil?"

"Yes, but what on earth for?"

He dipped a rolled piece of felt in the oil.

"Watch."

He burnished the surface of the plate with the felt and olive oil until it was smooth as a mirror. It took a good while.

"Now you can bring me some crumbs of stale bread," he said.

Mystified, I did as I was told. With the absorbent breadcrumbs, William removed the oil from the Plate, and so it was ready for use.

When William was ready to engrave a Design, he would incise a line with his Graver, which was a small steel rod about four inches long, with a rounded handle. He pressed the point of the Graver into the surface of the plate, and there would be a little curl on either side of the tool, called a Burr. Sometimes he would use dots or short lines, called Flicks. After painstaking work, there would emerge an image on the copper, people and trees and skies and buildings. The real magic came when the plate was printed.

We did not buy our own press until we started the business with the Parkers after William's father died. Before that, I had been to a print shop with William to see how it was done. The Printer presses ink into the lines engraved on the plate with a little cloth ball called a Dabber. The extra ink is rubbed from the plate, and finished by the palm of the hand, till it is quite clean.

I observed that a copper-plate Press is really a sliding board which passes between two rollers. You put damp paper carefully against the plate, with special blankets on top, and roll it under the rollers with enough pressure to force the paper into the hollows and pull out the ink. When the design comes out it is called an Impression. You have to re-ink the plate between Impressions. I became quite good at this. I especially enjoyed the smokey smell of the ink.

I noticed that William had different ways of signing his work. If he had engraved the design of Tom Stothard or some other artist, after his name he would write *sculpsit*, or just *sculp*. If he had etched it, which means the lines were incised by acid, he would write *fecit*. And if he had made up the design himself, he would write *invenit*. This language is called Latin, and all educated people know it.

"William, will you teach me to be an Engraver like you?" I asked him one day about two years after we were married.

He looked surprised.

"That is too hard for a woman, Kate. And it takes a long time to learn. I apprenticed to James Basire when I was fifteen years old, remember. But don't look so disappointed. I could teach you to draw and paint. Many women do that very well."

So I made myself a little Notebook of good drawing paper, to keep as a drawing book and a secret Journal, which I still have. William taught me to draw, first spheres and cones and squares, and later objects around the house, chairs and tables and bowls. Later, he also taught me to paint, and we painted all his own works together, by which time I did get to help him at the printing press. Of course, it was always really William's work, except that I did paint one very good picture on my own in later years, which I gave away. There were other drawings in ink and pencil, too, which I do not like to remember I made.

"Why on earth are you learning to draw?" asked Mrs. Blake when she heard about it. "Aren't two artists in the family enough?" She was referring to William and Robert. She went on, "It won't do you any good to pretend you are a Lady."

I thought it best to keep silent. I knew that drawing was an accomplishment of women like Mrs. Mathew, but that was not my reason for wanting to do it. It was something I did as Kate, not as Blake's wife. I liked the feeling when I had captured an Image on paper that had been before me, even if it was only a picture of a daisy in a milk jug. What I really wanted to draw was a portrait of William. Later, when I did so, it turned out to be one of my best works. I drew him in profile, his hair curling down his neck with a life of its own, and his eye serious.

"I like it," said William, "and now I will draw you."

And he drew me full face, with my hair loose. I think I rather resemble William in that drawing—but then, all of William's Portraits of people look like him.

William called me his Sweet Shadow of Delight. I liked the Delight part. But what did it mean to be someone's Shadow? Surely a Shadow had no substance of its own, it was only the dark reflection of someone. So was I only the reflection of William, the reflection of his own delight, and therefore sweet to him? Only that?

Old James, William's father, was sitting by the fire wrapped in a blanket. I recall it was a Sunday afternoon in early January in 1784, and William and I had joined the Blakes for dinner at their house in Broad Street. Robert and Cathy were present, too, and James, the elder brother, but not John.

Blake, *Full Face Head of a Young Woman.* Courtesy of Rare Books and Special Collections Division, McGill University Libraries, Montreal

Catherine Blake, *Portrait of the Young William Blake.* Courtesy of Fitzwilliam Museum, Cambridge

Mr. Blake said, "Kate, you should try to draw a portrait of Cathy for me."

Cathy blushed, and said, "Why me, Papa?"

"Because you are my only daughter, and because you are now twenty years old," he smiled at her. I said I would try, and she could come to sit for me the very next day. I thought Robert and William exchanged glances as if to say they did not think I could do it.

James said, matter-of-factly, "I had a vision last night."

Now it was known that Broad Street had been built upon the site of an old burial ground, and ghosts were said to be seen there. Certainly William had seen some in his youth, but we had never heard James make such a claim.

"And who was it?" asked William with interest.

"A man who died of the plague," said James. "Very sad, he was. He was looking for something he had lost."

"I sympathize," said Mrs. Blake.

"Did he wail?" asked Cathy.

"No, I did not hear him speak. He just looked."

"I know that kind," said William. "You must speak to them with your mind, and then their words will come to you."

This sort of conversation always made me uneasy. I did not think these things should be spoken of so matter-of-fact.

"I have never seen a Ghost," said Robert, "but I can imagine being one. I will appear to you, William, often, I promise."

William blanched. "Do not speak of this, even in jest, Bob! Heaven forbid that you should die just to appear before me as a ghost!"

"It is a comfort," said Mr. Blake, smiling, "to have sons who will see me as a ghost after I have gone."

"This conversation is getting morbid," said Mrs. Blake. "It is time for dinner for those of us in corporeal form!" We were all in a rather giddy mood after this, except for Cathy, who remained serious.

The next day Cathy came to Green Street to let me begin to draw her. She wore her brown hair curling under a little lacy cap, and she had on a pretty embroidered shawl. She sat quietly before me in a low chair; I sat facing her with my drawing book on the table in front of me. All was quiet in the room.

Suddenly a cup and saucer fell from the dresser and crashed on the floor. Before I could express my surprise, one of the plates came flying off the shelf and broke at my feet.

"What is this?" I cried out, "Did the earth shake?"

Cathy remained fixed to her chair, very pale.

"Oh, look!" she whispered, as the little wooden footstool by the fire began to move, and circled crazily about the room.

Then there came a knocking from under the table and I rose in fear, upsetting my drawing board and papers, and Cathy and I ran from the room and down the stairs, through the landlord's kitchen and out to the little garden.

"Oh, why is this happening to me!" Cathy began to weep.

"This has happened before?"

"Yes, a few times this year." She was shaking.

I calmed down soon, because after all, I was used to this sort of thing with William, although flying china had not been part of his repertoire. I made Cathy a dish of camomile tea to soothe her, and told her to try to keep a quiet mind, and these happenings would soon go away. I thought more than once in the days to come of my mother's apprehensions about the family.

From Kate's Notebook.
June 14, 1829. Lisson Grove.

Mr. Tatham is working hard at becoming an Artist. He is always trying some new material. First it was Watercolour, then Tempera, and now I think he is going to try to be another Flaxman, for he is turning his hand to sculpture these days. He is going to do busts of his clients: he has a way with heads. He says the clay feels good in his hands. He makes a movement here, a stroke there—he thinks it is like being God.

He had wanted to do a full length female figure of a wood nymph, and asked Maria to model, but she was shocked at the idea and refused, her fine black eyebrows arching in distaste. Now he has to find a professional model, always a risky business.

"Lucky Blake," he said to me, "to have a wife who would model for him."

We were in Frederick's art room, where all my inherited books and pictures by William are stored.

On the table were a pile of pencil sketches for designs of Dante's *Inferno*, which John Linnell had commissioned; odd, compelling images. There are scores of drawings and engravings of Biblical subjects. Especially fine is a large pen and ink drawing of the story of Job done early in William's career, *What is Man that thou shouldst Try him every Moment?* I posed as Job's wife. I had luxuriant hair in those days.

I saw Frederick picking up a group of illustrations which were just rough sketches, left unfinished at William's death. I had put them in a folder labeled "Five Illustrations to the Book of Enoch." Frederick knew the story—how two hundred angels, called Watchers of Heaven, became enamoured of the Daughters of Men and descended and copulated with them, begetting monsters.

The first drawing shows the figure of a lovely naked woman, enticingly curved, with full breasts and slim waist, gesturing with one arm outstretched as over her hover two angels, with rays of light like stars emanating from their huge phalluses. Another, titled *An Angel Teaching a Daughter of Men the Secrets of Sin*, pictures in faint sketch a descending angel reaching down with one hand and touching the vulva of a naked standing girl.

William must have been at least sixty-five years old when he sketched these. He still had sexual desires. Were these curvaceous women with their luxuriant curly hair memories of me in my youth? I smiled to myself and noted that Frederick was hiding his thoughts by pretending to be terribly interested in the clay as he returned to his sculpting.

"When did you first meet my father?" Frederick asked me just this morning. He invited me to sit with him in the Morning Room while Maria was preparing to go shopping for ribbons or some such thing. She was always shopping.

"Oh, about ten years ago," I told him. "Mr. Linnell introduced us. I remember William gave your father a copy of *America,* and Mr. Tatham gave us his book on Architecture."

"That was a long time ago," said Frederick, "but I remember well our dinner together five years ago at Mr. Linnell's house in Hampstead.

I was but nineteen then. I will never forget that he had a Vision, right there at the table!"

It had been King Saul. I remember William had trouble drawing that helmet and armour.

Frederick recalled that William said, "I can't go on—he is gone! I must wait till he returns!" as if the Vision didn't like to sit for his portrait for very long.

"Of course, Mr. Blake's best visionary portraits were the ones he did with Mr. Varley," I told Frederick.

That was in 1819, when we lived in South Molton Street and Mr. Varley's studio was nearby in Great Titchfield Street. Mr. Varley was a great astrologer. He cast William's horoscope and even published it in an Astologer's magazine, called *Urania*, I think. He wrote about William's conversations with William Wallace and Cleopatra while he drew them. He said that William's extraordinary faculties were the effects of the Moon in Cancer in the Twelfth House, and so forth!

William did not really believe in Astrology but Mr. Varley believed in William's visions. He kept all the portraits in a notebook.

I remember around that time at Mr. Varley's, William saw the Ghost of a Flea. It was horrible. He said it was covered with a scaly skin of gold and green, had a tongue whisking out of his mouth, and a cup in his hand to hold blood. Mr. Varley handed William a pencil and paper, and he drew the portrait. The Flea told William that all fleas are inhabited by the souls of men who were excessively blood-thirsty, and were providentially confined to the size and form of insects, otherwise, should he be the size of a horse, he would depopulate a great portion of the country.

Later.

Frederick is always asking me about William's Visions, and my own, too. He wants to see them himself. I know that he is on a spiritual search of his own. I suspect he dearly wants to be a preacher. He wants to feel the rapture.

Only yesterday Frederick held William's *Milton* in his hand, turning over the pages of the small closely written volume, which seemed to glow with an amber light because of their rich colours. This had been our own copy. I knew these words fascinated Fred, for they revealed William's calling:

> And did those feet in ancient time,
> Walk upon Englands mountains green:
> And was the holy Lamb of God,
> On Englands pleasant pastures seen!
>
> And did the Countenance Divine,
> Shine forth upon our clouded hills?
> And was Jerusalem builded here,
> Among these dark Satanic Mills?
>
> Bring me my Bow of burning gold:
> Bring me my Arrows of desire:
> Bring me my Spear: O clouds unfold!
> Bring me my Chariot of fire!
>
> I will not cease from Mental Fight,
> Nor shall my Sword sleep in my hand:
> Till we have built Jerusalem,
> In Englands green & pleasant Land.

I love those words, and that is why I copy them out again.

Part Two

LONDON 1784–1800

In thunders ends the voice. Then Albions Angel wrathful burnt
Beside the Stone of Night; and like the Eternal Lions howl
In famine & war, replyd. Art thou not Orc, who serpent-form'd
Stands at the gate of Enitharmon to devour her children;
Blasphemous Demon, Antichrist, hater of Dignities;
Lover of wild rebellion, and transgresser of Gods Law;
Why dost thou come to Angels eyes in this terrific form?

Blake, *America*, Plate 9, Copy E (1793). Lessing J. Rosenwald Collection, Library of Congress. Copyright © 2003
the William Blake Archive. Used with permission

4

In Which We Run A Print Shop and Meet Mr. Hayley

James Blake, William's father, died in the last week of June, 1784, in his sixty-third year. We buried him in the Dissenters' graveyard at Bunhill Fields on Sunday the fourth of July. It was a bright cloudless day, and our dark mourning clothes made us look like walking shadows on the green landscape among the tombstones. I felt sorry to say goodbye to James, who had always been kind to me, if distant. I also sympathised with Mrs. Blake, who was now left alone with young James to run the Hosiery Business and look after Cathy and Robert at home. But I felt sorriest for Cathy, who became even more the sole focus of her mother's attentions.

William reacted with great calm to his father's death, for he had all his life felt a stubborn resentment against old James. He believed that his parents preferred John, "the Evil one," as he would call him. I could see there was a kind of lazy charm about John, even though I disliked him, and he did seem to captivate James and Catherine. But William, resenting the situation, never forgave his parents. He was not hypocritical enough to pretend a Sorrow he did not feel, and did not shed a tear at the Funeral. I thought this rather harsh, because to me James had always seemed generous to William, and an amiable man.

. . .

Soon we received a pleasant surprise. James had left William a tidy sum of money, about one hundred pounds.

"We will start our own Print Selling Shop," said William to me, "and I know just the man to be partner!" So into our lives came James and Anne Parker.

James Parker had been William's fellow apprentice at Basire's Engraver's Shop. His people were originally from Wales, though now his father was a Corn Chandler in London. James was stocky, with dark hair and eyes and a fine singing voice. He had the dark moods of a Welshman, too. Why is it that Men are so prone to Melancholy?

His wife Anne was small, fair and cheerful enough. I never knew anyone so intent upon Sweeping and Polishing. I know this because once we became Partners, William and I moved with the Parkers to a house at 27 Broad Street, Golden Square, where we set up the Print Selling shop of *Parker and Blake*. (This house was right next door to 28 Broad Street, where the Blakes lived.)

Now we had a Shop on the ground floor, with a kitchen and sitting room above that, and bedrooms for each couple on the next storey. There was also a little attic room with windows, which we used to store boxes and extra supplies for the shop.

The most exciting thing about the move was that William was able to buy his own wooden Rolling Press for forty pounds, and from then on was able to see his own work through from beginning to end. That is how I came to know so much about Printing, too.

Living next to the Blakes and their Hosiery Business as we did, Robert and Cathy were often in and out, as was William's mother, who liked to check up on us, and was always looking at me keenly with her piercing blue eyes to see if I was with child.

There were few Print shops in London and we began to sell artists' work to many fashionable people who were Collectors. We had an oak table for the display of Engravings, and a long cabinet with draw- ers to store them. I loved being in the shop meeting people; Anne Parker preferred to do the cooking and cleaning, and so we divided the work along those lines.

One day in April of 1785 when I was busy in the Shop, and Robert was sketching an arrangement of tools in the corner, William and

James were tinkering with the Press in the back room. Suddenly into the shop stepped a handsome, fair man of about forty years. He was tall and military in bearing, though he used a black rolled-up umbrella as a walking stick, for he had an observable limp.

"Good afternoon," he said, in the accent of a Gentleman, "I am William Hayley, and I am looking for the Author of *Poetical Sketches*."

"Then you are looking for my Husband, sir," I said. "I am Catherine Blake."

He looked at me with keen blue eyes and smiled. I became uncomfortably aware of my ink-stained apron and the untidiness of my hair.

"I am happy to meet you, Mrs. Blake," he said. "John Flaxman has sent me a copy of your husband's book, and I have called to say that I am impressed by it."

William came out of the back room looking grubby.

"Mr. Hayley, here is William," I said.

William knew immediately who William Hayley was. He had heard all about him from John Flaxman. He was a famous Writer, and some called him the greatest living Poet in England. William told me later his poem, *The Triumphs of Temper*, had just gone into a twelfth edition, and Hayley's Collected Works were soon to be published. I must confess, when I tried to read Hayley's poems, I found them very long and dull. But he was such a kind man! He made William feel at ease right away by saying they had likely met years before, when Hayley had lived at No. 5 Great Queen Street, very close to James Basire's. He spoke warmly of Flaxman, whose works he often commissioned. And he was interested in William.

"I have seen your drawings of Joseph at the Royal Academy Exhibit," he said to William. "This is an interesting theme you are developing—the Prophet who is outcast from his own family."

William was more than pleased that Hayley noticed his work, and we spent an hour or so showing him other drawings. He knew a good deal about Art, because his best friend was the fashionable portrait painter George Romney. Romney had introduced Flaxman to Hayley, and because of that John obtained a wonderful commission to make a monument to Hayley's wife's parents in Chichester Cathedral. He had also made sculptured portrait heads of Romney and Hayley for the Library of Hayley's elegant house at Eartham in Sussex.

After a time, Hayley thanked us for showing him William's work, and took his leave of us, expressing a desire to meet again. Robert now came out of his corner, eyes wide, and asked William all about him.

"Is he very rich?"

"Very."

"Does he have many children?"

"No, only one son, near five years old, named Thomas Alfonso. And this son is not the son of his wife, Eliza, but of his housemaid. Flaxman tells me they all live together cordially at Eartham." William looked at me meaningfully. He was always trying to expand my horizons.

"What else did Flaxman tell you about Eliza?" I asked, rather interested in this broad-minded woman.

"Well, she is rather eccentric. She does not spend much time home with Hayley, but goes up to Bath and takes the waters, or comes here to London. She is much given to Melancholy, or else excessive high spirits."

"Well no wonder!"said I.

From Kate's Notebook.
April 28, 1785.

I have written a Poem, like William. Well, not really like William, but to see what it is like to write a Poem. I liked the feeling—but it took me a long time to get the words right. This is a fair copy I make now, without any crossing out of words:

The Crystal House

> I built a house of Cobweb
> And hung it in the Air
> A tear drop was each Window
> A Hope was every Stair.
>
> It glistened in the Sunlight
> It shimmered in the Wind
> It changed its Shape and Substance
> With every Change of Mind.

I saw it turn to Crystal
When in it You did dwell
But when you sighed, it trembled
And when you left, it fell.

That is how I felt for a long time after I knew that William wanted to make love to other women. He had told me how he felt about Nancy Flaxman, and then had never mentioned it again. But I know his heart. If not Nancy, then someone else will take his eye. I am always aware of his attraction to pretty women, and I feel Jealous when often there is no reason.

"A man is made to admire pretty women, Kate!" William exclaimed once when I saw him turn to admire the slim waist and pale bosom of one of the Mathews' guests.

I drew a breath to speak.

"And don't go quoting Scripture at me!"

I am Jealous of more than pretty women. When a young mother passes me in the street with a baby in her arms, I feel a pain in my heart that is surely physical. I imagine the babies that William and I might have: little dark haired boys with grey eyes—or a girl with black eyes and a little round face. I want a child so much, yet the years go by and in spite of all my prayers, I do not conceive.

From Kate's Notebook.
April 30, 1785.

I have a role in William's life as Witness of Visions. I sit, night after night, still as a statue beside him, and sometimes see what he sees. "Bring me my things, Kate," he says.

So I fetch his drawing paper and pens and charcoal pencils. He sketches sometimes during the visitations, sometimes afterward. William seldom seems afraid of what he sees, whereas I am afraid all the time. Fear is something I live with, like another person in the house. It was not there in the beginning, when what I felt most often was Awe. Then William began seeing stranger and stranger visions.

Just two nights ago, when the fire had sunk to glowing coals, we stared into it to see what faces might appear. William always likes to do this, then he draws the faces. He always sees different faces than I do—often they are Kings and Queens of Ancient Britain. I, however, never see anyone recognizable. On this occasion, I decided I, too, would draw what I saw, and was ready with paper and a piece of charcoal.

The room grew colder as the fire died down. I drew my fringed shawl close around my shoulders. William had said not a word for twenty minutes. I could not see at first what he was staring at, but gradually I did see something. A face, yes. But not a human face! What I saw taking shape in the flickering coals was the flat face of a Serpent. It had long, glittering, red eyes, and a forked tongue darting in and out. The head moved sideways and back in a hypnotic motion. I screamed, stood up and dropped my paper into the grate, where it burst into flame. The Serpent face disappeared.

"What happened?" William snapped to attention, turning toward me.

"The Serpent!" I whispered, shaking.

"But that is nothing to fear," he said. I detected a tone of disdain in his voice. "That is only Energy in its most potent form."

"No! It is Satan!" I cried.

A wave of resentment came over me. Always I have been expected to believe everything William says, and I have done so willingly. He knows so much more than I do. But not this time. I know what I saw.

Robert Blake was the only brother for whom William cared. James was busy managing the haberdashery business with his mother, and though William himself was now in business, they seemed to have little in common. Cathy had taken a great interest in Herbs and Healing, and often visited Mrs. Goodhouse, the Midwife, in order to learn from her. I was most interested in what she was doing. When Robert came down with a cough and a fever, it was Cathy who cured him with infusions of Lungwort and Dandelion.

I loved Robert like a brother. He never tired of helping me with my reading and writing, and we used to draw together also. He was now eighteen years old, slim and fair, with a sensitive mouth and the wide brow of all the Blakes. His innocent spirit seemed to shine out of his grey eyes.

One day in the shop, he helped me to serve Reverend Anthony Mathew and his wife Harriet, who were trying to choose a print by Tom Stothard. Anthony Mathew was a plump man with an air of one who expects to be waited on. Harriet wore as usual one of her frilly bonnets. William had been engraving many of Tom's designs for booksellers and had extra prints of several in the shop. We also had a few pen and wash drawings which I thought were a little messy, but the Rev. Mathew admired them for the rhythm of their curving lines. Robert could see that Harriet liked one line drawing of a rearing horse. It looked rather like Flaxman's spare style. Even though he was young, Robert was sensitive to others' feelings and complimented Harriet on her choice.

"I will have this one then!" declared Harriet.

As Robert was placing the drawing between two sheets of paper for her to carry it home safely, William came out of the back room to greet them, wearing his ink-stained apron.

"Well, my good man," said Anthony Mathew, "we have not seen so much of you these past months at our Literary Evenings."

"Pressure of business, sir," said William.

"Then you are not writing much Poetry now?"

"Not so much," said William. This was rather a sore point with us, as the shop did seem to be ruling our lives. Commercial engraving left little time for Poetry.

"Now this young man is the up and coming artist of the family." William turned proudly to Robert. "He studies at the Royal Academy, and no doubt someday will exhibit there, too."

Robert blushed, and after polite conversation, the Mathews paid for their drawing and took their leave.

William seemed agitated. I thought it best not to speak to him until later in the evening. I knew it bothered him that he was really in Business now, rather than spending all his time at art or poetry. He saw that John Flaxman was busy pursuing his Sculpture, and Tom Stothard was making a good living. We were doing well as a business, but William was not producing his own designs as often as he wished.

"Do you know what I want for Bob?" he asked me, as I sat mending that evening. "I want him to be free of Commerce! Let him paint and draw as much as he likes! We won't apprentice him to anyone but ourselves—he doesn't need a Trade. What does a trade do? It allows you to be Patronized, that's what it does!"

I recognized the resentment came from memories of the Mathews' evenings. But there was more on William's mind.

"Why do you think William Hayley came here?" he mused. "It is because he wants to do us a good turn. He wants to help us out. And it is all because of Flaxman!"

"But is not that kindness?" I asked, surprised. "John always tries to send business our way."

"That is just what I am talking about. Even John looks down on us these days because we are not Educated or polished enough in Company."

William was exaggerating, but he was very sensitive on this matter. John and Nancy were out in society a great deal, even though Nancy had to be a frugal housekeeper. They never abandoned us, but William was becoming conscious of their success. Not that William was doing badly himself. We were earning more money than ever in the Print Selling business, and he was busy with commercial engraving, too. In spite of his protestation against trade, he had also begun to teach engraving to Robert.

Thanks to Robert, I was now quite a good reader and writer. It was often an industrious picture in our room in the evenings, with William setting Robert an exercise with his burin on a copper plate, and me poring over a bit of writing that Robert had set me to copy. Sometimes James and Anne would join us before the fire and talk would become lively, for James was as outspoken as William.

One evening James said, "I hear the *Ladies Magazine* wants us to engrave some bloody fashion plates again. They are sending us a portrait by Romney of Mrs. Robinson in another new dress."

"I suppose if you were once the Mistress of the Prince of Wales everyone wants to know what you wear," said Anne, who was herself particular in the way she dressed.

"Is this really the kind of work we want!" said William, glumly.

"It is all money," said James. "Be glad of it!"

"William has grand projects in his head," said Robert. "Fashion engraving only gets in the way of his visions."

"Let us have some rum and water," suggested Anne, going for the mugs.

I found the bottle and a pitcher of water, and we served drinks around. "To Commerce!" toasted William. "To Matrimony's Golden Cage! Even Flaxman, to pay his bills, must work as a rates collector in St. Anne's Parish, ink-bottle in his buttonhole."

"I don't see anything so wrong about earning extra money that way," I defended John. I was rather miffed at the Matrimony-Cage remark. William was often too indifferent to money matters for my liking.

"Ah, Kate," said William to me, "you are an Angel as always. I am surrounded by Angels."

"Draw me an Angel, William," said Robert, tactfully changing the subject. "And what about a poem to go with it? Something like Shakespeare or Milton."

"Shakespeare is too wild," said William, "and Milton is too cold. I will outdo them both, see if I do not. But not tonight!"

Soon after this, I came across a print of one of William's early engravings. He had done it as an apprentice at Basire's, after a design of Michel Angelo, and it is powerful. It shows a muscular old man with a long beard, his arms folded across his chest, staring sadly at the ground. He wears a short garment that reveals his strong body, while he stands on a rocky cliff, overlooking the sea. It is *Joseph of Arimathea among the Rocks of Albion*—Joseph, who brought the blood of Jesus in the Holy Grail to England, who built the first Christian Church at Glastonbury. William told me that Joseph had been the first Prophet in England.

Something about the loneliness of the figure caught at my heart. There was so much of William there. Not the William that everyone saw, day by day, in his ink-stained apron, but the William I saw at night, wrestling with his visions, struggling with Ambition.

About a month later, in May, as I was attending to our Account Book in the shop, I heard voices raised in anger in the back room.

"I cannot do business in this way! Can you never complete anything on time?" It was James's voice.

"Business is not what we are about," snapped William.

"You are a Fool to speak like that! Business is exactly what we are about. Art is not only Inspiration, you know! Money is what we hoped to gain when we entered this partnership, and don't you forget it!"

James stamped out of the room and passed me as he went out the front door. He raised his hands in a gesture of exasperation. I had a sneaking sympathy for James, because William often chose to ignore the practicalities of life. Every so often he would forget to give me money for bread or meat, and I would simply place an empty plate in front of him at meal times. I had already begun to hide away a little leather bag of coins as a secret hoard of savings. I had accumulated one pound sixpence in a year!

William followed James out of the back room, looking glum.

"This cannot go on much longer," he said, not especially to me. "I cannot work with him always after me to finish in his time!"

Just at that point a customer came in to buy a Print, so I was not able to respond to William.

Anne that day cooked an especially good dinner—a lamb stew followed by a spice pudding, all washed down with good English ale. I thought that there were some advantages to living with the Parkers, but it did not surprise me that, after about a year at Broad Street, William wanted to move. Parker and Blake decided to each go his own way, though they often still worked together. William wanted his own place and so did I. In spite of the good meals, I had begun to find Anne's hustle and bustle rather annoying, and besides, she had a baby coming. I was relieved when William told me he had found us a house at 28 Poland Street, just around the corner from Broad Street.

From Kate's Notebook.
August 22, 1829. Lisson Grove.

Today, Frederick looked up from his novel to see me in my bonnet going past his study door, with parcels in my arms.

"Where are you going, Mrs. Blake?"

"Just a visit across the road, Mr. Tatham," I replied. "I am going to visit Mrs. Rivers and her unfortunate ladies. I will take them some apple pies."

Mrs. Rivers's unfortunate ladies are the worst kept secret of the street. In Mrs. Rivers's large house there always live two or three young gentlewomen, not often seen, who never use their real names. After a stay of some months, they depart, leaving behind their shame and indiscretion in the shape of a wee babe. Mrs. Rivers, through many subtle connections, seemed always able to place a child with a country family.

I know Frederick is fascinated by his infrequent glimpses of some young woman, large brimmed hat veiling her face and ample skirts disguising her condition, who might pass by his window. His imagination was overactive; he tended to dwell on the passion that produced the condition, and not on the shame and grief endured by the young lady, banished from her home, her relatives pretending she had gone abroad.

Sometimes Frederick would catch a glimpse of a slender ankle if the wind blew about a swirling skirt. I know he truly repents his thoughts, and prays fervently to be given a true purpose in life.

Fred was examining several small books of Emblems that I had given him to sell. William made them in 1793 and called them *For Children, The Gates of Paradise*. Then about ten years ago, he had revised them and written a prologue and other text, and changed the title to *For the Sexes, The Gates of Paradise*. There was even a small drawing of another title page: *For Children, The Gates of Hell*.

Frederick ponders William's long interest in the idea of Innocence, the innocence of both children and adults. It is a state of grace, a freedom from guilt or moral wrong that Frederick devoutly desires for himself. For twenty years after William first engraved these Emblems, the country was at war, the government invested in the slave trade, famine was abroad in the land, and the government was mercilessly oppressive. Fred has asked me more than once what sustained William's faith in Innocence. I remind him about William's wonderful kindness.

As he turned the small pages with their minutely clear engravings, Frederick was arrested by the image of a naked man prone upon the ground, while over him hovered a winged black devil with moon and stars in his wings. The title read, *To the Accuser who is the God of this World*, set over a coiling serpent. Frederick was startled. He read the verses:

> Truly My Satan thou art but a Dunce
> And dost not know the Garment from the Man

Every Harlot was a Virgin once
Nor canst thou ever change Kate into Nan

Tho Thou art Worshipd by the Names Divine
Of Jesus & Jehovah: thou art still
The Son of Morn in weary Nights decline
The lost Travellers Dream under the Hill

Frederic was shocked to the depth of his being. He asked me if William was truly saying that our idea of God in this world is really Satan. Was it Satan the Accuser who was responsible for Frederick's vague feeling of constant guilt? Did Blake really mean that under it all, Satan could still be Lucifer, the Son of Morn, his unfallen self? I assured him it could be so. Sighing, Frederick began to think then that there could be hope, even for him.

Later.

Maria was in a bad mood this afternoon.

"Frederick, this house is too small," she said, coming into his study, where we were talking, her arms filled with parcels.

"Why do you say that?" he asked. "I thought we were very comfortable here. We have three storeys and a nice little basement kitchen for Mrs. Blake—"

"But the rooms are so mean!" she interrupted. "I have just been calling at the Richmonds on York Street, and they have so much more space."

"And they have so much more money."

"Oh, why can you not do better," complained Maria. "Can you not ask your Father for a better allowance?"

"No, I will not. We must make do. Come now, sweetheart, cheer up. Show us what you have bought at the Haberdashers . . . new ribbons for a bonnet?"

Maria was momentarily distracted, but I saw that Frederick was plunged into melancholy. It probably occurred to him that the only way he could make money at the moment was to find buyers for Blake's work; I had allowed him a percentage of the sales. I was now free from want because of the sale of the *Faerie Queene* to the Earl of Egremont. I could see Fred was thinking that William's paintings and books would have a future value . . . they may be worth hiding away for a few years. I saw him, almost without intention, pick up a copy of the *Gates of Paradise* and put it in his desk drawer, under several papers.

5

In Which Two Sad Events Take Place

*L*ondon streets all have stories. Honey Lane is where people used to keep bees, and Black Boy Alley has a ghost. Poland Street, where William and I moved in 1785, was named for Polish people who came there twenty years before to set up their trades.

As I described it to Mr. Tatham, No. 28 Poland St. was a narrow, red brick house of four storeys, with two rooms on every floor, and a basement. We had never lived in so many rooms! We used the ground floor as a print selling space, with the rolling press in the back room. Underneath was the kitchen. Upstairs was our sitting room and a bedroom, and above that a room for Robert or a guest. We bought an extra chest for bed linen and a plain oak table and two chairs for the sitting room. Mrs. Blake gave me some red woolen material to make curtains for the sitting room and bedroom.

The Christmas season was upon us before I had time to recover from the move to Poland Street. Besides moving the rolling press, we had countless boxes of paper, racks of engraving tools, hammers, and expensive sheets of copper to cart along the streets. William had to see that everything was clean and orderly in his workroom. Our household possessions were my responsibility. I was slower than William to get organized, and was still unpacking bits of crockery as needed.

The days were dark by three o'clock in the afternoon, so we burned many extra candles which cast a lovely light as we worked at the printing press. William hung some of his collection of Prints on the walls and some of his own work, too, including the Dancing Man with arms outstretched that I liked so much from his mother's house.

I planned to give William a new shirt for Christmas, which I was secretly sewing whenever he went out. Cathy Blake came to visit one morning, and we sat doing needlework together. She was twenty-one years old now, with abundant brown hair worn in a little bun at the back of her head, with two curls free on either side of her face. I could never get my own black hair, which was curly, to behave so neatly. I wore it mostly up under a kerchief, or loose when William wanted to use me as a model. Cathy had not the bloom that one expects to see in a young woman. She had outgrown the Knocking Spirits, but there was something pinched about her. I put it down to her mother's domination.

At first she had not much to say as her needle went in and out of her embroidery, but then in a flood, she told me a surprising thing.

"I am in love with Thomas Holloway," she announced, "but you must not tell anyone." Tom Holloway, I knew, was an Engraver who had once lived on Broad Street. He was much older than Cathy, about thirty-seven years, and a widower.

"And does he love you, too?" I asked cautiously.

"Of course he does! Do you think I would be telling you this if he did not? He wants to marry me."

It seemed to me that she should be happy rather than Irritable.

"Well, that is wonderful," I said smoothly, "and does your mother approve? Does James?"

"That is the trouble! No—Mother does not want me to marry him. Just because he is older and has two little children! And of course James agrees with Mother."

I knew that Mrs. Blake was ambitious for Cathy, and would have liked to see her marry someone with more wealth than an Engraver. Yet I did not think that anyone Cathy chose would ever please Mrs. Blake.

"What are you going to do?" I asked. "Do you see Tom often?"

"I meet him when I go to Sarah Goodhouse for herbal instruction, once or twice a week."

"Has he formally asked your mother for permission to marry you?"

"Not yet. I know she will refuse. And then—and then, I will simply run away with him!"

I could say nothing, so much was whirling in my head.

"Who else knows about this?"

"Robert does. He takes messages between us sometimes. But these days his cough is so bad that I do not like to send him out in the cold weather."

"Please, Cathy, do not act hastily in this matter. Wait till after Christmas, and see if your mother does not come around. And consider whether you want to assume the care of two children."

"Yes, Kate. I have given all this much thought. How many chances at marriage do you think I am going to get? I am not beautiful, and I do not have much in the way of a dowry. Tom is a kind man, and I like his company. Mother is just being selfish—she wants me around for companionship and to wait on her when she is busy in the shop. I must have a life of my own!"

My heart was heavy for her. Marriage had seemed so simple for me. I always thought I would marry someone I loved. I did not have a dowry and never expected one. I just trusted that God had a plan for me, as indeed he did. I had my William.

The next day I asked Robert what he thought of Cathy's situation.

"I think Mother is mistaken," he said. "She should let Cathy go."

Christmas Day with the Blakes seemed rather strained. We all went to the Baptist Church for the morning service and then back to Mrs. Blake's house for a special dinner at two o'clock: a plump pullet roasted with chestnuts. For dessert we had a suet pudding made with raisins and ginger.

We had each dressed up in our best holiday clothing. William wore the new shirt I had made him, and I had a new fine red woolen dress with a low neckline bordered by a white lace William had just given me. I had knitted a bright green scarf for Robert, which he insisted on wearing indoors. We should have all been merry, but

Cathy looked quite downcast and that seemed to make everyone quiet. William suggested we sing some Carols, offering to accompany us on his tin flute.

We all sang "The Holly and the Ivy" which reminded me of playing games with the Holly Boy and the Ivy Girl during my country childhood. James and Anne Parker had joined us at the Blakes', and, of course, elder brother James was there. He had a good strong deep voice. Cathy sang with a pure soprano, but very shy.

James poured us all a glass of port and started on "The Carol of the Twelve Numbers." This is that curious song beginning, "I'll sing you one-ho! Green grow the rushes-ho." And it has the refrain, "One is one and all alone and ever more shall be so." It has a lovely tune and is a very mysterious song. You sing up to twelve numbers: One is one and all alone, Two for lily white boys, "clothed all in green-ho," Three for "rivals," Four for Gospel makers—that would be Matthew, Mark, Luke and John. Five is for "cymbals at your door," Six is for "six proud walkers." Eventually you get to Twelve for the twelve Apostles—and always the refrain, "One is one and all alone and ever more shall be so."

"I like that!" said William, when we were finished. "There is no fooling about with the Trinity in that song!"

"You mean no Father, Son, and Holy Ghost?" asked Cathy.

"Exactly. God the Creator is a Spiritual Body in the form of a man from all Eternity," said William vehemently. "There is no division."

"So what does that make Jesus, then?" asked James, with some irony.

"Jesus is God become human. There is no other God."

"So when Jesus was on earth, there was no God in Heaven?" asked Anne, surprised. I must confess, I had never thought of this before myself, though I had heard William express his belief in Jesus before.

"That is true. And when Christ died, the Father, Son, and Holy Ghost all died. The whole Life of the Infinite Power was dead."

"My father used to believe that," said Mrs. Blake, as if to herself.

"But that is horrible!" exclaimed Cathy. "What if Christ had not risen from the dead? There would be no God in the world!"

"More to the point," said James Blake, "how did Christ ever rise from the dead if there were no God in heaven?"

William had the answer for this, too.

"Before Christ came to earth," he said, "He had the foresight to appoint prophets, Enoch and Moses and Elias. They had the power to quicken life in Jesus."

"Well, I am so glad you have thought all this out," said James. It was becoming obvious that he was irritated by William. Robert tried to make peace.

"But it is not just William who believes these things," he said. "So do I. And so do the Flaxmans."

"Better minds than even those wrestle with the problem of the Trinity," said James, dryly. "I am content to leave the matter to the Wise."

"Pompous Ass," said William, under his breath.

The next day we were back to work as usual at Poland Street, cleaning the wooden press and arranging Prints on the walls. William had some work from a book publisher named Joseph Johnson of St. Paul's Churchyard.

As I set about my tasks, my mind was troubled for Cathy's sake. I could see no way out for her except direct disobedience. My Voices echoed in my ear, Trouble is coming. I had not heard my Voices for some time, as I paid so much attention to William's, but I heard them that day. The cold rain outside mirrored my mood.

Robert came through the door, dripping wet.

"Is Cathy with you?" he asked abruptly.

"No, I haven't seen her today," I said.

"She's not at home. Mother is frantic. I don't know where she could be . . ." Robert was shivering.

"Sit down by the fire," commanded William, bringing a shawl. "You are going to catch cold."

"Cathy was exceedingly melancholy after yesterday's conversation," said Robert suddenly. "The idea that God could die was very upsetting to her."

"But surely the idea that God could live as a Human Being is consolation," said William. "We are all part of the Divine Human Form, after all."

"Oh, William, be practical!" I exclaimed. "Cathy is a troubled girl. She needs the consolation of a Heavenly Father just now."

William seemed surprised.

"Haven't you seen what is going on?" said Robert, hugging the fire. "She is in love, and Mother won't allow it."

"Mother is a fool," said William, as if that solved anything.

Robert's damp shirt was clinging to him, and he looked pinched with cold.

"I must go out again to look for Cathy," he insisted. I think he had a suspicion where she was, and in the end, he was probably right.

"But it is raining so hard," I objected, "you will be chilled."

He would not listen. He borrowed a dry shirt and jacket from William and went out. He took Cold that night and never really was well from then on.

It became clear to me where Cathy had been when she came to my door about two months later, at the beginning of March, 1786.

A thin sunlight was filtering in the window that morning, which only highlighted how uncommonly pale she appeared.

"Kate, help me!" she gasped, throwing off her cloak and bonnet. "I am very sick!"

She almost fainted in my arms. William was not at home, and I had a hard time steadying her by myself.

"What is the matter? Why are you not at home?"

"Help me to your bed! Oh, I am so sick!" She retched miserably, as I ran for a basin and water. We struggled up the stairs. As I laid her on the bed, I saw to my horror the ugly red stain seeping through her skirts.

"My God, Cathy. What is wrong? I must send for the surgeon! You are bleeding!"

"No! Send for no one! I have taken Pennyroyal and Rue to bring down my courses and thank God they have come. It has been two months!"

"But there is so much blood!" I was crying. I could not imagine how I was going to prevent her from dying right there. The red stain spread all over her skirts. I brought towels and spread them beneath her, and they, too, turned crimson. Then I remembered a bottle of rum that William had stored in the cupboard. I ran to get her a draught. This restored her strength a little.

"We must just wait," she gasped. "I have seen this happen to patients of Mrs. Goodhouse. Soon the bleeding will stop, I am sure. Oh, thank God it has come!"

My soul revolted at what she had done. The realization that she had wilfully destroyed what I myself so longed for was a bitter taste in my mouth. I poured out a portion of rum for myself.

By evening, the bleeding had stopped. I gave Cathy a dress of mine to wear while I boiled up her clothing and our bed linen to get rid of the blood stains. William seemed to take it all calmly on his return. Reassuring his sister that we would look after her, he went out to tell his mother that Cathy was staying the night with us, which she sometimes had done in the past.

I asked Cathy about Thomas Holloway. It seems that he knew of her trouble and was willing to marry her right away, but he wanted to sail to America shortly. At this, Cathy hesitated.

"I do not want to leave England," she wept. "I am afraid to be alone in the New World! I do not have the courage."

I did not blame her. The tales we heard of the long sea voyage to New York or Virginia were frightening. Many died of illness on the trip, even those who could afford decent passage, or who could carry their own lemons against the scurvy. The weather, even in summer, could be ferocious, with gales coming out of the North, and icebergs still floating about. And then, when one did arrive in America, there might be wild Red Indians in the forests, ready to attack the new settlers.

Tom Holloway came one last time to see Cathy. They had to meet at our house in secret. I left them alone in the garden on a lovely April morning. Through my window, I could see them in earnest conversation, his dark head bent toward her fair one.

Go with him, I found myself silently urging. Change your life!

All I could see was that both of them were weeping.

So Cathy let go her chance of Marriage. After this, she became rather prim and subdued, and of a rather irritable disposition. She might have benefitted from Mr. Hayley's poem, "Triumphs of Temper," which was about Woman's Disposition, come to think of it. She now spent long hours studying Herbals, and accompanied Sarah Goodhouse on her rounds.

When William and I were in bed together, we used to have long conversations. Snug and warm under covers, exploring each others bodies sometimes while we talked, we told each other what was of most concern. In the day, William would sometimes be brusque or impatient with me, but close in bed, he was always gentle and patient. He would always console me each month when, once again, it was clear no child was coming.

"Do not cry, beloved," he said, "I, too, would delight in a child, but if we do not have one, we have each other. Never forget that."

Sometimes we read the Bible together, especially the *Song of Solomon*.

"I am the rose of Sharon," I would read, "and the lily of the valleys."

And he responded, "As the lily among thorns, so is my love among the daughters."

Then I would read, "As the apple tree among the trees of the wood, so is my beloved among the sons. I sat down under his shadow with great delight, and his fruit was sweet to my taste."

And William would laugh "Stay me with flagons, comfort me with apples, for I am sick of love."

Then I would laugh, for William was never sick of love.

William and I began to be real partners in Printing. He had been teaching me for a long time to assist him at the big wooden press. It was not usual for Engravers to keep Copper-plate presses in their houses, so we were proud of ours. It stood six feet tall, made of sturdy polished oak.

There were two other important tasks which went into Printing. One was the preparation of Paper, and the other was of Ink.

"We must print on the best paper we can afford," William always said.

So we bought wove paper from James Whatman, which was heavier than ordinary paper and did not have the chain lines that usual papers showed from the mould in which they were made. We dampened our sheets of paper the day before we were to print, passing five or six leaves through a flat tub of water two or three times, and then stacking them on a flat board to keep them very smooth.

Ink was a big part of our lives; it was messy, but I loved it. We used to make our own, mixing powdered pigment with burnt linseed oil. Burning the oil was a smelly business. First it was boiled, and then set on fire. This made the oil properly stiff to mix with the pigments. Then we would grind the oil and pigment on a marble slab till it was the right thickness.

The colours of inks were wonderful. At first we only used blue-blacks or brown blacks, but later when William produced his own books, we used red ochre, yellow ochre, raw sienna, burnt umber, Prussian blue. William taught me how to ink a plate with a linen dabber and to wipe off the plate's surface with the palm of my hand. What a mess! The Print is a Marriage of ink and paper, as Engravers always say. Or it is a baby, born from the marriage, under blankets on the Bed of the press. We hung the prints up to dry on a clothesline, like baby clothes.

From Kate's Notebook.
Tuesday, May 2, 1786.

We had a May Day celebration of our own yesterday. William and I walked to Hampstead Heath, where a fresh breeze blew over the meadows and the gorse hills were blooming bright yellow.

William made me take my hair down so he could see it blow in the wind, and we made love right there under the open blue sky. Then last night, he made love to me again, but this time I knew he wanted a Vision to come with Love, as it often does. He lit candles around the bed, and we burned a little bowl of sweet-smelling grasses that Cathy had given us. I massaged William's Body with lavender-scented oil, and he smoothed it all over me.

He entered me, and the Visions came. This time they were not Fearful, but Beautiful. Winged creatures, rainbow colours. It was like being in a garden on the moon.

I could not achieve Visions like this alone. William can, and I am in awe of him. But I wonder, why does a Child not come of all this Love?

Robert's cough was terrible to hear.

"He has a wasting disease, or else stomach trouble," Cathy said. "I wish I knew what to do!"

William would not admit there was anything wrong with Robert.

"It is just a passing illness," he would say, even though it never seemed to pass.

Mrs. Blake was philosophical. "If it is God's will that he be ill, there is nothing we can do." I thought this was a shocking attitude. I did not believe God would ever will anyone to be sick.

By January, Robert was confined to bed, weak and feverish. I went to see him late in the month. He lay in the middle of a small, white room at the top of the house. One square window showed a patch of cloudy grey sky.

On a little table near him lay a Bible, which he liked to have read to him, and a bouquet of dried lavender. Cathy had put it there to make the sickroom smell sweet.

Robert's delicate hands lay still on his blue coverlet, knitted only last month by his mother. His eyes, so large in his thin face, had that far-away look you see in the eyes of the dying. It was as if he already could see past the veil of everyday life to another realm. He was calm and smiling as I approached his bed. I bent over and kissed his forehead.

"Kate, remember to keep reading," he said to me. "Do not cry. I am only going into another room." Then a fit of coughing took him.

"I am so tired," he said. "It will be good to rest."

To my eyes, even in repose, Robert had an aura of light about him.

Cathy tried her best to find Infusions and Poultices to help Robert but he was wasting away before our eyes. Poor Mrs. Blake was quite unable to cope with the dying of her youngest son. She stayed in her sitting room and wept. James tried to keep the Business going. John Blake had joined the Army. So William just naturally assumed Robert's care.

In mid-January, he moved back to Broad Street to nurse Robert and never left his side for two weeks. He tended him night and day. Mrs. Blake or I would prepare a meal and take it up to them, but Robert could not eat by this time and William was scarcely interested.

"Please, William," I pleaded one rainy day, after I had climbed the stairs to Robert's room with a tray, "have some of this good beef soup. You must not get sick, too."

He looked right through me. I may as well not have been in the room.

"William!" I demanded. "Think of me. Even Robert does not ignore me. You must eat, even if Robert does not!"

Robert turned his head toward us. He looked so much older than his twenty-four years.

"Kate is right, Will," he said. They had always been Bob and Will to each other. "Look after yourself. I am happy . . . I know it is beautiful where I am going . . . I want to see it . . . it is my time."

Then he seemed for a moment to gain energy. He reached out for William's hand.

"But you, Will," he said, raising his head, "it is not your time yet. Do not let the Visions get in the way of your work. You must remember this!" And he fell back, exhausted.

The raindrops fell like tears against the windowpane.

Robert died on February tenth, 1787. The date is engraved on my heart. I was not in the room. William told me he saw Robert's Spirit released, rising from the Body and clapping its hands for joy.

We buried Robert on the eleventh of February in Bunhill Fields, near his father. Then William went home and slept three days and three nights.

6

In Which I am Introduced to Henry Fuseli
and Paradise Lost

All that William had left of Robert now was his Notebook, in which Robert sometimes sketched: he had liked to draw such imaginary scenes from Ancient British History as Druid or Roman times. There was also one lovely little ink and wash drawing of Shakespeare's fairies Oberon and Titania, reclining on the petals of a poppy. He had made that for me when we read *A Midsummer Night's Dream*.

When William took over the Notebook, it seldom left his hand, for William was always sketching or writing. I noticed that he left Robert's drawings at the front of the book and only removed a few ink stained leaves. The very first thing William sketched was a picture of the two of us in the early morning: William is sitting on the edge of our four poster bed, putting on his stockings, while I sleep on behind him in my mob cap. Underneath he wrote lines that made me laugh: "When a Man has Married a Wife / he finds out whether / Her knees and elbows are only / glued together."

William used that Notebook for drafts of poems and designs, and as a kind of Diary, too, writing all around his sketches. When he filled its fifty-eight leaves, he turned it upside down and started from the back again!

John and Nancy Flaxman attended Robert's funeral and were a consolation to us in the days immediately following. John, looking stooped and intense as ever, seemed to know how to comfort William best. He read to him from the works of Emmanuel Swedenborg, who believed that on the death of the material body, we rise again to our spiritual body, where we exist in perfect human form. Since this was William's experience with his vision of Robert, he began to read Swedenborg's book, *Heaven and Hell*, with interest.

"Swedenborg is revealing ancient secrets to the world," said John. "The Spiritual World exists in every material thing. I have always believed this myself."

John tried to cheer William up with another idea.

"Mr. Wedgewood is going to send Nancy and me to Italy to study Ancient Art," he announced, "and we thought we should find you a Patron, so you could come, too."

This was too stunning an idea for me to contemplate. On one hand, it would be the greatest chance of our lives to be Artists, but on the other, to be a stranger in a strange land was frightening. If we did not go, we would lose John and Nancy for years. In private, we dared to dream of the opportunity.

"Imagine being able to see the great Michel Angelo's sculptures," mused William.

We knew them well from other artist's engravings of them, of course, but it would be thrilling to see the actual objects. I am told the statues are of white marble. William often modelled designs on Michel Angelo's figures. To Copy well, he said, was speaking the Language of Art. It was learning the permanent images of the Imagination, where everything Real existed.

Eventually it was clear that no Patron was going to send us to Italy. We bid a tearful farewell to John and Nancy. I think I was a tiny bit relieved to have green-eyed Nancy out of William's sight for a while. He had never ceased to admire her.

"I like beautiful bodies," he told me once, "Male or Female. It is the Human Form Divine."

"Well, maybe not so Divine," I said. "Look around you. Most people in London streets are stooped, or bent, or lame, or blind!"

"We are all perfect underneath our Garment of Flesh," said William, "and that is what I see."

Spring came with its promise of new beginnings, and Robert's spirit seemed to comfort us. His presence was perceived as we walked on familiar paths outside London, walks that we used to take with him.

Bluebells appeared in the woods, a lacy carpet inviting us to explore. Here and there a great chestnut tree burst into bloom with huge ruby candles, and the cherry trees, like little May Day dancers, could be glimpsed beyond a hedgerow.

"Look there,"said William, "what do you see?"

"I see a Daisy."

"I see a young woman with a ruffled skirt."

"Well, of course, I could imagine that too."

"Imagine! That's it! That is just as real as the flower."

"Well, perhaps . . ." I was doubtful.

"Mental Things are Real!" said William vehemently. "I will prove it to you."

On all our walks we described to each other what we saw, first in the Outer World, then in the Inner. After a while, we had a whole cast of characters who lived in a land called Har: shepherds and shepherdesses, wicked stepmothers, and changeling children. Later we moved on to Kings and Queens, living in a land of Clouds, who had strange names like Enthinthus and Thiralatha.

"I know them all," said William, gesturing grandly to the Heavens, "most people would think they see Trees, but we know they are Giants, don't we, Kate?"

We never saw another Rose-tree, though William continued to call me by that name in private. I planted Lavender against the back of the house in Poland Street and enjoyed it twice, when its purple spikes bloomed, and when it was dried and scattered its perfume in our blanket chest. I sang as I went about my work:

> Lavender's blue, dilly dilly,
> Lavender's green,
> When you are King, dilly dilly,
> I shall be Queen.

I did not need to be Queen to be happy, I thought. I had William and a busy life. If only . . . but I tried to put the thought of a Baby out of my mind. We had now been married almost five years, and I had to accept the obvious. I would never bear a child. It was hard to get used to the idea of being a barren woman. Awful word, *Barren*. It reminded me of a stony, brown field—a field that should be ploughed, and then burst forth with bloom or grain. But what if the plough were faulty, and not the field?

William loved children. He was always so interested in their songs and games. The Blake haberdashery business supplied goods to the Parish School of Industry on King Street, Golden Square, where children trained to be housemaids and apprentices. Sometimes we accompanied James on a delivery. We always marvelled at the cheerfulness of the boys and girls, who had a hard life even now, and a harder one ahead.

"I think children must live in a world different from ours," I observed after one such visit. "Something protects them from seeing the harsh life."

"It is their innocence," said William. "It is like a country they live in, and we do not live there any longer. I have often thought that if we could only get back to that country, how happy we would feel!"

"Always protected," I said, remembering my own childhood with all my brothers and sisters.

"Yes, and absolutely the centre of the Heavens. Who wants to think he is only a body in space, circling around the sun? When you are a child, you are the sun!"

"But you know that self-centred, grown-up people are horrible to be with," I said. "You cannot think the world revolves only around you. Think of your mother."

"There has to be a difference in a child's innocence and an adult's innocence, that is true. The adult has to know life is not going to protect him, but he will be protected anyway by the memory of that other country."

"What if she's a girl," I said, a little miffed at his male examples.

"Well, then, she is herself a little world," said William. "She holds within her the space itself. And I know just where to find it!" He reached playfully for my skirt, and his hand went to my breast.

"You are too wicked!" I laughed. And that was the end of that conversation.

From Kate's Notebook.
June 14, 1787.

Robert appears to William all the time, but not to me, sadly enough. I would love to see Robert again. William says he looks as he did of old, healthy and smiling. I imagine that everyone in the Spirit Realm has a new body—one would surely not be perpetually old or crippled!

William suffers from Nervous Stomach, especially when his orders for Commercial Engravings are piling up, and he wants only to compose his own works. I see it as my responsibility to make his life Peaceful, so I run the house, organize our meals, fetch the water, and clean up the Workroom, day in and day out.

Mrs. Blake said yesterday, "Why do you bother to bake bread, when the Bake Shop is around the corner?"

"Because I like the feel of it," I said. "I like to knead the dough."

She looked at me as if I were odd. She does not realize that I think while I press the resilient dough under my hands. My thoughts help keep my Object in mind: I am William's Helpmate. Handmaid to the Visions.

At the end of Poland Street was an Ale-house. It was where the "Ancient Order of Druids" met, a convivial group. Ladies were invited some nights, when we could get a dinner for fourpence at a shiny mahogany table with black leather benches. The place had a comfortable atmosphere with its smoky tallow candles and the smell of roasted meat and beer mingling with the tobacco haze of the pipe smokers.

One evening when we had closed up the shop early to treat ourselves to dinner there, I saw the most extraordinary man. He was not very tall, but monkey-like and energetic, with a large head of hair powdered white and combed back from his face. He was gesturing with great animation in conversation with a friend, a dark-haired man who nodded at William.

"Who is that?" I asked.

"That is the Swiss painter Henry Fuseli," said William, "and he is sitting with Joseph Johnson, the book publisher, who sends us work often. I have not met Fuseli as yet, but you must know how famous he is since his picture *The Nightmare* was exhibited about five years ago."

"You mean that awful picture?"

It was of a young woman lying back in a sensual and contorted manner, with a horrible, leering, monkey-like goblin sitting on her stomach, and of all things, a horse sticking its head through the bed hangings.

"Yes, the one that caused a sensation."

"What kind of warped mind does the man have!" I exclaimed. And looking at him, I saw to my surprise that he was quite attractive in his energetic way.

A few weeks later, we met him at Johnson's house. Life is full of surprises that way, especially in London.

We had gone to one of Joseph Johnson's famous Tuesday dinners above his book shop at 72 St. Paul's Churchyard. Johnson was a small, dapper man, clean shaven, who was prone to attacks of asthma. He was a bachelor, rather secretive, but known for his generosity and kindliness. In religious matters, he was a Dissenter who published Unitarian tracts. He had liberal ideas and tried to publish cheap editions so that his books would reach as many people as possible. He wanted to raise the general level of education of people like me.

I hoped it would not be like the Mathews' evenings, where I was expected to be clever in conversation. By now I had a little more self-confidence—after all, I had read *Hamlet* and *A Midsummer Night's Dream* and *Macbeth*, and even *Gulliver's Travels*. I was also becoming a good Printer. Not many women in London could claim that. And I was pretty in a way that men seemed to find pleasing; more than one customer in the shop had commented on my black eyes and hair.

Johnson's eating room was a strange little upstairs space, where the white-plastered walls were not at right angles. The table was set at four in the afternoon for about twelve guests, and we ate plain boiled fish and vegetables, followed by rice pudding. I do not think the guests came to Johnson's for the food. No, it was for the talk.

"That is Dr. Joseph Priestley," William whispered to me, as we entered the room. "He is a famous chemist. He has discovered Inflammable Air to fill Balloons for travel. Some say he is an Atheist."

"And there is Mrs. Anna Barbauld, the writer of hymns for children," I pointed out. "Remember, we met her at the Mathews' house?"

Mrs. Barbauld approached us, smiling.

"How are the Visions, Mr. Blake?" She greeted us warmly, her lacy cap crisp amid her brown curls. I could never tell whether she was making a Jest at William's expense, or if she really believed in him. Her politics and ours were Radical, like Priestley's.

"The Visions are always with me," said William, half-smiling. "I see Plato beside us this very Moment." I wished sometimes that William would not be so truthful.

"Then you will want to speak to Mr. Thomas Taylor, who's a Neoplatonist," said Mrs. Barbauld without hesitation. "He is working on a Translation from the Greek, and has written a Treatise, *Concerning the Beautiful*."

William allowed that he would indeed like to meet Mr. Taylor and was soon introduced.

Talk was buzzing all around us—talk about the New Constitution in America, and about the new currency there called the Dollar. Voices spoke about the rumoured mental illness of King George, and about the young Prime Minister, William Pitt, and his efforts to suppress the Slave Trade in the Colonies. I began to feel that once again I was out of my depth in such a gathering.

And then I saw him again, Henry Fuseli. He was only a little taller than I, but his hair was powdered white and combed high, and his eyes were deep set and compelling. He saw me looking at him and said to Joseph Johnson, "Why, Joseph, kindly introduce me to these interesting guests." I noticed his heavy foreign accent. He had said *Vy* and *eenteresting*.

"I am pleased to present William and Catherine Blake."

"*Mein Gott*, you haff a beauty here!" Fuseli said to William.

I smiled, charmed at his frankness and energy. He was forty-six years old, the same age as Johnson, with whom he had been friends for many years. He also had a well-deserved reputation for womanizing, which he never denied. I had heard that he loved to make erotic drawings of women with odd hair arrangements. Strangely, he had studied theology in his youth in Zurich. I learned from Johnson later that he was also a writer and translator, and that he spent eight years in Rome studying Antiquities and Michel Angelo. He was soon to be an Associate of the Royal Academy.

William and Henry seemed to like each other right away. They had intense conversations about art and religion, always accompanied by much swearing and gesticulating on Henry's part. Henry gave William a copy of a book he had translated, Winckelmann's *Reflections on the Paintings and Sculptures of the Greeks*, little knowing that William had possessed his own copy since he was a student at Basire's. Neither man was very tall, and perhaps that is why they were each, in their own way, so combative. I had become used to William arguing in a group, and now here was another man who seemed also to thrive on controversy.

On one thing they always agreed, their high regard for John Milton's *Paradise Lost*. Hearing them discussing it so often, and especially Henry's quite shockingly admiring statements about Satan, I decided to read the poem for myself.

I found the volume among William's books, the leather binding worn with use. I lit a candle the better to see, even though it was a sunny afternoon outside. I placed the book carefully in front of me, and opened to Book One.

> Of man's first disobedience, and the fruit
> Of that forbidden tree whose mortal taste
> Brought death into the world, and all our woe
> With loss of Eden . . .

It started well enough, I thought, but soon the poem was nearly impossible. I could never find the end of any sentence. I was lost in a rush of words and allusions to places I did not understand. But I came upon a phrase which quite surprised me. Milton wanted to "justify the ways of God to man."

Is that not Pride? Is that not Arrogance? I had only allowed myself to think these things a little bit about William sometimes, when he would put the Artist on the same level as a Prophet in the Old Testament.

And then words caught me up, and I read with fascination as the picture of the rebel angels flung out of heaven, lying on the burning lake, came to life in my mind. When Satan rose from the waters, flames rolling off him, I was amazed. Then I read these words:

> The mind is its own place, and in itself
> Can make a Heaven of Hell, a Hell of Heaven.

In my inmost heart, I had always known this to be so, but no one had ever put it in words to me. I realized that William with his visions was always making his own place, and then drawing it, and so were Fuseli and Flaxman, and all the other artists we knew. With such knowledge, no hardships life threw in your path could ever undermine you.

After an hour, I put the book away, only to return to it the next day as soon as I had a moment alone. I read of the great consultation Satan held with four of his other fallen demons, whom we know as Moloch, Belial, Mammon and Beelzebub. Of them all, only Satan had the courage to try to find the world that God had created for Man. I saw why Henry spoke admiringly of Satan, though when you really considered it, his mission—to destroy God's creation—was not really noble at all. That night, I had bad dreams of dark cosmic spaces, where a bat-like human form flew and flew, looking for me.

William found me on the third day of my reading, puzzling over Book Three. I had to confess that I could not understand a good portion of what I was reading.

"We will read it aloud together," said William. And so began my education in earnest.

By August, we had become frequent visitors at Joseph Johnson's dinners, and Fuseli's calls to our premises had stimulated William to paint many pen and wash drawings of Biblical and Historical subjects. I often modeled for him for Job's Wife. I became quite stiff from crouching on the floor in Despair. Henry asked if I would let him draw my head with my hair all braided and coiled up, but I declined, pretending that I had not the time because of work in the print shop.

One night, very late, William woke me.

"Kate, I have had a dream of Robert," he said excitedly, "and he

Blake, *Satan Watching the Caresses of Adam and Eve* (Illustration to Milton's *Paradise Lost*) (1808). Pen and watercolor on paper. Reproduced with permission. Copyright © 2002 Museum of Fine Arts, Boston. Gift by subscription. 90.96

has told me a wonderful thing. It is a new method of Printing! It will combine words and design on one page!"

I nodded sleepily, and he talked on and on about this wonderful new method, his words flying above my head in waves of sound.

From Kate's Notebook.
November 10, 1787.

I cannot deny it any longer. I have been afraid to think . . . I was afraid I may be ill instead. But it *is* true—Sarah Goodhouse has examined me. At last, I am with Child.

From Kate's Notebook.
October 27th, 1829. Lisson Grove.

I see that Frederick's secret cache of William's work has grown considerably. I suppose I do not mind, though it troubles me to think I cannot trust him. Fred often asks for some of the Illuminated Books to read, and I give him happily any he wants, except for the one coloured copy of *Jerusalem*, which I keep beside my bed.

There is also the single copy of *Milton*, which I allowed Fred to read, but made sure it also returned to my bedside table. This book has no Frontispiece, only a Title Page which pictures the back of a beautiful naked man, clouds billowing around him, pushing one hand between the letters MIL TON. Under his feet are the words *To Justify the Ways of God to Men*. On the first page were words which I know went straight to Fred's heart, "Would to God that all the Lord's people were Prophets."

I know that more than anything in the world, Fred wants to be a Prophet. We lately attended a prayer meeting in a private home with Edward Irving. There had been about ten people present in a fine house on Great Russell Street. Irving looked every inch the Prophet himself, tall and erect, with his black hair carefully trimmed. He had spoken fervently, and led the prayer, taking as his text Numbers XI, verses 27–29: "And there ran a young man, and told Moses, and said Eldad and Medad do prophesy in the camp. And Joshua the son of

Nun, the servant of Moses, one of his young men, answered and said, My lord Moses forbid them. And Moses said unto him, Enviest thou for my sake? Would to God that all the Lord's people were prophets, and that the Lord would put his spirit upon them!"

One of the ladies present, a young woman with fair hair, fell to her knees and began to babble. Soon another woman did the same, and a man, and four people were speaking in tongues. I saw Frederick watch with horrified fascination, the urge to follow them rising in his chest. Even I was moved. The four who had spoken were now sobbing with emotion.

Irving calmed them and interpreted for them. He seemed to know what they had said.

"You are chosen vessels," he said. "The Spirit is abroad in the land. I have heard that in the West of Scotland there have been healings."

"How do we know this is not the work of the Devil?" Fred had asked.

"I am convinced it is the Word of God," said Irving. "Jesus had a human nature and spiritual gifts. So do we."

This was so like something William would have said. Greatly encouraged, Fred went home and tried to puzzle out more of William's writings. William was the closest thing to a Prophet that he had ever met.

7

In Which I Meet Mary Wollstonecraft

$\mathcal{N}$ow I come to that part of my story which grieves me terribly. I look over my Notebook, which I carefully do not show to Mr. Tatham, and see that I could not be completely happy about my Pregnancy because of Jealousy. Then, of course, I lost all enjoyment of life.

We had always been great walkers in and around London, touring the City in all seasons, rain or shine. It was always "Infinite London" to William, who could discern beneath the soot and grime of the narrow streets, through the calls of the Street Vendors, the smells of slop buckets and Candle-makers, and the jostle of the crowds, the lineaments of an Eternal City. The dome of St. Paul's beckoned us toward the river, looming over the spires of countless churches. On Westminster Bridge we looked back at the curve of the river's edge, at the masts of tall ships on the Thames. Once or twice, on a long summer's day, we had even crossed the Blackfriar's Bridge to Battersea to see my father, who always sent us home laden with vegetables.

In late October, after a frost, the flame of copper beeches on the edge of the fields seemed perpetually burning. On the roads around London, great oak and chestnut trees spilled their nut fruits on the ground, and meadowsweet still bloomed in the ditches. From Wimbledon Common you could watch sheep grazing, while a farmer herded his cows through fields that extended all the way to the River.

Even as the child grew in my belly, I had energy to walk. We sometimes strolled down Piccadilly to see the shops: there was a wax and tallow Chandler, a Breeches maker, and an interesting set of rooms where a Charles Fortnum, who had been a footman to King George III, sold the remains of wax candles from the Royal Household, and sometimes exotic spices from the East India Company. William bought me some preserved ginger to suck when I felt nauseated.

My favorite shop was the Showroom of the potter Josiah Wedgewood in Greek Street. On big round tables you could find a hundred lovely forms: teapots, vases, dinner plates, pitchers. Some had ornaments that we knew John Flaxman had designed. I gaped at the fashionable people in the shop.

I tried to make our own Showroom, too, as inviting as the China merchant's. I hit upon the idea of placing an easel near the door, where a Print in a carved frame could be displayed. Sometimes I would place one or two of William's own collection on a shelf as decoration, though they were not for sale. He had been buying Prints since he was a boy, all done by Italians, though I think he had a Hogarth or two.

William Hayley had come back to buy Prints from time to time, and it happened that he came again that winter.

He limped into the shop in December, leaning on his umbrella, his tall frame filling the small entrance. He had finely arched brows and a pleasant smile.

"I am glad to see you again, Mrs. Blake," he said, "but I see you are very busy. May I ask what you are doing?"

I was straining whiting through muslin as part of a method to prepare the white base for William's paintings. I think I must have had white powder all over my face and hands. I explained to Mr. Hayley what I was doing.

"What a helpmate you are to your husband!" he exclaimed. "How fortunate he is to have you by his side in all his endeavors."

I was quite embarrassed at this personal remark. I must have looked startled. Then Mr. Hayley did a surprising thing: he put out his hand and brushed his fingers across my forehead.

"You have powder on your brow," he said, smiling. I felt myself blush, inwardly scolding myself for behaving like a witless girl. He had that effect on me.

Mr. Hayley then became businesslike, and William emerged from the back room and helped him choose a Stothard engraving for his London lodgings.

From Kate's Notebook.
Thursday, December 6, 1787.

My Recipe for Preparing White Ground for William's canvasses:

Get the best whitening—powder it.

Mix thoroughly with water to the consistency of cream.

Strain through double muslin. Spread it out upon the backs of plates, white tiles are better, kept warm over basins of water until it is pretty stiff.

Have ready the best carpenters' or cabinet makers' glues made in a very clean glue pot, and mix it warm with the colour—the art lies in adding just the right portion of glue. The *Test* is, that when dry upon the thumbnail or on an earthenware palette it should have so much and no more glue as will defend it from being scratched off with the fingernail.

This, and the cleanliness of the materials are the only difficulties.

Sunday, December 9, 1787.

We are going to have a June baby, a child born under the sign of Gemini, the twins. What if we have twins! Gemini people are charming and love to talk. That means the child will be a great companion to William, who also loves to talk. William is a Sagittarian, the sign of the Archer, born on November 28. Archers are always stubborn, and hate to feel tied down. Now, I am born under the sign of Taurus, on April 25. That is the sign of the Bull. This means I am warm and affectionate, but also stubborn. So any baby of ours is going to be very strong-willed and a great talker, for not only do the Stars command it, the Child's Parentage does also!

William was excited about the new technique for etching plates revealed to him by Robert in his dream.

"Look at this, Kate!" He called to me one morning from his workroom. "I've done it! I've painted on the Copper with a brush! And the lines come out white instead of black!"

I ran to look at the little etching which William had completed. It was based on a pen and wash drawing Robert made before he died, called *The Approach of Doom*. A group of bearded old men in long gowns stood with their arms clutched around each other, staring at a big black cloud that seemed to be coming toward them. There is a kind of Nightmare feeling about the picture. Indeed, the outlines were white.

"What did you use on the brush to protect the lines from the acid?" I asked.

He waved his paint brush in the air.

"It's the Stopping Out Varnish that we spent our last shilling on! It works! I am working on Copper as if it were Paper! The black ink can't get into the varnished lines and the lines remain white!"

"And then did you go over parts of the design with a needle to add the texture?"

William was almost dancing around the room.

"Yes, that's it—there are so many possibilities here! I'm going to call it Relief Etching! I think with this I can write words on the pages. Just think—words and pictures on one copper plate! Kate, we might even get rich!"

I was as excited about my pregnancy as William was about his Relief Etching.

"Now you must have Sarah Goodhouse for your Lying-in," Mrs. Blake told me, as if I would have had anyone else. Is there anything worse than having someone direct you to do what you always intended?

"I would not have a male Physician attend you, who would just as well deliver a baby under a sheet and not even look at what he is doing for modesty's sake!" she went on.

"I think that is an old-fashioned worry," I said, "but I have faith in Mrs. Goodhouse." Mrs. Goodhouse and Cathy had kept me well supplied with herbal teas and oil of lavender to guarantee a safe delivery. Cathy knew a good deal about midwifery now, and was attentive to me. It was good to have her as a friend.

I had so many changes of Mood, I was like the Moon. I was so happy I could hardly stop smiling all day when I felt the first stirring of life inside me; and I loved the first gentle rounding of my belly. But then I began to get very black moods, when I felt unattractive, or when I craved an impossible orange at the end of December, when I was just too tired to work the press, and William had much work to do.

"William, what shall we name our baby?"

"Is it a boy, or a girl, Little Mother?"

"I think it is a girl. I keep talking to her in my heart, and she does a little dance when she moves."

"Then we should name her Thalia, one of the Three Graces."

I continued my reading of *Paradise Lost*. I found many difficult words, and William, who liked to study languages and already knew some Latin, helped me many times. I do not know why John Milton did not write clearer sentences; it must be that poets, when they tackle long, long poems, write long, long sentences. Yet after a while, Milton's language carried me along like a wave.

I was surprised at the admiration I felt for Satan in Book Two. And I was even more shocked at what I felt about God in Book Three. God sits on his throne in Heaven, and he sees Satan flying toward this world, and He knows what is going to happen, but he lets it happen anyway! Is that a merciful God? I know He says that He gave Adam and Eve free will, and they disobeyed of their own choice: "They themselves decreed their own revolt, not I." But still! When I made these observations to William, I was gratified that he agreed with me.

"Milton's God is a Tyrant," he said. "Milton is of the Devil's Party without knowing it. All the Energy in that poem is the energy of Revolution."

I thought Milton imagined Eden wonderfully, with two glorious creatures in it, Adam and Eve. However, I was surprised at the lines in Book Four:

> For contemplation he and valour formed,
> For softness she, and sweet attractive grace;
> He for God only, she for God in him.

Is not that like a man, I thought. Always wanting to be master. Surely, in Eden, Adam and Eve were Equal. I am sure she worked as hard as he did, naming the Beasts, and tending the Garden, and so on. Of course, William did not agree with me. As far as he was concerned, woman was made from Adam's rib, after Adam was created, and that gave Adam a direct connection to God, which Eve should properly respect. William could appreciate the Bible when it suited him.

I confess that all the Books about the revolt of Lucifer and the War in Heaven were a bit boring, until the Son of God appeared and drove his enemies over the wall of Heaven. I began to be more interested again in Book Eight, which is what I was reading the last week in February, when we were invited to a dinner at Joseph Johnson's to celebrate the publication of a new magazine.

I was looking forward to seeing Fuseli at Johnson's evening, and perhaps talking to him about Milton, because he always expressed such forthright ideas. In fact, he was among the company, but too much engrossed in conversation with someone else to have any time for me. For Joseph had a new project, and it was not just the magazine. Her name was Mary Wollstonecraft.

She drew people to her like a Magnet. It was not that she was beautiful, but that her pale oval face and prominent hazel eyes radiated intelligence. She was tall, with a good figure, and I judged her to be about twenty-eight years old. She wore a large beaver hat atop luxuriant brown hair, and a rather dowdy black dress that was a little untidy, fraying at the sleeves. She had slender hands with long, expressive fingers.

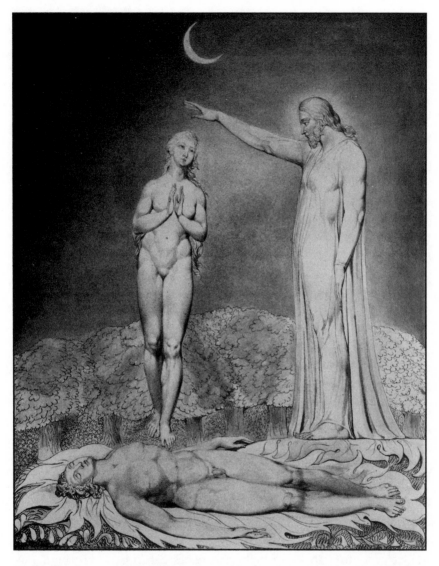

Blake, *The Creation of Eve* (Illustration to Milton's Paradise Lost) (1808). Pen and watercolor on paper. Reproduced with permission. Copyright © 2002 Museum of Fine Arts, Boston. Gift by subscription. 90.95

"Come and meet my new writer for our new *Analytical Review*," said Joseph in his breathy voice, as if showing off a new painting.

"Ah, Blake," said Fuseli to William as we approached, "here is someone with a Wit to match your own."

She looked at us with a smile. Something inside me said *Danger*. I was conscious of my matronly figure in contrast to her slim waist.

William bent over her hand in a courteous manner.

"I will be honoured to match wits with one so charming," he said. I could hardly believe my ears. William was using the very manners he so often ridiculed and rejected.

Henry, whose wide-set eyes often gave him a cat-like look, glanced at me and said, "Catherine Blake, Mary Wollstonecraft. Kate is Eve to William's Adam."

"Oh, I hope your Paradise has not left the Apple uneaten," said Mary quickly to me. "Knowledge is the only weapon we women have in this world of men." I smiled in spite of myself.

Fuseli was clearly captivated by Mary, and she by him. I watched their flirtation with interest, for I knew Henry had begun to court an artist's model called Sophia Rawlins, who was determined to marry him. He kept Sophia away from his social round and seemed to enjoy playing a double game. William and Mary were attracted to each other. I could not help seeing it. Their eyes kept meeting. That first afternoon at Johnson's lengthened into evening, and they were all three still deep in conversation. The topics ranged from religion to politics to ethics, and I could only listen for the most part.

Our meetings at Johnson's increased in frequency. Fuseli was always the star performer, with Mary a close second. She was writing articles for *Analytical Review*, and Johnson was going to publish her novel. He had taken a house for her in George Street, William confided to me, though he thought the relationship between them was purely of patronage and friendship. Johnson had really saved her from destitution, allowing her to work for him. I had to admire her, a woman alone in the world, making her own way. It was very hard, and she must often have experienced pain and jealousy at the way some women treated her. But she had her brilliant wit—that must have been some consolation. It was a consolation I never had. When the world treated me ill, I had to use cunning.

Mary was passionately interested in politics and followed the events in France with great interest as they moved toward throwing off the yoke of monarchy. She had her own ideas about differences between the sexes.

I ventured to suggest to her that Eve was really the most interesting character in *Paradise Lost*.

"Adam is completely taken with her when she is created from his rib, and loves the act of love so much that the Angel Raphael cautions him against too much passion. This gives Eve the power in their relationship, don't you think?" I asked her.

"Yes, I agree with you," said Mary, "and it is Eve who has the courage of her curiosity. And she uses her Reason. She sees that the Serpent has not died after eating the forbidden fruit of the tree of Knowledge. Why would Death be invented only for her and Adam? A hunger for Knowledge was her only fault, if that be a fault."

"But there is one thing about her that bothers me," I said. "Once she has tasted the fruit, she resolves to give it to Adam, too. This is a sharing of Knowledge, of course, but it also means he will no longer be Immortal if he takes a bite. In effect, she is willing to kill him."

"Well, she is willing to share her fate with him," said Mary. "It is not her best hour, that is true. She is at her best later. But Adam knows what he is doing; Eve was deceived by the Serpent. If disobedience is Original Sin, then he is more to blame than she."

"I have wondered why Disobedience is so Awful in the eyes of God," I confessed, "and I conclude that it is only a Parent who would think that way—a Parent who cannot stand to be contradicted. William says Milton's God is a Tyrant."

"Exactly!" exclaimed Mary, "Adam did not ask to be born. I always remember his speech:

'Did I require, thee, Maker, from my Clay
To mould me Man, did I solicit thee
From darkness to promote me, or here place
In this delicious Garden?'

Why, God created us for his own amusement."

"Do you not think, then, that the Son is the real hero of the poem?

He intercedes for Adam and Eve, and offers to die for them." I had not tried this idea out on William yet.

"Oh, yes, He well may be," said Mary. "He certainly represents Reason in its most exalted form. But Eve is the most complicated character, for God sends her a dream, remember, promising through her seed that Paradise will be restored. Adam was given all the Nightmare visions of human history, you recall, but Eve gets the promise that Jesus will be born in human form."

I must say, Mary had a way of making a woman feel proud of her sex.

She was not above feeling jealous of another woman if the regard of Fuseli or William strayed to someone else. One evening there was a flurry of attention when a most beautiful young woman, arrayed all in silk and sparkling jewels, was part of Johnson's usually rather plainly dressed gathering. All the men were drawn to her like moths to a candle.

"Who can that person be?" asked Mary of me, not expecting an answer. But I knew who she was, for she lived a few doors from us at 54 Poland Street.

"That is the famous singer, Elizabeth Billington," I told Mary, "otherwise known as the Poland Street Man-Trap, for she is so accommodating."

I was being catty, but I had suffered some pangs of jealousy myself from time to time, when I saw William in conversation with her on the street. Mrs. Billington had a great success at Covent Garden a couple of years before, and was a highly paid stage singer, considered the best in London.

"Fancy Joseph inviting a singer to his dinner," said Mary. "I wonder why he never mentioned it to me."

As the Spring came, and I grew more round and clumsy, I felt less inclined to attend Johnson's Tuesdays and to watch Mary weave her web around both Henry and William. William was sweet and attentive to me at home. We still worked together on his printing projects. Since he wanted to include words on his etchings, he was practising writing backwards on copper, so that the words would be right way up when printed. I was the judge of legibility. Nevertheless, he always seemed a little distracted, as if he were about to tell me something and always stopping himself.

"Will you have time for the printing when the baby comes?" he asked me one day in April, when we were out for a walk.

It was perfect weather, sunny with a little wind blowing about the new green leaves of the alders. We were in the South part of London, where the cornfields were beginning to grow and the larks could be heard, little circles of sound in the air above.

He did not wait for an answer, "Because if you won't have time, that is—I was thinking to ask Mary Wollstonecraft."

He might as well have taken a knife to my heart.

"What! You would replace me with her? Are you Mad? Do you think she would deign to work at a printing press?" I could scarcely control my anger.

"It would only be temporary; be calm, Kate. It would be some extra money for her."

"What do you mean? You would pay her? With what? Where do we have money for extra help? You have hardly enough commercial work for the two of us!"

There, I had said the unspeakable. William was not making a great deal of money.

I could still hear the sound of a lark, and it was such a contrast to my jealous heart that the afternoon seemed like a bad dream.

"Kate, be calm, you will make yourself ill. Why are you shaking? Sit here, under this tree."

We sat down among some daffodils. It was all beautiful—it should have been a wonderful interlude for us, but he was spoiling it.

"I do not understand your jealousy of Mary," said William. "She has not changed my feelings toward you at all. You must know that. You and I are inseparable, I have told you over and over. But she expands our horizons. We must include her in our lives."

"And what about Fuseli?" I cried, "Surely you know she is mad for him, and he for her. And he about to marry Sophia! He is unscrupulous!"

"He is an honest man," retorted William. "He is not a hypocrite. He does what he desires, and does not pretend otherwise."

"That is why you want Mary and me! Because Henry has two women! You are hateful!" And I began to weep. The baby kicked in my womb, and that only made me weep harder.

"You are impossible! Stop these tears, you will make yourself ill.

And it is not good for the child. I did not mean to upset you so much." William offered me his handkerchief which was smeared with ink, as usual. Something about that familiar sight comforted me, and I dried my tears.

"I cannot help what you feel for Mary," I said, "but I do not want her in my house. That is all I have to say."

From then on, I watched with a sick heart whenever I saw Mary and William in conversation. Envy entered my life in earnest, and I knew that the Ancients were right to make it one of the Seven Deadly Sins, and the poet William had read to me who compared Envy to a ravenous wolf who ate his own entrails suddenly made sense, because I felt it there, in my middle, burning.

We continued to argue as the time for my Confinement drew nearer. William never ceased to be tender and considerate, and we did have many good moments as we prepared for the baby. He built a lovely oak cradle, and Cathy and I made several little receiving gowns. Mrs. Blake had knitted a tiny white blanket. Early in June, as I was looking over these small articles, I cannot say that I was unhappy. It occurred to me that perhaps we were about to leave our particular Garden of Eden and were wandering inescapably toward the Eastern Gate.

It was Tuesday, June 10. I was out behind the house, hanging some laundry on the clothesline. I had felt rather energetic that morning, though I was very clumsy of movement, and being not very tall, I had become quite spherical in pregnancy. Suddenly I felt a flow of unexpected water, and a sharp pain across my abdomen. At last! It is time.

8

*In Which I Do Not Speak For Sorrow and See and
Hear Many Things I Should Not*

I have collected many documents for Mr. Tatham. Some I
have saved for many years, some I have copied, and some
I have written from my Imagination.

*From the Birthing Notes of Mrs. Sarah Goodhouse, Midwife.
June 10, 1788. London.*

I was called to attend young Mrs. Blake at 28 Poland Street. It was a
tall, narrow dwelling near the Public House, where all the artists
gather. She was already in hard labour, which surprised me, as her husband had come only an hour earlier to say her water had broken and
the pains were just beginning. She lay on a simple wooden bed with
clean linen, which soon enough needed replacing. She was breathing
unevenly and her forehead was damp, but even so you could see she
was a beautiful girl with her black eyes and dark curls. Her husband,
William, the Engraver, was very kind to her and continually stroked
her brow, saying over and over her name, Kate, Kate. He was a good-
looking man, not tall but powerfully built, with intense eyes.

When I placed my hands upon her belly, I could soon tell that something was amiss. The babe in the womb was not placed properly, and was presenting its breech to the opening, not its head. I spread the mother's legs, and probed inside as gently as I could. All was as I feared. In my experience it is possible to deliver a Babe so placed, and I immediately set about my task.

I told William to boil some ginger-root, which I gave him from my supplies, and with the water I placed compresses on the mother's belly, and oiled and massaged her privy parts. When she breathed a little easier, I gave her some tea, brewed from my secret herbs, which is an Opiate that never fails. This having calmed her, so that when her pains came she did not panic, I undertook the difficult business of turning the child.

At first the vigorous massage of the mother's belly seemed to work, but caused Mrs. Blake so much pain that I could not continue.

"For God's sake, stop—I cannot stand it. William, make her stop," she cried.

Pity overcame me; I knew time was running out because with my ear-horn I could tell the babe's heartbeat was irregular. Only one hope remained. I felt inside Mrs. Blake and with my two hands inside her almost above the wrists, I violently turned the child. The mother's screams filled the room, and she became unconscious, but at last the babe's head was visible. Dear God, let it be alive, I prayed as the labour continued, with the mother becoming weaker and weaker as each wave of pain washed over her. At last, the child slid into my waiting hands, all streaked with blood. It was a girl, perfect, but alas, dead.

From Kate's Notebook.
Wednesday, June 11, 1788.

> Silent as the womb
> Empty here I lie
> From my lips will come
> No lullaby.

Though I in secret cry
Revenge against the years
From my eyes will fall
No tears.

Tulips swell and die
A Rose fades in the wild
At my breast will sleep
No child.

From the Journal of Joseph Johnson, book publisher, of 72 St. Paul's Churchyard.
Wednesday, June 11, 1788. London.

It is the night after one of my Tuesday gatherings. A good selection of London's thinking men attended and conversation was lively, I am gratified to note. Fuseli was especially vivid, and engaged Priestley in argument, most amusing. I was just now sitting down to a late supper of cold chicken and a good glass of Claret, when Mary entered the room, much agitated.

"I have heard news of Catherine Blake," she said. "Her baby was born dead, and she is very weak. And more, she refuses to speak one word, and turns her face to the wall."

Now this is ill news indeed. Not only am I fond of little Mrs. Blake, but I know her husband would be much affected. He has been working for me designing book illustrations for some years—a singular man, much given to black moods, but essentially sweet of nature. Not exactly punctual with work, but it always gets done. One thing about Blake, his politics are sympathetic. He's a Dissenter and a reader of Rousseau like the rest of us. Now here was Mary, pacing the room, all in a Conflict of emotions. It is not just that babies die, or women die in childbirth, or get the Melancholy afterward: these things affect her in the Abstract, she philosophizes on the fate of her sex. But I sense there is more going on here. I have seen the way she looks at Blake.

Mary Wollstonecraft has a fine intelligent face, but at twenty-eight years, she is no beauty. It is her aura that is so compelling. Her Mood precedes her into the room. I recognize her talents and have taken a house for her on George Street. In return I am soon to publish her

Novel and her Stories for children. I was glad to become her Patron and save her from the fate of becoming a Governess again. Now that I have achieved fifty years, it is one of my pleasures to encourage young writers and artists.

Sadly enough, Kate Blake has never been at ease in our gatherings. Though she is of humble origins, she has been educated by her Husband and helps him in all aspects of his work. She has a good eye for Prints and knows a good Engraving when she sees one. But it is hard for her to hold a conversation with the likes of Mary or Fuseli. And Fuseli has been Blake's best friend since the sculptor John Flaxman went to Italy last year.

"I must pay the Blakes a visit," said Mary. "I know William would want me to visit Kate. Perhaps I can help her, for I too have suffered Melancholy. Perhaps she needs to be bled."

Mary always knows what to do for everything. No matter what I advised, she would do what she wanted, so I did not offer any advice. I do not think she should visit Kate.

. . .

I lie in my bed of sorrow and imagine many things. I hear voices, conversations.

"You have a visitor, Kate. It is Mary Wollstonecraft."

I thought, I will not speak. Especially to her. Leave me alone.

"Good Morning, Kate. Will you not look at me? I have come to offer my sympathy and help. I have not yet been a Mother, but my sister Eliza has suffered as you have. I know what fortitude is necessary."

Do you indeed? You with your eye always to the main chance, who flirts alike with my husband and Henry Fuseli, both married men. What do you know of my sorrow, of my emptiness. Where is my baby? Go away.

"She does not answer, William. Her eyes are dull. What have you done for her?"

"The Midwife has applied the leeches. She said time would heal her. I have prayed for her, too, but my Angels have not come, and to me Kate is like the cold moon."

Cold Moon? But it is a Black Cloud, William. Can you not see? And it is she, in her plain black dress and superior ways, and high flown ideas that men seem to find so fascinating.

"Kate, your grief is not yours alone. We must all help each other in times of trouble. Will you not be my friend, and let me help you and William?"

I am cold, and you are too bright for my sight. Go dazzle William and his damned Angels. Leave me alone.

They went into the next room. They thought I did not hear them talking.

"I have begun to write a poem for you, Mary. It is called The Crystal Cabinet."

"My dear Mr. Blake! How does it go?"

"Like this:

> The Maiden caught me in the Wild
> Where I was dancing merrily
> She put me into her Cabinet
> And Lockd me up with a golden Key
> This Cabinet is formd of Gold
> And Pearl & Crystal shining bright
> And within it opens into a World
> And a little lovely Moony Night
>
> Another England there I saw
> Another London with its Tower
> Another Thames and other hills
> And another pleasant Surrey Bower.

That is as far as I have written."

"William . . . what can I say? What will come next?"

"No good can come, can it? I will try to keep the Vision, but it will disappear. I will fill with woes the passing Wind, as the poets say."

"Give me your hand . . . you do know what great Affection I feel for you? And Kate? We wanted it not to be like other people's hidden affections . . . why is there not love enough in the world for all to share? Why should man and wife have to be exclusive of all others? I want to live in the Light!"

"And so do I . . . and so I have, till now. But the timing is all wrong. Friendship cannot exist without Forgiveness continually, and Kate cannot forgive."

Cathy comes to see me, and Mrs. Blake, but I do not speak to them. William is always near, stroking my hand, but I do not care. I will myself to become disembodied and fly where I wish, as I had done long before. I do not care that I am breaking my promise to William. I go to Mary Wollstonecraft's house in George Street. I watch and listen.

"What, Fuseli, are you here so early in the day? It is not respectable."

"Good God, Mary, what does that mean coming from you? Since when have we been concerned about respectability? Damn respectability!"

"So now you are swearing at me in two of your eight languages. It's a good thing your Swiss accent is so endearing, my love. You are in your usual good mood, I see. Pray, what brings you to my sitting-room at ten o'clock in the morning?"

"I hear you have been to see Blake."

"Oho. And what do you care? You are recently married, or have you forgotten that already?"

"Unfortunately, no. But . . . I could not let Sophia down. It makes no difference to you and me. Come, Mary, let us not quarrel . . . my God, are you still wearing stays? French women are giving them up, you know . . . ah, that's better . . ."

"Oh, Fuseli, you are as insinuating as a cat . . . oh, no wonder I can't resist you. But you must not concern yourself with me and Blake. We are spiritually connected, just as you and he are. So the three of us are One. You are not jealous, I hope?"

"Such bloody idealism! It is the consequence of your youth. Let us go to bed, Mary, I want to look at you again. See, I have made some sketches of our last time together."

"So now you woo me with erotic drawings! They do nothing for me, Henry—put them in the fire! I need only you . . ."

The three of us are One, she said. Oh, Mary, you are playing a dangerous game.

From Blake's Notebook.

> A Flower was offrd to me
> Such a flower as May never bore.
> But I said I've a Pretty Rose-tree,
> And I passed the sweet flower o'er.
>
> Then I went to my Pretty Rose-tree;
> To tend her by day and by night
> But my Rose turnd away with jealousy:
> And her thorns were my only delight.

From Kate's Notebook.
Saturday, July 5, 1788. London.

William has given me paper and ink, and I think perhaps it helps. I pin the words like butterflies on the page and they stay in place, instead of scattering, bright wings flying off in the summer air. I hear more clearly without Speech. I see feelings in the air in rainbow colours. William thinks I am getting better.

Sunday, July 6, 1788.

In the mirror I see a woman, not rounded, flat as earth, thin as a virgin. Her face is smooth, even pretty. No one knows she died. I am going out today into the Cries of London's streets. I will put on a mask. They will think I am Kate.

Monday, July 7, 1788.

Last night I know that William saw a Vision. It came to him on fiery wings, burning in the dark, to set his brain alight. I saw it too, but did not dare to ask: Where does Love live? Is it in the Sunlight, as he says, or safe in a moonlit Marriage bed?

Letter From Mary Wollstonecraft to Henry Fuseli.
Tuesday, July 8, 1788.

My Dear,

How can I go on in this manner? Each time you leave me to return to Sophia I am in Misery. Why have you taught me to experience such Sensations, only to recollect them in Loneliness? You have had me plait my Hair for your eyes only in elaborate coiffures—and then you show me drawings of Sophia in even more exotic Rolls and Curls, all created for your Pleasure, even as I have done. Do you enjoy torturing me?

My solace is Work, and I thank God and Joseph Johnson for that. He has published my novel, *Mary,* as well as the children's story book, and I am busy writing Essays for his new magazine, *Analytical Review*— are you not doing the same? I hope my books are successful; I feel I must leave my Mark on the world somehow. You at least can claim notoriety if not Genius with your Nightmare picture—after all, you are in the Royal Academy because of it!

The talk at Joseph's gathering tonight was all about kings...the madness of King George and the bankruptcy of the King of France... so now you are thoroughly informed of my concerns this week. I hope to hear the same from you.

Joseph told me you dined with Blake yesterday. I have not seen him for two weeks at least. He is not like you—or rather, Kate is not compliant like Sophia—and Blake will not abuse her Feelings. So he has remained polite but distant. Still, I feel a Spiritual Bond. Pray, tell him of my Affection.

> Come Soon, my Henry,
> Your Mary

From Kate's Notebook.
Saturday, July 12, 1788.

Now here is something wonderful, a gift—Henry has given me a kitten. She loves to curl into my lap, a ginger ball, with greeny eyes and furry tongue. I have named her Marigold. Poor William, caught with me in Sorrow's cloud. No sunlight—no, nor Marigold for him. I feel such Pity. Shall I offer him a Rose instead?

Letter to William Blake from Kate, n.d.

Dear William,

Since you have given me the pen and paper, I will use them to help me express what I cannot say aloud.

I remember when we first married you spoke to me of Freedom and not Binding down our Joys, and it all sounded so blissful and exciting. I was a country Girl and not unaware of the ways of men, after all. Then you tested those ideas with Nancy and I hated it. Now you have met Mary, who shares so much with you in realms I cannot follow.

I cook your meals, and sew your shirts, and make our candles, and help with the printing press—but it isn't enough for you, I realize. And now I can't even give you a child.

I want to forgive you for deserting me—oh not in Body, but in Spirit. But I cannot do it. We lie in bed like two bodies in a Tomb. I do Pity you, as I see you, too, are troubled and lonely.

But for now I have nothing to give. Well, the little cat rubs against my skirt and wants her supper. I will leave this letter at your plate this evening.

Your Kate.

Fair Copy of a poem in Blake's Notebook.

London

I wander thro' each charter'd street,
Near where the charter'd Thames does flow.
And mark in every face I meet
Marks of weakness, marks of woe.

In every cry of every Man,
In every Infants cry of fear,
In every voice: in every ban,
The mind-forg'd manacles I hear

How the Chimney-sweepers cry
Every blackning Church appalls,
And the hapless Soldiers sigh,
Runs in blood down Palace walls

But most thro' midnight streets I hear
How the youthful Harlots curse
Blasts the new-born infants tear
And blights with plagues the Marriage hearse.

Note delivered by Messenger to Mary Wollstonecraft from Henry Fuseli. Tuesday, August 12, 1788 at 5 P.M.

Mary, I need your help. Blake has collapsed—some sort of gut trouble. But there may be more to it as he has been in Despair of late. Go for Kate at Poland Street and accompany her here to Johnson's book shop in St. Paul's Churchyard. I have sent for the Surgeon.

Make haste—Henry

9

In Which I See A Ghost

It is hard to believe, but at last I saw Robert's Ghost with my own eyes, and I heard him read aloud to William. It was the evening after William's illness. Mary, Henry and I were in the sitting room, worrying, when I heard a noise above in the bedroom where William lay. I went up quietly so as not to disturb him. Then I heard a voice. My heart stopped, for it was Robert. I peeked into the room, and there he was at the head of William's bed, looking as he did when he was alive and well. If I had not known he was dead and buried, I would have thought he was there in the Flesh. He was reading a poem aloud:

> "I wonder whether the Girls are mad
> And I wonder whether they mean to kill
> And I wonder if William Bond will die
> For assuredly he is very ill
>
> "He went to Church in a May morning
> Attended by Fairies one two & three

But the Angels of Providence drove them away
And he returnd home in Misery

"He went not out to the Field nor Fold
He went not out to the Village nor Town
But he came home in a black black cloud
And took to his Bed and there lay down

"And an Angel of Providence at his Feet
And an Angel of Providence at his Head
And in the midst a Black Black Cloud
And in the midst the Sick Man on his Bed . . .

Hmnn . . ."

William said, "Robert, is that you? Are you here? Or have I died?"

"No, William, you did not die. You had bad food," replied Robert.

"Oh, good. I thought Death would be more glorious. But I am sore, and I am so hot. Where is everybody? Doesn't anyone care that I am sick? Where is Kate?"

"They are all downstairs worrying about you. Mary, Kate—your two Angels—and Henry."

"Angels! They are killing me with their Feelings. Kate and her Melancholy, and Mary gone to Fuseli. And I stopped seeing Mary, Robert—but Kate did not change! Pale and cold, pale and cold. It is destroying me . . . I can't even work anymore. . . . and I'm so hot!" He threw off his covers.

Robert said, "Work is all that lasts, William. What have you done with the idea I gave you—about etching the words and designs on the same copper plate?"

"I did two little philosophical books . . . and I started a poem about the lost baby, but I haven't finished it . . . The Book of Thel it will be called."

"Does Kate know?"

"No."

"When did you write this?" said Robert, waving the paper he was reading from.

"About three days ago."

"Hmnn . . . it's not one of your best . . . but I expect it expresses your state of mind right now."

William groaned. I went into the room, scarcely knowing what to say. Robert disappeared.

"William?" I placed my hand on his brow. "Oh, William you have a fever! Oh, please look at me!"

William said, dryly, "It's good to hear your voice, Kate."

"Please get better. Everything will be the way it used to be if you'll just get better."

"No, Kate. Things will never be the way they used to be. You turned me away. I don't feel the same."

I began to weep. At this point, Henry came into the room.

"Mein Gott, what is going on here? Blake, are you sensible? You look flushed. Kate, pour him some water. Blake, you must rest and keep drinking water. You have given us all a fright."

William sat up gingerly. "Ah, Henry! I have written you a poem . . . 'The only Man that eer I knew / Who did not make me almost spew/Was Fuseli he was both Turk and Jew/ And so dear Christian Friends how do you do . . . '"

"By God, Blake, that's a good one! You can't be too sick if you are still rhyming. Mary is here and wants to see you."

I looked glumly on as Mary entered, her skin pale against her black dress.

"My dear Blake! How are you today? I am so sorry this has happened."

"Mary, you do me good just to look at you. You are bright as the morning."

I said tearfully to Fuseli, "He loves her, Henry. He doesn't love me anymore."

Mary sat in a chair at William's bedside.

Henry said to her in a low voice, "Say your piece and leave. He looks seriously ill to me. And remember, you are my lover, not his!"

Mary said, "You must get better, dear William. We have work to do together, remember. We will be friends for life."

"Yes . . . but you will have a hard life, sweet Mary. I see it . . . I see Fame . . . and Scorn . . . And thine is a Face of Sweet Love and Despair . . . And thine is a Face of mild sorrow and Care . . ."

"He is raving," I said.

"And thine is a Face of Wild Terror and Fear . . . That shall never be Quiet till laid on its bier . . ."

This alarmed Mary. She rose and rushed out of the room, Henry following. I stood transfixed, for Robert reappeared, in shimmer of light.

"Brother, let it go. You have frightened her."

"But I see . . . oh, God, I see Mary . . . and a baby, and blood . . . so much blood!"

"To whom are you speaking, William? Who is here? Mary did not have a baby . . . I did! It was me, William . . . Kate!"

Robert said, "Be calm now, brother. . . . Sleep."

William fell back on the pillow, and Robert faded away, giving me a long look in parting. I smoothed William's brow, straightened the covers around him, and left the room, shaking.

For the next two hours, Henry, Mary and I sat around the oak table in the sitting room, drinking wine by the light of a single candle.

"When I was a girl," said Mary, "I always wanted to be beautiful, like you, Kate—and get married, and have children and a household like everybody else. But nobody cared much for me, not my mother . . . or father . . . and even the family money went to my brother, as well as any affection or respect."

I cradled my kitten in my lap, and said, "I was the last of nine children. My mother was worn out with childbearing. As soon as she stopped suckling one, another would be on the way. I never thought I would have trouble childbearing. But as for money, well, we never had any. My father had a market garden. I didn't even know how to read properly till William taught me. I wish I were clever like you, Mary."

"Ha! What do women need brains for?" said Henry, pouring more wine all around. "Do they make Mary happy? I love women . . . and men, too, sometimes . . . but all they need is a capacity to Feel! That's what I like about William. He feels things . . . things that nobody else does."

"And he sees things, too," I said. "Visions of God . . . and Prophets from the Old Testament . . . his Imagination frightens me sometimes."

"Do you know what he told me once?" said Mary. " 'Everything possible to be believed is an image of truth.' I love his mind."

"And he loves yours. I can understand that." I drained my glass. The room looked a little blurry.

"Blake has good taste in women, by God!" exclaimed Henry, "But he will never be rich, you know. He doesn't care what anyone thinks. God, I hope he lives!"

I cried, "He has to live . . . of course he will! And I know what will make him better!" I stood up, "Come, we'll go see him."

I led the way into the bedroom, carrying the candle. William raised himself on one arm as we came in.

"I feel very strange. How long have you all been here?" he said. "Have you seen Robert?"

I answered, "He is not here now, William, but he watches over you."

I felt his forehead. "You are not as feverish, I think. So perhaps you will understand what I have to say. Listen to me, please, all of you. William, you love Mary better than me . . . it's all right, I understand. She is special. You must take her to be your Wife . . . and I will be Housekeeper to you both."

I had long thought about this. I knew it was an idea dear to William's heart, but never before to mine. Now, I thought I knew how to save him and our life together.

"What?" exclaimed Mary.

"*God's Teeth!*" said Henry.

"We will all three live together in perfect Love and Harmony," I continued, "and you can paint, and she can write . . . and I will look after you both."

I began to tremble, and I fell to the floor, feeling faint. The room spun around. William stared in shock as Mary and Henry, exclaiming, lifted me to the bed and lay me beside him.

Mary said, looking at Henry, "What an amazing idea."

And then I saw Robert emerge from the shadows, with the poem in his hand, and he read in a voice that sounded just like William:

I thought Love lived in the hot sun shine
But O he lives in the Moony light
I thought to find Love in the heat of the day
But sweet love is the Comforter of Night.

Seek Love in the Pity of others Woe
In the gentle relief of anothers care
In the darkness of night and the Winters snow
In the naked and outcast Seek Love there.

When I recovered and found myself lying next to William, I suddenly felt very happy and knew I had done the right thing and he and Mary and I would live blissfully together in Everlasting Joy and Love. I confess I rather forgot about Henry and Sophia—five people in one marriage was more than I could imagine, I suppose.

William just looked at me as if he had never really seen me before and I saw something like Pity in his eyes until he smiled at me and kissed me tenderly, and fell asleep himself. Mary and Henry kissed me, too, and went away, saying they would see us the next day, when William was sure to be better. And, as I had known all along, his fever broke that night and did not return, and early in the morning he took up his pen and wrote the lines in his Notebook he had recited to me during our courtship:

> He who binds to himself a joy
> Doth the winged life destroy
> But he who kisses the joy as it flies
> Lives in Eternity's sun rise

Then I knew William was himself again. When I brought him his morning tea, he had written yet another poem:

> Come hither my sparrows
> My little arrows
> If a tear or a smile
> Will a man beguile
> If an amorous delay
>
> Clouds a sunshiny day
> If the step of a foot
> Smites the heart to its root
> Tis the marriage ring
> Makes each fairy a king
>
> So a fairy sung
> From the leaves I sprung

> He leapd from the spray
> To flee away
> But in my hat caught
> He soon shall be taught
> Let him laugh let him cry
> He's my butterfly
> For I've pulld out the Sting
> Of the marriage ring

Oh, he *was* in a good mood. And from that day he recovered his Strength and Energy.

As the morning progressed, I began to feel a little nervous about what I had proposed . . . I mean, we had only a narrow four storey house, with two rooms on each floor, and the downstairs was the Printing Room and Kitchen. So where would my room be, once Mary took over the bedroom with William? She would want the third floor as her study. I supposed I would go in the attic, under the roof. Would William pay any attention to me once Mary was here? Would I love her as a sister when I could see her every day, taking my place in William's bed?

I confess to feeling a little sorry for myself, and I shed a tear or two as I began to bake some bread, but I heard William calling me and so I went upstairs with my hands and apron all floury, and there he was dressed and sitting on the edge of the bed, and he had the Bible in his hands and he read aloud as I came into the room: "Thou hast ravished my heart, my sister, my spouse; thou hast ravished my heart with one of thine eyes, with one chain of thy neck. How fair is thy love, my sister, my spouse! How much better is thy love than wine!"

I knew how to respond. I chose another verse: "As the apple tree among the trees of the wood, so is my beloved among the sons. I sat down under his shadow with great delight, and his fruit was sweet to my taste."

That is how I knew that William loved me again and would not take Mary for his second wife. Just the idea that I would not stand in his way should he want to was enough to keep him from doing it.

As for Mary, she really just wanted William to keep paying court to her great intellect, which of course he always did, and she was a great admirer of Good Conversation, which William always provided, but it was Henry with whom she really wanted to live.

. . .

How much can one woman cry? I seemed never to finish with Tears. They came welling up out of a great emptiness and loneliness that William could not fill. My arms yearned for the babe that was gone and for a child I knew I would never have. After a time, I wept less, or at least, more inwardly. I was cheerful by nature, and my Melancholy days became bearable as I went about my work, learning more how to print and colour William's designs.

The next year, 1789, was better for us. William made a beautiful book, *Songs of Innocence*, finished by hand with watercolours. I got to paint a little on the designs, too. Then in July the Revolution started in France, and that is all Mary, Henry, Joseph and everybody else could talk about.

It did seem as if a wonderful New Age would begin, a time when you would be free to live without a government oppressing you, or feel you were inferior if you were only the daughter of a market gardener. William called himself a Son of Liberty and took to wearing the red cap of the Revolutionaries when he went out.

In 1790, Edmund Burke published his book about the Revolution in France and everyone became nervous about change. Mary wrote a response about the rights of Man, which became the talk of the Town. Joseph's friend Tom Paine wrote one too. Anyone wanting reform of Parliament was under government suspicion, and everyone at Joseph's dinners, especially. Joseph was going to publish a poem of William's called *The French Revolution* but then lost his nerve, as it was a bit too radical, and England had become quite frightened that the idea of Revolution would spread across the Channel. So the poem remains in proof and I don't suppose anyone will ever read it.

From Kate's Notebook, n.d.

Mary has just come to call, and she told me that Joseph has urged her to write about the Rights of Woman, since her essay on Man was so successful. She is seriously thinking about it. She says women are human beings, not just sexual creatures, and just as rational as men. Mind has no sex, she maintains. We are robbed of our Dignity because we are totally dependent upon husbands for our maintenance. We should be free to Love where we wish without the idea of Possession being part of the relationship. Mary thinks Society is wasting half its members; women should be trained like men for Professions and Careers. Oh, I think her ideas are marvellous. I've heard William say some of the same things about Love—but I'm not sure how Henry will take it.

Mary also told me that someday she is going to suggest to Sophia that she, Mary, would join the Fuseli household as a Spiritual Wife. Somehow, I don't think that's going to work.

10

In Which We Give A Party

There is a Grain of Sand in Lambeth that Satan cannot find
Nor can his Watch Fiends find it: tis translucent & has many
Angles.

—WILLIAM BLAKE.

*A*s we were beginning to make a little money with William's
engraving commissions, we moved in the autumn of 1790
across the river to Lambeth. Number 13 Hercules Buildings
was a handsome, three storey brick house, the largest in the row, with
pleasant green open fields behind. Here we had proper space to work
for the first time in our lives. It was a grander dwelling than I had ever
imagined I would live in, a new house of ten rooms. Two rooms on
the ground floor had each a marble fireplace and panelled walls;
William chose the second of these, which looked out on a proper garden, for his painting and printing room. The kitchen was in the basement, and had lovely blue and white tiles on the walls.

I had a little sitting room of my own on the second floor, where I
was able to have my own spinning wheel and store wools for my

embroideries and tapestries. There was colour there, and indeed all over the house, with William's paintings on the walls, and one or two of Henry's in the sitting room. William had a Trade Card which read: *Mr. Blake Engraver, Hercules Buildings, Westminster Bridge.*

When people came to discuss commissions, William received them in the panelled front room, which we had painted pale blue. The black and white engravings looked particularly good against that colour, I thought. William had been doing well, with commissions from Johnson and Fuseli, and among other things he engraved was an illustration of the famous Portland Vase, the one exhibited at Wedgewood's in Greek Street.

Then there were, of course, his six illustrations for Mary Wollstonecraft's *Original Stories from Real Life.* I particularly liked the frontispiece to that, for William used me as the model of a slim-waisted woman in a large bonnet, with arms outstretched over two young girls. The grapevine in the background could have been inspired by our own luxuriant vine, for we now had also a pretty garden, with a grapevine against the house, and a little fig tree against the wall, and beds of marigolds and daisies.

After we had been a few months at 13 Hercules Buildings and were well settled in, we decided to give a party. It was a Twelfth Night celebration, January 6, 1791, and I planned it and prepared for it for a month.

First, the guest list. Unfortunately, the Flaxmans were still in Italy, but of the oldest friends, we invited Tom Stothard and his wife Rebecca, and George Cumberland and his plump, amiable wife, Mary. Then there were the Parkers, of course, and Fuseli and his wife, Sophia. It was unusual for Sophia to accompany her husband. Henry usually kept her at home. She was a good-looking woman with a fine figure and rather sharp features, whose hair was always elaborately arranged.

Mary Wollstonecraft came, too, of course, feeling rather displaced by Sophia, I imagine, so she stayed close to Joseph Johnson, and one of his new writers, Captain John Gabriel Stedman, who was visiting from Devon. He wanted William to engrave many plates for his narrative of five years expedition to Surinam, in Guiana, on the wild coast of South America, where he had spent five years in the early Seventies.

We also invited our neighbour Philip Astley, who had the next garden but one from us. He owned a Theatre about three streets away, with a very popular Circus. Rumour has it that he can talk to horses; he certainly can train a horse to do any trick: I have seen it with my own eyes. At William's behest, we included the golden-haired singer Elizabeth Billington and her husband, James, the musician. Elizabeth arrived in dress of sprigged muslin with a neckline so low you could see her pink nipples.

Dr. Joseph Priestley also came, who was that very year to lose his house and laboratory in Birmingham to a violent mob. He had been worried for some time about the safety of his property, for Dissenters like us who supported the Revolution in France in 1789 were suspected of being subversive. Most of the group only wanted to see tax reform. Of course, Dr. Priestley, outspoken in his support of the Revolution and of English Parliamentary reform, was the obvious target of a suspicious mob. At our party, that trouble was still in the future.

Priestley was deep in conversation with Thomas Christie, a handsome and witty Scotsman of about my age, who had founded the *Analytical Review* with Johnson, and worked with Mary. He had rushed over to France as soon as the Revolution was underway to see events for himself in the very first month. He had thought it admirable. He believed in actively working to improve conditions of life for Humanity, and he thoroughly approved the moves for civil liberty in France. Of course, he was a canny Scot, and William said he was also intent on going into business with people involved in the Revolution.

Among our guests, the painter George Romney was also present, along with his good friend William Hayley, who happened to be in London on business. We even invited William's brother James, and his Mother, and of course Cathy, who was a great help to me.

For the first time in my life, I had a little maidservant named Bessie, whose room was on the top floor of the house. It was rather hard for me to have someone else underfoot, but for the party she was very useful. We baked for a week beforehand. We made Bath cakes with caraway seed, a Saffron cake, and an old-fashioned almond cake. We invited everyone for dinner at about 3 P.M. Our main dish was a good roast sirloin of beef, served with a rich gravy. We also made several onion and potato pies to go with the beef. These were a great success with their mace and nutmeg flavouring and the layers of dried apple and hard-boiled egg that goes into them, too. There was plenty of ale and wine to go around, and though I must confess to being a quiver of nerves before the party began, as the afternoon wore on and the noise level of conversation in the house rose higher and higher, I realized that everyone was having a fine time.

"My goodness, Kate," whispered Cathy to me, "have you seen how Henry Fuseli is flirting with Mrs. Billington? His wife looks very out of sorts!"

I had, in fact, earlier in the evening noticed Henry and Mrs. Billington in the hall, deep in conversation, and had not missed the fact that Henry had his hand in Mrs. Billington's very available bosom.

Mary had decided to ignore Fuseli for the evening, and, handsome in a new black silk gown, concentrated on conversation with Johnson and John Gabriel Stedman. He was indeed an interesting man. He had a forthright manner about him, and a solid physique, rather like William. His memoirs of his life in Surinam, where he had been a Soldier of Fortune, were full of gruesome accounts of the cruel suppression of a revolt of Negro slaves. He also told the story of his love for a young mulatto slave girl named Joanna, whom he saved from being brutally flogged.

"She was given to me by her mother," I overheard him say to Mary, "and I loved her for four years, and a babe, too. But I left her behind when I came home to Devon."

"What happened to her?" asked Mary, who was always interested in the fate of women.

"She died about six years after I left," he said, simply. Stedman was also an artist and one of the illustrations in his book which William engraved, was a picture of poor Joanna.

"She was still a slave?" asked Mary.

"Alas, yes," said Stedman, "I could never purchase her freedom. I fear she was sold at auction after I left, and in my dreams I saw her tortured, insulted, and bowing under the weight of her chains, calling to me."

"How tragic!" exclaimed Mary, much moved. "What an odious thing is slavery!"

"It is an abomination!" cried William, who had joined the group. "There will be no liberty or equality among us till slavery is abolished!"

"Too many London Merchants have a vested interest in slavery for it to be abolished soon," said Joseph dryly.

"And too many aristocrats," added Mary.

I excused myself from that conversation just then to attend to Mr. Hayley, who was sitting alone by the fire. I offered him a piece of almond cake.

"Ah, Mrs. Blake, how charming you look!" he said. "Your black eyes reflect the firelight most remarkably." As usual, I blushed under his gaze. I enquired politely after the health of his wife and son.

"My wife and I live apart a good deal," he said, "but the boy does wonderfully well. He shows talent as an artist, and he has a facility with languages. And by the way, he was delighted with William's *Songs of Innocence*. Did I detect your hand in the colouring?"

I confessed that I had helped. Though the ink was the same in each run, the designs in each copy were coloured a little differently.

"And the poems themselves—they are quite wild and natural, would you not say? Did you not contribute to them, too?"

"Only one," I admitted. "I thought of a line. It was 'Little lamb, who made thee?' But William took it from there."

I was really quite in awe of the man: he was, after all, one of the most famous poets in the country, and here he was in my sitting room, looking at me intently, and seemingly interested in what I had to say. He turned to George Romney, who had entered the room, and called him over.

"Romney, does not Mrs. Blake have something of the air of Emma Hart?"

Now it was Romney's turn to blush, it seemed. I did not know then that Emma was his favourite model, and he was in love with her, but she was now mistress of Sir William Hamilton, Ambassador to Italy, and soon to be his wife.

Romney said, "Indeed she has. Mrs. Blake, do you model?"

"Only for my husband, sir," I said. I felt Mr. Hayley's deep-set eyes on my bosom and waist, and divined his thought. I deemed it best to change the subject.

"Allow me to find you both some wine," I said, and left with as much composure as I could muster.

I passed Thomas Christie and Joseph Priestley in animated discussion.

"Did ye know, Priestley, that Johnson is bringing out a second edition this verra month of Mary's *Vindication of the Rights of Man?*" Thomas said in his soft Scots burr.

"It is a rather indulgent work," said Priestley, with a wave of his hand. "Rather scatter-shot, I thought. I am very interested in all the responses like hers to Burke's *Reflections on the Revolution in France*, of course. His is the voice of Reaction; he is very afraid of losing the rule of law. He made a good argument, we must admit."

"But Mary's response was popular," Christie replied, "and now Johnson is going to put her name on the second edition. I ken that will make her famous."

"I hear she is now thinking of a *Vindication* for women," said Priestley. "That will be something to see."

Later, I went out into the garden for a breath of air. There was a cold, clear night out there, with a blaze of stars across the sky. The candles from the rooms inside cast a golden glow on the garden. I could distinguish two figures near the wall to my right, walking up and down, deep in conversation together. It was William and Mary. They were not touching, yet there was a connection between them, a similarity in the way they paced, the angle of their heads bending together.

With a pang, I realized there were places I could never go with William, where Mary went all the time. And Henry and Dr. Priestley and Joseph Johnson—in fact, almost everyone at the party could reach William on a plane I could never inhabit, no matter how hard I tried.

"You did well, Kate," said William late that night, after everyone had gone. "It was a fine evening. I do enjoy good company and good food. I appreciate all the work you did." He moved his hand lightly over my cheek and down my neck to my breast, as he kissed me tenderly. So there was something I could do for him.

From Kate's Notebook.
February 10, 1791.

It rained today, so I undertook to tidy William's painting room. There were always books piled on the floor, and powders for inks on the shelves, and paper drying on the racks. Then there were portfolios of drawings stacked on the side table. I decided to sort those first. Idly, I opened one that did not look familiar. It was one of Fuseli's. And then, shocked, I realized it was one of his sets of erotic drawings. Repelled and yet fascinated, I regarded the images of women and men in strange positions of sexual congress, of women partially clothed with hair in elaborate creations, baring their bosoms or their buttocks.

Then I realized that these women all looked exceptionally cruel or dominating. These were not scenes of love, but of lust. There was no word in my vocabulary for what these women were doing, but inflicting pain seemed to be their prime motive. There were drawings of Male Members, erect and not erect. There were drawings of Vulvas with wings. And always there were women with hair braided in impossible shapes, breasts bared over transparent flowing skirts, threatening a recumbent male.

As I turned these pages, a strange thing began to happen to me. I began to feel a wave of heat in my nether regions, such as I would feel if William stroked my breasts. I touched my right nipple: it was hard and upright. I stroked my own breast, hypnotized, and soon I sat on a chair and touched myself where usually only William would touch me. My fingers felt a wetness, and I moved them rhythmically, pleasuring myself.

I felt wave after wave of warmth suffuse my loins, and I gasped involuntarily. Then I saw a shadow out of the corner of my eye, and I realized that William had entered the room. He took in the scene at one glance. He said not a word, but coming to me, placed his head between my thighs, and moved his tongue on me as I had moved my fingers. It was as if butterflies were caressing me. I had never experienced such pleasure.

"Oh, do not stop," I moaned.

And then he took me in the usual way, right there on the floor, his Maleness hard in me. We lay together as the passion subsided, smiling at each other. He put his hand on my slippery Womanhood, and again I felt a circle of heat.

"Again?" he smiled. I did not have to answer. With his fingers he again brought me to climax, but then he did a new thing. He brought his erect Member to my mouth.

I must have looked startled, for he said, "There is no shame. Pleasure me as I have pleasured you."

So I took his Member in my mouth, and moved my tongue over it gently.

"Ah, harder," he said. So I sucked him repeatedly, as hard as I could, choking a little, feeling repelled and excited at the same time. There was a salty taste in my mouth, and suddenly a spurt of liquid. Startled, I swallowed, wiping my mouth with my fingers.

"You have swallowed my Essence," said William. "Now we are truly one flesh. I would not have asked were you not ready."

Our physical bond is very great. Now I will not be able to enter the painting room without this memory!

From Blake's Notebook, 1791.

What is it men in women do require?
The lineaments of Gratified Desire
What is it women do in men require?
The lineaments of Gratified Desire

From Kate's Notebook, n.d.

Since that day in the painting room, I now look at the roles of Wife and Harlot in a new light. What is the relation between them? Are women so cold and prudish that harlots are necessary? Do men have to buy what they do not find at home? And why are there women so poor that they must sell themselves on the street for bread? And why do other women use their bodies to marry wealth, and yet are not considered whores?

William said that we had a Sacred Marriage, and the Energy generated from our love was making him Inspired. Indeed, he was working very hard, and making the most unusual designs of his own, when he was not toiling over commercial engravings. He would make love to me so often and at such unexpected times that I was embarrassed lest the maid Bessie may notice, so I decided to let her go.

We began to print a work of William's called *The Marriage of*

Heaven and Hell. William had been writing this off and on for several months. It was an odd collection of poetry and prose, tales and aphorisms, in which he commented on many things: the Bible, Milton and Swedenborg; things Angels had told him, things Devils had told him. Some of it came from our sexual life together:

> The lust of the goat is the bounty of God.
> The cistern contains; the fountain overflows.

Body and Soul had no boundaries; this we had experienced for ourselves. So I understood when William wrote this passage:

> Man has no Body distinct from his Soul; for that call'd Body is
>   a portion of Soul discern'd by the five Senses, the chief
>   inlets of Soul in this age.
> Energy is the only life and is from the Body and Reason is the
>   bound or outward circumference of Energy.
> Energy is Eternal Delight.

In this work, the Devils have all the best lines. For example, I love this observation by one of them:

> How do you know but ev'ry Bird that cuts the airy way,
> Is an immense world of delight, clos'd by your senses five?

William made up what he called "Proverbs of Hell," which would certainly destroy our way of life if we took them to heart, for example, "The road of excess leads to the palace of wisdom." Or, "He who desires but acts not, breeds pestilence."

We chose six Inks for the first run: green, yellow ochre, raw sienna, raw umber, and olive green and brownish red. We had used these for *Innocence* and *Thel*, too. As to the Watercolours with which we painted the images on the plates, why we made our own. We had pigments of Prussian blue, gamboge, yellow ochre, rose madder, vermilion, and others, which we mixed with gum arabic, or more often carpenter's glue for body and adhesiveness, and then a mix of glycerine, honey and a drop of ox gall. William said that the sacred Carpenter, Joseph, had revealed that secret to him.

We would choose a wash for the print, and then gradually layer on the colours until the pages glowed like jewels. I was always pleased when William asked me to paint a series of pages. Each copy of the book was thus a little different from the others in the run, each one unique.

It had been the same for the *Songs of Innocence*, too, and *Thel*. Those designs had been gentle and pastoral, but the designs for *Marriage* were brilliant with flames and naked bodies floating or falling. Some pages were mostly words with tiny figures entwined between the lines, and many little serpents and birds emphasized sentences. As I sewed these books together between plain paper covers, I smiled at the little animals and figures. I certainly did not understand everything he had written, but the last line of the book summed up much of William's thought for me: For every thing that lives is Holy.

From Kate's Notebook.
Monday, April 4, 1791.

Today as I was sorting pages in the Painting Room, preparing them for colouring, I marvelled at William's clear handwriting—because he had to write on the copper plates backwards in order for them to print forward. He dips his brush in the sticky stopping-out varnish thinned with a little turps and composes on the copper plate.

I have tried to write like this myself, but cannot do it. It seems to me that if you can write backward, you must think differently than other people. My name backwards is *ekalB etaK*. William is *ekalB mailliW*. He has to think of himself backward whenever he signs his work.

I wonder, is it this other self who is responsible for William's contrary Nature? Because he is often prickly and argumentative. Why can't I be prickly sometimes? Why must I always be sweet-tempered and give in? I'll wager ekalB etaK would not be so amiable.

. . .

One day in Spring, Mary Wollstonecraft came to call on me. I found this most surprising, because we had not been on intimate terms, though our relations had been cordial. I could tell she was much agitated and needed to talk.

"I have few women confidantes," she said earnestly, after I bid her be comfortable in our sitting room. She was looking rather tired, and her brown hair was hastily tied up behind her ears. As usual, she wore a black gown.

"It helps to talk about one's troubles, sometimes," I told her as sympathetically as I could.

"It is Henry," she said. "I do not know what to do about him. I cannot get him out of my mind. Do you know he took both Sophia and me to a masquerade at Covent Garden? Together!"

"What happened?" I was surprised at Fuseli's nerve.

"Well, we were annoyed by a man in a devil's costume, who so abused Henry that he simply went home. And he left Sophia and me alone."

"It just reveals that he does not want confrontation," I suggested.

"He has taught me to scorn convention," said Mary, bitterly, "but he retreats into it with Sophia at every opportunity."

"You would be open about your feelings for Henry?"

"Yes! I would tell everyone if I could, and I would have him love Sophia, too. I would wish we could all love each other openly without jealousy."

"I do not think that is realistic."

"What? And you are Blake's wife? Would you not find him lovers to share your bed as you once offered me? He wants that, does he not?"

These words froze my blood. I felt betrayed, though I should have known William still shared his thoughts with Mary. There was a poem of his in manuscript, of which I had seen a page, called *Visions of the Daughters of Albion*. The heroine, Oothoon by name, had a speech which echoed exactly Mary's sentiments. Oothoon said she would catch for her lover "girls of mild silver, or of furious gold. . . . I'll lie beside thee on a bank and view their wanton play / In lovely copulation, bliss on bliss . . ."

I had hoped that William had transferred his fantasies to the poem, but I now worried that in contemplating Mary's continued infatuation with Fuseli, he yearned for one of his own.

At the bottom of our garden there was a little summer house, covered in a luxurious grape vine. Here William and I would sit secluded on a warm spring evening, and sometimes we would remove our clothes, and naked to the evening breeze, enjoy looking at one another. We would read *Paradise Lost*, Book Nine, when Adam and Eve are in the Garden of Eden. That evening, after Mary's visit, I ventured to ask William if he was satisfied with me as his wife. He held me close and I reveled in the protection of his broad shoulders.

"I will always love you, Kate," he said. As I watched the moon rise above us, I knew suddenly that its silver orb was at the same time inside me, too, and as William and I moved together, the moon shattered into a million stars.

11

In Which I Experience Jealousy and Go To Dover

I always liked to visit Covent Garden, a spacious Piazza on the north side of the Strand, faced by the handsome church of St. Paul. All around the perimeter were Arcades built under the upper floors of the houses, rather like cloisters in a church garden. A wooden rail surrounded the square, and in the middle was a tall column often festooned with garlands. At one end vendors of fruits and vegetables with their covered wagons sold their wares. Actors and mimes strolled among the throngs of visitors: there was always something going on in the Square, perhaps a visiting Circus or a troupe of musicians, clinking their tambourines.

The Theatre was a grand place with wrought iron doors. We crowded into a small, dark entry to present our admissions to *Love In A Village*, a comic opera. Suddenly we were in a beautiful space, brilliantly lit by a huge chandelier, sparkling with reflected candles. Three tiers of seats rose up on three sides, with elaborate railings all around, and oil lamps casting even more light. The stage was hung with a green curtain. The walls were painted red and gold and the ceiling displayed beautiful plaster scroll designs, but I was surprised to find we sat on plain backless benches.

The audience was made up of all classes and sizes, some fashionably dressed and some poorly dressed—all were noisily talking and calling to each other. The noise did not really stop even when the performance began, because aristocratic Ladies with feathers in their hair were calling to each other from their boxes. I looked in amazement at some of their lovely jewel-coloured satin gowns—most wore short jackets with close half-sleeves, and a cambric kerchief at the breast. The fashionable Gentlemen were no longer powdering their hair, but tying it back, and some were wearing it close-cropped. William wore his black jacket and breeches, but some men wore tight pantaloons with cutaway coats. I had put on my best gown, a simple pink taffeta with ruffled sleeves, and a wide low collar with a gauzy bouffant insert across the bosom.

Fuseli and Sophia were with us. Sophia as usual had her hair in elaborate braids, and something about her shrewd expression reminded me suddenly of the women in Henry's erotic drawings. Poor Mary, I thought.

"It is too warm in here!" Sophia complained, fanning herself irritably.

"Why don't you svare, my dear," said Henry. "It will make you feel better." Swearing was Henry's favourite means of relieving tension.

I was delighted with all the noise and movement and gaiety of the theatre, and when the music started, I was transported. The green curtain rose to reveal an amazing sight: a real garden with statues, fountains and flowerpots and several arbours with real roses at their gates!

Two young women were seated in the garden on pretty chairs, Rosetta and Lucinda. They were discussing marriage: Rosetta was Elizabeth Billington, who had given us the tickets, costing two shillings each. She was the first to sing an Air by herself. It went:

> My heart's my own, my will is free,
> And so shall be my voice;
> No mortal man shall wed with me,
> Till first he's made my choice.
>
> Let parents rule, cry nature's laws;
> And children still obey;

And is there then no saving clause,
Against tyrannic sway?

I thought, William must be enjoying these sentiments! And indeed, he was seemingly transfixed by Elizabeth's performance. She had a voice of astonishing range. Her high notes were pure, and her low notes alluring. I was not surprised to hear that she was very well paid. Her costume was in the fashionable shepherdess style. Her hair and figure were charming. I had to admire her.

As to the Comedy itself, well, I must confess that the plot of young people escaping from arranged marriages was amusing, but so far from my own Experience that it did not really appeal to me. There was much Posturing on the stage, with exaggerated Gestures. I liked the dancing, though, that concluded each Act. In the bright light we could see each actor clearly and the musicians in the orchestra pit, too. The audience applauded every song, shouted its approval, booed when it felt like it, and laughed loudly at other times. All was very lively indeed.

"If you like Theatre," said Henry to me, "I must take you to see Mrs. Siddons at Drury Lane. She is Tragedy personified, by God."

William, who used to love to go to musical comedy at the Haymarket when we first came to London, but had never taken me, said, "I don't think Kate would like to be made sad but, come to think of it, she'd be a fierce Lady Macbeth herself!" I poked him in the ribs with my fan.

After the performance, we went backstage to congratulate Elizabeth. She had a tiny, hot dressing room, where she received us with only a silk dressing gown over her naked shoulders and petticoats. Her golden hair cascaded down her back

"Blake!" she said first to William. "I am so pleased you came." For a split second, I imagined that something passed between them, a look, a flicker.

"Kate!" she turned to me. "I hope you enjoyed the performance. And you, too, dear Mr. and Mrs. Fuseli."

We all assured her that we had, and she and her husband joined us while we promenaded around the square, jostling in the crowds, watching a troupe of jugglers and clowns. It was while I was admiring a particularly skillful juggler that I turned to share my amusement with William, and saw it. Elizabeth passed a folded note to him. He put it in his breast pocket and turned away from her.

I felt a shock go through me. I remembered Henry's advice to Sophia, only I could not think of any words to swear by. Then one came to me: I had heard Mary use it.

Merde, I said.

From Blake's Notebook.

> My Spectre around me night & day
> Like a wild beast guards my way
> My Emanation far within
> Weeps incessantly for my Sin

Henry told me about it. I went to the Royal Academy in his company, just to see Sir Joshua Reynolds's portrait of Elizabeth Billington. It was called *Portrait of a Celebrated Figure*, but everyone knew who it was. There she stood, full length, in a flowing robe, holding a book of music, while a chorus of little angels sang above her, and her luxurious hair blew in some heavenly wind.

"Joseph Haydn says the angels should be listening, not singing," remarked Henry.

Elizabeth in the picture was supposed to be St. Cecilia, the patron saint of music, because Elizabeth was a child prodigy at the harpsichord before she began taking singing lessons from James Billington. Now she was the most famous singer in London.

"She fights with her husband all the time," said Henry. "I think he beats her, by God! She likes men with a temper." He said this as if to himself. I remembered them together at our party.

"What am I to do?" I thought in despair. Another talented woman, a woman who would be a magnet for talented men like Henry and William. How can he take me to bed every night, and yet love her, too? How can I ever hold my own now?

From Kate's Notebook.
Thursday, December 1, 1791.

He is with *her* tonight. I know it. I imagine them together, lying naked in her bed. Her hair is long, and lies over her breasts, and he revels in it. I pace the room, cursing them, crying. When William comes home, I throw a cup at him, and insult him. *Bastard,* I cry, *Adulterer!*

From Blake's Notebook.

> Oer my Sins Thou sit and moan
> Hast thou no sins of thy own
> Oer my Sins thou sit and weep
> And lull thy own Sins fast asleep

Through it all, we work. I have banished him from my bed, but not myself from his printing press. We have a truce of sorts during the day, when we talk of mundane things and life goes on much as usual.

We finished several copies of *The Marriage of Heaven and Hell.* I realized that William wrote it to shock his readers into looking clearly at the usual categories of Good and Evil: "Good is Heaven. Evil is Hell." These sentiments are not good enough. Without Contraries is no Progression, he wrote. The life-forces have to work together, as in a marriage: Opposition is True Friendship. Well, I thought, we have enough Opposition in our marriage right now to be the best of friends—and I did not feel that we were achieving a great reconciliation!

I saw in this work that William had turned against some of the teachings of Swedenborg, accusing him of spiritual Pride, and the mistake of trying to eliminate evil in the interest of good.

"Swedenborg thinks that our rational faculty can put away evil," he told me, "but spiritual reality cannot be comprehended by Reason. Too much Faith in Reason is the great Sin of our age!"

Well, that's all very well, I thought, if you are a man who talks regularly to Spirits and the Ghost of your dead brother, but does not have the Wit to use your Reason and see that you are destroying your own wife by your selfish behaviour.

I did not realize it then, but we were more prosperous in those days than we were ever to be again. Our house in Lambeth was large and comfortable, and we had accumulated a few pieces of Silver Plate for our table. I took great pleasure in it, for I had never dreamed of possessions like this when I was a young country girl. And I now had two gowns as well as my everyday grey morning dress, and three pieces of Belgian lace for collars. But my Pride in these possessions was a sin of which I was soon cured.

One rainy morning in January of 1792 I had gone to the Fish Market, and William was off buying a piece of copper plate. I returned, cold and wet, to find the front door ajar. Since I did not expect William back as yet, I was alarmed. I hesitatingly peeked inside, and my heart sank. Chairs and tables were overturned, chest drawers were opened, and household effects scattered everywhere. *Thieves.* And indeed, my silver Platter and Porringer were gone, and the two silver serving spoons. Then when I went to my wardrobe, I saw to my distress that my Lace was gone, and my best pink gown, and two of William's shirts.

When William returned a short time later, he found me sobbing, this time, at least, not over him.

He put his arms around me and said, "Kate, they were only Material possessions. They are not worth your tears."

"But the Silver—it was worth at least £60!" I wept. "And your shirts . . . they took me weeks to make! And my gown . . ."

The feel of his strong arms around me was comforting. I had not realized how much I missed the physical closeness of him.

"We can buy you another gown," he said to soothe me, stroking my hair, "but you do not need raiment to be beautiful."

This made me cry even harder. He was trying to make peace between us. He could never understand my jealousy.

"Why can you not comprehend that my relation with Elizabeth is not making me love you less?" he had asked during a quarrel at Christmas time. "Why can you not accept it as you did with Mary?" We were in the Painting Room, mixing smokey-smelling inks.

"Because Mary was a meeting of minds," I had cried. "I know I can never be all things to you. But Elizabeth! Why do you need her?"

"Elizabeth is joyful," said William. "And she wants nothing from me but joy. She does not quarrel and moan!"

He went to his work table and snatched up a piece of paper.

"Read this," he said.

In his fine, spidery handwriting, I read these words:

> I cry, Love! Love! Love! happy happy Love! free as the
>   mountain wind!
> Can that be Love, that drinks another as a sponge drinks water?
> That clouds with jealousy his nights, with weepings all the day:
> To spin a web of age around him, grey and hoary! dark!
> Till his eyes sicken at the fruit that hangs before his sight.
> Such is self-love that envies all! A creeping skeleton
> With lamplight eyes watching around the frozen marriage bed.

So this was how he saw me. Shocked and sickened, I had hurled a pot of green ink at him, and run from the room.

Now, distressed at the Robbery, and wanting William's comforting presence, I was almost ready to give in. Forgive him, my inner voice said, Accept him. But some stubborn streak in me rebelled. I pulled away from him.

"I will clean up this Robber's mess," I said to William. "You can go back to work, you are way behind as it is. Stedman is writing you about his plates, and you owe the Flaxmans a letter. I am quite capable of getting over this, thank you."

He looked at me, shook his head, and left the room.

Mary Wollstonecraft was suddenly famous. She had, in a burst of energy, written her tract on women's rights and education in December, and Joseph had published it right away. *A Vindication of the Rights of Woman* was at once in great demand. Everyone was talking about it.

Her indignation at the waste of women's potential in our society seemed to hit just the right note, and I could not help agreeing with her, though she had more experience than I of women who lived only as Ornaments and wasted their lives, totally dependent on their husbands for the necessities of life. Of course, I myself was dependent upon William, but we did at least work together, and so had William's mother with his father. In some ways, tradesmen's wives were more independent than women of the upper classes.

Poverty and prostitution were the lot of most women who had not the protection of men through marriage; it was a rare woman like Mary who could make her living on her own, and she received much criticism from men. I heard she had been called a "hyena in Petticoats" after writing the *Vindication*. Even Fuseli was not complimentary, and this was not surprising, since I could tell he thought women should stay at home and wait on their men as his own wife did. I was not sure what William thought about Mary's book, though I knew he admired her ideas about the improvement of both sexes if women were treated as rational human beings, and properly educated, and treated as moral equals of men. He certainly admired her ideas on love.

Fuseli's attitude to Mary was something of a mystery to me. He seemed very involved in her family affairs, even giving her brother Charles a birthday present of ten pounds. He seemed to take up a great deal of her time and kept her from receiving other suitors.

Mary, of course, professed to be uninterested in marriage. Divorce being almost impossible in England, the law forced people into awkward arrangements. We knew that the Hayleys lived separately, and Thomas Christie's French mistress, Claudine, was living now in England awaiting Christie's child and her divorce from her French husband. But Fuseli enjoyed his marriage to Sophia even while he maintained an emotional hold on Mary. Eventually it all came to a head.

Mary, Fuseli, Sophia and Joseph Johnson were planning to make a trip to France together in August.

"We are going to Paris for about six weeks," Mary told me. "We all want to see first hand what is happening there."

She said that since the Fall of the Bastille, the King of France had uneasy relations with the Assembly. Ordinary citizens who desired a more active say in political life had been infuriated last year when the new Constitution ensured that only people with property would elect members to the new Assembly. They called it an aristocracy of wealth.

"Yet the new constitution seemed successfully to have made a change from Absolute monarch to Constitutional monarchy," explained Mary, "but then the King spoiled it all."

It seems that last June the Royal Family attempted to disguise themselves and furtively took a coach to flee from France. At Varennes, 140 miles from Paris, they were recognized and forcibly taken back to Paris.

"As Louis and his Queen, Marie Antoinette, entered the city," said Mary, "a strange silence fell over the assembled crowds as they passed. It was like a Funeral. And now Louis is like a prisoner in his own Palace."

William had told me that other Monarchies of Europe were nervous at what was happening in France. There had been a Treaty issued by Austria and Prussia, calling on the powers of Europe to restore the French Monarchy. This had prompted the Legislative Assembly to attempt a war against Austria only two months ago, in April. William had heard news of it in a Coffee House. At Johnson's dinner we were told it had been a disaster for poorly trained French troops, who retreated in headlong confusion. And this was the situation that Mary and Fuseli and Johnson wanted to see for themselves.

I had never paid a great deal of attention to Politics, in spite of being surrounded by people who could talk of little else. But I had in the past few years absorbed enough information about events in France to be curious, too. Some people, like William Hayley and George Romney, for instance, had gone to Paris in 1790, and had a fine time, and visited the artists David and Greuze. Forward thinking people were hopeful then that a Constitutional monarchy would work in France.

I was interested in Mary's plans, but not at all prepared for her next statement to me. We were sitting in our summer house at the end of the garden in July. It had been a hot summer, and we were both in thin wrapped dresses. Mary had a good figure and carried herself well. She sat up very straight and said to me, "Would you consider coming to France with us. Please?"

I was taken aback. Why me? I thought. What could I possibly add to their group? I was no thinker—but then, neither was Sophia. Then it began to dawn on me: Mary needed a buffer between herself and Sophia.

Mary's long fingers played with the hem of her sleeve as I paused.

"You will keep us all cheerful, Kate," she said.

"You want me alone?" I asked. "And not William?"

"I want you as a sister," she said, "for my own company."

I felt a nervous flutter somewhere in my middle. I had never been away from William since we were married, almost ten years ago. Yet I had to admit our marriage was not going well at present. We were living under the same roof, polite and distant. Except when we were not polite. He may or may not still be dallying with Elizabeth Billington, but I did not trust him anymore. I was jealous and resentful, and I wanted to hurt him as he hurt me. Perhaps the means lay in Mary's invitation.

"Yes," I said, "I will come."

We were to leave on the twelfth of August by coach to Dover, from there to cross the Channel by ship. William was aghast when I announced my plans. We had finished our supper, and were sitting across from each other at the oak table in the light of the summer evening.

"You would leave me alone?" he asked, incredulous.

"You won't be alone," I retorted. "Cathy will come in and cook your meals."

"That's not the point, and you know it!" he cried. He ran his hand through his unruly hair in a familiar gesture that caused a little pang in my heart.

"And it's dangerous, besides!" he said vehemently. "I cannot understand why Fuseli and Johnson will risk their safety like this. Mary is headstrong and fearless, she will do anything . . . but Fuseli! It is not like him."

"What do you mean, dangerous?"

"Don't you know the people of Paris are restive? They are going hungry while the King delays the Constitution. Did you not hear how some angry men invaded the Tuileries and forced Louis to wear a red liberty cap? And others are working to restore the monarchy as it was before. Don't you know that the Duke of Brunswick has threatened to destroy Paris if any violence happens to the Royal Family?"

I did not know any of these things, but blindly trusted Mary and the rest. I was not going to let William stop me.

"I am going away for a while, William," I said. "It will do us good to be apart. I do not want to live with you any more just now. I just want to go away," I ended rather lamely.

"My God," was all he said for a long moment. Then he added, "Female Love is a terrible thing. I won't pursue you. *I won't!*" And he brought his fist down on the table so that the bowls and plates jumped up and fell down again with a clatter.

I did not really want William to pursue me all the way to France. What could he have been thinking of?

The plan to set off by coach on the twelfth of August, to sail on the fourteenth from Dover to Calais, and to go from there by coach again to Paris, was fully organized. Mary and the others had letters of introduction to people in Paris; Mary had already received a visit at her house from Talleyrand, the Bishop of Autun, to whom she had dedicated her book. He was sympathetic to the Revolution and to the education of women, I gathered.

I did not have a large travelling bag, as I had only two dresses to pack and an assortment of shawls and laces. But I did take along my Notebook, and pencils to sketch with. I had always been good at saving money, and felt a little guilty taking ten pounds of our savings with me, but then, I thought, it was I who saved it.

The turnpike road to Dover was well travelled and safe, but it still took most of a day, with frequent stops to change the horses. Fuseli and Johnson had hired a post chaise with a postilion. I thought it very elegant with its four shiny wheels and four black horses.

I boarded it conscious of my heart beating with excitement. It was a hot, bright day and sitting close-pressed between Mary and Sophia and across from Henry and Joseph, I became immediately aware of a combination of smells—human sweat, a hint of lavender scent emanating from Sophia, the familiar pungent smell of horses in summer. And Joseph carried a camphor-dipped handkerchief, in which he buried his nose frequently, to prevent his asthma.

·   ·   ·

William had insisted on taking me to board the coach. His demeanor was very glum.

"By God, Blake, you look like a Funeral Attendant," said Henry. "Can't you giff us a smile?"

William smiled wanly.

I was touched that he was concerned for me. We had earlier exchanged a few words about my trip. Very early in the morning before departure time, we were eating a bowl of berries picked from the nearby hedgerows.

"I never thought of you as headstrong," William had said. "I thought you had Spirit and Energy . . . but this is Foolhardiness!" When William spoke, I thought of Capital letters, the way he printed.

"I may be foolish," I said, "but I am following my desires, as you do, and as you always advocate. He who desires but acts not, breeds pestilence if I may quote!"

"You are quoting out of context," he retorted, and I noticed he lapsed into silence. He tried another tack.

"Kate, I love you," he said.

The early morning sun shone on his still golden-brown hair, giving off glints of fire, and his gently curving mouth smiled at me tentatively. The taste of bramble berry was both sweet and sour to my tongue.

"I do not know what I feel, William," I said. "All I know is that I want to go away, and this is the best way to do it. I cannot stand the thought of you and Elizabeth Billington. I have things to think about."

"I think of you as my Rose-Tree," he said, "but now I think you are blighted! It is Jealousy that will destroy you . . . it will destroy us both!"

And we left it at that.

From Blake's Notebook.

> Thou hast parted from my side
> Once thou wast a virgin bride
> Never shalt thou a true love find
> My Spectre follows thee behind

As we bounced along to the clip-clop of the horses, I began to feel queasy. Cathy had advised me to take along some fresh ginger-root, which she had kindly found for me, to ward off motion sickness. I was saving it for the sea voyage, but I nibbled a little in the coach.

I was glad of our first stop at a posting inn, and not only for the relief of motion, but for relief from the tension of the atmosphere between the other occupants of the coach. Silent voices kept pressing in on me.

Mary, of course, was the center of all Energy. Joseph Johnson, whose attitude to her was an odd mixture of paternal and cavalier, seemed annoyed for her sake at every comment of Fuseli's. Fuseli, for his part, always seemed to be watching the interplay between his wife and Mary, his body-mate and his soul-mate, I supposed, though no doubt Mary was sometimes his body-mate, too.

I could never see the demure Sophia without being reminded of the Cruelty of her expression in her husband's erotic drawings, the bare breasts like orbs of power above elaborate corsets, or the curvaceous bare legs and backside revealed by a parted skirt, while she stood before a dressing table with phalluses for table legs. I knew that what two people do in the Privacy of their bedroom was no one else's concern, but unwittingly I had become a party to this knowledge. It had become part of my attitude to Henry, and even to William, who, after all, shared Henry's enjoyment of those pictures. Sophia's power over Henry was based on her dominating eroticism on the one hand, and her obedient submission in the eyes of the world. She made my skin crawl when I was not feeling Pity for her.

Henry was a compelling study: a man of Genius, I had no doubt, but unselfconsciously selfish. He loved Mary's admiration; he loved knowing that she was obsessed by him, and that part of the obsession was half sexual fascination, half intellectual power. And now that Mary was famous, he seemed to me to be a little jealous of her. He never complimented her on her work, and called her "the assertrix of female rights." I found that embarrassing. Mary must have been hurt many times by his little jibes. To me, Henry was at all times polite, for William's sake I am sure, because he was as fascinated by William as Mary was with him, and perhaps for the same reasons.

Mary's colour was high with the heat of the coach and inn and the stimulation of the trip. She was looking particularly well, her hazel eyes and brown hair contrasting with her fair skin. Her charms were not lost on Henry, who could not take his eyes from her face.

"What do you think we will find in Paris?" Mary asked Joseph, as we ate our simple lunch of bread, cheese and ale.

"Well, there was a peculiar alliance of the Gironde and La Fayette, but it cannot have continued," said Joseph, referring to the group in the French Government that was the spearhead of the Republican movement. The Marquis de La Fayette was the leader of the National Guard of Paris, a hero of the Revolution in 1789.

I remembered that William had admired La Fayette, who had been also a hero of the American Revolution, and a friend of George Washington and Thomas Jefferson. Although an aristocrat, he believed in liberty and humanity and wanted to see a limited monarchy in France. William had written of him in his poem, *The French Revolution*, the one that Joseph judged too dangerous to publish.

"Both groups thought a short war would further their own ends," continued Joseph. "The Gironde believed that war would incite a general uprising against all the monarchs of Europe, and La Fayette hoped he would return with a victorious army and crush the radicals. Then he would be the power behind the throne."

"But it did not happen that vay," interrupted Henry. "Robespierre was right, it was dangerous, and the French army was not trained. I heard that three regiments deserted to the Austrians!"

"Since then, Paris is full of rumour," said Joseph. "I heard news two days ago that there has been a call for the immediate abdication of the King, and the indictment of La Fayette for treason. Treason against the people of all things! As if he had not always wanted the best for the people!"

"But will this not be a dangerous time to go to Paris?" asked Sophia in a small voice. I was beginning to feel a little nervous myself. I had been so keen on leaving William in a burst of independence, that I had not really listened to him about the political situation in Paris.

"We are not afraid of a little danger, surely," said Mary intensely. "We must go to see history being made!"

"Of course, I am not afraid," said Sophia, regaining her composure immediately, and glaring at Mary, "only using common sense."

"I have taken the liberty of asking Christie to keep us informed," said Joseph, interrupting, and refilling his tankard of ale. "He is closely informed of news in France, and frequents the Coffee Houses. He will send us a message if need be."

"There now, by God," said Henry, "all you fair ones need not worry."

"My dear Fuseli," smiled Mary, delicately biting a piece of cheese, "you underestimate us as usual. I know I speak for Sophia and Kate both when I say we are not worried at all. We are all Democrats and long to see parliamentary reform in England. To see government becoming populist in France is as fascinating to the Female mind as to the Male!"

"A toast then, to *Liberté, Egalité, Fraternité et Fémininité!*"

By nightfall, after long hours in the coach and several more stops to change horses, we approached Dover. I had never been so close to the sea. As the sun set in a golden pink sky I looked eastwards over the darkening slate grey water rimmed on one side by luminous chalk cliffs, and my heart leapt at its vastness.

Out there was France, another country, and beyond that the rest of Europe: cities which I never expected to see, languages I had never heard, and people I would never meet. There were blue hills and valleys and winding rivers and canals I could scarcely imagine; sailing ships and barges, the spires of churches and the towers of castles. The hugeness of the world weighed down upon me, and I wished that William were there by my side. Somehow his love affair with a beautiful actress seemed less important the farther away I travelled.

I knew how William adored the physical beauty of the body; how he painted it almost to the exclusion of everything else, for to him it was the proof of the Incarnation, the Human Form Divine. Elizabeth was beautiful and graceful and sang like an angel; she was famous and wealthy, too. How could I really blame him? I had thought, when our own lovemaking became so frequent and spiritual, that he would not think of desiring anyone else. I certainly did not. I realized now that with William, almost the opposite happened. Love for him was not exclusive: he would want to expand to include others.

I sighed and brought my attention back to the interior of the coach and its inhabitants as we hurried down the narrow cobbled streets toward the city and the Inn where we were to spend the night. We were all tired and a little grumpy, looking forward to a hot dinner and a good bed.

Mary was watching Sophia with half-closed eyes, pretending to be asleep. Henry had been attentive to Sophia on this trip, calculatingly fanning Mary's jealousy. Joseph looked abstractedly out of the window, fatigued from the tensions of the trip and worried about the future, I suspected. I heard a shout from above, and the coachman pulled up our four horses with a clatter. A young groom appeared and began to unhook the horses, and our bags were lifted down from the top of the coach as we dismounted.

Our Inn, called the Pale Horse, was comfortable, but crowded. My room was low ceilinged and tiny, tucked up under the slope of the roof, with plain whitewashed walls, a low beam across the ceiling, which rose at an angle above it, and one small window. There was scarcely room for the bed and a table to hold the candle and a chamber pot. Being of small stature, I could move about easily enough, but a tall person would have to duck to avoid the beam. Out the tiny window, I could glimpse the courtyard below, where coaches were passing in and out, horses were whinnying, and people were milling about with their grooms and luggage in the dying light of the evening. I heard a babble of voices with words in French as well as English. A sudden excitement washed over me. I am really here on my own!

As it was a warm night, I did not take a shawl with me when I joined the others for supper. I removed the plain collar of my travelling gown, and left the neckline bare and cool. It was perhaps a little revealing of my bosom, but no more than Sophia had exposed for the whole trip, I thought. I carried a little fan that Cathy had given me.

Our Host at the Inn was a large, jolly man, and his wife was the exact opposite, thin and severe, but she sat us down politely enough at a big wooden table, and her husband filled up our pewter tankards of ale. The room was already full of the noise of revelry and the clinking of glasses. There was even a fiddler playing a squeaky tune by the fire, which was burning even though it was a summer night.

"Here's a plate of cold meat and potato for ye, ma'am," said the hostess, and I realized just how hungry I was. Mary smiled at me as I began to eat with relish.

"Do you see we have another guest at our table?" she whispered.

Then I saw that across the table and next to Henry sat a handsome young man with his black hair tied back neatly, wearing an open necked shirt which revealed an expanse of smooth chest and a St. Christopher medallion.

"Who is he?"

"His name is Paul-Marc Philipon, of Paris," said Mary in a low voice. "He says he is a cousin of Manon Roland de la Platière, wife of the Minister of the Interior. They are Girondins, and therefore active in the Revolution. Paul-Marc is on his way to London to raise money for their cause."

Paul-Marc acknowledged me with a nod, and an intent glance.

"Madame Blake, I am pleased to meet you," he said, after an introduction by Mary. He spoke English haltingly but well. There was something unsettling to me about him. He regarded me seriously. At last he said, after a draught of ale, "You are French, perhaps?"

So my Huguenot ancestry was obvious to him. After all, we did look alike, both with black hair and dark eyes.

"My Grandfather was," I replied.

"And your husband . . . ?"

"My husband is English," I said. To fill in the pause that followed, I added, "He is an Engraver."

"*Mon Dieu!* So am I!" He smiled, and his face relaxed, so that I could see a vulnerability and gentleness about his mouth. "My uncle has a very big workshop full of apprentices, and I am only a few years working since I learned from him. Perhaps I will meet your husband in London?"

"Perhaps," I said, "but I am going to Paris now."

"What? *Mais non, Madame!* It is too dangerous for travellers!"

There it was again, that warning. Never having been in danger in my life, perhaps I was unaware of what it meant. I could only shrug, and say that it was not my decision whether to go to Paris or not, I was part of a group. Someone gave me a glass of wine, and I drank it without eating much supper, as I was engrossed in conversation with Paul-Marc. I could feel his eyes on my bosom as I fanned my neck in the heat of the night.

I drank more wine that evening than ever before in my life, and only remember the laughter and the noise, and Mary and Joseph in good humour, and Henry and Sophia making amusing conversation, and Paul-Marc always seeming to be nearby. We somehow borrowed a torch and all went for a walk after dinner in the dark grounds of the inn, skirting the stables, where the horses rested quietly, and looking out to the sea where the ocean could be seen moving in the bright moonlight.

Then Paul-Marc saw that I was safely in my room, and bade me goodnight with a polite kiss on my hand. I sat on the small bed, wearing only my shift, and began to brush my hair in preparation for sleep. I was really too excited for sleep, my head spinning with the admiration of an attractive man, and the prospect of a voyage across the Channel the next day.

There was a soft knock on my door.

"Come in," said I, thinking it was Mary.

Paul-Marc stepped into the room. I drew in my breath in surprise.

"You did not bar your door, *Madame*," he said. "Did you know I was coming?"

"N-no," I said. "It did not occur to me. You should not be here, Sir. It is not seemly!"

He ducked under the beam and sat on the bed next to me, all in one fluid motion. He smiled into my eyes, and our spirits danced in recognition. His hand went to my breast, and I could feel the warmth of his fingers through the thin shift.

"Kate." He spoke my name as if he knew me well.

"You must go! I did not mean . . ." I pushed him away, but his hands had slipped my shift from my shoulders and I was naked to the waist in the candlelight.

"*Ah, comme tu es belle!*"

My heart was pounding in a mixture of dismay and exhilaration. Had he really found me so attractive? Then as my common sense told me it was just a young man's lust, my own desire surprised me. My heart pounded in spite of myself. I did not resist his kiss.

As I lay back on the bed and he slipped the shift from my hips, a voice in my ear said, Kate.

I sat up. Paul-Marc was now naked in front of me, beautiful as any statue I had seen in engravings. It was not he who had spoken.

"Did you hear a voice?" I said, shaken.

He gently pushed me back on the bed, and knelt above me, covering me with kisses. It was as if the wind were bearing me away. Then again I heard a voice, and this time knew it was William. Kate.

"Stop, Paul-Marc!" I cried. Paul-Marc, who was not bent on rape, only a love encounter, stopped.

"What is wrong? Do I hurt you?"

"No. It is my husband!"

"Here? Where!" He sat up and looked around at the shadows in the room.

I felt the hairs rise on my neck. In the corner of the room, I saw the familiar figure of a man, a man with curly hair and broad shoulders. He stood there, not quite square on the floor, but seeming to float about a foot above it, a shadow but not a shadow, for I could see the glint of copper in his hair as the candlelight fell upon it.

"Do you not see him?" I gasped.

"*Non*, I see nothing."

"Paul-Marc, you must go!" I whispered urgently. "It is a sign from God. My husband is here, in this room! I know it!"

Paul-Marc crossed himself.

"I do not think so," he said nervously, "but you are shaking, *chérie*." He handed me my shift, and pulled on his trousers.

I was overcome with embarrassment.

"I am sorry," I whispered, "I should not have . . ."

"Madame, I understand," he said, "I have frightened you. It is too soon, that is all. But we like each other, *n'est-ce pas?*"

"Yes."

"Then we will meet again." He bent and kissed each breast and then my mouth, and was gone. I saw that the corner of the room was empty. William had gone also.

In the morning, I packed my travelling bag and went down to the kitchen to meet the others for breakfast. I had not slept the entire night. I could not understand what had possessed me to allow myself to flirt with a man so frankly that he felt free to come to my bed. I may have been angry with William, but was I capable of revenge in kind? Evidently I was. But was William watching over me, or was the vision a figment of my own guilty conscience? I looked nervously around for Paul-Marc, but thankfully he was nowhere to be seen. No doubt he had left for London, and at least I was off to Paris.

. . .

I saw that Henry, Sophia, Mary and Joseph were already seated in a close circle, looking at a paper that Joseph held in his hand.

"Ah, there you are," he said to me. "We have news. Not good, I am afraid. It is a message from Thomas Christie, and it came by rider very early this morning. The poor man must have galloped all night to reach us."

"What does it say?"

Joseph placed his spectacles on his nose and read: "You must not go to Paris. Royalists are fighting Sans-Culottes at the Tuileries, and a massacre is underway. The King has fled to the Assembly building. Robespierre will be in charge of France. I urge your immediate return to London."

"This is too bad," said Henry, "but I recommend we take his advice and go back."

Sophia murmured agreement, but Mary looked defiant.

"But what an opportunity!" she exclaimed. "We must not stop now! I would go on to Paris! We still have to sail to Calais, and then it will be another two days by coach . . . things will have changed completely by the time we get there!"

"Things could be worse by then," said Joseph, "and besides, Paris is rather nasty at best, with its narrow, dark streets, and conceited people. And now the common people will be more ill mannered than ever. Christie's advice is good."

"What do you think, Kate?" said Mary to me, hoping for support.

"What are *Sans-Culottes?*" was all I could think of to say.

12

In Which Some Surprising Things Happen

*T*he others in the coach were dozing or lost in their own thoughts. Mary lapsed into silence. It was such an anticlimax to have to return to London. I did not know how I was going to face William. My little bid for independence had failed, and I felt guilty besides.

Mary told me, as we rattled along the London road, about the *Sans-Culottes*.

"The word means 'without breeches,' " she said. "It used to refer to men who are not wealthy—French tradesmen and wage earners, who wear trousers rather than the knee-breeches of the upper classes. But now it means the politically active and the radical revolutionaries."

"Who is Robespierre?" I asked her. I wanted to understand why we had turned back.

"He is a leader of the Legislative Assembly and was public accuser until recently. He is supposed to be incorruptible and a powerful orator, to boot. He and his associates Danton and Marat are all admired by the *Sans-Culottes* and will no doubt fashion a new regime in France. That is why I wanted to see it myself. But Joseph and Henry fear bloodshed."

. . .

London was hot and dusty as we arrived. It must have been the hottest summer in years. I dropped my bag in the hall, and William came out of his workroom in surprise.

"Thank God you are back!" He exclaimed, and gave me a warm embrace. I hugged him back, glad of his reassuring arms, though I felt undeserving. Could he really know about Paul-Marc?

"What made you turn back? Did you hear of the massacre at the Tuileries?"

"Yes. Thomas Christie sent a message to Dover. We got it at the Inn."

We went down to our kitchen, and William made tea. He looked at me across the table and said, "I had a vision while you were gone."

I thought, "Oh, no, he did see me with Paul-Marc!" But I said nothing.

He went on, "It was horrible. I saw guns and soldiers, and fear and confusion. I saw blood . . . so much blood in the streets. And all I could think of was you, of reaching you and telling you to come home."

"And d-did you see me in your vision?"

"Not exactly. I felt your presence, but there was something else barring my way. Did you not feel my concern? We used to have a spiritual connection . . . I thought our minds were One, once."

"William, I did feel your presence," was all I could say.

That week, as I resumed my duties about the house, I felt a dull sadness, as if I had let William down somehow. I don't know why, because he had been unfaithful to me and seemed to think it perfectly natural. Was this a natural difference between men and women then? Were women meant to be faithful and men to wander? Or was I sad because I did not tell? We had always been honest with each other, and now I had a secret. Not a very big secret, that is true, but I wondered if I would ever see Paul-Marc again. I wondered if he would find work in London as he hoped.

On our arrival back in London, Mary was very melancholy. I had never seen her so listless. About three days later, I went to call on her at her house on Store Street, behind the British Museum, where she had moved almost a year ago. In front of her house lay fields and nursery gardens.

I found Mary in a nervous state.

"I have had a terrible experience!" she said. "I am glad you have come. I can tell no one else about it!"

I could see she had been weeping, and her hair was in disarray. In her sitting room, I perched on a small upright chair, and she paced back and forth.

"I could not stand the situation between myself and Henry any longer," she began. "You can understand that?"

I nodded.

"I had to be near him, to see him every day. So I remembered what you offered to do for William once, after he got sick."

"You mean . . ."

"Yes, I went to see Sophia this morning."

I could imagine that. Sophia sitting imperiously on her sofa, Mary pacing as she was now, intent on her own thoughts, thinking Sophia could understand.

"I told her I could not live away from Henry any longer. I must see him every day. He was necessary to my mental life. I proposed to live with them in a Spiritual Marriage."

I bit my lip to prevent my exclamation. How could she have expected Sophia to listen to this?

"What happened?"

"First she laughed," said Mary miserably, "then she shrieked at me: 'Get out!' she cried, 'and never come near this house again!' She also called me names which I shall not repeat." Mary was shaking at the recollection; she added, "She has no Intellect at all, and not a shred of Understanding. How *could* Henry have married such a harridan?"

I felt very sorry for Mary, but at the same time wondered how she could have expected any other reaction from Sophia. And why had Henry not seen this coming? I knew he was becoming increasingly irritated by Mary, and would carry her letters unopened in his pocket: I had seen them there this very week.

"What shall I do now?" cried Mary. "I am so humiliated. Henry will never take my side against his wife."

I sensed there had been a conflict of envy between Mary and Henry ever since she had become famous.

"I think it would be a good idea for you to go away for a week or two," I said. "Take a holiday and calm yourself. Can you visit relatives somewhere?"

Mary agreed with me, and left London the very next day for three weeks. Sophia was not discreet about repeating Mary's proposal to be a spiritual wife, and the gossips were busy. Even Joseph threw up his hands.

William, however, was sympathetic to Mary, as always. He wrote a poem about her, with these lines: "O why was I born with a different face? Why was I not born like this Envious Race/Why did Heaven adorn me with bountiful hand/And then set me down in an envious Land." It made me cry to read it. "All Faces have Envy sweet Mary but thine."

William was working on his own poetry and engraving all the time, to the detriment of his commercial work, I feared. Our accounts were showing less and less profit, but the manuscripts in the Notebook and on loose papers strewn about the workroom kept growing. He was putting together a book of poems to compare with *Songs of Innocence*, calling them *Songs of Experience*.

"They are about the other aspect of human life," he explained to me, "when we realize to our sorrow that we are not the centre of the world around us. Experience is a Contrary State from Innocence."

For me, the differences in the poems were made plain by comparing the two frontispieces. In *Innocence*, a piper with his flock behind him, gazes up at a little naked child flying freely above his head. In *Experience*, a shepherd holds the little naked angel on his head, and both look out at the reader. It is as if Imagination is not so free in Experience, but confined to the head alone. William hated to think how the conventions of life restrained us. In this book, he called them "mind-forg'd manacles," and in more than one poem, I felt he was writing directly to me. In *Experience*, he has Earth say she is imprisoned by Jealousy, and complains:

> Does spring hide its joy
> When buds and blossoms grow?
> Does the sower

Blake, Frontispiece to *Songs of Innocence*, Copy B (1789). Lessing J. Rosenwald Collection, Library of Congress. Copyright © 2003 the William Blake Archive. Used with permission

Blake, *Songs of Innocence and of Experience*, Plate 29, Copy C (1794). Lessing J. Rosenwald Collection, Library of Congress. Copyright © 2003 the William Blake Archive. Used with permission

Sow by night?
Or the plowman in darkness plow?

Break this heavy chain
That does free my bones around
Selfish! vain!
Eternal bane!
That free love doth with bondage bound.

And there were many more poems in that vein about love and human emotions, and how destructive they can be, yet all with beautiful designs of trees and flowers and people.

One day when he was working on the manuscript, William asked me what I thought of the sentiments in what he considered rather political poems, *The Chimney Sweeper*, and *Holy Thursday*. These had the same titles as poems in *Innocence*, so the reader was bound to compare the ideas.

I had loved *The Chimney Sweeper* of *Innocence* whose faith allowed him to survive the horrible truth of his daily life. Now in *Experience*, the little chimney sweep, "a little black thing among the snow," is completely clear-eyed about the hypocrisy of his parents and the government that allowed children to work like that:

And because I am happy & dance & sing
They think they have done me no injury:
And are gone to praise God & his Priest & King
Who make up a heaven of our misery.

"I have always hated to see the little boy go up the chimney when he comes to clean it," I said, thinking of the skinny little bare-headed boy of about nine years, who came to our house about twice a year, "but I never thought that the Government or the Church was behind it."

The poor little mite would come down all black with soot, his eyes staring hugely out of his darkened face, sores on his knees and elbows. He would put on his filthy clothes, and sweep up the soot from the hearth into his bag. I would give him a piece of bread and cheese, which he would gobble up in a moment, and then he would smile just for a second, and be off.

"*We* are the Government and the Church, Kate," said William. "Men and women like ourselves letting it happen, thinking that Custom is unchangeable. Or not thinking at all."

"And believing it will all be better in the next world," I reflected, "we excuse present misery in hope that Heaven will take care of it."

"The Human Race has been creating stories to excuse itself for Ages past," muttered William. "I am working on my own version of the Bible, as a matter of fact."

This did not entirely surprise me, since William was daily in conversation with some Prophet or other. I had become so used to these visitations that I had ceased to think of them as extraordinary. They were just part of our life.

From Kate's Notebook.
August 18, 1792.

William and I have been married ten years today! We celebrated this—and my return from Dover—with a walk to Covent Garden, where William bought me a bouquet of cornflowers and daisies from a Flower Seller, a ragged girl in an old straw hat. The sun was shining as we strolled down to the Thames Embankement. We watched the sailing ships and river craft, and enjoyed the familiar fishy smell of the River.

After a while, we turned back towards Oxford Street, where William paused in front of an Apothecary Shop.

"It is a good day to speak to the Prophets," he announced. "I have an idea." He opened the door and went in. I was mystified, especially when he purchased tincture of Opium for less than a shilling.

"Are you unwell?" I asked. "Have you more pain in your bowels? Why do you need Laudanum?"

"I am well," said William. "Only wait and see what we are going to do with this!"

As soon as we reached home, William sat me down on our bed, and fetched two glasses of water. Into each of these he measured one teaspoon of the Laudanum.

"Now we are going to drink this," he said.

"But why?" I protested. "We are not sick!"

"Because I want to Enhance the Eye of Imagination," said William, raising his glass as if in a toast. "We will have a new kind of Vision, I think. Henry told me about it."

As usual, I obeyed, yet I was full of misgivings as I drank. The dusky brown liquid tasted like medicine. I lay on the bed, waiting to see what would happen. Soon enough I felt a torpor in all my limbs, and a feeling of exquisite peace. It was early afternoon, and the August sunlight was pouring in our bedroom window. I caught sight of the bouquet of daisies I had placed on our blanket chest. Each flower with its fringe of white petals was piercingly clear to me. Each yellow centre seemed like an eye looking back at me. The veins of each leaf were like little roads to an unknown country. I had never seen anything so clearly.

But this was as nothing compared to what was happening to William. He sat upright, alert, and stared into space. Although it was a warm day, I felt suddenly chilled.

"What do you see?" I whispered.

"I see the huge figure of a man," he said quietly, "but he has the head of a Dog."

I froze.

"Get him out of here!" I cried. "He cannot be anything but Evil."

William stood up. He raised his right arm.

"Begone!" he shouted.

The chill disappeared from the air. William brought me a clear glass of water.

"I am sorry," he said. "This was not the Vision I had hoped for."

I could not say a word, but I took him in my arms and comforted him as a mother would a child.

William's mother sickened and died in September. Her death little affected me: I had long since become used to her criticisms, and merely tolerated her. She was usually busy with her own concerns and James's at the Haberdashery, and she cared only for her daughter Cathy.

Mrs. Blake was laid to rest in Bunhill Fields next to her husband and Robert.

"Poor Mama," wept Cathy, "I will miss her."

We were back at the Blakes' house on Broad Street after the funeral. William said not a word.

James, now a portly man of business, took charge of everything.

"She wished you to have her silver sauce boat, William," he said, presenting it to us. William did not reach for it, so I took the graceful silver dish.

James said, "Mother never understood you, William. She thought you would become a famous artist or writer, especially after all those stories you told about seeing God when you were a boy."

"Sorry," said William.

"Have you seen God lately?" asked James.

William knew when he was being chaffed.

"I have indeed painted His Image many times," he said. "He looks like you and me or any man."

James threw up his hands, and Cathy smiled. It seemed strange to me that William did not really grieve over his mother. It had been the same with his father; only Robert had moved him. I wondered if he would weep for me, if I died.

In October, William began working on a poem about the American Revolution of 1776, called *America a Prophecy*. He was using larger copper plates than he ordinarily did, and the designs covered more of the page than the words. These were marvellously energetic designs, swirling with flames and soaring figures. There was a character in the poem called *Orc*, a young man with flaming hair, just like William himself. Orc was the spirit of revolution, who ultimately came to France. There was also the opposite of Orc, an old man called *Urizen*, who was the spirit of repression and conventional government. You knew these two figures were related because William presented them in the same pose, sitting with raised knee and outstretched arms.

"Are you suggesting that the old government and the spirit of revolution are just the old and new forms of the same Energy?" I asked him, as I began to prepare the paper for printing *America*.

"You are a quick study, little wife," he said, smiling.

We were getting on well these days. Elizabeth Billington was away touring, and I had stopped feeling guilty about my encounter with Paul-Marc. William was feverishly engraving his own projects, though I knew he was late with plates he had promised John Gabriel Stedman.

He was late because he had been distracted by occasional Opium use. I myself had not tried it again after the first experiment. Eventually, I persuaded William to put it aside, because he did not need it to achieve Visions. It angered me that he thought he needed it. It cheapened the visions in my eyes, and I felt somehow disappointed in him.

We had heard news of the September massacres of priests and prisoners in Paris, and William became grave and decided not to wear his red liberty cap any more. It was hard to espouse democratic principles when things seemed to be getting out of control across the Channel. By October, Joseph Johnson's asthma attacks were becoming so frequent he even requested of William that his sister Cathy, now known as a healer, find him a remedy. Cathy told me privately that she thought Joseph's attacks were caused by worry about the political situation, constricting his throat. Mary Wollstonecraft, back in London after a few weeks away, was avoiding Fuseli entirely and planning to return to France by herself, still hopeful all would turn out well there. She left the first week of December, intending to be away only six weeks.

It was at Joseph's house that William had a conversation with Tom Paine. He was one of Joseph's authors—the powerful one who had written *The Rights of Man* and inspired Mary to write her book—and he had been at Joseph's dinner with us. He was active in French affairs, and because he supported the Revolution, and even called for the overthrow of the English monarchy, he had been indicted for treason in England and was awaiting his trial, dining out cheerfully among his friends.

"I should be terribly worried in his shoes," William remarked.

In Paris, Tom had been made a French citizen. He had just been elected to the National Convention as a deputy for Calais when we saw him. He was not planning to return to France for a few weeks, but as he took his leave, William suddenly stopped him, laying his hand on Paine's shoulder.

"You must flee England soon," he said, with an intense light in his eyes, "or they will detain you before your trial. Do not delay!"

Paine shook William's hand and left, saying he would take the warning seriously. We heard he was subjected to indignities at Dover two days later, at the hands of customs officers, but he was allowed to return to France. I do not think he ever set foot in England again.

"Do you not think it is dangerous to suggest evil is so admirable?" I asked Henry one day when he came to show William some sketches for a Milton project.

Henry was organizing a Gallery of the Miltonic Sublime: all paintings and engravings were illustrations of *Paradise Lost* or other of Milton's poems. There had been a successful Shakespeare Gallery like that in London to which Henry had contributed, though William had been overlooked, much to his chagrin. Henry believed that a Milton Gallery would have a similar success: all paintings were to be done by him, and William would be the principal engraver. He was fascinated by the character of Satan: he saw him as a heroic rebel, and drew him, and eventually painted him, as powerful and godlike.

"Dangerous to whom? Art is decoration, that is all," he said. "Art is neither good nor evil—it has merely to depict human nature."

I privately thought, that explains some of your perverse erotic drawings. I knew William did not agree with Henry's theory of Art. They loved to argue with each other about it, and Henry would often use William's ideas and figures.

"Your husband is damned good to steal from!" he exclaimed on more than one occasion.

When William first taught me to draw, he would set me to copying the figures in old Engravings. Since boyhood, he had cherished a collection of Drawings and Engravings of old and modern artists.

"It is the best way to learn," he said. "Copy forever is my rule!"

I took to it well, and soon realized that I did not have to copy just the Old Masters, but it was amusing to copy John Flaxman. He had a long, flowing line, and drew Greek heroes in action.

One day, instead of copying, I drew a figure of Hector as if Flaxman had done it. It happened that I left it on the table, and William passed by.

"I didn't remember that I owned that one," he commented. "John is accomplished, isn't he?"

He had thought it was by Flaxman! Was I really so skillful? I did a few more drawings in this style over the next months, and kept them aside. I intended to show them to William, but for some reason, I never did.

Now, looking over my secret portfolio, and worrying about our lack of money, something came over me, a terrible, wonderful thought. What if I could sell the drawings? The Flaxmans were not in England, so they would never know. I would not tell William, of course. It was dishonest. I knew it. But what harm would it do, if no one ever knew? It would bring no harm to John if someone thought I owned one of his drawings, and had sold it.

I noticed that my hand was trembling as I chose a sheet of drawing paper and picked up the pencil.

Paul Colnaghi looked carefully at the drawings. He held them close to his eyes, and tilted them this way and that. He was dark and foreign looking, the busiest Print Seller in London these days. We were in his shop in Pall Mall; he stood near the bow window.

"Where did you get these, Mrs. Blake?"

"They are part of my husband's collection," I said calmly. "John Flaxman is a friend." I had rehearsed this well.

"They are very fine," he said, looking up. "Do you have others?"

"Perhaps we could sell others." My voice did not quiver.

And thus began my career as a forger.

William was working on too many projects at once, and only a few of them would bring in money. I was beginning to be alarmed as Christmas approached, and Stedman kept writing for news of the engravings for his *Narrative*. It was a relief to me when William announced one evening that he had found an assistant engraver to come in the next day to help him catch up on his commercial work.

"I am pleased to hear this!" I smiled, "Will we give him dinner?"

"Yes, he will eat with us," said William, "but do not go to much trouble. He is a Frenchman, and I do not know what they like to eat."

"A Frenchman?"

"Yes. His name is Paul-Marc . . . something."

Mary wrote frequently from Paris. The mood in Paris was serious; they had put the King on trial. Mary had seen Louis XVI being driven through the streets to attend his defense. Joseph read us a letter from her, describing the silent streets lined with guards, and her feelings after:

> I have been alone ever since; and, though my mind is calm, I cannot dismiss the lively images that have filled my imagination all the day.— Nay, do not smile, but pity me; for, once or twice, lifting my eyes from the paper, I have seen eyes glare through a glass-door opposite my chair, and bloody hands shook at me. Not the distant sound of a foot-step can I hear.—My apartments are remote from those of the servants, the only persons who sleep with me in an immense hotel . . . I wish I had even kept the cat with me!—I want to see something alive; death in so many frightful shapes has taken hold of my fancy.—I am going to bed—and, for the first time in my life, I cannot put out the candle.

I shuddered for her, and for France. Each day brought graver news, for the French people seemed determined to bring down their King. I admired Mary's courage in wanting to witness these events.

Whenever Paul-Marc and I were alone together, we discussed this situation in Paris. His appearance in my home as William's assistant had been a delightful shock.

He arrived one morning at 8 A.M., smiling as he came in the door. William introduced us. I felt I had to pretend I had never met Paul-Marc before. I do not know why.

"Welcome to our home," I said to him. I know I blushed.

William looked at me with interest. I was not usually so shy.

"Madame, *mon plaisir*," said Paul-Marc, bending to kiss my hand, still smiling.

Paul-Marc arrived early every morning and stayed till after dinner at sundown. We all worked together, the men at engraving, and me at printing or general help. I could not but compare the two: William short and powerfully built, energetic and dominating, Paul-Marc tall and slim, with dark eyes, perhaps ten years younger than William. As soon as we were alone that first day, Paul-Marc had cupped my face in his hands and kissed me.

"I 'ave found you again, *ma petite*," he said. "I knew it would be so."

I, too, had thought long about him, and knew it could not be so. I could be no more than a Spiritual lover of Paul-Marc. It was not possible for me to betray William in his own house, in his own city. I had felt guilty enough when I was in Dover and on my own. A little voice kept saying, But William betrayed you. Don't you want to be even? And I answered myself, I am even. Someone else loves me. Besides, I was Blake's wife and I felt that he expected loyalty of me, even though he would speak of love, free as the wind. It did not seem right for me to be other than as loyal as possible, even if my heart broke in the attempt.

The trouble was, I had fallen in love with Paul-Marc. What had started as an adventure had turned to real Affection. There was a part of me that responded to Paul-Marc on a Spiritual level. It was as if I had known him before. He felt it, too. We talked all the time—of the weather, of our printing work, of William, of our childhoods. We never engaged in physical intimacies, only kisses.

If William knew, and I am not certain he did not, he was indulgent.

"Why don't you two take a rest from the Shop," he would say, wiping the ink off his hands on his apron. "Walk out a little and enjoy the Air. I want to read for a time."

So we would go off together, to Covent Garden, or down to the Thames Embankement. London life teemed around us, the cries, the smells. We were happy just to be in each other's company, with little thought of the future.

Paul-Marc was engaged in a dangerous enterprise. He was raising money among the Dissenters in London, those who supported the revolution, and sending it to the Gironde, the party in which his cousin Manon Roland was active. This was dangerous because we English were turning against the revolutionaries, especially since the September massacres, and the trial of the King. Paul-Marc could be arrested as a spy if he was not careful, accused of plotting revolution in England.

It was a mid-January morning in the New Year of 1793, and we were waiting for William to return with new copper plate and some paper supplies, when I asked Paul-Marc about the King's trial. He had taken my hand in his for a moment, and I felt I should distract him.

"The Gironde do not want this trial," said Paul-Marc. "It will divide France. But Danton and Robespierre see us as supporting the Royalists if we do not cooperate." He did not drop my hand.

"What does your cousin think?" I asked.

Now he released my hand and took a letter from his pocket.

"She has written me that she is ashamed since the September Massacres. She writes . . . I will translate . . . 'You know my enthusiasm for the Revolution; well then, I was ashamed. Our Revolution has been sullied by rascals; it has become ghastly.' *Mon Dieu*, I must go back very soon, Kate."

My heart sank. If he went, when would I ever see him again?

At this point, William returned bearing heavy packages, and we helped to unwrap them.

"We were speaking of the situation in France," I told him, as Paul-Marc and I began laying stacks of paper on the side table.

William's thoughts immediately went to Mary.

"I am glad that Mary has the company of Thomas Christie and his wife in Paris," said William. "Joseph sends her money orders through him. He knows Danton, too, I hear, so Mary is just where she wants to be, witnessing history."

"She has seen the downfall of the monarchy," muttered Paul-Marc, stacking the two heavy copper plates William had carried home. "I fear she will see the execution of the King. The Assembly have found his secret correspondence with Austria, and they accuse him of plotting against the revolution."

"Is not the King's person inviolable?" asked William.

"Some say he is now only a simple *citoyen*," said Paul-Marc. "They call him Louis Capet."

"I heard something at the Coffee House, today," said William. "They are calling for a vote, tomorrow, January sixteenth. It will decide whether to execute him or not."

Paul-Marc crossed himself.

"*Mon Dieu*, it is worse than I thought. I must go back to Paris, soon, Monsieur Blake. I will finish our work, and then I must go." He glanced briefly at me.

Paul-Marc did not stay for supper that night. He was visibly distressed and preoccupied. As he said his goodbyes and closed the door behind him, William turned to me and said, "You know, Kate, I always feel that I have seen Paul-Marc before."

The terrible news came a few days later that King Louis XVI had been executed on January 21. In the morning rain, his head was cut off with a new instrument called the Guillotine. From the scaffold he had cried, "People, I die innocent!"

I did not know how to comfort Paul-Marc.

"We are a nation of regicides!" he cried. "We who wanted revolution did not want this to happen. All Europe will be against us now."

I decided it would be good for Paul-Marc to walk with me along the river bank below our house. I had kept Paul-Marc at a distance for several weeks, and he had accused me of cruelty, but seemed to understand my feelings and did not press me. Now that he was so distressed, I felt that I wanted to comfort him, almost as a mother would comfort a child.

We sat together on the river bank, a little way from new construction of houses and warehouses, and watched the ships moving up the Thames. It was cold and clear, at the end of January. I was muffled up in my coat and bonnet, and he had a scarf wound around his neck over a big greatcoat. His olive complexion had a ruddy glow in the winter air. He put his arm around me. I did not move away.

"*Je regrette, ma chérie*," he said, "we must part soon. I would have liked to know you better." He looked into my eyes and kissed me full on the lips. Again, I did not move away.

"I do not think your husband would mind this," he said. "I have read some of his work. He believes in the Divine Power of Love. He would not blame you."

I kissed him back, and for the moment believed what he said.

In the month ahead, Paul-Marc and I would walk daily through the cold city streets, on the pretext of some errand or other, but always really to be able to talk alone to each other. We confided in each other as true friends, and I even told him about my secret drawings. I think he was appalled, but he said nothing.

I took him to see Sir Joshua's portrait of Elizabeth Billington at the Royal Academy. I had heard that she was back in London, but I restrained myself from asking if William was visiting her.

"How can I compare with someone like her?" I asked Paul-Marc. "Or Mary Wollstonecraft for that matter? I have no gifts! I am only an ordinary woman."

"You are a true heart, Kate," he comforted me, "and you are precious to William. You are his friend and comfort."

He took my hands in his and looked at them. They are small and square, and had become roughened because of all the work I did in the house and print room. "Not the hands of a Lady," I remarked, ruefully.

"With these hands, you make it possible for him to create, *n'est-ce pas?*" said Paul-Marc, his black eyes intent. "Who else cooks his food, makes his shirts, prints his work! If only things were different, I would take you away from him! We would run away to France together!"

My heart was in turmoil most of the time that February. The French had declared war on England and Holland, and Paul-Marc had to return to Paris by the end of the month. Each morning I awakened with dread. As I poured water in my basin to wash my face, a wave of nausea would overtake me, as if I were with child. Paul-Marc had become dear to me. I had not admitted to myself before I met him that I had become lonely in my marriage. William spent much of his time in the company of his Imagination, or hard at work. Of course, I loved him; he was the rock upon which my life was built. Yet Paul-Marc provided me with the companionship that had faded from my marriage.

Paul-Marc left London without my ever giving myself to him bodily, but in my mind and heart, I had committed adultery with him many times over. Did William know? This question burned in my brain. He was usually acutely sensitive to what was around him, but where I was concerned, all was taken for granted. Unless it was I who did not read the signs. I looked closely at what William was working on.

William was printing and colouring *Visions of The Daughters of Albion*, the long poem that I knew was about Mary and her ideas of love and slavery and the emancipation of women. Yet I felt that one plate expressed my own personal torment: a naked female figure

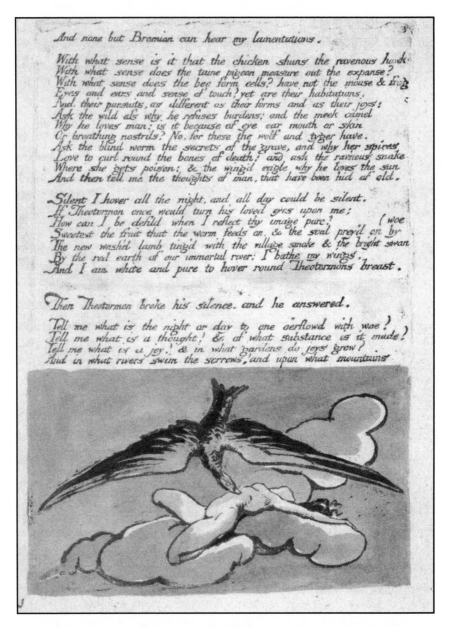

And none but Bromion can hear my lamentations.

With what sense is it that the chicken shuns the ravenous hawk
With what sense does the tame pigeon measure out the expanse?
With what sense does the bee form cells? have not the mouse & frog
Eyes and ears and sense of touch? yet are their habitations.
And their pursuits, as different as their forms and as their joys:
Ask the wild ass why he refuses burdens: and the meek camel
Why he loves man: is it because of eye ear mouth or skin
Or breathing nostrils? No, for these the wolf and tyger have.
Ask the blind worm the secrets of the grave, and why her spires
Love to curl round the bones of death: and ask the ravnous snake
Where she gets poison: & the wing'd eagle why he loves the sun
And then tell me the thoughts of man, that have been hid of old.

Silent I hover all the night, and all day could be silent.
If Theotormon once would turn his loved eyes upon me;
How can I be defild when I reflect thy image pure?   (woe
Sweetest the fruit that the worm feeds on. & the soul prey'd on by
The new washd lamb tingd with the village smoke & the bright swan
By the red earth of our immortal river: I bathe my wings.
And I am white and pure to hover round Theotormons breast.

Then Theotormon broke his silence. and he answered.

Tell me what is the night or day to one oerflowd with woe ?
Tell me what is a thought? & of what substance is it made?
Tell me what is a joy? & in what gardens do joys grow?
And in what rivers swim the sorrows? and upon what mountains

Blake, *Visions of the Daughters of Albion*, Plate 6, Copy J (1793). Lessing J. Rosenwald Collection, Library of Congress. Copyright © 2003 the William Blake Archive. Used with permission

fallen backward on a cloud, writhing as a huge eagle seems to pierce her heart with his beak. In the poem, it was the heroine Oothoon, a free spirit, tormented by a conventional lover, but to me, it was as if my own conventions were tormenting me, preventing my spirit from soaring. William's own words burned into my heart with a terrible irony: *How can one joy absorb another? Are not different joys / Holy, eternal, infinite! And each joy is a Love.*

Mary wrote from Paris. She had been invited to present a paper on education to a committee of the Girondins, and Thomas Paine was working on a committee for constitutional reform. William was happy to hear this, as we had not seen Tom Paine since last September.

"It is good that Mary has found congenial people and interests in France," said William. "The Gironde are a progressive group."

I thought of Paul-Marc's cousin, Madame Roland, and wondered if Mary had met her. Paul-Marc had described her as a beautiful woman, with a great flair for dramatic action and a desire to be perfect in all her various roles. Paul-Marc apprenticed to her father, a Parisian engraver, and so had been her friend since youth. She married Roland when she was twenty-six, had one daughter, and no more children. She was not really happy in marriage, Paul-Marc thought, and liked to dominate her husband. She was active in politics. Her dinners and salon were an influence in the Gironde, when her husband was Minister of the Interior. She was just the sort of woman Mary would like. I hoped they had met, because then Mary would have some contact with Paul-Marc and I might hear news of him.

From Kate's Notebook.
March 2, 1793.

Such an odd thing has occurred, I do not quite know what to make of it. Last night, William and I were sitting by candlelight, he reading and I mending. Usually he would say, "Bring me my things," and I would know a Vision was present, and would fetch him his drawing materials. But this time, it was not William who had the Visitation: it was I.

And strangely, it was not present to my sight, but to my hearing. Of course, I have always heard Voices, though not like this. This voice took over my entire body. You must write, it said, write down what is dictated.

I reached for William's pen and ink bottle and a piece of paper. William did not at first realize what was going on. He continued reading.

Then the voice began to dictate. It was a feminine voice. I began to write rapidly:

> Hear me, I am Enion, Mother of Life!
> I am made to sow the thistle for wheat; the nettle for a
>   nourishing dainty
> I have planted a false oath in the earth, it has brought forth a
>   poison tree
> I have chosen the serpent for counsellor and the dog
> For a schoolmaster for my children.
> I have blotted out from light and living the dove and
>   nightingale
> And I have caused the earthworm to beg from door to door
> I have taught the thief a secret path into the house of the just
> I have taught pale artifice to spread his nets among the
>   morning.

I gasped; I could hardly stop writing, but I did not understand a word. William looked up curiously as I continued writing, possessed by the words:

> My heavens are brass my earth is iron my moon a clod of clay
> My sun a pestilence burning at noon and a vapour of death in
>   night.

"What are you writing?" asked William, putting down his book. "The voice," I whispered, "the voice in my head. Can't you hear it?" My hand trembled; wanting to write again. William came and stood beside me, and began to read as I wrote the next lines:

> What is the Price of Experience do men buy it for a song
> Or Wisdom for a dance in the street? No, it is bought with the price
> Of all that a man hath his house his wife his children
> Wisdom is sold in the desolate market where none come to buy
> And in the withered field where the farmer plows for bread in vain.

At that point, I fainted. At the same time, William exclaimed, "My God!" and caught me as I fell.

When I revived, William brought a cushion to my chair and a glass of water. He sat beside me and questioned me intently: How did I feel just before I heard the voice? How did I feel during the writing? Did I see any light in the room?

He examined the paper carefully.

"I know who Enion is," he said. "She has lived in my head for some time. And there are others."

He raised me up from the chair and took me in his arms. He carried me to bed and by the light of a single candle made love to me, over and over.

So now I can compete with Elizabeth.

Mary wrote to us about her life in Paris. She was often in the company of Thomas Christie and his wife. Surprisingly, his wife was not the French mistress, Catherine Claudine, who had borne his infant daughter at the end of July. No, in September Thomas had married Rebecca Thomson of Finsbury Square, heiress to a carpet manufacturer. I had thought at the time that it was another example of how poorly women were treated by men, used and discarded at will. I was surprised that Mary had any regard for Christie, though of course they had written together for Joseph's *Analytical Review*. Mary wrote:

Thomas's sister Jane and I are being coached in French, but I fear I am not improving as quickly as I would like. It is hard to concentrate, for Thomas's baby daughter Julie has joined the Christie household, Thomas having persuaded Mme. Claudine to give up her baby to him.

I felt a pang of jealousy when I read those words. How easily it was for these people to have a child in their household. There seemed to be no shame attached to these relationships. Perhaps William and Mary's ideas of freedom from the bonds of convention were really taking place in France. It must be heady stuff for Mary.

Soon the letters came less frequently, for the mail boats stopped running in March. Joseph told us that life was becoming difficult for aliens in Paris. There were shortages of food and candles and riots in the streets. Why did not Mary come home?

I found out why, eventually. She had met an American army captain, Gilbert Imlay, and was in love.

In the weeks following the Spiritual Writing, William treated me as if I were a precious and breakable object. It was wonderful. If he found me scrubbing the kitchen floor, he made me stop and rest. He brought me tea in the middle of the day. He bought me a new black shawl of a soft knitted wool. And every evening, for several weeks, I sat still as a terrified bird and waited for Enion.

13

In Which We Have News From France

*P*aper was stacked all over William's painting room. Printed designs hung drying from lines strung across the room, glowing with watercolours. It was becoming difficult to move without knocking something over. William had been working intensely for months. His visions were transformed from his mind to the copper plate and from there to the printed page, where we painted them. I was constantly urging him to do some commercial work, as my little hoard of shillings and pence was now sadly depleted. William thought he might soon have a sale of his work, but in the meantime, we had to eat.

"Have faith, Kate!" William would say cheerfully, picking up his pen. And then I would see him look off into space at some point of light, and sit that way, rapt, for half an hour.

The characters in my own imagination began to have lives of their own. Enion had a husband named Tharmas.

Sometimes they quarrelled. One night, under her spell, I wrote:

I have looked into the secret soul of him I loved
And in the Dark recesses found Sin and cannot return.

And the voice of Tharmas replied:

> Why wilt thou Examine every little fibre of my soul
> Spreading them out before the Sun like Stalks of flax to
>   dry . . .
> The infant joy is beautiful but its anatomy
> Horrible Ghast and Deadly . . .
> Thou wilt go mad with horror if thou dost Examine thus
> Every moment of my secret hours.

It was then I realized that these characters were not in reality Spirits possessing me. It was that I was reading William's mind. I did not tell him this, for reasons of my own. He needed me now, not just for the work I did for him. I was now a Muse.

My visits to Paul Colnaghi were not frequent, because I knew enough not to flood my market. What few pounds and shillings I made, I kept hidden away in my kitchen, and I spent carefully. It gave me a good feeling to know I was contributing to our welfare, helping William even though I knew he would abhor the means.

I discovered that I could also draw like Henry Fuseli, who was most prolific and could not remember half of what he produced—especially the drawings he did for Gentlemen. I knew where William kept *his* Private collection of Fuselis—those depictions of large-bottomed women with elaborate hair arrangements. Why should I not try some like that? Mr. Colnaghi, eyes wide open, paid me very well for those.

We resumed our habit of taking long walks in and around London. We each had a hickory walking stick, and William carried a knapsack with a bit of bread and cheese in it, two tin cups and a bottle of good ale. He always wore black clothing and his wide-brimmed beaver hat, and I wore a straw hat tied down with a scarf. It was Spring, and the air was soft. The little fig tree in our front garden was green and leafy, but the streets of the city depressed us, as War was in the air. There was a campaign in Flanders, and general Melancholy and furtiveness in the faces of the crowd.

All around us in Lambeth Marsh there was always much building going on, filling in to make firm land. Now there was a wine factory, a Pottery or two, and dye works. The fields we could see from our window were becoming crossed with new roads for the traffic from Westminster Bridge.

One early morning, we walked south toward the lovely hills of Camberwell. The birds twittered in the hedges, while the Lark sang in disappearing circles of melody, higher and higher above the fields. The corn at Peckham Rye blew in the light breeze.

"Look, I'll make you a crown of daisies," I teased William, who had presented me with a wild rose from the hedge. I wove him a little circle of flowers as he ate some cheese. The air was so clear it seemed to reflect light from every living thing.

At midday we turned west toward Southfields, intending to circle back and stop for the night in Battersea to see my father, who now lived alone, my brothers and sisters all having married now with children of their own. In fact, my sister Sarah had married Henry Banes, a Merchant, and they lived in London, though we saw them infrequently. I reminded myself to call on her more often . . . it was just that she had so many children, and it reminded me of my own Barren state to see them.

We had reached the hill at Southfields, when, looking ahead towards London with its distant church spires, pink and gold in the afternoon light, William suddenly stopped. A stricken look came into his face, and he staggered.

"What is it? Are you ill?" I cried, grasping his arm.

"Oh, God, it is what I see!" he cried, standing now stock still. "It is dark, dark, dark! But there are bursts of light all around. I can hear the light! Can't you hear it, Kate?"

"No, no I cannot!"

William was unusually agitated: his visions were often of only one or two persons. This seemed different.

"The light!" he cried again. "Ribbons of light, crossing in the air!"

He raised his arms up to the sky.

"That sound!" Now his hands went to his ears. "That awful

wail . . . I have never heard such a sound! Can you not hear it? It is a scream from heaven!"

"William, it is a Vision!" I cried. "Calm yourself!"

"Oh, My God, there are horrible metal birds, blotting out the skies," he shouted, "Oh, horrible, horrible! The noise—the earth cracks! *Fire.* Oh, Kate, it is the Apocalypse! I see it! I see it—as did John of Revelation."

William fell to his knees as if in prayer.

"London is burning!" he wept.

"No, William, it is only a dream. It is a Spring Day! The sun is shining!"

"The Spirit is in me," he whispered. "There is a War in Heaven. The metal birds are fighting it. The noise is like a thousand cannon firing all at once! Oh, Jesus Christ, I cannot bear this!"

He fell to the ground in a faint.

That Vision troubled William all his life. He never could puzzle it out. I later thought it was about the Wars in France, which went on for many years when Napoleon Bonaparte came to frighten us. William never thought that. He maintained it was his own private Vision of Apocalypse and wrote different accounts of it in several poems over the years. When we returned home, he straightaway wrote this on a scrap of paper, and later it became part of *The Book of Urizen*:

> Sund'ring, dark'ning, thund'ring!
> Rent away with a terrible crash
> Eternity roll'd wide apart
> Mountainous all around
> Departing; departing; departing:
> Leaving ruinous fragments of life
> Hanging frowning cliffs and all between
> An ocean of voidness unfathomable.

And there was something that troubled me greatly. In his Notebook he wrote:

I say I shant live five years
And if I live one it will be a
Wonder   June 1793.

The day after he had written these words, William dressed in his good black jacket and said he was going out. He did not tell me where, and I was immediately suspicious. But what to do? I could have stayed home and fretted for the day, but I decided I was no longer going to be so complaisant. I pulled on my bonnet and shawl and followed him furtively, across Lambeth Bridge, through the narrow lanes, to Poland Street. Of course, I suddenly realized, Elizabeth is back in London.

"Why do you do this to me? What does she do for you that I cannot do?" I cry.

"It is useless to compare: she makes no demands, that is all."

"And I do? What do I demand, for God's sake!"

"When I first married you, I gave you all my whole soul. I thought that you would love my loves and joy in my delights, seeking for pleasure in my pleasures."

"You asked the impossible, you know it!"

"Then you were lovely . . . mild and gentle. Now you are terrible in jealousy and unlovely in my sight!"

"Then you need not look at me any longer!"

From Kate's Notebook.
August 1, 1793.

I have never been more Humiliated in my life. I never thought William could be so unfeeling. I have just come back from Vauxhall Gardens, where Henry Fuseli and I went for amusement this evening while William was supposedly having a business dinner with George Cumberland. I suffered a little pang of conscience regarding Henry but felt that he of all people would forgive me, if he knew about the drawings I pretended he had drawn.

I thought it was kind of Henry to offer to take me to see the Pleasure Gardens, which we did not often find time to visit. It is a wonderful place with trees and gravel paths, colonnades and arches, with tea shops and restaurants, and hundreds of hanging lanterns. There were bands playing. I enjoyed the music as we walked near large paintings called transparent pictures, which were installed here and there, lighted from behind so they looked like stained glass.

And then it was that we saw them, Elizabeth and William, her arm through his as if she owned him. They passed us, not noticing we were in the crowd.

Henry said, "Do not fret, Kate. Men will be men. Women must accept it."

But I thought, How could he go out in public with her, for all the world to see? How could he thus abandon me to public humiliation? I had never felt so betrayed, even when I first knew of William's affection for her.

And to think I had let Paul-Marc go back to France unloved because of some scruple I had about William!

From Blake's Notebook.

> Dost thou not in Pride & scorn
> Fill with tempests all my morn
> And with jealousies and fears
> Fill my pleasant nights with tears

From Kate's Notebook.
August 18, 1793.

Our Anniversary—our eleventh. A good time to take stock. I have an unfaithful husband, and no children. I refuse to believe it is all my Fault, or it is the Nature of Husbands to be unfaithful. No! Something is going very wrong. For the first time in our marriage, I am beginning to fear that William is not stable, that his Visions are coming from a Disturbed Mind.

Last night was especially upsetting. In our bed, in the midst of embracing me, William suddenly started up, threw off the bedclothes, and exclaimed, "Be Off! You are not Kate! Fiend!"

"Are you speaking to me?" I cried. He had taken the candle from the table and was holding it above the bed. I covered my nakedness. His features were contorted.

"You are not Kate!" he repeated. "You are covered with scales! You have eyes in your breasts!"

"My God, William, you are Mad!" I cried. "Calm yourself!"

As suddenly as the Fit came on, it passed. He sat on the side of the bed, his head in his hands.

"Forgive me," he said, "I am over-tired."

"You do not love me at all," I began to weep, "or you would never have a dream like that."

He denied it many times over. He covered me with kisses. But my heart has turned to ice.

Letter to William and Catherine Blake from Mary Wollstonecraft. September 15, 1793. Faubourg St. Germain, Paris, France

Dear Friends:

I write not knowing if or when you will receive this letter, which I am sending to England in the safekeeping of a friend, who will take great risks for his cause. The bearer is Paul-Marc Philipon, who is, I know, acquainted with you both. As you are aware, he is a cousin of Manon Roland, an admirable woman with whom I am acquainted, but who was alas, arrested on the first day of June, while I was living safely in Neuilly. M. Philipon will take this letter to Joseph Johnson at St. Paul's Churchyard from whence Joseph will see that you receive it.

"So Paul-Marc is back in London," William said as he read the letter aloud to me. "He is a brave man to bear the horrors of Paris these days and trade them for the growing political oppression in England. You must find him and offer him dinner here."

"Oh, yes," I said.
William read on:

I scarcely know how to begin to tell you of the feverish events I am witnessing: even Thomas Christie and his family were arrested early in August, but thankfully released. They have gone to stay in Geneva. I am safe enough for the time being, and will mix good news with bad to tell you of the events of the past months. In April of this year, I became acquainted with a singular man, a captain of the American Army. His name is Gilbert Imlay. He is a businessman and a writer, having published last year in London a book about the western territory of North America; this year he will publish a novel, *The Emigrants*. He is a handsome man of thirty-nine years, tall and thin, with a great appetite for life. He has roamed the American wilds, contrasting that new world with this corrupt European one; like me, he does not believe in corrupt institutions such as marriage. Well, in short, I am in love with him and he with me.

We have the most harmonious mental and spiritual relationship. Not only that, we have lived as man and wife for over four months. I was offered the use of a small house in Neuilly all summer, to which I retired because the situation in Paris was so alarming, with the Guillotine set up in the Place de la Révolution, the tocsin sounding every day, and citizens denouncing each other. It was too horrible.

Neuilly was Paradise. You remember the Garden, Kate, from *Paradise Lost*?

Neuilly is a tiny village to the Northwest of Paris, surrounded by green woods, which stretch as far as Versailles. My little house stood in a garden lush with roses and prettily shaped bushes; there was an old gardener who also tended the grape vines which made a pretty arbour nearby.

Here Gilbert visited me, and we achieved the utmost physical and mental harmony. Now our union is to be blessed with a child! Gilbert has registered me as his wife with the American Embassy, for safety's sake, so that I may be protected as an American citizen, for many English are being arrested and detained.

"Well, that's the least he can do," muttered William. "Robespierre wanted to expel all foreigners two months ago!"

I thought, "A baby coming!"
William read on:

Unfortunately, my dear Gilbert has had to go off to Le Havre on business. He left almost as soon as we were settled here in Paris together. He expected to be back soon, but unfortunately has been several times delayed.

"My God," interrupted William, "can't she tell he's a cad?"
"How can you tell?" I retorted.
"Read between the lines," William said. "He's left her alone there and he is spending all his time in Le Havre."
William read again:

To occupy my time, I have been working on a book—*A Historical and Moral View of the French Revolution*—and I fear I must tell you that I spend a good deal of time visiting friends who are imprisoned. I have been told it is dangerous to be writing a book, and even more dangerous to send letters to England...but I am proud that I can work while I do suffer the early weeks of pregnancy, and the longing for my dear Gilbert. Friends tell me I look well.

I have referred to the Guillotine, that instrument of death that the Committee of Public Safety, which now rules France, uses to rid the country of its enemies. It is used on men and women without distinction, and because it was a woman, Charlotte Corday, who stabbed Marat to death, the cause of women's education and rights, to which I am ever devoted, has suffered a setback. Corday's act horrified the country, and she was soon sent to the Guillotine. She was only twenty-five years old! They are turning against women in public life here—Robespierre is known to be a misogynist—and that is why they have arrested Madame Roland.

Of course, it is not only the cause of women which is being crushed here; all human decency is being lost. Devotion to Revolution has become a collective dictatorship of ten men—illegal tyrants! Informing on one's friends is considered a civic duty. I do not know what will happen next, but fear not for me as I am safely known as an

American wife. I will try to write again in a few weeks. Perhaps I will join Gilbert in Le Havre if he does not come back for me soon.

> Your devoted Friend,
> Mary

Note delivered to Mrs. William Blake from Paul-Marc Philipon. Thursday, September 26, 1793. London.

Chérie . . . I am once again in England, as you will have heard. It has been a difficult journey. Come to me at 18 Blossom Street, Spital-fields. I beg this of you.

I found Paul-Marc ghost-thin and weary, but somehow handsomer than I remembered. His dark hair was still neatly tied back in a block, though his clothes were rumpled. When he hugged me, he smelled of Cloves. He no doubt was trying to ward off the stench of the streets, for Spitalfields was a poor area, inhabited by French Protestant silk weavers, who crowded into their little houses along with their looms. Mrs. Blake used to buy goods from them, I remembered.

"Ah, *Mon Dieu*, I did not think to ever see you again," Paul-Marc whispered, his lips in my hair.

"Nor did I. But, here you are, and this time, I won't let you go!"

We clung to each other like two children in a storm, crying and laughing in turn. The little room became warmer and warmer, sunlight streamed through the narrow windows, and glowed on our nakedness.

I was so happy.

"*Je t'aime, ah, je t'aime*," Paul-Marc murmured. I told him that I loved him, too.

My true friend had returned. For a little time, we experienced a world of our own, whose borders were the confines of a narrow bed in Spitalfields.

I do not think that William ever knew I had loved Paul-Marc. William, who saw so many things, did not see what was right in front of his nose. Or perhaps he did see, but accepted it the way he had expected me to accept Elizabeth. I suddenly understood how you could love two men at once, for each love was different. I felt estranged from William, but deep in my heart I still loved him. I did not love him any less because I cared for Paul-Marc. In fact, I wanted us to all be together as much as possible. I thought it might have a calming effect on William.

As William had suggested, I did invite Paul-Marc to dinner. It happened that John Gabriel Stedman was in London, staying with us for a few days. He had made the trip from Tiverton in Devon to see Joseph Johnson about his book on Surinam. William liked this rough ex-soldier, and Stedman had entrusted various business dealings to William, who had worked on engravings for the book during the past few years. He had almost finished the last ten plates. As we were all acquainted with Joseph, he was a lively topic of conversation at the dinner table. Paul-Marc was devoted to him.

"Monsieur Johnson has supported the cause of the Gironde from the beginning," he said, in his gentle way. "I am grateful to him eternally for helping me travel across the Channel."

"Hmph. I call him a scoundrel!" muttered Stedman. "I have no satisfaction from him as a publisher! Delay, delay! And he changes my manuscript continually."

"He is a well-meaning man," said William, as he helped me serve the rabbit stew and potatoes. "He keeps a good table, and his support of Mary Wollstonecraft when she was alone and unemployed in London was a true Christian act."

"Christian maybe," said Stedman, "Jacobin more like it!"

"And is that so bad?" asked Paul-Marc, rather surprised. To him it was hardly a sin to be a democrat.

Stedman banged his fist on the table, his face reddened and he exclaimed, "I am a Monarchist, Sir!"

Now Paul-Marc's face flushed, but he kept silent.

William tactfully turned the conversation back to Johnson, and Stedman's book. He showed us the proof of an engraving he had done for one of Stedman's illustrations, "A Negro hung alive by the Ribs to a Gallows." It was horrible. The black cross-hatched image of an almost naked man, suspended from a gallows, a hook through his ribs. A skull and bones littered the foreground, and two skulls on poles receded into the horizon, where a tiny ship sailed away.

"This is powerful," said Paul-Marc. I saw his fingers shake slightly. It was too close to home, too like the Guillotine.

William now decided to cheer up the evening by showing our guests a little emblem book he had published in May, called *For Children/The Gates of Paradise*. He was charging three shillings for it, but so far had only sold one or two copies.

"What is this!" exclaimed Stedman, turning to the Frontispiece. "A little worm-child on a leaf, with a caterpillar above? 'What Is Man?' A good question!"

The little designs were only about two inches square, child-sized.

"I like the first Emblem," I said. "Look at the woman picking babies out of the ground as if they were vegetables! 'I found him beneath a tree.' Would not a child laugh at that?"

"These are *trés bon*," said Paul-Marc, with the practised eye of a fellow engraver, looking at the tiny emblem of a ladder to the moon, with a little figure at its base. The title was "I want! I want!"

"It would be a wise child who could understand these," observed Stedman.

Another evening, we had Paul-Marc to supper when Cathy was visiting. I noticed that she always had a high colour when Paul-Marc was around. She had met him on his first visit, when he had been William's assistant. That evening, she was wearing a becoming blue dress and brought us a huge bouquet of daisies and fresh thyme. Paul-Marc remarked on the flowers, which I put on the table.

"Have you passed by Covent Garden today?" Cathy asked him. "That is where I bought these."

William was at the table, too, though he had his nose in a book.

I surveyed them all, as I placed bread and cheese before them. Paul-Marc raised his eyes, and meeting my glance, smiled.

Cathy noticed.

"Are you interested in herbs?" she asked Paul-Marc.

"Cathy is learning a great deal about healing with herbs," I remarked.

Paul-Marc smiled at me again.

"Allow me to help you pour the Ale," he said. As he passed by, he touched my shoulder lightly. I saw Cathy's eyes on us.

"Would you like to see my herb collection, Paul-Marc?" Cathy asked, drawing his attention.

"Ah, of course," he said.

William did not even look up from his book while we ate supper. It was only when Paul-Marc was leaving that he said, "You must come more often. There are two women here who enjoy your company."

From Kate's Notebook.
September 30, 1793.

Enion came again. Under her spell, I wrote :

> Tharmas reared up a form of gold and stood upon the glittering
>   rock
> A shadowy human form winged and in his depths
> The dazzling as of gems shone clear, rapturous in fury
> Glorying in his own eyes Exalted in terrific Pride
> Opening his rifted rocks mingling together they join in burning
>   anguish
> Mingling his horrible darkness with her tender limbs then high
>   she soar'd
> Shrieking above the ocean; a bright wonder that nature
>   shuddered at
> Half woman and half beast all his darkly waving colours mix
> With her fair crystal clearness in her lips and cheeks his metals
>   rose
> In blushes like the morning and his rocky features softning

I blushed to read this. Was it me and Paul-Marc, or was it William and Elizabeth? William read it, and embraced me with Passion, as he always did when I heard the voices. But this time, I was severely distressed, for it seemed to me that I was betraying now Paul-Marc as well as William. The marks of both were impressed on my body.

.   .   .

> O Rose thou art sick.
> The invisible worm,

That flies in the night
In the howling storm:

Has found out thy bed
Of crimson joy:
And his dark secret love
Does thy life destroy.
William Blake, *Songs of Experience.*

The winter of 1793 was a dark time for England, for France, and for us. Armies were mustering in the fields around London, where grain should be growing, and what grain there was mostly went to feed soldiers on the continent. There was a shortage of bread in England—another reason for Riots in the streets. The days grew shorter and colder. The Queen of France was guillotined on the sixteenth of October. Paul-Marc wept when he told me. My heart turned to stone.

I was already grown thin and sleepless because of conflicting emotions over William and Paul-Marc, and in addition, I worried over Paul-Marc's political activities, his collecting of documents and monies to aid his cause, and the news we were frequently hearing that the Mountain, that group in Paris which opposed the Girondins, were the directors of the Terror. Once again, Paul-Marc prepared to leave London, knowing that his cousin Manon had been arrested, and hoping to save her—how, I did not know.

"Why do you have to go back?" I asked. We were walking around Covent Garden, stealing an hour or two together, pretending to shop for cabbages at the barrow boys' stalls.

"It is my fate, my little one. It is my country, so I must help. Europe will never be the same—I must be part of the change." Paul-Marc's dark eyes regarded me gravely, and then his lips curved in a gentle smile.

"Do you believe in God?" I asked suddenly.

"Of course. You do too, *n'est-ce pas?* And your husband—he sees Him, I think."

"Then I will pray to keep you safe. He will listen, because I have always tried to be good."

"But you feel guilty now—so you are worried He will not listen."

Paul-Marc bent down and kissed the top of my head. He could always perceive my thoughts.

"But I *am* guilty, and not just about us." And I reminded him about the forgeries.

He was grave.

"My poor little one," he said, stroking my cheek, "you have done this terrible thing only for your husband, I know. But it is dangerous. Tell no one else."

Later, lying with him in his tiny room in Spitalfields, bodies close under the quilt, I felt his gentle touch bring an overwhelming tenderness to my spirit, and a yearning for him that was not assuaged by our physical union. Sick with foreboding, again and again we moved together in that dance that is also a struggle, a pressing of flesh and a storming of a gate that opens at last into a quiet garden.

He was to leave the next day. I could not bear the thought. I cut off a lock of my hair and gave it to him—it was all I could think of to give. He gave me a little silver brooch in the shape of a rose that had been his mother's. We both wept. I left his little room in Blossom Street and walked home alone, through the narrow, darkening streets, avoiding the beggars, seeing nothing but my own despair.

Cathy Blake confronted me one day.

"How could you have let Paul-Marc go away again without saying goodbye to me?" she demanded, her face pinched and white.

I was aghast. I had not realized the depth of her feelings.

"You never think of anyone but yourself!" she accused me. "I know Paul-Marc liked me, he was so kind to me. He came to see all my herb collection, did you know that?"

I had a vague recollection of his mentioning that.

"You kept him to yourself and William," she almost shouted at me, "and now he is gone!" She began to weep.

"I did not know you cared for him," I whispered. "He could not have responded. He had too many responsibilities in France. He had to return."

"That's what you say, but I know you kept him from me, Kate! You only wanted him to admire you. I could see it, even if William was blind!"

We were in the kitchen, where I was trying to make soup for supper. Paul-Marc had been gone about a month. How could I not have been aware of this? Cathy was so lonely and vulnerable. I could tell she was full of animosity to me.

"The situation is not as you imagine," I said defensively.

"Oh, of course, what do you care about my feelings!" And she picked up her shawl and left the house, banging the door behind her.

From Kate's Notebook, n.d.

I have just now presented William with a little leather pouch for his tobacco, which I bought with my secret earnings. He was so delighted it was worth the pangs of Conscience. But I am greatly bothered.

Is there not a Mystic Bond between the Artist and his Work? Am I not breaking this Bond by pretending to be Flaxman or Fuseli? Will God ever forgive me for what I am doing? Will William, if he ever finds out?

William had written a Prospectus, for he was going to have a Sale of his Art. (A copy is among the papers I have given to Frederick.)

TO THE PUBLIC
October 10, 1793.

The Labours of the Artist, the Poet, the Musician, have been proverbially attended by poverty and obscurity; this was never the fault of the Public, but was owing to a neglect of means to propagate such works as have wholly absorbed the Man of Genius. Even Milton and Shakespeare could not publish their own works.

This difficulty has been obviated by the Author of the following productions now presented to the Public; who has invented a method of Printing both Letter-press and Engraving in a style more ornamental, uniform and grand, than any before discovered, while it produces works at less than one fourth of the expense.

And so it went. Among the works on sale he offered engravings on Historical subjects and his Illuminated Books. *America,* in Folio with eighteen designs cost 10s.6d, and *The Book of Thel,* in Quarto with six designs cost 3s. *Songs of Innocence* and *Songs of Experience* were 5s. each. I advised him to ask as much as 3s. for *The Gates of Paradise.* He concluded:

The Illuminated Books are Printed in Colours, and on the most beautiful wove paper that could be procured.

No Subscriptions for the numerous great works now in hand are asked, for none are wanted; but the Author will produce his works, and offer them to sale at a fair price.

I privately thought some of this was arrogant, but William had great faith in his work. And the books *are* beautiful. Their pages glow with reds and yellows, every outline crisp and clear. There are tiny figures between letters, there are little toads and worms and snails, there are green tendrils of plants between lines, there are birds in the skies. And there are those gesturing, striding, swirling figures. And there are Words: Tyger, Tyger, burning bright . . . Yes, the books are beautiful, but hardly anybody bought them.

William retreated into his own world. He laboured all the time, doing only enough commercial work to put food on the table. He was obsessed by his own complicated books, which he called Prophecies. He was writing a poem, *Europe,* which he planned to print the next year.

It was a history of the rise and fall of all the tyrannies that bind us—religion, law, reason. I could not understand much of it, but my Voices had spoken of a new woman, Enitharmon, and now she was the central character of William's new poem. "Go tell the human race that woman's love is Sin . . . " she says, " . . . Forbid all Joy and from her childhood shall the little female spread nets in every secret path." I detected a resentment against the female sex in those and other lines, and I wondered guiltily if William knew about me and Paul-Marc, or had he become disillusioned with Elizabeth? Henry told me that she and her husband were planning to live in Italy next Spring.

One person who did come to buy books was William Hayley. I had not seen him for some time because he lived mostly at Eartham in Sussex. I had heard that his wife, Eliza, from whom he was separated, lived in London, so he wished to avoid her. Now he was looking through the books and engravings in William's painting room, still tall and military of bearing, his hair powdered in the old-fashioned way.

"I have good news, Mr. Blake," he told William. "John Flaxman has written to Romney that he will be returning to London in about six months."

"That is good news, indeed," said William. "He has been seven years in Italy. What treasures he has seen." He did not tell Hayley that we too had received a letter from Flaxman with the same news. And it had put me in a flurry of Nerves, for reasons I could not divulge.

"And he has promised to instruct my son Thomas Alfonso in the Fine Arts. Tom has a great talent, you know."

"So I have heard," said William, tactfully telling a white lie. He had only heard it from Hayley himself, who never tired of talking about his gifted boy.

"Tom will live with the Flaxmans here in London while he is studying," said Hayley, "so you will be able to meet him."

And I thought, Nancy Flaxman will be back just as Elizabeth Billington leaves. Will I never have any respite?

While I was thus being eaten up with guilt and jealousy, fear for Paul-Marc's safety and worry about William's state of mind, William came back from an evening at Johnson's with another letter from Mary. He had not broken the seal, and we read it together.

Paris, November 28, 1793.

My dear Friends:

It seems that a young Mr. Williams from the Lake District has risked a trip to France to see his pregnant *fiancée*, and has been prevailed upon to return with letters from one or two exiled English citizens, like myself. So I am entrusting this to him, and pray it will find you well.

As you see, I am still in Paris. I am still with child, and Gilbert is still in Le Havre. My acquaintances have guessed my condition, and I told two of them simply that I was with child, and let them stare! All the world may know it for aught I care! Yet I wish to avoid the coarse jokes of some men.

I do often consider the differing roles of men and women regarding children. In the natural world, a male bird protects the female, but for us it is sufficient for a man to condescend to get a child, in order to claim it. A man is a tyrant.

"It sounds as if she is waking up to Gilbert Imlay's true character," said William. "Read on," I said.

Yet a man must make a living, and my dear Gilbert assures me that we are only separated that he may look after me in future. Our little one is due next May, but do you know that France has established a new Calendar, and has renamed all the Months of the year? The child will be born in *Floréal, l'an II*.

"That is a pretty name," I said. "Do you think that is what she will name her baby?"

I am consoled by Gilbert's letters in his absence, and can still walk about Paris on some days and see elegant carriages in the streets. But still, we know the Seine is running red with blood. So many wonderful talents are being slaughtered by these stupid men. Now even Danton is advocating clemency.

And sadly, I must report to you that Madame Roland was sent to the Guillotine. Her last words were memorable, "O Liberty, what crimes are committed in thy name..." I heard also that her husband has committed suicide. And I must tell you of another sad death this month: her courageous cousin, Paul-Marc Philipon was also executed. I know you are both acquainted with him and will be saddened to hear.

"Oh, A Contemptible Act!" exclaimed William. "We were both fond of him. And he was so young! Kate, are you ill?"

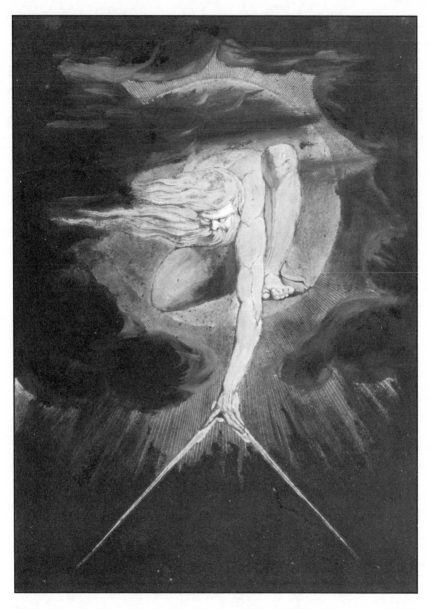

Blake, *Europe*, Frontispiece, *The Ancient of Days* (1794). Courtesy of Yale Center for British Art, Paul Mellen Collection

"Yes," I said. "I am very ill. I do not want to hear any more of the letter just now."

There is a painting that William made that winter, a painting of God. An old man bends out of a red orb, and while a great wind blows his white hair and beard, he leans down, and with his left hand holds compasses to measure and divide the firmament.

That is God, I thought, The Ancient of Days. The God who let Paul-Marc be killed, the God who took my baby. I hate Him.

14

In Which William Almost Fights a Duel and Mary Almost Drowns

From Kate's Notebook.
Tuesday, December 24, 1793.

*J*t is Christmas Eve. Bleak Midwinter. My heart is bleak, too. How do I survive, day by day? I am going through the motions of everyday living. I cook meals, I mend clothes, I clean the house, I work with William on the Printing Press. But I have no joy in life. I grieve over Paul-Marc. Dead. How could he no longer exist? I did not see him that often, so it is hard to believe he is not still there, somewhere in Paris, walking narrow grey streets in his big great-coat, slightly stooped, looking serious. I need him to help me endure. Oh, why is he gone? Is it because *I* had to be punished?

We are going to Church for Christmas Day at the Baptist Church at Grafton Street. William always likes to go to Church at Christmas, though his ideas of God are not always the same as the minister of the Church. And mine are not like anybody else's. I think the God of this world is cruel and vengeful: just as Milton showed in *Paradise Lost*, He is a tyrant. God turned Adam and Eve out of Eden, even though they repented. And in the Book of Job, why would God play tricks on Job with the Devil's connivance? There is something mean and spiteful about God. William is always praying—but to whom? He'll say it is the Human Imagination, The Poetic Genius, or Christ. William will never call the subject of his pages God, but neither will he deify Reason, as his Dissenting friends do. William is writing his own Bible, but I can't understand it.

Sometimes I wonder how closely his designs are related to what William is feeling. He has been unusually silent of late. I think he may be slipping into Melancholy. He never talks to me anymore about Paul-Marc, or about Elizabeth for that matter, though I know he must see her still, so I do not know what he feels, except when I look at his pictures. He has invented a huge serpent for the title page to *Europe*, a serpent with four huge coils, and a tongue of red flame; on the opposite page is his portrait of God, leaning down and creating the world with his compasses. So is that the world God created? The Serpent world? We will be printing these designs soon, I know. William is even now painting colour directly on copper to get a new effect. I will ask him, perhaps.

The designs of *Europe* are so frightening! Assassins lie in wait behind huge rocks; two women crouch before a fire with a dead baby at their feet; people die of plague as the bellman passes by. And some of William's words show such resentment of women: there is a poem in his Notebook with the lines:

> Till I turn from Female Love
> And root up the Infernal Grove
> I shall never Worthy be
> To Step into Eternity

> And to end thy cruel mocks
> Annihilate thee on the rocks
> And another form create
> To be subservient to my Fate

So perhaps he is angry with me, after all.

. . .

"Come, Kate, we are going out to celebrate the New Year. I will take you to see a Panorama."

William stood before me, full of energy and magnetism, his shirt a bit smudged with ink, but he was wearing his good trousers and his new shoes with buckles. He seemed his old self again.

"Really? I have only just heard of it . . . is it really a circular room all painted with a beautiful view?"

"So I believe. I think we will view a panorama of London as if seen from Southwark. But it is more than just a room . . . it is a circular building in Leicester Square, near where we used to live when we first married. It has only just opened as an amusement. Come, dear, you need a holiday!"

I was touched and pleased by William's gesture, and curious as to what a Panorama really was. I put on my coat and best blue bonnet, and we set out for Leicester Square, locating the entrance on Cran-bourne Street.

William paid 1s. apiece for us, and we walked through a narrow passage that led to a huge ground floor space, about ninety feet in diameter. In the centre we mounted a circular platform with a balustrade. From here we could see an immense circular canvas, about thirty feet from the edge of our platform, depicting Blackfriar's Bridge as if from the Albion Sugar Mills at Southwark, spanning the Thames with many little watercraft on the River, and the dome of St. Paul's on the far shore. This view surrounded us on all sides, and in the middle of our platform was a column which supported another platform above us. This we reached by climbing three flights of stairs at the side of the building. I was quite exhausted, arriving panting at the top. But William, who was in fine fettle, had got there well ahead of me.

"Just look at this!" he cried, thrilled.

For indeed, up here was a perfect illusion of being in the midst of a new space. A skylight was the only source of light, but here it was deflected by a canopy so that the scene was illuminated by an unseen sun. Up here we were in the Lakes or in Scotland; it was more than just looking at a picture, for there were no frames to separate us from the prospect, and nothing external to measure distance by, so that we were enwrapped by the view.

"Can you imagine what this would do for a battle scene!" said William. "You would be right in the middle of it!"

"That is the next project, Sir," said a voice next to us. It was William Hayley, smiling in recognition. "And permit me to introduce Robert Barker, inventor and artist, owner of the Panorama."

"We are indeed happy to meet you, Sir," said William, "and to see you again, Mr. Hayley."

"It is always a memorable occasion when I can meet Mrs. Blake," said Hayley, gallantly. "It makes a memorable experience even better. Are you troubled by Vertigo up here? Many people are."

"Not at all." I felt myself colouring under Hayley's steadfast gaze.

"I was just saying to Mr. Barker that the sketches of London downstairs would make a fine book if engraved," Hayley said.

And so it transpired that William was asked to do engravings of the scenes depicted on the Panorama, the sketches being done originally by Barker's son, Henry. But as I remember, it was one of those projects that William was dilatory about, and I do not know what became of the engravings, or if he was ever paid for them.

The experience of the Panorama was a lovely memory for us both, and I noticed afterwards that William's designs strove for an airy atmosphere that would try to take one out of the frame of the picture into another dimension.

"Hayley certainly has an eye for you, Kate," remarked William as we walked home. He seemed quite amused by the idea.

"He makes me uncomfortable," was all I said.

Mary Wollstonecraft went to Le Havre in January to join Gilbert Imlay, although he had not asked her. She had sent news of herself to Joseph, who had been asked to send her money. Poor Mary! For one so proud, it must have been terrible for her to ask for help. She must have decided Imlay would have to support her if she joined him.

Joseph said Imlay had taken lodgings for them in the home of an English Soap Merchant, and Mary worked on her book about the Revolution while she awaited the birth of her baby. Imlay seemed to go to Paris frequently.

Mary wrote that she liked living in France. Even throughout the troubles she found that life was better for the Female Sex there. Her reputation was not ruined because she had an unconventional liaison and was expecting a child. Nevertheless she called herself Mrs. Imlay.

Letter from Mary Wollstonecraft to Catherine Blake.
August 25, 1794.

My dear Kate,

I write to tell you of my good fortune in being delivered of a daughter on May 25, three months ago. She is a fine baby, and her birth was easy. Her name is Françoise, but we call her Fanny.

Gilbert and I love her tenderly. She is a fine baby, with a fuzz of brown hair and brown eyes. She is growing well, and sucking so vigorously Gilbert says she will soon be writing the second part of the Rights of Woman! I was up and about eight days after the birth—most women here stay indoors for a month, but my mind was ready, and so I bade my body to do what I wished.

You perhaps have heard that the Terror is over. Robespierre is dead. He was shot through the jaw, and then guillotined. Perhaps he had attempted to shoot himself, no one knows. He who had desired to make the Terror an instrument of Virtue to cleanse the Revolution of its enemies, had become himself an enemy, denounced as a tyrant. Danton had already been executed in April. It is reported that he called out, "Infamous Robespierre, the scaffold claims you!... You'll follow me!" And so it proved.

Gilbert has gone to Paris to see what is happening, and today he has written that he must go to London. He will send for me and Fanny within a few weeks. Perhaps you and William will meet him!

Your devoted Friend,
Mary

William said, "Indeed I have met him. He is a vainglorious lout, albeit a fine figure of a man. And he has an eye for women. He will break her heart."

William worked continually on his own Bible, which he called *The Book of Urizen*, followed by *The Book of Ahania*, and *the Book of Los*.

It was as if, after seeing the Panorama, he was at home in the Cosmos: all Space and Time were part of his Imagination. The characters illustrated in these poems are all in tremendous pain: they clutch themselves in agony, or they thrust upward with terrible burdens. It was as if he wrote about himself:

Here alone I in books formd of metals
Have written the secrets of wisdom
The secrets of dark contemplation

I knew that William was one of those men who think all the time, no matter what they are doing. He was always trying to make sense of religion and politics; he would never accept anyone else's ideas before trying them out on the anvil of his own mind. That is why his favorite character was a blacksmith, whom he called *Los*. It is Los who creates Urizen, who is the God of William's Bible. William thought of himself as Los. He knew he had Genius, and I knew it, too. That was why it was so hard to see that the public did not recognize it. And privately, I continued to worry about William's state of mind.

We were working harder and harder, drumming up commissions for commercial work, and William was all the time working on his own visionary projects. We were always good friends, though there was a veil between us since Paul-Marc had died. I could not talk about him and William never mentioned Elizabeth Billington, yet I knew there must be more than political and religious reasons for William's dark images. It happened that in the summer of 1794 I had new insight into what was going on.

William had gone away to spend a day with George Cumberland, who was planning a book on art. I was busying myself arranging papers in the Painting Room, when a knock came at the door. I answered myself, because we had no servant. And there stood Elizabeth Billington.

She was dressed elaborately in sprigged silk, with a green shawl that must have come from an Indian Maharajah. Her fair hair was high, and her bosom cut low, and it was heaving.

"May I speak with you privately, Mrs. Blake?" She had always called me Kate before. Her eyes were deep blue and imploring.

In surprise, I ushered her into the house, and led her to the sitting room, where we had a couple of oak chairs and a tea table. I was glad I had put some daisies in a tankard that morning to decorate the table.

Elizabeth's slender fingers played with the fringe on her shawl. I was conscious of my own work-worn hands. I folded them firmly in my lap.

"You know that your husband and I are . . . friends, I think?" There was a slight hesitation in her voice.

"Yes."

"Let me assure you, I would not be here except . . . except that I do most sincerely care for him."

"Really."

"Mrs. Blake, this is very difficult for me. I know you must think it very odd that I am here . . . but you see, it is for William's safety!"

"What do you mean?"

"It . . . it is my husband, James. He is a violent man." She paused.

It occurred to me that here in my rather humble sitting room was one of London's most famous singers and actresses. And she seemed to want something from me.

"Of what concern is your husband to me?" I tried not to be unmannerly, but I rather enjoyed the moment.

"It is just that I know he is desperately jealous. And he has taken it into his mind that William Blake has cuckolded him . . ."

"Well, has he not?" I looked at her sharply, suddenly curious in an almost lustful way, imagining the soft curves of her body, the pale breasts, the hollows of her collarbones. I saw her through William's eyes. Yet I felt an attraction to her myself; she had beautiful eyes, and if it is true that the eyes are the windows of the soul, then she had a beautiful soul. I realized that strangely, I liked Elizabeth, even while I resented that she had a part of William that I felt was mine.

Elizabeth paused and fingered a curl at the nape of her neck.

"William has been a wonderful friend to me, I will not deny that. I am sorry if you have been distressed. But you must listen, there is not much time! James is going to challenge William to a Duel!"

I could hardly keep from laughing. A Duel? Who could imagine William in a Duel? He had never even held a Pistol as far as I knew.

"Are you serious?"

"Yes, of course. Do you think I would be here if I were not? James is going to visit you this evening and challenge William. Oh, please, take William away. . . . Do not let this happen! James is a good shot! And think of the scandal!"

I calmed Elizabeth as best I could, and sent her away with the assurance that I would warn William and we would leave the neighborhood this evening, though I did not think for a minute that we would. I saw her leave with a curious wave of affection for her. We were sisters in a strange sort of way.

I did not know whether to be alarmed or not at her news, but I did think I should tell William.

Suddenly I pictured a scene: it is early morning in a wood near London. Four men are gathered in a close group—suddenly they part, and William and James, choosing pistols, walk fifteen paces in opposite directions. They turn. There is the loud report of gunfire. William falls to the ground. Dead.

Oh, William, how could I live without you? What would I do? Who would look after me? Oh, poor William. I knew he would never survive a duel.

And then James would be tried for murder. I saw that scene in my mind, too. The dark-robed judges with their white wigs, solemn faced, sentencing James Billington to death. And Elizabeth weeping. And I would weep, too. And all of London would buzz with gossip, because Elizabeth was famous, and her husband had shot the engraver, William Blake. Henry Fuseli would say, Damn it, Kate, you shouldn't haff let him do it!

I said to William at dinner, "Your mistress was here today."

He dropped his fork.

"Who do you mean?" he hedged.

"Do you suggest there is more than one?"

"Kate! Please. Was it Elizabeth? Here?"

"Yes. She is concerned for your safety. Evidently James Billington is going to defend his wife's Honour and challenge you. Imagine—a Duel!"

"My God!" exclaimed William, actually blushing.

"What will you do?" I asked. "Shall we leave town?"

"Of course not," he said. "I cannot take this seriously."

At that very moment, a knock sounded at our door. I suddenly became genuinely afraid.

William opened the door, and there stood James Billington, resplendent in a cutaway coat, white breeches and high leather boots. Next to him stood another man, equally well dressed, who was introduced as Elizabeth's brother, Michael.

"Do come in," said William.

"I have come to challenge you," said James, stepping into our sitting room. "You know the reason, I think." He was a good-looking man with something mean about his mouth.

"Oh, indeed?" said William, coolly. "Pray, be seated, gentlemen."

I hovered in the doorway.

"Some port, please, Mrs. Blake," said William, taking charge of the situation. I hurriedly went to fetch a decanter and glasses and when I returned, the men were in earnest conversation.

"So you wish to meet me with pistols in Hampstead Heath tomorrow," William was saying.

"And you must choose a second," said Michael. He seemed shy and reminded me of Elizabeth. I had heard he was also a musician.

I had an incongruous flash of little cat-like Henry Fuseli bearing pistols for William.

Suddenly a strange thing happened. William began to speak, and none of us could take our eyes from him. He spoke of Love, between man and woman, between man and man. He could see no Sin in Love, he said. As he spoke, an aura appeared around him. I do not know what else to call it. It was light, outlining all his figure. I have seen auras before, but never like this.

James and Michael could see it, too. They blanched and clutched the arms of their chairs. The light became brighter, brighter than the candles illuminating the room. William seemed to be taller and larger. He dominated us all. He spoke of Brotherhood, of Imagination and Spirit.

James was the first to break down.

"Ah, Mr. Blake, will you forgive me?" he said. "I was mistaken to come. I mean you no harm."

"Elizabeth is fortunate to know you," mumbled Michael.

The light continued to glow around William as he ushered them out of the house. I stared in amazement at my own husband.

He looked at me, a little smile hovering about his lips.

"A soft answer turneth away wrath," he quoted.

The Flaxmans returned to London and took a house in FitzRoy Square. They invited us around in February of 1795 to take tea. William was delighted at the prospect of seeing them again. I went with some trepidation. Would they somehow find out about the forgeries? I had stopped selling drawings when I first heard they were returning. It had been seven years since they had gone away, seven years in which John Flaxman had become famous and William Blake had not.

It was one of the coldest winters in years. The Thames and its canals froze for several weeks, but the sun shone, making the frost sparkle on the window panes. I dressed carefully in the sunlight, arranging my worn lace collar over my plain brown wool frock. I had at least new lace cuffs, which came just below my elbows. I knew I was thinner than I had been a few years ago, but I still had enough bosom to fill the neckline of my dress, and I had carefully arranged my dark hair which was still curly and abundant, though showing a few strands of grey—after all, I had thirty-six years now.

It was my hands which would give me away, I feared. They were small, but strong and square, and slightly reddened with work, hands which Paul-Marc had kissed. My nails were worn down, and there always seemed a bit of ink or paint that clung to their corners. Oh, well, I could hide them in my shawl, which William had given me for Christmas, a lovely bit of fringed silk. I suspect it had come from Elizabeth, who had departed for Italy with her husband. I had taken a deep breath of relief when I heard they had gone.

John Flaxman greeted us warmly. He looked older, still frail and stooped, but he had an air of authority about him that he had lacked before. I could tell by his face that he found me changed. Nancy was plumper than before, but no less friendly, which I found comforting, because she was used to keeping company with grander folk than William and me. Their sitting room was painted pale green, with many of Flaxman's fine line drawings of Homer's *Iliad* framed in gold leaf on the walls. (They seemed like old friends to me!) Otherwise the room was bare of decoration, with only chairs and a table or two of some highly polished wood. We were introduced to a young man of about fourteen, who turned out to be William Hayley's son, Thomas Alfonso.

"Tom, here, is our young Sculptor," said John. "He is my Apprentice now." Tom was a slight, sensitive-looking lad, with long, light brown hair. I did not suppose he had his father's Passion for galloping over fields on a good horse.

William Hayley himself arrived a short while into our visit. He was all smiles.

"Do you know," he said to me, "Tom is reading History and Greek and Latin with the Flaxmans, and Mrs. Flaxman has taught him to play *Begone dull care* on her pianoforte! And he is learning to model in clay."

I found his pride in his boy touching. The Flaxmans were childless, like us, and I could see that this young man filled a void in their lives. Worldly success was not everything.

I decided I was not even going to think about worrying whether William would be attracted to Nancy Flaxman again. There they were, sipping tea together and smiling. He was telling her of his latest Project, a series of large Colour Printed drawings, mostly on Biblical subjects, though he planned a picture of Isaac Newton, too. Each print was finished by hand

I could have told her how we kept the copper plates warm on our coal-burning kitchen-range, along with the Colours in their little pots. We put the pigments right on the plates. But I do not think anyone was very interested in my part in William's work. Except perhaps William Hayley. He always found some excuse to begin a conversation with me. He asked me about my Health. I confessed to a few fleeting pains in the joints of my hands.

"Ah, I know the very remedy for that!" he exclaimed. "I am something of a physician, you know. I look after all my tenants at Felpham. Now what you must do is get some comfrey root, and mash it up, then spread it upon a small piece of leather. Then you apply this to your joints. It will provide great relief, believe me!"

I said I would try it. I knew that Cathy would have some dried comfrey root in her stores, and in the summer I could always find it growing tall in the fields. But fancy Mr. Hayley being interested in physic!

When I later remarked on this to William, he pointed out that Hayley loved to do things for people. He was always ministering to Romney, who had the Melancholy. Looking back, I think now that it was too bad he could not save his son Tom, who died only five years later, some say from forcing him to do too much, but in reality it was a curvature of the spine.

"I am concerned for Mary," said William, returning from St. Paul's Churchyard one evening, looking quite serious. "Gilbert Imlay has a new mistress. He is never going to send for Mary and her babe."

I felt a deep sorrow for her. She had written me not long before that Gilbert was a fine man and they would soon be reunited in London. Mary could never bear to be wrong about anyone.

"She is short of money," said William. "I can't see how she can support herself and the child's nurse."

The baby was weaned now, running about happily, Mary had said. I suppressed a pang of envy. Mary seemed to be living life; I seemed always to observe it. Certainly, Mary was unhappy now, but she still was in charge of her own fate, even though it might seem to some that she was buffeted by Passion and only reacted to that. It was true that it had been to escape the humiliation of her love for Fuseli that she had left for France. Once there, she had written a book, and had a baby, and experienced the Revolution. I knew no other woman who lived independently; all were in the shadow of their husbands, like me and Nancy Flaxman. Even Elizabeth, who had a great talent, was at the mercy of her violent husband.

Soon I was surprised to receive a note from Mary. It was from 26 Charlotte Street, London: I am back in London. I would be happy to have you call on me.

I went the next day. She was living in barely furnished lodgings. Mary herself looked lovely. Motherhood had softened her features, and her brown hair was softly arranged. She embraced me warmly.

"Ah, Kate, how men do use us!" she exclaimed. I wondered if something about my appearance had prompted that remark but said nothing.

"Here's my little cherub!" Little year-old Fanny came toddling into the room, accompanied by her nurse, Marguerite, who spoke French to her.

"What a lovely child," I said, touching her brown curls.

"You know, I wanted to raise her in France," said Mary. "I felt a real horror at having to come back to England. She would be raised freer in France. I am so unhappy here."

There was not much I could say. Then she told me something shocking.

"I took too much laudanum last week," she confessed, pacing up and down the room. "Poor Marguerite was quite beside herself. She tried to give me reasons for living. She even called Gilbert!"

"Oh, Mary! Think of your child!"

"I did. She would be better off with Gilbert. I really do not see much use for my life. But Gilbert does have a plan for me, it appears. He is sending me to Scandinavia."

It was so like Mary to have something unusual like this to announce. It seemed that Gilbert had shipping interests in Sweden and Norway, and his cargoes had gone astray. He wanted Mary to straighten things out. She was going to depart in June.

"It is a clever man that can send his discarded mistress on a sea journey to the frozen North for his own business interests!" observed William.

Mary wrote many wonderful letters of her travels in Scandinavia to Imlay. I know this because Johnson later published them as *Letters Written during a Short Residence in Denmark, Norway, and Sweden*. She was a great Observer of people and landscape and foreign customs, and a courageous traveler. She had taken her baby with her. It was a journey to remote places, taken with a heavy heart. When the letters were published, they were very popular with the Public. By then, Mary had experienced the depths of despair and yet another suicide attempt, for she faced the fact that Imlay would never live with her as her husband.

I had seen her shortly after her return from Scandinavia, once again in her lodgings in Charlotte Street. Her face was drawn and tired.

"How many proofs of his indifference must I suffer!" she

exclaimed. "Gracious God! I have tried to be tranquil, to suppress my emotions, and all I do is stifle all the energy of my soul!"

And then she confided in me that she had even questioned a Servant of Imlay's about his living arrangements, and discovered that he had yet another lover, an Actress. I was humiliated for her. Yet, I envied her still, for she had a plump little daughter running about, bringing smiles to every face. She was living out her own beliefs of sexual freedom and honesty. I observed that she was taking no solace in this. She was saying alarming things.

"I have written to Gilbert," she said, "and I have told him I shall plunge into the Thames where there is the least chance of being rescued!"

"You cannot mean this!" I exclaimed. "Think of your baby!"

"She will be better off with Gilbert," said Mary. "I shall appear to him in memory. He shall be full of remorse!"

There is nothing one can say to people like that. Mary was bent on self-destruction. She did indeed jump into the Thames. She chose a rainy night in October and leapt off Putney Bridge.

I imagined it all . . . how she must have set off in the rain, walking towards Battersea, where, soaked through, she rented a small boat and rowed upstream to Putney Bridge. I imagined the thoughts that were in her mind, illogical thoughts: He will be sorry; he will weep for me. Or self-pitying thoughts: I am worthless; I have accomplished nothing.

She would have had to pay a halfpenny at the tollgate after she beached her boat under the old wooden bridge. She must have concealed herself on the bridge in the alcoves where foot passengers could protect themselves from coaches. Her clothes would be drenched, her hair wet. She would be shivering. No longer thinking coherent thoughts, bent only on her dismal desire to end her suffering, she climbs on to the wooden railing of the bridge, hampered by her sodden clothing, and jumps.

She told me later that she was surprised by pain. She floated, she did not sink, and choking and gasping, the agony in her chest roused her to coherent thought.

I should have chosen another way to die. And then she mercifully lost consciousness. She had been seen. The watermen rescued her, took her to a Public House in Fulham, and called a doctor.

Mary convalesced at the home of Thomas and Rebecca Christie in Finsbury Square. The Christies had last year returned to London from France, where Thomas's French mistress had sued to regain custody of their daughter. Little Julie was happily playing with baby Fanny the day I paid Mary a visit. Rebecca was a good friend to Mary, as they had all lived in Paris during the Revolution, and I supposed that they had introduced her to Gilbert Imlay, as Thomas was now in business with him. I could tell that Mary was hoping Gilbert would call while she was staying with the Christies. Her scheme of making a travel book of the letters she had sent him from Scandinavia came to her there.

I think Gilbert Imlay was one of those men who cannot bear to be unkind when you are in his company but will write you the most devastatingly cruel letters when you are out of it. That seemed to be his pattern with Mary. She was always clinging to a faint hope that he would return to her and the baby, because he never managed to say frankly to her that it was not going to happen. Mary even moved her lodgings to Finsbury Place to be closer to him and the Christies. But Imlay and his actress had gone to Paris for several weeks.

"I exist in a living tomb," said Mary to me, "and my life is but an exercise in fortitude continually on the stretch."

At last things came to a head. Imlay had been back in London about a fortnight when Mary happened to call in at Christies' home one evening, her baby accompanying her. The house was bright and comfortable, with a marble fireplace at one end always glowing with a coal fire. The room was full of company, Mr. Imlay among them. Above the hum of conversation, Rebecca heard Mary's voice in the passage, and hurried to her.

"Pray, do not come in, Mary," she said, "for Gilbert is in the room."

"But why should I shrink from the presence of one who has wronged me!" Mary exclaimed.

She strode into the room, her black skirts billowing, with two-year old Fanny at her side, and led the child purposefully to where Imlay sat. He stood up in a gentlemanly manner and instantly suggested that the three of them retire into another room.

"He was then so kind to me," Mary told me later, "that once again I gave myself up to castles in air, and imagined a future with him."

But he disappointed her again. Briefly, she thought he would take her to live with him and his mistress in the kind of *ménage à trois* she had once suggested to Fuseli, but that never happened.

Once Mary saw clearly that Imlay would never renew their connection, she finally cast him out of her heart. I had seen her do this with Fuseli. It took her a long time and much grief to quench her emotions, but she eventually accepted the situation. Yet I never after heard her say anything critical of either Imlay or Fuseli. It was as if, because she had loved them, they were still the best of men.

William had a busy year. He finished all his work for Stedman, who had sent us a plump goose for Christmas. In June, Stedman had visited us in London for two days, and given me a little blue sugar bowl. We had printed and coloured a complete set of the Illuminated Books, now on larger paper, and besides these, William produced a set of twelve Colour Prints. These had a wonderful rich dense texture because he painted them upon common millboard with oil colours, and would take a print from that, and recolour it. These designs expressed William's ideas on religion and science and many other mysterious ideas besides.

I liked especially the design called *The Elohim creating Adam*. William said this was the name of God in Genesis. He painted him as an old man with eagle wings hovering over the prostrate form of Adam, whose body is encircled by a worm. Adam's arms are outstretched as if he were on the cross to mirror the creating arms of God. Both appear to be in pain.

The companion piece to this is *Satan Exulting Over Eve*. Here Eve is prostrate on the ground. She looks dead, though her hair is spread out luxuriantly around her. She reminded me of Elizabeth. Eve is wrapped about by a serpent, almost embraced by it. I know William was expressing in these paintings his ideas of our human Fall from the Eternal into Mortality.

From these paintings, I could read William's state of mind. There was a portrait of Isaac Newton, bending down as if he were a young naked "Ancient of Days," creating with his compasses diagrams of science in an undersea world, our world of mortal life. He cannot see anything but his diagrams, so concentrated is his gaze. And there was Nebuchadnezzar, the King, gone mad, on all fours, becoming a beast, becoming what he beheld. William's pictures reflected a dark vision

Blake, *Satan Exulting Over Eve* (c. 1795). Courtesy of Tate Gallery, London/ Art Resource, New York

of the world, but a vision not without grandeur and passion. One cannot paint darkly if one does not have a vision of the light.

It was, I thought, another aspect of a view of the world like Mary's, a passion for life, but less hopeful of the outcome. Mary revelled in her Sensibilities. I could never be like her, so ready to abandon myself to Feeling, to cast myself into a cold river for love. But of course, I was no Genius. I had no maid named Marguerite to help with the tasks of everyday life as Mary did. I had no Wife to mend my clothes and empty my chamber-pot as William had. I think it is everyday life that keeps one in good Sense.

From Kate's Notebook.
Friday, January 8, 1796.

William is writing again, a long, strange work he calls *Vala*. This is the reason I heard the voice of Enion, and a few times she has returned, but mostly now she belongs to William. He is trying to account for nothing less than the way the human mind works, and the reasons for our political troubles:

> Enion blind and age-bent wept upon the desolate wind
> Why does the Raven cry aloud and no eye pities her?
> Why fall the Sparrow and the Robin in the foodless winter?
> Faint! Shivering they sit on leafless bush, or frozen stone

This winter we have famine abroad in England, and rioting in the streets for bread. People want peace with France, but the government spies upon everyone. William believes we must keep our thoughts secret.

"There is a British Inquisition," he said, "and a Black List of English Jacobins." We dare not speak out for Peace or Reform of Parliament. In the margin of *America*, William etched the words which showed his dismay and fear:

> The stern Bard ceas'd, ashamed of his own song; enraged he
> swung
> His harp aloft sounding, then dash'd its shining frame against
> A ruin'd pillar in glittering fragments; silent he turn'd away
> And wander'd down the vales of Kent in sick and drear
> lamentings.

That day we had indeed walked down the Old Kent Road. After that, though he still wrote against War and he still prophesied a new revolution, despite what had happened in France, William never wrote very clearly about it. He hid his thoughts in "wild and whirling words"— I remember that line from *Hamlet* when I read Shakespeare with Mary.

15

In Which Mary Marries and Dies

I observed to Mr. Tatham that the next four years brought us to the New Century, 1800. Time passed swiftly because so much happened, fate catapulting us eventually to Felpham and the sea. Before we reached there, we had to live through disappointment and death.

William had received the biggest commission of his life from Richard Edwards, a young bookseller in New Bond Street. It was to complete a series of watercolour drawings by the end of 1796 for the text of the poet Edward Young's *Night Thoughts*. They would then be engraved in a large format, and be a most popular book, for Edward Young was much read. There was to be a picture for all five hundred and more pages of the poem, but only about two hundred were to be engraved.

William agreed to do the job for twenty guineas, which I thought was much too little, but he said he expected a steady income from the engravings. God knows, we needed it now that my secret source of extra money had ceased.

The drawings were interestingly placed to surround the text of the poem, and he chose a line for each page to illustrate. The full title of the poem was *The Complaint and the Consolation: or Night Thoughts on Life, Death, and Immortality*, so one can imagine how serious it was. Young's ideas were very like William's, with an exalted vision of human destiny, and the thought that Angels were merely "Men of a Superior Kind."

One night, William was reading Young's line, "who can paint an Angel," and he said aloud, "Aye, Who can paint an angel?"

And a voice said, "Michel Angelo could."

William looked around the room to see who had spoken, but he only noticed a greater light than usual.

He said to the voice, "And how do you know?"

And the voice said, "I know, for I sat to him: I am the archangel Gabriel."

William said, "Oho! You are, are you? I must have better assurance than that of a wandering voice; you may be an evil spirit—there are such in the land."

"You shall have good assurance," said the voice. "Can an evil spirit do this?"

William looked whence the voice came and was then aware of a shining shape with bright wings, who diffused much light. As he looked, the shape dilated more and more.

"He waved his hands," said William, "and the roof of my study opened—he ascended into heaven. He stood in the sun, and beckoning to me, moved the universe. An angel of evil could not have done that—it was the archangel Gabriel."

Henry Fuseli was always a little skeptical when William told him such things.

"Damn it, Blake, if you vant to be a member of the Royal Academy, you can't talk like that!" And he was right, because though we heard a rumour that William might be accepted into the Royal Academy, he never was.

Night Thoughts did not appear till the winter of 1797, and then only in a single volume containing Four Nights, with only forty-three engravings. About two hundred copies were printed, and some were beautifully coloured, though not so beautiful as the watercolours, in my opinion. They were displayed in Edwards's shop with the book, because William had done all 537, and they were large and striking. Soon Edwards went out of business.

In the designs for *Night Thoughts*, I saw the recurring figure of Jesus Christ. There were Nine Nights, and it was all about the Fall and Redemption, the central idea being about man's struggle with doubt. I think William recognized this struggle, and the picture of the dynamic figure of Christ rising in a great triumphant leap told me how deeply he lived the religious life.

I had taken to going to The New Jerusalem Church at Store Street on Sundays without telling William. Even though I had not sold a forged drawing for months, my Conscience was not clear and vague nightmares of Guilt and Discovery plagued me. I feared the wrath of a judgmental God.

In Church, I loved the hymns, the music, and the moments of silence and peace. The sermons reminded me of William's poem, "The Divine Image":

> Then every man in every clime,
> That prays in his distress,
> Prays to the human form divine
> Love Mercy Pity Peace.
> And all must love the human form,
> In heathen, turk or jew.
> Where Mercy, Love & Pity dwell,
> There God is dwelling too.

I could cease to hate God if I thought of Him in Human Form as Jesus. That was, after all, the form of Paul-Marc, of William, and myself. The tyrant God, the Ancient of Days, was like a weight on my soul that I was glad to shrug off.

The Flaxmans admired William's work on *Night Thoughts*. John asked William to illustrate Thomas Gray's *Poems* for Nancy's library. It was a Birthday Gift for her. He wanted them in a similar manner to the Young, with the designs surrounding the poetic text. John

Blake, line engraving for Edward Young's *Night Thoughts* (1797), Title Page for Night the Fourth, *The Christian Triumph*. Courtesy of Yale Center for British Art, Paul Mellon Collection

commissioned 116 watercolours. On the last page, William wrote a little poem to Nancy, "A little Flower grew in a lonely Vale/Its form was lovely but its colours pale . . ." He always liked to play the Nature Poet for her.

It used to annoy me that we would go to visit the Flaxmans and William would behave like a Gentleman instead of the honest Engraver he was, and even John and Nancy would behave as if they had always been well-off and bred to better things. I would sit silent, wrapped in the Indian shawl that William had given me, and pretend that I was the songbird in the cage that Nancy kept in the sitting-room, and observed the group with a bird-like eye.

The room was lit by several candles, quite extravagant, I thought. One night, another couple was present, a Mr. and Mrs. Thomas Butts. He was a small, neatly made man with lots of fair curly hair, very well groomed. Mrs. Butts was plump and blonde. She talked of her many daughters and her large house in Great Marlborough Street. I had seen the two of them at the New Jerusalem Church. They were Swedenborgians like the Flaxmans. Mr. Butts was chief clerk in the War Office, and he spoke as if he were a man of means.

The men were discussing the influence of Sir Joshua Reynolds, the first president of the Royal Academy, who had died in 1792.

"That Man was hired to depress Art!" said William vehemently. "I heard him myself as a student, giving a discourse in the Lecture Room. It was all about General Beauty and General Truth! To Generalize is to be an Idiot!"

"I am inclined to agree with you," said Mr. Butts, "though Reynolds was a great painter of portraits."

"I have seen his portrait of Elizabeth Billington," I volunteered in a small voice. "It was very like her."

William coughed.

"It was certainly in his Grand Style," he said dryly.

"I hear that James Billington has died of Apoplexy in Italy," said Nancy, "but Mrs. Billington is still pursuing her operatic career."

"I am sorry to hear she is alone," said William.

What Irony, I thought, that she should be deprived of a husband, when I feared that her husband would shoot mine.

"I doubt that Mrs. Billington would be alone for long," said Nancy, cheerfully. "She and Lady Hamilton are acquainted, I believe."

"Lady Hamilton—didn't she used to be Emma Hart?" asked Mrs. Butts. "The one that Romney loved to paint? Don't we have one of those pictures, Mr. Butts?"

"I do believe so, my dear," he replied. "He has a great facility with colour. I hear you are a great colourist, Mr. Blake. May we come and see your work some time soon?" And that was the beginning of our friendship with Mr. and Mrs. Butts.

"I have created a System," said William to me one day as were busy at the Press. "I have been struggling for a long time, but I see now that Four Mighty Ones Exist in every man."

"What do you mean?" I asked. "Four Mighty Whats? In every Man? What exists in every Woman?"

"Do not mock me, Kate. Four Mighty Ones exist in Man and Woman. They are parts of our Mind. Consider: We are creatures of Reason; we can weigh and measure—pass the dabber, please—we can choose our actions. That is One Mighty One. I have named him *Urizen.*"

William finished inking with the dabber and I placed a sheet of damp paper on the bed of the press.

"Yes, I can see that," I said, "and what is another?" Oh, watch the registration, there. I lined the paper up exactly.

"You can guess, surely. If you are not Reasoning, what are you doing?"

"Feeling?"

"Exactly. That is the Second Mighty One. I have named him *Luvah.*"

"And the Third Mighty One?"

"Ah, that is the best. It is what we cannot do without. He creates the world for us: he is the Imagination. I call him *Urthona.*"

"I have pulled the bed under the roller . . . there, the first impressions are done. And so what is the Fourth Mighty One? I cannot think what Faculty is left."

I removed the impressions, and placed them on a table, while William inked the plates which were to be the next batch. Then I printed again.

"What is left is very important. It is the force which holds the

Mind together, the Parent Power of Thought and of Speech. *Tharmas*, I call him."

Now all the leaves were printed, and I hung them to dry on a clothesline above our heads.

"And do these Mighty Ones not have Female Partners?" I asked.

"Of course they do," said William, "only I have not named them just yet, except for Enion and Enitharmon, of course. But I'll tell you something else. They have different names in the Fallen World."

"This is too complicated for me," I said, trying to wash some ink off my hands.

"By God, you are a good 'printer's devil,' Kate," said William, kissing my neck. "I'll have to work you into my System."

"You'd better!" I said.

Mary Wollstonecraft had moved yet again, in order to start a better life. She settled with Fanny and her maid, Marguerite, in a pretty little house off the Pentonville Road in Cumming Street. She began to go out into society again.

She was still famous for her book on the rights of women, and for her travel book on Sweden, so many single women sought her out. The great actress Mrs. Siddons called on her, and Mary met her brother, the actor John Kemble. In my experience, actors and actresses only brought trouble, but I suppose it was different for Mary. She went to the theatre a good deal.

She was often in the company of William Godwin, who was a famous atheist thinker and writer. He was a big, good-looking man, who in my view had a great opinion of himself. But it was probably deserved, for in 1794 he had published a widely-read book about crime and human morality called *Adventures of Caleb Williams*. We had seen Godwin occasionally at Johnson's, where Mary, too, had first met him a few years ago. She had annoyed him by talking too much, I recall, when he had wanted to talk to Tom Paine. But now, they were talking to each other all the time, and loving each other's company.

I believe that Mary set out to marry William Godwin quite purposefully. She always maintained that she did not believe in Marriage—nor did he—but she did have little Fanny to support, and she did see the sad spectacle of actresses who were abandoned by their lovers and were not getting any younger. Godwin was much admired by a number of literary women, each of whom made Mary jealous. In any case, she became his mistress. I know this because she showed me a love letter he had written to her: "For six and thirty hours I could think of nothing but you. I longed inexpressibly to have you in my arms. Why did I not come to you? I am a fool . . ." And so it went, an honest letter, longing for her. Mary had not had a man love her since her brief experience with Gilbert Imlay, and she liked the act of love. She was not ashamed of her own nature; that was one of the things that kept us friends. I was neither a literary lady nor an actress nor a writer, but I could talk to her frankly of women's matters, and Mary was always curious.

"Does the act of love bring you pleasure every time?" she asked me once.

"Not every time," I answered truthfully, "but almost."

She blushed. "Godwin is a good lover," she admitted, "though he likes to pretend his passion is all in the mind."

"William considers sex a Mystery," I confessed. "It is something he needs to be creative. Desire is almost as important as the act for him."

"Ah, yes," she said, as if remembering something. I felt an old resentment surface.

She told me that she was writing a novel called *Maria, or the Wrongs of Woman*, all about the hardships of being Female in our time, and our lack of legal rights. She also wanted to describe honestly the sexual feelings that women experience. I wish Mary had let me read some of that novel, though I do not think she ever finished it. I used to think it was lucky I had married William, for a Country girl could come to a terrible End in the City. Had not Mr. Hogarth shown us just such a story in *The Harlot's Progress?*

Mary's romance with Godwin was not without its storms and jealousies. Godwin did not believe in Marriage in principle, and Mary began to worry that she was pregnant. When he went to the theatre with Mrs. Inchbald, an actress and playwright whom Mary considered one of her chief rivals for Godwin's affection, she staged a terrible row.

"You are cold and bitter," he told her. "Your moods crush me."

Mary said to me in February of 1797, "I am with child again, and

I cannot face the thought of being unmarried and bringing another child into the world, even though my theatrical friends seem to think Fanny and I are fashionable."

I thought how well Mary looked, with high colour and her brown hair carefully arranged these days. I knew that she was terrified that Godwin would treat her as Imlay had done and abandon her.

Thankfully, Godwin was not like Imlay. He swallowed his principles and married her on the twenty-ninth of March at St. Pancras Church, just across the fields from where Mary lived. They moved into a new house together, No. 29 The Polygon, a handsome three-storey house, and Godwin took separate rooms for a study.

Mary was almost house-proud as she showed me the rooms. She had taken her furniture out of storage, and displayed some pretty blue and white China from the Wedgewood pottery. William and I had called to congratulate her and Mr. Godwin, who received us cordially. Since he was so long known for his ridicule of the married state, he was eager to prove he had not lost any independence, and told us of his spacious rooms for study where he spent most of the day.

I heard that Mary's theatrical friends laughed when they learned she had married and did not call upon her. I suppose they felt she had let them down. Mary even invited Fuseli to dinner with William and me, to show him how well she was doing, I suspected. Fuseli was bored by the company. "By God, if it were not for you, Blake, I would die of Boredom! That Godwin is Dullness personified!"

I think Mary may have found her husband a bit boring, too, and his unrelenting atheism was not congenial to her as her pregnancy progressed. I took her with me to the New Jerusalem Church from time to time. I think she repented of her suicide attempts. She looked forward to a new baby, and her little Fanny was a charming, bonny child. It did seem that her life had changed for the better, or at least it was more secure for her, and she and Godwin took to calling each other "Mama" and "Papa" in an affectionate manner. If Mary felt a loss of independence amidst her domesticity, she did not show it to me.

Mary was going to be attended by a Midwife, Mrs. Blenkinsop, the matron in charge of the Westminster Lying-In Hospital. By now Cathy Blake, who had been trained in herbs and midwifery by Mrs. Goodhouse, happened to be an assistant of Mrs. Blenkinsop, and visited Mary several times previous to her confinement.

Cathy was now a tall, calm young woman, with a superior air. Since Paul-Marc had died, she remained distant with me, though she visited us once or twice a month. She was still fond of William, and would bring him herbs to make infusions which calmed him when he was hard at work. It was Cathy who told me the harrowing story of Mary's labour.

"It was on Wednesday, the thirtieth of August that Mrs. Godwin's pains began," said Cathy, "though of course we had visited her several times previously. She was so calm and agreeable, and told me and Mrs. Blenkinsop to call her Mary. Was not that thoughtful? She did not expect any problems with her delivery, as she had experienced an easy time with little Fanny. She said she expected to go down to dinner the day immediately following the birth! I thought this was quite unusual, because most women I had attended kept to their chambers a full month after delivery. But Mary was determined, and of course she was in perfect health.

"I was pleased that she had chosen women to attend her, instead of a male Physician. Mr. Godwin was away in his rooms across the street, and Mary would send him notes on the progress of her labour. Mrs. Blenkinsop and I arrived about two in the afternoon, and we took her up to her bedroom on the second floor. Her little girl, Fanny, was looked after by her nurse, Marguerite. We expected the labour would be over by ten at night—about that, at least, we were not so wrong.

"Mrs. B.—as I like to call her—believed in the use of a birthing stool, but Mary preferred to lie in bed with her feet propped against a log of wood. She asked her husband not to come in till the baby was born, so he had gone out to dinner. Towards the end of her labour, the pains were very hard. We applied ginger poultices to ease her. By this time, it was late at night, and we placed many wax candles about the room. They cast dancing shadows on the walls, like dark sprites.

"'It is not like the first time,' she gasped. 'Why? Why?'

"'The child is pressing on your spine,' said Mrs. B. 'It is common, do not worry. Cry out if you wish.'

"We gave her a little drink of water between pains. She did cry out, but I admired her self-control very much. I had heard women cry more. As the baby crowned, I massaged her with butter.

"The baby was born about twenty minutes past eleven o'clock that night—a fine baby girl. I think perhaps Mary wanted a boy, because she had said it would be nice to have one child of each sex, but she smiled at her newborn. Mary's brown hair was wet with perspiration, and stuck to her forehead. I bathed her head with a cool cloth.

"'Tell Mr. Godwin he has a daughter,' she whispered to her maid, who was also present.

"'But he cannot come up yet,' said Mrs. B., looking at me significantly, 'you must pass the placenta first, Mary. One more contraction, now.'

"But the placenta did not come. We gave Mary a small drink of spirits to give her strength, for she was bleeding greatly, but no longer in pain. By three o'clock in the morning Mrs. B. and I were terribly alarmed, for the placenta was not delivered, and that meant that the womb would not contract, and bleeding continued. And not only that, we feared that infection would soon occur.

"'Send Mr. Godwin for Doctor Poignand,' said Mrs. B., by now exhausted and hot herself. We were working furiously to stop the bleeding.

"Mr. Godwin, much distressed, went out into the night to find Dr. Poignand, the Chief Man-Midwife at the Westminster Lying-In. He arrived, very serious in expression, a short stocky man. Mr. Godwin was so upset at the sight of his wife, bleeding and fainting, that he could not stay in the room. Mrs. Blenkinsop and I held Mary's shoulders while Dr. Poignand inserted his hand in Mary's womb and felt about with his fingers.

"'I fear the placenta is in pieces,' he said. I am not sure that Mary heard or understood him, for she was in and out of her senses from the terrible pain.

"As the sun came through the window at six, we were still at work, and Dr. Poignand struggled on until eight, when he thought that he had removed all the pieces of the placenta in the womb. Mr. Godwin came to see Mary, who was sleeping at last, and the baby in her cradle beside her. But Mrs. B. and I knew that infection was almost certain to set in. We cleaned up the bloody sheets and bowls in silence.

"We went home for a few hours rest, and returned before noon on Thursday with Dr. Poignand, to find Mary and Mr. Godwin cooing over their baby. Mary seemed to be doing well, and began to suckle her child. Fanny was allowed to see her new sister.

"'What is the name of the new baby?' I asked Mr. Godwin.

"'It is Mary, after her mother,' he said with a smile all around.

"On Friday, Mr. Godwin went to his study as usual, and later was called upon by Mr. Joseph Johnson, who, I think, told you and William that Mary was safe, did he not?"

From Kate's Notebook.
Tuesday, September 12, 1797.

I have now to record the sad last days of my friend Mary Wollstonecraft Godwin. Everyone thought she was going to recover. But on the Sunday after the birth, Mary had terrible shivering fits, every muscle of her body trembled, and her teeth chattered. She told me it was a struggle between life and death when I went to see her with Cathy. Dr. Poignand had come again, and another physician friend of Mary's, a Dr. Fordyce. There seemed to be people coming and going all the time.

"Please, Kate, tell them not to set dinner in the room below mine tonight," she asked. "I cannot bear the noise."

Meanwhile she was suckling the baby, but Dr. Fordyce did not think she should continue. Mary reluctantly gave her infant to a wet-nurse, and little Fanny was sent to stay with friends. That was the last time Fanny was to see her mother.

"I will come back tomorrow, Mary," I promised as I took my leave. Mary waved wanly at me, but she was shivering again.

Cathy looked very grave.

"I fear it is the onset of the Poison in her blood," she said. "There is no treatment for such infection."

It was then I really understood that Mary was going to die.

What a terrible waste, I thought. A beautiful, brilliant woman who has so much to give to her own sex, whose whole life has been devoted to the improvement of the lot of women, and she is dying of a disease only women can get. A disease I will never die of.

She lingered for another week. Poor Godwin called in every doctor he knew—a Dr. Clark, and a Dr. Carlisle also. Dr. Poignand gave up calling. Cathy said he knew the case was hopeless. Mary lay passive and weak, her mind wandering.

"Oh, Godwin, I am in heaven," she murmured. They gave her wine, thinking it would help.

Godwin tried to talk to her about the children, for he knew the care of the little girls would fall to him alone now, but all she could say as she lay pale on her pillow was, "I know what you are thinking of, but I cannot talk about them now."

Mary died at twenty minutes to eight o'clock on the morning of September tenth. William could not speak when Johnson came by with the news. But I remembered the poem William had prophetically written about her:

> O Why was I born with a different Face?
> Why was I not born like this Envious Race
> Why did heaven adorn me with bountiful hand
> And then set me down in an envious Land . . .

And I remember the lines later:

> All Faces have Envy sweet Mary but thine.
> And thine is a Face of sweet Love in Despair
> And thine is a Face of mild sorrow and care
> And thine is a Face of mild terror and fear
> That shall never be quiet till laid on its bier.

16

In Which My Cards Are Read and I Paint A Picture

*H*enry paid us a visit shortly after Mary's funeral. It was mid-September, and still warm and summery. The air was heavy in our little garden at Hercules Buildings where we sat taking tea in the late afternoon, remembering Mary.

"She was a damn fine woman," said Henry, "but too intelligent. No woman should be intelligent."

"She had a vision that the world could be improved," said William. "I admired that." He poured himself China tea from our little pot. It was a treat that Henry had brought us.

"How can a woman be too intelligent?" I ventured.

Both men looked uncomfortable.

"Don't be difficult, Kate," said Fuseli. "A woman should know her place, that's all."

"Women have too much power as it is," said William. "They rule us from cradle to grave." He stood up and surveyed the garden, most of which I had planted.

"Milton had it right," said Henry, who was much involved in his Milton Gallery project. "He for God; She for God in him."

"That is true," said William. "The female life lives from the light

of the male. See a man's female dependents, and you know the man."
He sat down again and took a scone I had baked and brought out for
them for tea.

I could not believe my ears. Poor Mary would turn in her grave.

"And just what does that make me!" I exclaimed indignantly.

"A perfect Wife!" smiled William. Did he mean it? I was not sure I
liked that compliment. It was condescending, somehow. Why had I
never seen this before?

"A woman whose Ruling Passion is not Vanity is Rare, by God!"
Henry declared, taking a piece of seed cake from the plate I had provided.

"Such a woman I adore," said William. Was that me?

Suddenly Enitharmon, one of the characters in William's poem
Europe, came into my mind:

Enitharmon laugh'd in her sleep to see (O woman's triumph)
Every house a den, every man bound; the shadows are filld
With spectres, and the windows wove over with curses of iron:
Over the doors Thou shalt not; & over the chimneys Fear is
     written.

It began to make sense. How threatened he was by Femaleness! I
inwardly wept, O Mary, why are you not here when I finally see what
was behind your life's work?

I had thought we were partners. I worked the Printing Press; I
coloured his designs. For that matter, I kept the accounts, what few of
them there were. We were not exactly prosperous. My fingers were
beginning to get arthritic from being constantly in cold water from
cooking and cleaning. But I had thought I had William's respect. Now
I was not so sure.

There was also the private poem, *Vala*, that he was writing on the
discarded proof pages of Edward Young's *Night Thoughts*. He did not
exactly keep it secret from me, but he did not offer it to me to read, as
he had with other works. I read it when he was not home.

I surmised it was going to be divided into Nine Nights, like *Night
Thoughts* had been, for now its full title was *Vala, Or The Death and*

Judgement of the Ancient Man, A Dream of Nine Nights. Some of the characters I had met before were there: Enion, Los, Enitharmon. It was a poem full of couplings and quarrels, spirits and flames. Los and Enitharmon were married, I think. They reminded me of William and me. But the poem seemed to take place in air, in space. He was writing the first twenty pages or so in fine copper-plate script, so I surmised he intended to engrave it, though he never did.

In truth, I could see that the poem was about more than individuals. Vala is a goddess; she is Nature, and before she exists is the Song of the Aged Mother, Enion, who used to visit me. She sings about the Four Mighty Ones in every Man that William had told me about. William said they are the Four Zoas of the Bible, the Riders in the Chariot of the Prophet Ezekiel, the four living creatures with human likeness. William had seen that they are a part of the human mind, and written the line: "Four Mighty Ones are in every Man," but even I could see that all their troubles stem from their Female counterparts. Men fall in love with an Object of Desire, only to be ruined. But since Vala appeared to me to be Nature herself, how could a man not fall in love with the sun and moon and stars and the green earth?

I took some flowers to Mary's grave, little single-petaled pink roses that still bloomed in early October. There was already in place a gravestone:

MARY WOLLSTONECRAFT
GODWIN
Author of
A Vindication
of the rights of Woman
Born 27th April 1759
Died 10th September 1797

In the soft evening light, the churchyard of St. Pancras was peaceful and deserted. The yellow stone of the church glowed.

"Dear Mary," I whispered, "I hope you are at peace. I will try to defend Womanhood in your place, if only in my own life."

Even as I said the words, I felt my heart sink with worry at my inadequacy, my lack of education and lowly place in society. I wondered what would happen to Mary's two little girls; I heard that Godwin cherished the children and was desperate to find a good nurse for them, Marguerite the French nurse having returned to Paris. Gilbert Imlay had gone to Surinam with Thomas Christie, so there would be no help from him. I wished I could have helped with the children. I went home and petted our old cat Marigold, the tabby Henry had given me so long ago. She was the only child William and I ever had, unless you count the Illuminated Books we produced.

I did not have many women friends now. Cathy Blake was rather distant with me, though polite enough. Nancy Flaxman and Mrs. Butts were kind always, and also Mrs. Cumberland, but they were busy with a social round in which I was not often included. Mary was gone. In retrospect she had become a friend, because we shared much experience, but I had never been completely at ease in her company. So I found myself seeking my sister Sarah's society.

Sarah, tall and vivacious, took after my father's side of the family. She had the dark eyes of all the Bouchers, but her skin was fairer than mine. Her hair was distinguished by a grey streak along one side, and she wore it plainly in a bun at the nape of her neck, with curls over the ears. My own hair was curlier and more unruly than hers, so I always put it up under a mob cap. Sarah had crinkly lines at the corners of her brown eyes from smiling. She lived with her husband, Henry Banes, in the Strand. Her large family seemed only to give her pleasure. She had five children, three of whom were still at home, girls aged ten, twelve and fourteen, who called us Aunt Kate and Uncle Will.

One Sunday in late October we had dinner with the Banes. That night the talk was political. The young General Napoleon Bonaparte was sweeping over Europe, and Britain was the only country still at war with France.

"Thank God for Admiral Duncan!" said Henry, raising a glass of wine as if in a toast. "He has destroyed the Dutch Fleet at Camperdown well and good."

William liked Henry, a good-hearted, stout man, who was a Russia merchant and exporter of English cloth. Henry had keen blue eyes and large hands and wrists. We always ate a well-roasted joint of beef at Sarah and Henry's house, and Sarah boiled water for tea in a big copper urn they had from Russia.

"Thank God we need not fear an invasion from France for the time being," agreed Sarah passing a plate of sweets. We had all worried about that.

"Oh God, to find some place on earth where the accursed politics of Europe are unknown!" exclaimed William running his hand through his hair, which then stood out in fiery ends. "What has our country come to—hanging the Irish, establishing the human flesh trade, and spying on each other!"

"Mr. Cumberland said he could hardly order his breakfast in a Coffee room without some stranger seating himself opposite to eavesdrop on his business," I contributed.

"One dare not speak one's mind, let alone write about it!" muttered William.

"You refer to the Gagging Acts," mused Henry. "I could not believe that Bills outlawing large meetings and political lectures would pass Parliament last year . . . why, they repealed the Bill of Rights of 1689!"

"We have friends in the London Corresponding Society," said Sarah. "They have reorganized so that no more than fifty people will ever meet at once. That way they can get around the law against mass meetings."

"It is a terrible thing to fear to speak," said William. "It saddens me greatly. And I know Joseph Johnson is being watched for what he publishes. Home Office Informers are everywhere. Liberty of the press is in peril! Living in London is like a dead weight on us all."

Henry refilled his glass, and William drained it at one gulp.

I was troubled by this conversation, as I had not realized how much the general political atmosphere had affected William. I had been too concerned with Mary. Yet William had been depressed by her death, too, and also by the news we had in the spring that poor Stedman had died, having only just seen his book finally published. And the very month of Mary's death came the word that her friend Thomas Christie had died of a fever in Surinam. It was a sad time.

William's health suffered at times like this, when his spirits were low. He had pains in his bowels, and days when he did not wish to eat. I had to do something, but what?

From Kate's Notebook.
February 14, 1798.

This is the day the birds are supposed to find their mates, St. Valentine's Day. I don't even hear sparrows twittering today, it is so cold and rainy. I want to record here that about two weeks ago, William Godwin published the *Posthumous Works* of Mary Wollstonecraft and his own *Memoirs* of her, and there is a real storm brewing about them. I do not understand how Godwin could reveal so much of Mary's private life to the Public. He wrote about everything, about Imlay and the baby Fanny, born out of wedlock, about her suicide attempts, about their living together before marriage . . . I suppose he thought he was pointing out how admirable she was, but people are scandalized.

Joseph published the *Memoirs*, and he told us that he and Godwin had no idea that the public would react thus against them. Isn't that like men! It does not help the position of women to show that their Chief Defender of Equal Rights flouted nearly all society's laws. Godwin makes Mary into a passionate heroine, living for love . . . but he says nothing of her serious arguments in A *Vindication of the Rights of Woman.* Fuseli said that Godwin asked to see Mary's letters to him, and that he refused and swore at Godwin. Good for Henry!

I think I may have found something to help change our fortunes for the better. Sister Sarah noticing my low spirits, confided that she knew a group of Wise Women who possessed Charms which would change our luck. I was shocked.

"What do you mean? Are they Witches?" I asked her.

"That is not the right word at all. Men who are afraid of women, or physicians who do not like Midwives are all too ready to cry *Witch!* And they have burned and tortured good women and called them that name simply because they knew herbal cures or had healing powers."

Then I asked her who her friends were, and if I might meet them. She said she would see, and she would let me know soon.

Sarah called upon me a week or so later, and said that if I would care to attend a Meeting with her, the Wise Women would welcome me. I was not to tell William where I was going, and I should not talk about what I saw there. It was a Secret Society, she said, such as many men have these days. So why should not women enjoy their own society also?

"This is the house of my friend Mistress Owen," said Sarah, as we approached a tall narrow house near Covent Garden.

It was March, and a full moon was rising behind the dark outline of the houses on the street. I felt nervous, and a little worried that I might be doing something heretical. Did these women believe in God? But then, did I myself really believe in God? William calls the God that everyone else believes in Nobodaddy! William certainly does not believe in that God. I tried to keep my confused thoughts under cover.

"Do not worry," said Sarah. "We are all very kind women. You will be welcome."

We entered a simply furnished room where five women were seated at a round table, with a candle burning in the centre. Other candles were lit about the room, and a lovely fragrance, something strange and spicy, was in the air. I noticed that all the women were wearing simple white robes, and when Sarah removed her cloak, she too was wearing one. All stood to greet us.

"Welcome, sisters," said Mrs. Owen, a pleasant, plump woman with a Welsh lilt to her voice, "and especially I welcome you, Kate, as a trusted visitor to our group. Here we all take names of Flowers. You may call me Sister Violet, and here are Sisters Marguerite, Iris, Hyacinth, and Lavender. Sarah is Sister Gentian, and you will be Sister Rose."

I felt as if I were taking part in a children's pantomime, yet there was something very serious in all the pleasant faces looking so intently at me. Sister Marguerite, a slim young woman with dark eyes and hair, fetched small bowls and proceeded to pour tea for each of us.

As I looked at each woman in turn, I noticed that each wore about her neck a little round silver pendant made of interlacing circles.

"Our meeting will now begin," said Sister Violet. We sat down at the table, and each woman clasped the hand of the one beside her so that we each had both hands clasped around the table.

"Ours is a Spiritual Sisterhood," said Sister Violet, as if explaining to me, "and we begin with a prayer."

We bowed our heads, and Sister Violet spoke.

"O sacred Name, Name which strengthens the heart of woman, Name of life, of salvation, of joy, precious Name, resplendent, glorious, agreeable Name which saves, conserves, leads and rules all, precious Mother, be with us tonight."

A shiver went through me as I realized we were praying to a *woman*. I wondered if it could be a prayer to the Virgin Mary as the Papists make. But no, Mary was not named, and as the prayer went on I realized the Sacred Mother was someone else, someone or something more powerful, who could not be named. Panic rose in my chest, and I began to breathe quickly. Sarah noticed.

"Calm yourself," she whispered, "breathe deep."

I took the fragrant air into my lungs as the group chanted in unison. I began to feel a deep peace within me. Sister Iris, a fair woman with grey eyes, took out a little tin whistle and piped a mysterious air. All became silent.

Then Sister Violet said, "It is time for the Wishes."

Each woman around the table was given a small piece of paper. In turn, we were told to write with a quill pen our deepest desire in a sentence.

Please, I wrote, Let Something happen to cure William of his Melancholy and change our Fortune.

The slips of paper were then collected by Sister Violet, who prayed over them and, one by one, burned the papers at a little altar in the corner of the room.

Then Sister Violet sat down again at the table and spoke.

"Sisters," she said in her pleasant Welsh voice, "it is time for business. There is an illness in the City that many of us have been called upon to treat. We must discuss our Remedies."

Of course. These women must be Healers and Midwives. Cathy must know them. But I did not know that Sarah was among them.

"I have found a remedy for the terrible cough," said Sister Lavender, a thin, older woman with long grey hair simply tied back.

The others were very attentive.

"You must make a poultice of mustard-flower, crumbs of bread, and vinegar," she said, "and apply it to the chest for as long as the sick one can stand it. The heat will draw out the phlegm."

"But that is an old Remedy!" exclaimed Sister Iris.

"There is nothing wrong with the Old Ways," commented Sister Hyacinth, a pale young woman who up till that moment had sat silent, as if in deep thought.

"I did not mean to criticize," said Sister Iris, "it is only that my own mother gave me that Remedy."

"There is also an Ague prevalent in London this month," said Sister Marguerite, as she refilled our bowls of tea. "I have been asked to help several small children. I have had success with a decoction of Agrimony."

I listened with interest, as William frequently suffered from the Ague, especially if we walked North. I had usually given him a drink made of the flowers of Hops.

This talk went on for some time; it seemed the chief business of the group. They spoke of Childbirths and Healings, learning from each other. I realized that Sarah, like Cathy, was a healer, though Sarah did not deliver babies. But there was something more. I discovered that Sarah had a gift of second sight. I should have known it, for I myself had some spiritual gifts, which I shared with William. It ran in our family. But Sarah had concealed her powers from me till now.

"It is time for the Readings," said Sister Violet to Sarah. "Sister Gentian, please proceed."

From the folds of her gown, Sarah withdrew a small packet wrapped in black silk. She carefully unwrapped long cards, with strange designs beautifully painted upon them in blue and red and gold. Curious figures were portrayed on the cards, with names printed at the base, in French: *La Papesse, Le Pendu, Cavalier de Coupe.* I shivered. I knew it was against the law to import playing cards into Britain. Where had Sarah got them? What were they?

"This is the Grand Tarot," said Sarah, divining my thoughts. She chose several cards from the deck, and laid the others carefully aside.

"I have brought you here, Sister Rose," she said to me solemnly, "to help you, as I know you are troubled. The cards will tell me, and you, much that you need to know. The cards know all our secrets."

Sarah spread some cards out face down before me.

"Choose one," she said. "It will stand for you in the reading."

I was drawn to one card, I don't know why. When I turned it over, it was the image of a woman, with a crown on her head, in a red gown. The name of the card was *Reyne de Coupe.*

"Well chosen," said Sarah. "That is the Queen of Cups, your card." She gestured at the smaller pile of cards on the table.

"These are the Major Arcana. There are twenty-two cards. You must pick them up yourself and shuffle them. And while you do it, think on your life."

I did as I was told. The cards were large, and hard to shuffle. I thought of how hard I worked for William, and how I loved him in spite of my disillusionment over his feelings for other women; I thought of Paul-Marc and my guilt over my love for him, and my sorrow at his death. I thought of Mary and her strange, flamboyant, short life. And I thought of our depression now, our bleak life in London, and how I wanted something good to happen.

"Now choose one of these. It will stand for your recent past."

Everyone in the room was silent, watching. The candles flickered. I was nervous.

I chose a card. Everyone gasped. It was a skeleton. *Le Morte.*

Sarah placed this card across the Queen of Cups. I was stunned; of course, it was true: Mary had died, Paul-Marc had died, even Stedman had died. And something was dying between William and me.

"Now shuffle all the cards together," said Sarah. I had noticed that there were four suits, Swords, Cups, Coins and Sticks, and each suit had an Ace, King, Queen and Knave, like other playing cards.

"What do these mean?" I asked.

"These are the Minor Arcana," said Sarah. "They correspond to the Four Elements of Air, Water, Earth and Fire. Each Element has a meaning." This did not clarify much for me, but I thought it interesting that so much seemed to depend on *Fours*, rather like William's Four Mighty Ones.

Sarah placed the cards face down in a fan shape before her, and contemplated them. Then she chose a card and placed it beneath the other two. It was the Two of Swords.

"The problem you have is in your marriage," said Sarah. "You feel bound and constrained. You are not expressing your emotions. There is tension here."

The card was beautiful. Its background was blue, and in the centre was an eight-petalled flower in yellow and red and dark blue, with four leaves above and below. Two curved black swords, like Saracen's blades, curved around the flower.

I privately thought that Sarah did not need cards to see that about my marriage to William. She could have observed it for herself. Then she went on.

"Ah, but there is improvement ahead. Here is the Nine of Cups. That means better times are coming, some material well-being. But you must be careful not to lose your artistic vision."

She chose another card and placed it on the right side of the cards.

"This is the Near Future," she said, "ah, *La Roue de Fortune*. The Wheel is turning in your favour. Things will change, Kate. You will move. There will be new people, new scenes, away from London."

This surprised me. I could never imagine myself or William out of London.

"Now for your Self," said Sarah, picking another card. It was the Ace of Swords.

"You are unclear about what you want, are you not?" she asked.

"Well, yes, I suppose so."

"You must develop a clear vision of what you want," said Sarah, authoritatively.

She chose yet another card.

"This is what is around you," she said. The card was *Le Bateleur*. The Magician. The image on the card was a curly haired man in a large brimmed hat, wearing a jacket with wide multicoloured sleeves, standing in front of a table with cups, daggers and odd objects.

"Of course," she said, "The Maker. It is William. He is so powerful; he dominates your life." I began to think that even if Sarah knew all this already, it was odd that the cards that appeared should be the ones that told her what she already knew. I felt myself shivering.

"Now for your hopes and fears: ah, the Eight of Sticks, reversed. You are afraid your current life will go on forever without change. But we have already seen change coming in the cards. Now for the last card."

It was an amazing card. A naked woman knelt by a pond, and above her many stars of yellows and reds and blues burst from a black sky.

"*L'Etoile*. The Star!" said Sarah. "That is lovely. This means much hope and aspiration in the future. Peace and promise. Remember this, Kate. Hold the image in your mind no matter what happens."

The reading was over. Sarah put the cards away in their black silk wrapper. Sister Marguerite, the old one, said to me, "You had strong cards. Mind them well."

Soon the Meeting ended with a song and more prayers, and then we drank a delicious cordial, and a plate of sweets was passed.

"Come again," said Sister Violet to me. I did go to other meetings, but in the next year it became so dangerous to meet that Sarah would not always inform me. Even a small group of women could be considered seditious by the government of William Pitt.

From Kate's Notebook.
February 28, 1798.

It is the morning after the Tarot reading. Last night, I dreamed a dream of Paul-Marc so real that I was not sure when I woke which State was which. But I realized that Paul-Marc was no longer real, so his appearance was the Dream. He appeared in my kitchen, looking as he often did, a little rumpled, a little shy.

"*Ma petite*, come outside," he whispered, "I want to show you something." I went with him, as one does in dreams, quick as a thought. We stood in the back garden, under the grape arbour, which was a mass of bare, twisted vines. Paul-Marc held out his hand. In it, he held a Pearl.

"It is for you," he said.

He placed the luminous drop in my hand. I had never held a precious stone before. I closed my hand over it, and awoke with my fist still clenched.

What had he given me?

All morning I have had Paul-Marc as my companion. Gradually it has come to me that the Pearl he gave me was Confidence. Paul-Marc had loved me for myself. He did not have an instinctive dislike of women as Fuseli did, and I fear, as William has. No, Paul-Marc loved me alone, as a friend *and equal*. That was indeed a Pearl.

From Kate's Notebook.
April 14, 1798.

We have just learned that Joseph Johnson has been arrested! It is all because he sold a pamphlet which the government considered seditious. He has been sentenced to six months in the King's Bench Prison, not far from us here in Lambeth. Poor Joseph! How his asthma will suffer! And William is in an agony of concern and worry.

He does not sleep, and he sees shadows where he used to see Visions. He rages, "The Beast and the Whore rule without control . . ."

I do not know what to do. I think of the Cards and hold fast to The Star. Change is coming. It must come.

From Kate's Notebook.
Wednesday, October 29, 1798.

I have been reading a new little book of poetry that Joseph Johnson gave me. It is called *Lyrical Ballads, with a Few Other Poems* and has been published anonymously, but the author is surely a Great Talent. Most of the poems are like the ballads one can buy on the street, but yet there is something different about them, they are about country people, or abandoned women, or children. They also are about Nature. Being a farm girl myself, I really liked the simple way the poet talks about Nature. For instance, he writes:

> One impulse from a vernal wood
> May teach you more of man
> Of moral evil and of good
> Than all the sages can.
>
> Sweet is the lore which Nature brings;
> Our meddling intellect
> Misshapes the beauteous forms of things—
> We murder to dissect.

I thought that very fine. And there was also a poem about a little girl who insisted that she had six brothers and sisters, even though one had been dead for years.

These poems are not as complicated as William's *Songs,* but there are two surprising poems in the collection that are different from anything I have ever read before.

One is called *The Rime of the Ancient Mariner.* It is very frightening and mysterious, all about a seaman who killed a beautiful bird for no reason, and was horribly punished, along with all the rest of his crew, while he alone survived after a long voyage through strange seas. He describes the most wonderful things:

> And now there came both mist and snow,
> And it grew wondrous cold:
> And ice, mast-high, came floating by,
> As green as emerald.

And there are scenes of heat, too, where the Mariner is punished with thirst:

> Water, water, everywhere,
> And all the boards did shrink;
> Water, water, everywhere,
> Nor any drop to drink.

This Mariner, who had been so oblivious to nature that he killed a beautiful bird for no reason, finally through his sufferings looks with love on water snakes, which flashed in the sea with golden fire. I was amazed by that poem, the mystery of it, the picture of the sea with snakes writhing in it, the angels who help him, the horrible idea that the Mariner would have to tell his story for ever and ever.

And then there was a poem at the end of the book, different and religious, called *Lines Composed A Few Miles Above Tintern Abbey*. It described a place to which the poet had returned, and a vision that place brought to him, a vision of all things being One, "a joy whose dwelling is the light of setting suns, / And the round ocean and the living air, / And the blue sky, / And in the mind of man . . ." Oh, it was beautiful, but so sad, so sad. Such a sense of loss was there.

"What do you think of these?" I asked William. He looked up from the book he was reading, pen in hand, writing in the margins.

"Those Poems are written by a Spiritual Man," he said, "but the Natural Man rises up in him at war with the Spirit—and then he is no poet, but a Heathen Philosopher!"

"Merely because he loves Nature!" I exclaimed.

"The Natural World is a Trap," William's eyes grew intensely blue, "you should know that, Kate."

"I don't care," I said. "I love Nature! I love the larks and the sun-flowers, and the River . . ."

"That's because you are a Woman," said William, as if that explained everything. He went back to his reading.

"Even the Bible has some Nature Poetry," I retorted. "What about this?" And I quoted from the *Song of Solomon*:

> A garden enclosed is my sister, my spouse; a spring shut up, a fountain sealed.
> Thy plants are an orchard of pomegranates, with pleasant fruits; camphire and spikenard,
> Spikenard and saffron; calamus and cinnamon, with all trees of frankincense, myrhh and aloes, with all the chief spices . . .

William seemed amused. It was good to see him smile. He rose from his chair, came over to me, and took the pins from my hair. It spilled down over my shoulders.

He looked at me with Desire. I had not seen that in a long time. He undid my bodice and slipped his hand into my bosom.

"I am come into my garden, my sister, my spouse," he quoted. "Come, let me eat my pleasant fruits."

His tongue caressed my nipple. I opened like a flower.

William had been writing furiously for days in his copy of *The Works of Joshua Reynolds*. It is a collection of the famous artist's Discourses on Art, some of which William had heard at the Royal Academy years ago. Curious as to what William had written, I turned the Title Page to see this written on the back:

> Having spent the Vigour of my Youth & Genius under the Opres-sion of Sr Joshua & his Gang of Cunning Hired Knaves Without Employment & as much as could possibly be Without Bread, the Reader must Expect to Read in all my Remarks on these Books

Nothing but Indignation & Resentment. While Sr Joshua was rolling in Riches Barry was Poor & Unemployed except by his own Energy Mortimer was calld a Madman & only Portrait Painting applauded by the Rich and Great. Reynolds and Gainsborough Blotted & Blurred one against the other & Divided all the English World between them Fuseli Indignant hid himself I am hid

"I am hid." This almost broke my heart. It was near the end of June, 1799. Fuseli's Milton Gallery had opened in May, and was not doing well with the public. They liked the Shakespeare Gallery better. In May also William had exhibited his painting of "The Last Supper" at the Royal Academy. There had not been much comment there, either, but Mr. Butts liked it, and I thank God for him. He commissioned William to do fifty small pictures illustrating the Bible. This puts bread on our table. And Flaxman gave us eight pounds for engraving three plates. The cards were right, things were changing . . . but slowly.

On Tuesday evenings, Mr. and Mrs. Butts usually called on us. I served tea from a white China pot. Then on Wednesdays, William visited them at their large house in Great Marlborough Street, where William took tea from a silver service. I did not always attend, as I welcomed an evening with my own thoughts. I was often tired in those days with all the work about the house, helping with whatever work William was doing, and sewing and mending our clothes. The Butts were very kind to us, and Thomas Butts gave William many commissions. On one occasion, William insisted I come along with him, as there was going to be a musical evening, and he wanted me to sing.

As usual, there were a great many young women about, for the Butts ran a school for girls, had several daughters and two maidservants. Mrs. Butts liked to do needlework and I complimented her on her fine stitching. It happened that she asked me to help her with a design for a hare in long grass that she had seen and wanted to capture. This made me feel useful, so I sang my song with confidence I rarely felt in company.

Mr. Hayley came to London to see the Milton Gallery. We saw him at the Flaxmans' house. His son Thomas was said to be gravely ill in

Sussex. Hayley was full of news about a Turret he had built on his "Marine Villa," as he called it, at his village in Sussex, and the Library Thomas had helped design. How well I was to know it! But there was other news.

"You know, Mrs. Blake, that I am a widower?" He said this with something of relief in his voice. I knew that his estranged wife Eliza had long been a financial burden to him.

"I am sorry for your troubles, Mr. Hayley," I said.

He looked down at me, smiling. He had fine eyes, I thought.

"Your sympathies mean much to me," he said. I felt uncomfortable at this, as I often did with Mr. Hayley.

Hayley then told me he wanted William to make an engraving of a little medallion of a likeness of his son that Flaxman had executed. I think he wanted to be of help to us.

Other of our friends did send work our way. George Cumberland introduced us to Reverend John Trusler, a clergyman who wrote helpful instructional books, like *The Way to be Rich and Respectable*. We should have taken his advice. He asked William to complete four watercolours on the topics, *Malevolence, Benevolence, Pride, and Humility*. But it all came to naught, for he did not like the work William did.

William was furious at his comments.

He wrote Trusler an angry letter in August:

> I really am sorry that you are falln out with the Spiritual World ... I feel very sorry that your Ideas & Mine on Moral Painting differ so much as to have made you so angry with my method of study.

That was only the beginning. He went on:

> You say that I want somebody to Elucidate my Ideas. But you ought to know that What is Grand is necessarily obscure to Weak men. That which can be made Explicit to the Idiot is not worth my care.

Trusler could not have liked this. And William continued:

I percieve that your Eye is perverted by Caricature Prints...Fun I love, but too much Fun is of all things the most loathsome. Mirth is better than Fun & Happiness is better than Mirth—I feel that a Man may be happy in This World. And I know that This World Is a World of Imagination and Vision.

And then he wrote the most beautiful lines, which always recall to me William's keen grey eyes, unruly hair, and air of magic:

I see Every thing I paint In This World, but Every body does not see alike. To the Eyes of a Miser a Guinea is more beautiful than the Sun & a bag worn with the use of Money has more beautiful proportions than a Vine filled with Grapes. The tree which moves some to tears of joy is in the Eyes of others only a Green thing that stands in the way. Some See Nature all Ridicule & Deformity & by these I shall not regulate my proportions, & Some Scarce see Nature at all But to the Eyes of the Man of Imagination Nature is Imagination itself. As a man is So he Sees.

And I thought, too, that there was something here that reminded me of the poet of *The Rime of the Ancient Mariner*, whoever he was.

From Kate's Notebook.
Thursday, November 14, 1799.

Tears are dropping on my page as I write. I have been thinking of Paul-Marc because news comes from Paris that there is a *coup* and Napoleon Bonaparte has become First Consul of France. We English fear Napoleon, but Paul-Marc would have been happy for his country. My grief surprises me. Have I not put him behind me? Why can the past come back so sharp, so unexpected?

Late Wednesday evening, January 1, 1800.

A new Century has begun! We celebrated with Mr. and Mrs. Butts, who gave a fine midday party. The dinner was delicious boiled mutton with a currant sauce, all served very prettily with little cauliflowers and turnips cut in dice. We drank mightily, and sang well into the night. Mrs. Butts wants me to call her Betsy, but something inhibits me from doing so, at least in writing.

About this time, I read the most shocking book. It was a novel, called *The Monk*, which caused a sensation when it was published first in 1796. It was called Immoral and Impious. Its author, Mathew Gregory Lewis, became known as Monk Lewis. I had long wanted to read it, and finally Henry Fuseli lent me his copy.

The story was complicated, but mainly it was about the Lust and Sins of a Monk named Ambrosio, and this was shocking because he was supposed to be a Man of Holiness. I could imagine that Henry would be titillated by the graphic description of seduction, but even more by the account of the Damnation of Ambrosio. Yet another story in the Book moved me.

It was the story of Agnes, a young woman in love with Raymond, who had entered a nunnery after she had thought mistakenly he had deserted her. Accident again united them, and she violated her vows of Chastity. The wicked Mother Superior kept her horribly hidden and in chains, and when she gave Birth to her baby, it soon died. When Agnes was discovered, she was half-naked, and her long hair concealed her face; one arm hung listless, while the other held the small bundle of her child close to her bosom. And she wept so piteously over her baby, about how lovely it would have been. My tears fell, too, when I read that passage.

And so I decided to paint a picture of Agnes, grieving over her dead baby. I took canvas and temperas, and painted her in profile, on the floor of the cell, bent in Despair. William said it was a very good painting, and Henry said it looked just like one of William's temperas. Well, I suppose it did, but it was not William who painted it, it was me.

I had shed many a tear when I painted the picture; then I decided to give it to Mrs. Butts, who was so often pregnant, and so fond of her children. She liked it and hung it in her hallway for all to see. I was proud of that painting, and felt when I had finished it, that something inside me was at rest.

From Kate's Notebook.
May 6, 1800.

We heard through Flaxman that poor young Thomas Alfonso Hayley died, and his father is distraught. William had been working on the engraving of the medallion for him. He sent Hayley a letter of condolence in which he told Hayley how thirteen years ago he lost a brother, yet he converses with his spirit daily. He wishes the same for Hayley and his son, "The Ruins of Time builds Mansions in Eternity."

From Kate's Notebook.
Sunday, July 12, 1800.

Oh, I am so excited I can hardly write a legible line. The most wonderful thing has happened! Mr. Hayley invited William to visit him in his village of Felpham in Sussex, and he suggested that we move there, and William work for him in his various literary enterprises, and help him decorate his Library at Turret House in memory of his son. William loved Felpham, and said we would go, and we are going to move lock stock and barrel to Felpham in September to live in a cottage that William has leased from the owner of the Inn, and William said it is lovely and large and the sun shines all the time at lovely Felpham.

Part Three

FELPHAM 1800–1803

Blake, *America*, Plate 16, Copy E (1793). Top Figure. Lessing J. Rosenwald Collection, Library of Congress

17

In Which We Live In Felpham
and See Much of Mr. Hayley

William and I discussed the move to Felpham at every opportunity.

"There are pitfalls, of course," said William one eve-ning in August, eating his fish stew with relish. "Mr. Hayley can be dictatorial. But I welcome this opportunity to leave London, which has become so oppressive."

"I have not lived in the country since we were married," I said, passing the bread. "It will be wonderful to have a garden again."

William took a draught of Ale.

"I have an idea that we should ask Cathy to join us for a few weeks," he said. "She will help us get settled."

Now I took a drink of Ale. There was sense in William's idea. Cathy had been much grieved at Paul-Marc's death, and a distance had grown between us. She remained devoted to William and I knew she would come. Our preparations began.

Letter from William Blake to Mr. John Flaxman.
Buckingham Street, Fitzroy Square, London.

Felpham, Septr. 21, 1800, Sunday Morning

Dear Sculptor of Eternity
We are safe arrived at our Cottage which is more beautiful than I
thought it. & more convenient. It is a perfect Model for Cottages & I
think for Palaces of Magnificence only Enlarging not altering its proportions & adding ornaments & not principals. Nothing can be more
Grand than its Simplicity & Usefulness. Simple without Intricacy it
seems to be the Spontaneous Effusion of Humanity congenial to the
wants of Man. No other formed House can ever please me so well nor
shall I ever be perswaded I believe that it can be improved either in
Beauty or Use
Mr Hayley recievd us with his usual brotherly affection. I have
begun to work. Felpham is a sweet place for Study. because it is more
Spiritual than London Heaven opens here on all sides her golden
Gates her windows are not obstructed by vapours. voices of Celestial
inhabitants are more distinctly heard & their forms more distinctly
seen & my Cottage is also a Shadow of their houses. My Wife & Sister
are both well. courting Neptune for an Embrace
Our Journey was very pleasant & tho we had a great deal of Luggage. No Grumbling all was Chearfulness & Good Humour on the
Road & yet we could not arrive at our Cottage before half past Eleven
at night owing to the necessary shifting of our Luggage from one
Chaise to another for we had Seven Different Chaises & as many different drivers. We set out between Six & Seven in the Morning of
Thursday with Sixteen heavy boxes & portfolios full of prints . . .
You O Dear Flaxman are a Sublime Archangel My Friend & Companion from Eternity in the Divine bosom is our Dwelling place I look
back into the regions of Reminiscence & behold our ancient days
before this Earth appeard in its vegetated mortality to my mortal vegetated Eyes. I see our houses of Eternity which can never be separated
tho our Mortal vehicles should stand at the remotest corners of
heaven from Each other.
Farewell My Best Friend Remember Me & My Wife in Love &
Friendship to our dear Mrs. Flaxman whom we ardently desire to

Entertain beneath our thatched roof of rusted gold & believe me for ever to remain

Your Grateful & Affectionate
WILLIAM BLAKE

I cannot say that I left Hercules Buildings without regret. It had been our home for ten years, and held many memories. Mary had visited us in that house and Paul-Marc, too. William had invented his Illuminated Books there, and I had learned to be a good printer along with him. It held the imprint of our everyday lives, our laughter and our tears. We would likely never have such a grand house again. And yet we both ardently desired a new beginning, which Felpham and Hayley promised.

What is worse than Moving House! We did not have that many worldly goods, but between our household pots and pans and our clothes and few bits of furniture, to say nothing of the copper plates and all William's books and engravings and Print Collection, we had sixteen heavy boxes besides the Press.

I became so tired I developed a terrible Headache and I had to call Cathy to minister to me. I needed her help now, and to her credit, she came. She was to stay with us in Felpham for a few weeks.

Because I was unwell, William had to write Hayley on the sixteenth of September:

Leader of My Angels,

My Dear & too careful & over joyous Woman has Exhausted her strength to such a degree with expectation & gladness added to labour in our removal that I fear it will be Thursday before we can get away from this City ...

Eartham will be my first temple & altar My wife is like a flame of many colours of precious jewels whenever she hears it named Excuse my haste & receive my hearty Love & Respect

I am dear Sir
Your Sincere
William Blake

My fingers Emit sparks of fire with Expectation of my future labours

I thought that was so sweet of William to describe me like that, but it was true that I had seldom been so excited and happy as I was in those days before the move.

I had sent a letter myself to Nancy Flaxman, which I asked William to write for me at my dictation, as my handwriting was never that neat. We called on them on Sunday afternoon, the fourteenth, at Hampstead, to say farewell. We hoped they would visit us at Felpham in the summer. We were so grateful to them for encouraging this relationship between Hayley and ourselves. I inwardly wept to think I may have wronged them. No one but myself bore that burden.

When we finally were packed into our first Chaise early in the morning of September eighteenth, we set off across London for the trip of about Sixty Miles along the Petworth Road. London seemed to us like a terrible desert, a wasteland of stone and brick and mud. When we reached the open country, it was as if a veil was lifted and all seemed clear and bright in the morning light. The wide September sky arched over fields of corn as we travelled towards the sea, though the corn was withered, as it had been a bad harvest, and there were riots in London over the high price of bread. Our hearts lifted as we travelled farther and farther from London.

William had never seen the Sea. As it glimmered in the distance, he became increasingly excited. The hills of the South Downs seemed like mountains to us. Even Cathy, who was usually quiet and withdrawn, became animated and cheerful. We sat eating bread and cheese, while we shifted Chaises at an Inn.

"I think I could become a Traveller," she said, "living under the Sky, eating simple food, and learning from the simple folk I would meet on the road."

"What if you met a Highwayman instead?" said I, not entirely in jest.

"Then I would charm him into taking me with him," she

laughed. "How interesting would my life be then!" That made me a little sympathetic to Cathy. Her life was indeed dull, living with James Blake and his family, with no prospect of a household of her own.

I was in a dither of excitement to see the Cottage that William had rented for us at Felpham. When at last we approached it down a country lane, it was half past eleven at night, and all we could do was find our bedrooms by candlelight and wait till morning to look around.

It was a lovely Cottage. From the outside, it was set at right angles to the Lane, so you saw first the steep line of the thatched roof like a tall A with the chimney up the middle. There was a blue clematis clambering over the gate, set in a low, flint wall. The whitewashed cottage was made of flint and cobbles.

There was a small garden in front, and beyond that, a view of cornfields, and then the sea, only a short way down the lane. In the back yard was an Elm tree.

Inside, it was a long, shallow, two-storey house, one room deep, with latticed windows. We had three rooms downstairs, the middle one immediately became William's work room. The first was the sitting room with a fireplace, and the last one was the kitchen, small, but cozy with a real cooker, not just a fire. From this room, a narrow staircase wound up to a nice large bedroom with a fireplace, which William and I used.

There was another staircase, wider, at the entrance to the house, in the sitting room, and this stair led up to two other bedrooms, with quaint rounded ceilings. We were all charmed by the place.

We heard larks every morning, and many other birds that awakened us with the sun. They were so noisy! From our bedroom window, we could see two windmills to the west towards the village of Bognor, and we had a wonderful view of the endless sea, stretching to the Isle of Wight. To the east, the high cliff of Beachy Head gleamed in the distance. Once outside, the smell of the sea mingled with the wild purple thyme that grew under our feet and in the meadow.

"If I should ever build a Palace, it would only be this Cottage, enlarged," said William.

Our landlord was Mr. Grinder, the proprietor of The Fox Inn, which was just a few steps up the Lane from our gate. This was quite a large public house with a timbered ceiling and dark wood panelling, topped by cheerful yellow painted walls. The Fox was named after a Revenue Cutter whose picture was on its sign. We spent many a convivial evening at the Fox, though I later came to think of it with Rue.

That very first day at Felpham, Cathy and I decided to try the Sea. Of course, we neither one of us could swim, but as William said, we "Courted Neptune for an Embrace." I found it quite a cold Embrace.

We shrieked and ran about, splashing each other.

William evidently wrote Mr. Butts about it, because he wrote back the wittiest letter:

". . . Your good Wife will permit, & I hope may benefit from, the Embraces of Neptune, but she will presently distinguish betwixt the warmth of his Embraces & yours, & court the former with caution. I suppose you do not admit of a third in that concern, or I would offer her mine even at this distance. . . . Allow me . . . to lament the frailty of the fairest Sex, for who, alas! of us, my good Friend, could have thought. . . . So Virtuous a Woman would ever have fled / From Hercules Buildings to Neptune's Bed?"

William, being unable to pass a day without work, settled in at once to finish a water colour or two of the Three Marys he had promised Mr. Butts. Cathy would take them back with her in the last week of September. In the meantime, we explored the village of Felpham. Chichester was only seven miles distant, a handsome City, to which we could walk quite easily. We found that in Felpham, meat was cheaper than in London. William considered it a wonderful omen when on the first morning after our arrival, he went out the gate and overheard a Plowboy saying to the Plowman, "Father, The Gate is Open."

From Kate's Notebook.
Friday, October 3, 1800.

William was sitting on the Sea Shore yesterday morning and had a wonderful Vision. He said that the Light was reflecting off the Sands, and each particle of light was a Man, and every stone and herb and tree that he saw was in Human Form, and that finally all Human Forms became One, and he was part of it, and so was I and Cathy, and Mr. Hayley, and Mr and Mrs. Butts also.

I am now baking bread.

Mr. Hayley came again today. He has been busy organizing work and introductions for William. He is a Great Man in these parts, quite famous for his Medical Potions, and for riding pell mell across the fields on his big black horse with his umbrella open over his head! He has a nick-name here, I discovered. They call him Felpham Billy! We are not allowed to forget that he is famous as a Poet, though we knew that in London. I, though, cannot read his verse for boredom.

But I cannot deny that Mr. Hayley is Kindness itself. He is now planning to raise money for the Widow Spicer by writing a poem about her dead son, *Little Tom the Sailor*. He has asked William to illustrate it. The proceeds will go to the Widow. So William is working on this now, and we will print it up as a broadsheet right away.

"You are looking fetching today, Kate," Hayley said this morning. He always compliments me, and it always makes me self-conscious. "I hope you are comfortable in the Cottage."

"Oh, yes, sir, indeed we are," I replied, not telling him that the sitting room fireplace smoked rather too much.

"I have brought over a pony for William to ride," he announced. "His name is Bruno. I will soon take William calling on friends in Lavant. And I have brought you something, too." I hoped it was not a horse. The idea of William on a horse was more than I could contemplate at the moment.

Hayley went outside and returned with a little yellow bird in a white cage! "It is a Canary," he said, "to sing to you. And with you." He smiled down at me with his piercing grey eyes. I was quite overcome with shyness, which is rather odd for a thirty-eight year old woman.

William Hayley was full of plans for William; he loved to manage people. I wondered how long William was going to endure this kind of control on his time, but he was remarkably patient and endearingly grateful for Hayley's patronage. By November, Hayley had William at work on an ambitious project to paint on canvas a series of Heads of the Poets to be used as a frieze in the new Library at Turret House. There were twenty Heads, including one of poor Thomas Alfonso. He was in the company of Milton, Cowper, Homer, Camoens, Spenser and others. Cowper had been Hayley's very special friend who had lately died, quite mad. William enjoyed that commission.

It had rained a bit, and for some reason with the rain came pains in my knees. I was cold all the time. I was not used to the damp air of the Sea shore. I tried to alleviate the pain with a little oil of eucalyptus, and ignore it, but it prevented me from working at the Press.

In spite of my rheumatic knees, I liked to walk on the beach with William. We admired the vast expanse of steely November sky, and the blue-grey sea, but I hated the bitter wind that went bone-deep and made my ears ache.

"We see this bleak weather this morning," William said, "because our Spirits are bleak."

"Speak for yourself!" said I. Sometimes he irritated me when he was like this.

"You do not see the Misery?"

"No, I see ordinary life going on around us. The Baker is delivering his buns to the Fox, the Fishermen are setting out for the day. It is raining, but the clouds are breaking up on the horizon. Better weather is coming."

"The Eye altering Alters all," mused William, who was given to quoting cryptic aphorisms.

"Who said that?"

"I did."

"So you think you are the Centre of the Universe! Whatever you see, is all there is?"

"Well, of course," said William, warming to his subject and almost visibly emerging from his gloom, "I have just written some poetry about this very thing. Let me say it for you.

The Sky is an immortal Tent built by the Sons of Los
And every Space that a Man views around his dwelling-place
Standing on his own roof, or in his garden on a mount
Of twenty-five cubits in height, such space is his Universe;
And on its verge the Sun rises & sets, the Clouds bow
To meet the flat Earth & the Sea in such an orderd Space:
The Starry heavens reach no further but here bend and set
On all sides & the two poles turn on their valves of gold:
And if he moves his dwelling-place, his heavens also move
Wher'eer he goes & all his neighbourhood bewail his loss:
Such are the Spaces called Earth & such its dimension:
As to that false appearance which appears to the reasoner,
As of a Globe rolling thro Voidness, it is a delusion . . ."

He stopped reciting, and looked at me for my reaction. It was so beautiful, I started to cry, and William cheered up completely.

Mr. Hayley was intent upon introducing William to his friends in the neighbourhood, especially to a Miss Harriet Poole, who lived in the village of Lavant, some three miles north of Chichester. She was a lady of literary interests, to whom Hayley was in the habit of reading his poetry. And so it happened that on many Tuesdays or Fridays William would accompany Hayley to breakfast with Miss Poole, whom they called "Paulina." Hayley would ride his horse Hidalgo, with his perpetually open umbrella over his head, rain or shine, and William would ride Bruno, and I was always relieved to see them both back home in one piece.

I began to wonder if Hayley had a romantic attachment to Miss Poole, and then I began to suspect that it was William who was attracted to her, for when Hayley persuaded William to begin to paint Miniatures, hers was one of the first he painted. It seems that William had a talent for Miniature Painting, and soon Hayley had procured many commissions for him, so many that William began to be irritated, for he never seemed to have time for his own writing. And Hayley had a habit of popping in unexpectedly, for Turret House was only a quarter mile or so up the road, and so William could never be sure of the peace and quiet that were so important to him.

From Kate's Notebook.
Monday, February 2, 1801.

Today, when William was out walking on the beach, Hayley came by. I was alone in the kitchen, kneading bread, flour up to my elbows, hair askew.

"Oh, Mr. Hayley," I exclaimed, answering the door, "you must forgive me, I am baking."

"Please, carry on, Mrs. Blake," he bowed courteously, ducking his tall frame under the low door as he entered. We walked through the sitting room and painting room into the kitchen, where a fire was burning, and the dough was on the table. He watched me intently as I kneaded, and finally wrapped the dough in a towel and laid it aside to rise. And then he did the most disturbing thing. He came over to me, and brushed his hand over my cheek.

"You have flour there," he smiled.

I was quite taken aback at his familiarity, and yet I had a flash of memory. He had done this before. I did not know what to say and I was afraid of offending him, so I brushed my own hand over the side of my face and stammered, "Can I make you some tea?"

And that is how William found us, calmly taking tea together, and he happily joined us. I have not told William about this, as it seems so silly.

In May, William wrote to Thomas Butts and told him about the Miniature painting, and invited Mr. and Mrs. Butts to Felpham. He had also invited the Flaxmans to visit, but John declined, as he said, "I am bound to my sculpture and I cannot make my rocks travel with me."

The Butts came to Sussex, along with their son Thomas Jr., and stayed in nearby Bognor. I suspected Mrs. Butts was in the family way again. When I saw a pregnant woman, I always had a little pain in my heart. William painted miniatures of the three Butts, and very good likenesses they were, too. But such activities were beginning to bore William.

"I cannot believe I am spending my time in such trivial pursuits!" he exclaimed one night, throwing down his brush and pacing about the room. "I should be writing!" Sometimes, when he did take time to write, I would see him stare abstractedly into space for what seemed like hours.

Mrs. Butts was so complimentary about the painting of *Agnes* I had given her, that I decided to paint another picture. This time I had an idea of a subject from the Bible—it was to be a Nativity scene, with a star shining through the window of the Stable. Mary would be supported by Joseph, and the Christ Child, already like a Cherub, floating in the air. I thought that Elizabeth and her child, John the Baptist, would be there, too, to receive the Baby.

First I did a sketch in charcoal on paper. I intended to paint it in tempera on canvas as I had before.

"Why, that is very good!" exclaimed William when he saw what I was doing. I was shy of showing it to him, but he had come upon me unexpectedly in the garden where I was drawing under the Elm tree.

"Is that Elizabeth with John the Baptist on her lap?" he asked.

"Yes."

"That is Original," he said. Then, "Kate, would you mind if I painted that Subject, too? You have given me an Idea."

What could I say? It was my idea? I mean, artists have been painting Nativity scenes for hundreds of years. But I did resent William's taking my idea. It destroyed any desire I had to finish the picture. When I saw his painting, which he created in tempera on copper for Mr. Butts, I felt quite resentful. It was not as I would have done it.

Perhaps this was an Emotion William felt regularly around Mr. Hayley. Perhaps this was why I should never have copied John Flaxman and Henry Fuseli.

Mr. Hayley used to like to read to us passages of his latest project, which was the Life of his friend, the late poet William Cowper. He put William to work engraving five plates for it. Poor Cowper had been prone to madness, and William sympathized much with him. William knew that some people thought he, too, was insane because he saw Visions.

"Do you know, Kate, that Cowper came to me in a vision," said William, as he was working on the plates for Hayley's biography.

"Oh, really," said I, "and what did he say?"

"He said, 'O that I were insane . . . can you not make me truly insane. I will never rest till I am so. O that in the bosom of God I was hid. You retain health and yet are as mad as any of us all—over us all—mad as a refuge from unbelief—from Bacon, Newton and Locke.' "

I was startled at William's insight. People thought anyone mad these days who confessed to a deep religious belief. William was considered Mad by some people; I knew this and so did he. He bore it patiently, because he said we lived in an Age of Science.

Science and philosophy were dominated by Newton and Bacon and Locke, though I did not understand their ideas. I knew that Cowper suffered from religious mania and believed himself Damned, and that Mr. Hayley had been a true friend to him for many years. Whatever his faults, Mr. Hayley had a kind heart.

Sometimes I thought long about Hayley's life, for some of it had been certainly sorrowful. His marriage to Eliza obviously had not been happy years. His son Thomas, of whom he was so fond, was the child of his housemaid, and poor Thomas died so young. When I thought about the loss of his child, my heart went out to him. Even though my own baby never really lived, I mourn her to this day, so I sympathized with William Hayley.

Yet there was more, too, because I had to admit that I was flattered by the attentions of a famous man—a learned man at that. But at the same time I was flattered, his attentions made me uneasy. Why, I wondered, had he chosen to befriend us? Surely William had something to do with it. Hayley was fascinated with William, as many people have been. There is something magnetic about William—his eyes, his aura. Perhaps I was jealous of that, and wanted to deflect some of Hayley's attention to myself. And yet I felt that his interest in me was improper. William, too, had conflicting feelings about Hayley.

For William, in the depths of night, would often wake and write his long poem, *Vala*. He seemed to write as if from Divine Dictation, and he would be terribly agitated as he wrote, it was as if he were letting go of some great rage, otherwise inexpressible:

> . . . Fury in my limbs. destruction in my bones & marrow
> My skull riven into filaments. my eyes into sea jellies
> Floating upon the tide wander bubbling & bubbling

Uttering my lamentations and begetting little monsters
Who sit mocking upon the little pebbles of the tide . . .

In the morning, when I looked at these pages, I saw to my alarm
that he had begun to draw in the margins horrible things, erect Male
Members, figures with breasts but also with huge male Organs, men
copulating with men, and strangest of all, a naked woman with an
altar or chapel where her sex should have been.

From Kate's Notebook.
Wednesday, April 2, 1801.

I have been plagued by rheumatic pains and the Ague for several days.
William has sent for Cathy, who came down in a not very good mood
but she cheered up when she saw I was sick so she could have William
to herself. They are now on a walk to Bognor, where they will take tea.
I do not feel like providing a meal today.

Why does this happen so often? Mr. Hayley came by, all smiles, bearing a bouquet of daffodils. This time he gave me a little hug as he
left—brotherly affection, he called it. How do I let him know I do not
care for these attentions, without offending him? We are so dependent
on his Patronage!

"Is it true you might become wealthy and famous if you became a
Portrait Painter?" I asked William. It was something Hayley had suggested to me.

William was sitting by the kitchen fire, reading and writing in a
book, as he always did. His clothes were ink-stained, as usual, and his
hair rather long, since had not allowed me to cut it for some months.
He had a little grey in his hair now, though it still glowed copper in the
firelight. Aside from that, he was as powerfully built as ever, and did
not look his forty-four years.

William looked up in surprise.

"I have thought of that," he said.

"And?"

"And I have rejected the idea! My visions are angry with me here. I am not doing what I was meant to do. I am *not* a Portrait Painter, whatever Hayley wishes. I will engrave his silly *Ballads*, but I thank God Mr. Butts still asks me for paintings!"

I sighed and said no more. It was the second time he had chosen to ignore worldly success; he might have succeeded in the Print Trade. There were many Print shops in London now, but we had been one of only a few. William had let that go. And now, he was chafing under Hayley's kindly meant direction. Were we never to have any worldly success?

It was always because of his Visions and his Writing. No one paid much attention to William as a poet, though some of his Illuminated Books still sold, and we printed new batches from time to time. But he wrote all the time, that odd, long poem *Vala*, and now I had seen that he had begun another manuscript which he called *Milton*, and kept in a separate folder.

He had begun to write it one bright day. We were in the garden when suddenly I felt as if the Sun was coming nearer and nearer. The light was terrible. I cried and hid my face in my hands. Through my fingers I saw William stagger backward as if struck by lightning.

But William saw an Angel, descending from the sky over our Cottage. He rose up, joyful. And William recognized the Angel as the Spiritual Form of John Milton, who then entered into William himself. William, elated, knew he, too was a Prophet, as Milton had been in *Paradise Lost*. It was not the first time William had been visited by the Spirit of Milton. It had happened, too, in Lambeth at Hercules Buildings. But this time, William knew it was time to write.

From Kate's Notebook.
Tuesday, December 29, 1829.

Though I have given Mr. Tatham many Letters written by William, he has collected the letters of some of William's friends, also—especially Mr. Hayley's. Frederick is especially interested in our stay at Felpham, for he knew William became Inspired there.

Fred has described to me a dream he recently experienced.

He is in a field somewhere outside London, where the sky is wide and grey. He sees himself from above, wearing a threadbare jacket and riding breeches, and a worn travelling pack is on the ground beside him. He is speaking earnestly to a motley group of farm people: he has the impression that he is preaching to them. They are looking at him with incomprehension, and he is becoming more and more agitated. He feels a terrible urgency to be understood.

"But you must be warned!" he is almost shouting. "Ye have been warned! Shut not out your Saviour!"

They turn their backs on him. Humiliation washes over him in waves, and he awakens shivering.

Poor Frederick.

18

In Which Our Stay in Felpham Becomes Unpleasant

From Kate's Notebook.
Wednesday, July 1, 1801.

I am feeling jealous of William's interest in Paulina at Lavant. He is always riding over there with Mr. Hayley to take coffee and enjoy literary conversation. I cannot believe I am still feeling Jealous! I am determined to rise above it.

Yet often I do resent all the attention William receives, while I slave away in the background. No one pays attention to Wife, even if she is a Printer herself. And I am an Artist too! I can draw like a Flaxman and paint a watercolour like a Blake—what useless gifts! I even see William's Visions. Oh, I truly am a *Shadow* of Delight, as he still calls me.

I wonder if William would care if he knew about Hayley's little attentions to me? If I am being honest with myself, I know I am rather flattered by them. After all, he is regarded as a very important man of letters. The other day, I even let him give me a little kiss on both cheeks, in the French manner, when he left after delivering a treat from his cook.

William, too, is sometimes flattered by Hayley's attentions. He does not always chafe at his company, for Hayley is always in good spirits, and William is prone to Melancholy, even in Felpham.

I got William out of one of his black moods the other day by asking him about a Vision I knew he had experienced recently while walking from Felpham to Lavant to meet Cathy at the Coach station. She has been here again on one of her interminable visits.

It had been a lovely sunny day, and William had fancied Angels in the bowers of Hawthorne that bordered his path, when he saw his Father hovering upon the wind, with his brother Robert, too, and behind him his brother John, who had died in the army in the Netherlands.

"They wanted *me*," said William. "Sometimes the dead do that, you know. They come for you, mostly in dreams. But you must not go with them then. And you know how I can always see two Forms of things?"

I nodded.

"Well, I saw a Thistle across my way. But it also appeared to me as an old man with grey hair. And he said, 'Don't go back. Life will only bring you Poverty, Envy, old age and fear. All joys will be tainted.' He sounded just like my Father! But I defied him, and struck the Thistle with my foot."

"Then what happened?"

"I struck the Thistle with my foot, I struck the old man in my path! I cried to Heaven in defiance! I will not accept that every duty in life and every joy be tainted with sorrow. Then the Sun appeared to me as Los, my Spiritual Form, the Blacksmith of my poems, the Forger in Fire. And I was inspired with Arrows of Thought. My mind like a bowstring was fierce with Ardour! Life is Good, Kate! Yes, I will go on with my work, and so complete my Spiritual Tasks!" And he cheered up then for several days.

Well, at last I myself have been invited to meet the sainted Paulina. We are all to go to her house in Lavant next Wednesday.

Wednesday, July 7.

Harriet Poole—Paulina—is plump and pretty, and she has set her cap for Felpham Billy, if I am any judge of character! How stupid I am to have been Jealous!

. . .

In October, Great Britain and France signed an agreement to end the War, and William was elated. He thought that we might even go to France and see great Paintings. He wrote to Flaxman:

October 19, 1801.

> Peace opens the way... The Kingdoms of this world are now become the Kingdoms of God & his Christ, & we shall reign with him for ever & ever. The Reign of Literature & the Arts Commences... Now I hope to see the Great Works of Art, as they are so near to Felpham, Paris being scarce further off than London. But I hope that France & England will henceforth be as One Country and their Arts One, & that you will ere long be erecting Monuments in Paris—Emblems of Peace.
> My wife joins with me in love to You & Mrs. Flaxman...

The Peace of Amiens was not finally signed till March of the next year. Fuseli and others did get to Paris, but we never did.

Every November I could count on William being in the Slough of Despond, and this year was no different from any other. His black mood came upon him. This time he seemed to be deeper in Spiritual Struggle than ever. He tried to pray but no words would come; his Visions fled.

"It is a dryness of the Spirit," he told me once. "I am parched. I cannot Believe."

To me, Unbelief was not so painful. I did not care whether God existed or not after Paul-Marc died. I carried on from day to day, not thinking. It was not till real trouble came that *I* began to pray again. But William was not like me. His faith was central to him. He had to believe in Christ or he was plunged into Despair, for Christ was part of William's Imagination, and if that light was gone, then William could not create.

. . .

Early in the month, William announced that he had invited Cathy to come for another visit.

"She will cheer me up," he said. I was not overjoyed, but could hardly complain if he thought she would do him good. Also, it would bring us news of London.

Cathy arrived on Tuesday, the fifteenth of November—a cold, windy day. The sea was steel-grey with caps of white foam, and the sky was troubled. She looked pink-cheeked and energetic as she entered the house with her baskets and bags. As was her custom, she immediately took charge.

"Let us make some tea. I have just the tonic!" Cathy always brought us herbal teas.

That night, as I prepared the evening meal, I was aware that William and Cathy were talking together intensely in low tones. Oh, well, I thought, she always likes to have William to herself. I realized that Cathy had few people in her life to care about, and she was closest to William. What I perceived as her jealousy of me was born of loneliness.

The next morning, William asked me to go to Bognor to pick up some drawing paper he had ordered. It was but a short walk westward, and I did not mind going alone, but I thought it almost rude of him. If he wanted to be alone with his sister, I surely would not stand in the way.

"I will stop for the afternoon in Bognor," I told them, as I tied on my Bonnet, "and be back just before sunset."

As it happened, I completed my errands in Bognor in good time, and decided to return early, as the wind was rising. It was mid-afternoon when I opened the door and called a greeting.

William and Cathy were seated before the fire. They looked at me, suddenly guilty.

"What are you doing?" I demanded, dropping my parcels.

I could see that before them on the low bench before the fire was a small dish full of dry leaves.

There was a brief silence, then both of them began speaking at the same time.

"Stop!" I raised my hand. "I can see you are up to something. But why the Secrecy? Why send me away? What are you keeping from me, of all people!"

"It is too dangerous for you," said William.

"It is a powerful potion," said Cathy, pointing at the dish.

"What on earth for?"

"For Visions," said William simply.

"It is called Devil's Trumpet," said Cathy, "and I have dried it. We will burn the leaves and inhale the smoke. But I have warned William. It can make one go Mad."

I threw off my coat and shawl and left them in a heap on the floor. I picked up the dish of dried greenish brown leaves. It had an unpleasant smell.

"But why, why do you need this, William?" I cried.

"Because the Visions have deserted me," he said.

"But surely this is not the way to bring them back!" I protested. "Surely you must be worthy of your visions."

He said nothing. I turned to Cathy.

"And what exactly is this Devil's Trumpet?"

She took the dish from my hands.

"It is *datura stramonium*. Sometimes it is called Jimsonweed," she said, "because rumour has it that American Soldiers in Jamestown in 1676 ate some shoots and went mad with hallucinations for several days. But it is far older than that. It is said the Delphic Oracles inhaled the smoke."

She opened a small wooden box, and took out a small clay pipe.

"So this is why you asked Cathy here," I said to William, sick at heart. Cathy went on preparing the pipe, stuffing the bowl with dried leaves.

"You are not going to leave me out of this," I said, seating myself between them before the fire. "I am William's wife!"

"Very well," said Cathy, "I will administer this to you both. But I warn you, do not take too much into your lungs. It is dangerous and bad for the liver. Pace yourself slowly. And think good thoughts."

My heart began to beat faster. The afternoon was darkening, and the firelight cast shadows in the room. Cathy, illuminated by the fire, seemed like a strange Priestess. She gave the pipe to William, who lit it with a small stick ignited by the coals. I did not care for the smell of the smoke. William inhaled the pipe, and passed it to me.

I inhaled, coughed, and drew more of the acrid smoke into my lungs. I was looking into the glowing coals of the fire. And as I looked, a whole world opened up in the flickering glow. I entered the heart of the fire, and yet was not burned. It was as if I were surrounded by luminous halls of gold. I looked over at William.

He was not alone. He was surrounded by creatures with vast, fiery wings. His angels had returned to him! His face was so beautiful!

I looked down at my own open palm. What intricacies of lines, cross-hatches and patterns. What perfection in the articulation of the fingers! I began to weep for Joy at the Beauty of everything I saw.

Cathy was watching me.

"How do you feel, Kate?"

"I feel as if I could fly!" I cried, standing up. "I know I can fly! I have to go outside."

I knew where I was going. I sensed that Cathy and William were right behind me. It was still light enough to find my way to the beach, where the sound of the sea roared in my head. The tide was high. I was almost flying already.

Our Lane ended at a small pier, which extended several feet over the water. I ran to the edge of the pier, and leapt into the welcoming air. I flew.

Voices came to me through a fog of Pain.

"She breathes! Oh, thank God!" It was Cathy.

My chest felt crushed. A searing pain went through my right arm as I tried to move.

"Kate, Kate, my beloved. Open your eyes." It was William.

I felt the stony beach under my cheek. I realized I was lying wet through from head to toe. There was the salt taste of the sea in my mouth. Suddenly I threw up.

"That's it, lass," said a strange, deep voice. "She will recover now. Put her to bed."

Strong arms picked me up. I could see a black beard and a fisherman's cap above dark eyes.

"Thank God you were here," I heard William say. "Thank God for your boat and hook."

Every breath I took was painful. As the fisherman carried me back to the house, I began to remember what had happened and the wonderful sensation of flight.

Late that night, I awoke from sleep to find William keeping watch over me. I felt weak and bruised, but no bones had been broken. I smiled at him.

"I put you in danger," he said. "Forgive me."

"You know I do."

"There is something I must know," he took my hand in his. "Before you went to the shore—did you see the Angels?"

"Yes," I answered.

At Christmastime, Mr. Hayley gave a party at Turret House. It was a very grand affair, with boughs of greenery and holly everywhere, and candles lighting up every room till they became quite hot and stuffy! The place is called Turret House because of a funny turret Mr. Hayley had built on the front, so that he could climb it and see the ocean.

The big square house stands on a sloping lawn, surrounded by Shrubs and lofty Elms, and is approached by a handsome flight of stone steps. Mr. Hayley prefers to live there now, rather than at his big house at Eartham, because of memories of his son Thomas. It is in Turret House that William designed the Heads of Poets for the Library, and some of them were there on display.

Mr. Hayley invited many grand people to his party, and seemed to like to show William and me off to them, as if we were new possessions, even though we had been there over a year.

"This is William Blake, Painter, and his lovely wife Catherine," he would say. That is where I first met Lord Egremont from Petworth, and Lady Hesketh, an imposing woman who was a cousin of the poet Cowper, and Mr. Rose, the Lawyer.

By now, I knew how to behave in Company, and wore my hair up high in curls at the back. I drank several glasses of sherry, and let Mr. Hayley kiss me three times under the mistletoe.

By February, I was beginning to feel ill much of the time. I had a cold almost every few weeks, and my joints ached. It was the damp ocean air, and the aftermath of nearly drowning. I asked Cathy to bring me some laudanum down from London.

There was no doubt that the Devil's Trumpet had returned Visions to William. He was elated, and had smoked the weed twice more. I, too, was fascinated by what it did to us. Such images appeared as can hardly be imagined. Yet I knew it was taking a toll on our health.

William had experienced fever and headache. I noticed that the pupils of his eyes were sometimes dilated, and I experienced an irregular heartbeat that frightened me. But it was hard to give up the Sensations, though I knew we should.

William was spending nearly every evening now at Turret House because Hayley was teaching him Greek. William has always found learning languages easy. So there he would go, up to Hayley's Library, where they would sit at a long oak table and translate the *Odyssey*. Mr. Hayley, who carried on a voluminous correspondence with many friends, would catch up on his letter writing while William studied.

Letter from William Hayley to a friend.
May 16, 1802.

...you will be anxious when I tell you, that both my good Blakes have been confin'd to their Bed a week by a severe Fever—Thank Heaven they are both revived, & He is at this moment by my side, representing on copper an Adam, of his own, surrounded by animals, as a Frontispiece to the projected Ballads.—

Adieu my dearest Johnny, give me speedily a good account of yourself & your works—accept our united Benefaction & believe me

Ever yr sincere & affectionate

Hermit

"How is your System coming?" I asked William one day in Spring, when we were digging the vegetable bed in the garden. I was going to plant carrots and parsley in alternate rows.

"It is complicated," said William, resting his spade. "Do you really want to know?"

"Of course I do!"

"Well, I've decided there are Three Classes of Mortal Men, and I've called then The Elect, The Redeemed and The Reprobate."

"Oh," I said, pulling a weed.

"Shall I go on?"

"Well of course! Don't you think I am capable of understanding?"

"It's complicated, that's all. Take the Elect. They are the Righteous ones, the Pharisees of this world, from before Time began. They'll never change. I also call them Negations. We know many people like that—Hayley, for instance."

"Hayley ! Kind, mild William Hayley?"

"The Mild are the Worst Kind! They kill you with kindness. Corporeal friends are Spiritual Enemies sometimes."

"Oh," I said, turning over the soil with my trowel.

"Now the next two classes, the Reprobate and the Redeemed are more important, because they are Contraries, and they get the business of life done," said William, warming to his subject.

" 'Without Contraries Is No Progression,' " I quoted a line from William's *Marriage of Heaven and Hell.*

"You remember!" He was pleased. "Yes, you see the Reprobate are the Prophets, outcasts in the community. They work upon the Redeemed, the timid and good-hearted, until the good men are roused to action."

"A clash of a Prophet's wrath and an Artist's Pity?" I ventured.

William's eyes flashed.

"You've grasped it! That's the formula for the New World! All will appear renewed in the Divine Vision. Listen, Kate, I know where John Milton went wrong in *Paradise Lost.*"

This conversation was moving too fast for me, but I did not let William see. I kept silent, and made a furrow, ready to scatter my carrot seeds.

"I have written many lines of an epic poem about it," William went on, "for my idea is to bring him back to Earth to redeem himself and his vision. He became too Rational . . . his God became the God of the Deists, a tyrant removed from Creation. His works, his Emanations, his wives . . . he has to renew them all! It is a long poem—I am not sure when I will finish it."

He went back to his digging, and I planted the carrots. *Milton,* too, was like a seed which grew over time, and reflected our lives in secret ways by the time it was finally engraved, many years later.

From Letters to Lady Hesketh, from William Hayley.
July 6, and July 16, 1802.

...Blake is in bed under care of perhaps the very best wife that ever mortal possessed, at least one that most admirably illustrates that expressive appellation a Helpmate.

...Heaven has bestow'd on this extraordinary mortal perhaps the only female on Earth who could have suited Him exactly—They have now been married more than 17 years and are as fond of each other, as if their Honey Moon were still shining—They live in a neat little cottage, which they both regard as the most delightful residence ever inhabited by a mortal; they have no servant:—the good woman not only does all the work of the House, but she even makes the greater part of her Husband's dress, and assists him in his Art—she draws, she engraves, she sings delightfully, and is so truly the Half of her good man, that they seem animated by one soul, and that a soul of indefatigable Industry and Benevolence—it sometimes harries them both to labour rather too much...I endeavour to be as kind as I can to two creatures so very interesting and meritorious...

I know that William never told Hayley about the poetry that was so important to him, and about his System, his view of mankind, and the work he was now outlining, the poem about John Milton, who was to return to Earth to redeem the mistakes he had made about God and Women. William instinctively knew that Hayley, kind as he was, was not a kindred spirit, and was, as well, a not very good poet, in spite of what the London literary world seemed to think. More than that, we were dependent upon Hayley, and sometimes the fact that we were his social inferiors, though never mentioned by him, was inadvertently suggested, by a wave of the hand, or a casual remark. One thing I knew about William Hayley: he really liked and respected Women. He had no hard edge underneath, as Fuseli had, and William had—no fear of female power. And for that, I admired him.

From Kate's Notebook, n.d.

Oh, God, I do not know what to do, where to turn.

Hayley is becoming reckless, too familiar. And yet he means no harm. But I cannot let this go on. Today he surprised me in the garden. It was a hot day, so I was wearing only a thin shift, and my arms were bare.

"Oh, Mr. Hayley, you startled me." I reached for my shawl.

"My dear, you are beauteous as the Morn," he said, coming up to me. He looked at me frankly. I blushed.

"You should not stare, Sir," I said.

He boldly put his hand to my shoulder, and moved my shift. One breast was bare.

"Sir, you should not!" I protested.

"Ah, Kate," he said, "Forgive me, you are so beautiful. May I not gaze at you, as I would the Moon?"

And he pushed down the other side of my shift. My breasts were naked before him for a moment before I covered myself with my arms and ran inside.

I felt uncomfortably like one of Mr. Hayley's Greek statues.

From Kate's Notebook.
October 15, 1802.

This has been a beautiful month of cool sunny days and golden harvests. The sea sparkled this afternoon as I walked on the shore, collecting shells. I should have been happy, but instead my thoughts were troubled. I recalled last night when I had stayed by William's side, witnessing his Visions.

He had smoked Devil's Trumpet yet again. I have never lost the feeling that there is something Dishonest about the Visions he achieves this way. I have stopped smoking the leaves myself, for not long ago, I found myself once more sitting on the Pier, but this time throwing into the water all the Shillings and Pence I had so carefully saved in my Purse, watching with deep fascination the concentric circles in the water.

I want William to stop using the weed, but I do not know how to persuade him against it. It has helped to keep his Black Mood away, after all.

Last night, to increase his Pleasure, he smoked the Pipe before taking me to bed.

"You are a whole World of Delight," he said, "our five senses contain worlds within worlds."

I closed my eyes, the better to share in his experience. Sometimes I have wept for Joy when he made love to me so. But last night was different.

Love did not go well. Something cruel entered into William and he was not Gentle. He called me strange names, *Gonorill*, and *Cambel*, and *Rahab*. He spoke these names with Disgust. He had travelled to some Shadowy Land which I could not see. But I could sense something awful. It was like the Grey Presence I had seen so long ago when I had been out of my body. This Presence was in the room with us.

William groaned, writhed, and babbled.

"Chaos," he whispered.

His eyes were open and staring, but I knew not what horrors he saw. Then I felt the Grey Presence come closer. I crept out of bed and wrapped myself in a quilt. I knew that only I stood between the shadow and William. My heart was a terrible pulsation. I had never been so aware of what it was—Life—a heart beating. If it stopped, I would die.

I picked up the candle and held it aloft.

"In the Name of Jesus Christ," I cried, "leave this place!"

Something snarled.

Then I was conscious of words in my head.

I will leave with either him or you.

So that was it. We had called up something truly Evil from the Spirit Realm. William had always said that Evil was part of being Human, but I was not so sure.

In my panic, I could think of only one name.

"Robert!" I cried. "Help me!"

William and I found ourselves safe in our bed this morning. I cannot remember anything after I called Robert's name. William will not tell me what he saw.

．　．　．

The day after William and I had the terrible encounter with the Grey presence, or Spectre, as William called it, we had a terrible argument. I insisted he give up Devil's Trumpet.

"I think your visions are Evil! They come from Hell!" I shrieked at him.

We were in the garden, piling up leaves for a bonfire. I was going to heat some stones and bake potatoes under them. No matter what, we had to eat.

"No!" he shouted, throwing down his rake and heading back into the house.

I followed him, weeping in frustration. Then I tried a different tack.

"How will you ever know if your Visions are again True, if you use the leaves?"

He sat down at the kitchen table, silent. I felt that he had heard me.

"Do you think Robert would have come unless you were in great danger?" I asked.

William held his head in his hands.

"You are right," he said, "I have lost the way. It is because of the emptiness that I looked into a year ago, before Cathy came with the Devil's Trumpet. But I have since seen an even worse Void."

"It is over now, my dear," I put my arms around him. And although I did not have any great conviction, I said, "Your Visions will come again."

Excerpts from a long Letter from William Blake to Thomas Butts. November 22, 1802.

Dear Sir,

My Brother tells me that he fears you are offended with me. I fear so too because there appears some reason why you might be so. But when you have heard me out you will not be so ... But you will Justly enquire why I have not written All this time to you? I answer I have been very Unhappy & could not think of troubling you about it or any of my real Friends (I have written many letters to you which I burnd &

did not send) & why I have not before now finishd the Miniature I promisd to Mrs. Butts? I answer I have not till now in any degree pleased myself & now I must intreat you to Excuse faults for Portrait Painting is the direct contrary to Designing & Historical Painting in every respect...

And now let me finish with assuring you that Tho I have been very unhappy I am so no longer I am again Emerged into the light of Day I still & shall to Eternity Embrace Christianity and Adore him who is the Express image of God but I have travld thro Perils & Darkness not unlike a Champion I have Conquerd and shall still Go on Conquering Nothing can withstand the fury of my Course among the Stars of God & in the Abysses of the Accuser My Enthusiasm is still what it was only Enlarged and confirmd...

Accept my Sincere love & respect

I remain Yours Sincerely
WILLIAM BLAKE

Now I a four fold vision see
And a fourfold vision is given to me
Tis fourfold in my supreme delight
And threefold in soft Beulah's night
And twofold Always. May God us keep
From Single vison & Newtons sleep

. . .

I own that I allowed Mr. Hayley a certain Familiarity in the autumn of 1802. He asked me to model for him; he was going to try his hand at drawing.

He would come to the Cottage when William was working in the Library at Turret House. Often William knew he was visiting me, but he did not know I was posing for Hayley. I do not know why I did not tell him. I think I was ashamed; but I also found it exciting.

At first I wore my own clothes. Then Mr. Hayley brought me a kind of Grecian gown to wear, very thin and revealing. He asked me to strike Attitudes, and showed me some drawings that Romney had done of Lady Hamilton. I had an amusing time, dancing a few steps, then pausing.

"Oh, that is Capital!" exclaimed Hayley. "Do it again, Kate."

Now my sleeve had fallen open to reveal my bosom.

"Will you not let me draw you Nude?" he asked quietly.

I thought, *Why not?* It was flattering, at my age, to have a man look at me as an object of Art, perhaps of Desire.

I dropped the garment, and turned hesitantly toward him. The sunlight shone full upon me, the fire kept the room warm.

"How lovely you are," said Hayley.

The room became very quiet as he sketched. But sometimes he did not sketch, only looked.

I heard a sudden footstep. The door opened.

"My God," said William, "what is going on here?"

Lines from William Blake's Notebook

> To H—
> Thy Friendship oft has made my heart to ake
> Do be my Enemy for Friendships sake

"He looked at you with Lust," said William, "as I do now."

Our bedroom was lit by only one candle. He moved it closer to me.

"*I* will look at you," he said. "Remove your nightgown."

I did as I was told.

Naked in the candlelight, my breasts heaving, I let my husband look at me as if I were an artist's model.

I lay back on the bed, on my side, the curve of my hip enticing him, my nipples like rose hips, erect. His hands cupped my breasts, and he kissed them, and my body, all the way down to the warmth between my legs. His tongue fluttered over me. I wanted him inside me, I wanted him gasping into me, I wanted him pushing against me with all his Maleness.

And then, together, we entered another Space. It was like whirling through a vortex and on the other side was silvery Moonlight, Perfect Peace, and Rest.

When I reflected on my behaviour with Hayley and William's response, I concluded that it marked an important milestone in our Marriage. It was as if we acknowledged the Struggle between us.

Why had I responded to Hayley's attentions in that way? I liked him—I felt a bond with him because we both loved William in our different ways, and I did feel a spark of attraction between us. I always had.

But I wanted also to make William jealous, as he had made me jealous in the past. I seemed to hear the ghost of Mary whispering in my ear, "You are a Person in your own right, Catherine Blake. No matter how devoted a wife, you are his Partner in Work, and his Comfort in Sickness and in Health. You still have fine black eyes and abundant hair and full breasts, so you wanted William to see that other men desire you. But is that really the way to make him respect your mind and Female Being? Is Lust the only Weapon you have?"

No, Mary would not approve. But sexual magic was important to William, and I knew I could always reach him that way. But there was often a reaction, too. After lovemaking, he would keep to himself for a while. He was afraid of too much closeness, still, after all these years. He could not bear to feel dominated by anyone. I wanted more from him than he could give me—I had wanted a child. Had he felt inadequate? Did he think he should have had more Worldly Success? Or had he felt that I had failed him by not giving him a son or daughter? Did he feel betrayed that I doubted his visions? Could we ever forgive each other?

Letter to James Blake from William Blake.
January 30, 1803. Felpham.

Dear Brother,

Your Letter mentioning Mr. Butts's account of my Ague surprized me because I have no Ague but have had a Cold this Winter. You know that it is my way to make the best of everything. I never make myself nor my friends uneasy if I can help it. My Wife has had Agues & Rheumatisms almost ever since she has been here, but our time is almost out that we took the Cottage for. I did not mention our Sickness to you & should not to Mr. Butts but for a determination which we have lately made, namely To leave This Place—because I am now certain of what I have long doubted Viz that H. is jealous...& will be no further My friend than he is compelled by circumstances.

The truth is As a Poet he is frightnd at me & as a Painter his views & mine are opposite he thinks to turn me into a Portrait Painter as he did Poor Romney, but this he nor all the devils in hell will never do. I must own that seeing H...Envious (& that he is I am now certain) made me very uneasy, but it is over & I now defy the worst & fear not while I am true to myself which I will be. This is the uneasiness I spoke of to Mr. Butts but I did not tell him so plain & wish you to keep it a secret & to burn this letter because it speaks so *plain*...

I am now Engraving Six little plates for a little work of Mr. H's for which I am to have 10 Guineas each & the certain profits of that work are a fortune... We are very Happy sitting by a wood fire in our Cottage the wind singing above our roof & the sea roaring at a distance but if sickness comes all is unpleasant...

I go on Merrily with my Greek & Latin: I am very sorry that I did not begin to learn languages early in life as I find it very Easy. Am now learning my Hebrew...I read Greek as fluently as an Oxford scholar & the Testament is my chief master. Astonishing indeed is the English Translation it is almost word for word...

My wife joins me in Love to you both...

William said very little about my modelling for Hayley; he even offered to instruct Hayley in drawing. This, of course, put an end to the sessions. Hayley continued on pleasant terms with us, though I know that inwardly William began to dislike him, and became ever more irritable as the weeks went by. For my part, I felt embarrassed in the company of Mr. Hayley, and regretful that our intimacy was terminated so abruptly. He was a kind man, and I did not like to hurt his feelings.

To smooth things over, I undertook to print the whole number of the six plates for Hayley's *Life of Cowper*, which William had finished. Everyone was very pleased with them. The Publishers gave me 10 Guineas each. This gave me confidence that between the two of us, we could make a living again when we returned to London in the Fall, because we had determined to go back. Yet we needed a nest egg in order to set up Printing when we got there. Where was that to come from? William seemed oblivious to the problem, but I worried all the time.

My uneasy state of mind was at odds with the season. Spring came early and the daffodils bloomed in the corners of the cottage garden, followed by blossoming cherry and apple trees all around Felpham. William's Spiritual Visitors were coming again regularly, and he even wrote from their dictation many long night.

I should have been happy, but I had a premonition. I heard a Voice of my own: Watch and wait, watch and wait.

From Kate's Notebook.
May 15, 1803.

Today William and I walked to Chichester, to buy some meat at the Market at East Street. It was a lovely Spring day, with puffy white clouds in the sky, and a fresh breeze. We got to Chichester in good time. I always love to see the spire of the Cathedral as we approach. Today there was an unusual buzz in the market, and over the lowing of the cattle in their stalls, we managed to learn the bad news: the Peace of Amiens has ended, and we are going to be at war again with France!

From Kate's Notebook.
July 21, 1803.

There are Soldiers all around Felpham these days. The First Regiment of Dragoons are stationed at Chichester. Some soldiers are billeted at the Fox, and I think the officers look very smart in their red jackets and tight white trousers. Many beacons made of tar-barrels are being erected along the coast. It is feared that Napoleon's fleet is going to invade England!

William is despondent at the breakdown of the Peace. Although he had been in sympathy with the democratic aims of the French Revolution, he is English to the core, and loves his country. He hates Tyranny in the form of Government, any government, and sees only that Famine and War result. I see him writing furiously every evening.

. . .

"Did you know we are in Beulah now?" asked William, putting his arm around me.

We were walking on the stony beach skirting Felpham. The full moon was so bright it cast shadows, while the sparkling edges of the black waves spilled onto the beach and broke into shining rivulets. You could not see the stars because the moon was so bright, but the sky arched over us like the comfort of a mother's arms.

"What is Beulah? The land in the Bible? The married land?"

"Yes, that's it. The name given to Palestine that the Lord delighted in, according to Isaiah. In my System, it is a state of Mind we can reach when we want to rest from the world and take Pleasure, and find Inspiration." He spoke softly.

I thought that was a good state to be in. Then I asked, "What is your name for the place you go when you are Writing or Seeing Visions?"

"I call that Eternity," said William, flicking a stone into the waves and bringing up flakes of silvery moonlight.

"Do you have a name for everyday life? I mean, we live in a Material World, and we aren't usually in Beulah or Eternity."

"Oh, yes, I have a name for that too. It is called Ulro. A horrible place."

I was offended.

"Everyday life is not so horrible," I said. I felt I was defending the realm of women. "We find pleasure in the world around us, in our food, in our friends."

I took off my shoes and began to wade in the water, which was warm at the edges and cold farther in.

"Well, to tell you the truth, I have considered that," admitted William, following me into the water. "I think I will call this Vegetative world we live in Generation. It will be the good part of Ulro. But Wars and Sorrows and Fears and Bad Dreams—that's the state of Ulro!"

"But this is Beulah, is it not?" I laughed, pulling him down into the moon-drenched sand.

Eternity. Beulah. Generation. Ulro. Names I was to become more familiar with in the years ahead, the years when William in obscurity, wrote and wrote, and engraved and coloured shimmering designs that few people ever saw. I knew they meant something important; they held a wisdom he expected certain readers to understand. Only I could not, myself, really understand all those pages. I pretended I did, though.

Chichester on Market Day was full of people and animals. The streets were narrow, so I clutched my portfolio of drawings carefully to my chest. I had slipped away from William with the excuse that I wanted to purchase some candles, but I really wanted to visit the Print Shop on the High Street to see if I could sell a drawing or two. I had not tried to forge drawings for almost four years, but now things were getting desperate. I knew our savings would never cover our return to London.

It was one of those summer days when there are billowing clouds high in the sky, and sunlight comes and goes. A shaft of light illuminated the dim room as I entered the Shop.

There was a counter ahead of me, and behind it two men were bending over some work. One was old Mr. Seagrave, the Printer, but the other—*the other*—was tall. He looked somehow familiar. I remember thinking it odd that he wore a heavy Greatcoat in spite of the season.

My insides heaved. Of course it was not possible. He was dead. But he looked so like Paul-Marc. Just for a minute, I thought . . .

Then he looked up at me. My knees gave way, my heart heaved to my mouth, and I fell to the floor.

I heard a voice, well remembered.

"*Mon Dieu,* it is you! I have searched for two years, ever since I returned . . ."

Yes, it was Paul-Marc. Alive.

They gave me Brandy. I recovered and shook from head to toe. He showered me with words.

"No, no, I did not die. I escaped the Guillotine, but had to let it be known that I was dead. They wanted me dead . . . Ah, *Kate,* how I have dreamed of you!"

"But it has been ten years," I gasped. I could hardly speak, he was clasping me so hard. He was the same, but not the same. His features were sharper.

"Where have you been all these years?" I whispered.

He looked carved from stone.

"At first, in hiding—hard years," he said, "then in Egypt, with Napoleon's army—in Egypt, where our heroic Bonaparte deserted us after Nelson's victory! He left us to rot in the heat with the flies and our dysentery! *Merde!* And Bonaparte returned to become a hero."

His voice was bitter. It was not a tone I remembered. He told me his story:

"When I left England, I was young and strong and full of hope that in the end all would be well in France and I would return. I had loved you, another man's wife, and you had loved me. This knowledge protected me from Despair, even though I did not know when I would see you again. But to see you I vowed to do.

"Then—the Terror engulfed me. I was to be executed in November of 1793, the same month as my poor brave cousin, Manon Roland. I will not tell you of all the horrors of my escape, but to hide among dead and bleeding bodies—ah, I dream of it still. At last, through the alleys and sewers of Paris I made my way to the countryside. I lived as a farm labourer, always moving from place to place, pretending to be a peasant. This is how I lived for four years. My name was Jean-Louis Carpentier. Sometimes life was not so hard, the countryside was to me beautiful, especially in Provence. But I was out of place, out of time. My poor country suffered, but now was at war with only the British.

"Finally I came to see that my only hope of regaining a position in life was to join the army of Napoleon. Only in him was there any hope for France.

"Do you think badly of me for fighting against your country?" He paused.

"Oh, no, no," I murmured.

As if to himself, he went on, "How else was I to find a place in life again! How else could I hope to be worthy of your affection? In the army, I could admit to being able to read and write, I could have a commission—I could be paid. And so it was I sailed from Toulon with Bonaparte's Egyptian campaign. I was seasick all the way to Malta, but recovered in time to fight the Egyptian Mameluke Army . . . they ran from us! Then on to Cairo. I was proud of my uniform, the white breeches, blue jacket, high leather boots. I allowed myself a moment of vanity, thinking you would admire me."

I smiled in sympathy, and took his hand.

He went on, "I nearly died in the desert of thirst and fever and starvation, like most of my compatriots. My men fought bravely, but we were weakened by wounds and malaria. When Nelson surprised the French Fleet at Aboukir Bay we were trapped. Our illustrious Bonaparte managed to sail home and left us to fight alone, like dying animals in the desert. Vive la France! Indeed, I am bitter. It was a year before I could get back to France. And everyone was gone. And yet . . . I have seen the Pyramids. And I am again a Printer in England, and can support a Wife."

Paul-Marc had found a chair for me, and was sitting beside me, holding my hand. I could not stop shaking. My thoughts raced. I wondered why he had come back to England, how he had managed to get here in that brief time after the Peace of Amiens.

He partly answered my silent questions by adding, "I wanted to see you again, my Kate. You were all that kept me alive in Egypt—and before that."

"But who told you we were in Sussex?"

"There was talk in the Coffee Houses. Blake the Engraver has gone to Felpham. Is that so strange?"

It was then I noticed the cane leaning nearby against the counter, and saw that Paul-Marc limped painfully as he rose to find my shawl and place it around my shoulders. He saw my gaze.

"Yes, I have been wounded. My leg is not as it was, and never will be. And I have fevers."

"But you are alive!"

"If you can call it living. I am myself not as I was, *chérie*. I have not much joy of life."

It was hard for me to keep from weeping. He needed my love and sympathy, I could see. I was in turmoil. Was this unbelievable meeting a sign from God? I felt drawn to him.

"So you are still forging drawings?" His voice was bleak. I hated to hear those blunt words, though he spoke them softly. The Shopkeeper had tactfully gone into the back room.

"We need money."

"I am not one to judge you, Kate," he said, "you must judge yourself. *Il faut manger pour vivre.*"

I hastily gathered my drawings, which had fallen from my portfolio when I fainted. This was not the time for that business.

"Come, tell me more of your story," I said. "Let us go sit in the Cathedral garden and talk." I still had an hour before William would expect to meet me. Even in my shock and excitement, I knew I could not tell William of this.

In the cool shade of the golden Cathedral, we held hands and spoke of our lives. Soon I realized that it was not the old Paul-Marc who had returned. There was ice in his heart. And there was a terrible need.

"Chérie, God has led me to you at last. He has forgiven me for the terrible acts I have committed in War—I have been allowed to see you again, to touch you. Le Bon Dieu has given you back to me."

My heart yearned toward Paul-Marc, even as something inside me withdrew from the old intimacy. It had been a long time and too much had happened. I was not the Kate he remembered, and yet . . . I trembled in confusion.

I touched his cheek.

"I have thought of you many times, too," I said.

"You cannot know how to think of you has kept me sane!" He hugged me close to him, "I promised myself to find you . . . all these years . . . to come again to England . . . it is too much!"

He wept from all the Emotions he was feeling, and I wept from Sympathy and Apprehension. He seemed to expect us to resume our Friendship as it had been. He told me more of his life in the intervening years—of his privations, of scrounging for food, of eeking out a living as the Labourer, Jean-Louis Carpentier. He told me even of Women he had loved, "but I pretended they were you."

I experienced then a physical pain near my heart.

Finally, he spoke the words I feared.

"Now that I have found you," he said, "you must soon come away with me. I have dreamed of you long enough."

His dark eyes were intent on mine. I looked away.

"No, my dear," I whispered, "it is not possible. I am William Blake's wife, and can belong to no one else after all these years." I was surprised at my own words.

"You do not love him!"

"I do."

There were tears inside me as I spoke, but I knew the Truth absolutely.

"*Je ne comprends pas* . . . I do not understand!" His voice was suddenly cold.

"Paul-Marc, surely you must see that things are not the same . . . we are older . . . life has taken us in different paths. I thought you had died."

"I must see you again!" Paul-Marc's eyes were angry. His hands were on my shoulders.

"No, it cannot be," I said softly, "it was only a dream—you must forget me."

I pushed him gently away.

"No, I will not! *Jamais!* You have been all that has kept life worth living. I cannot forget you! And I cannot believe you can forget *me!* I know you love me. I can see it in your eyes."

"Oh, Paul-Marc, how could I forget you? I loved you once—I have cherished your memory all these years—but my life is with William."

He stood up awkwardly and looked down at me.

"Promise me you will meet me one more time," he said. It was a demand, not a request.

I was weeping. I rose and faced him.

"But where?"

"Near Felpham—on the footpath to Bognor—at noon—in two days." He grasped my hands tightly.

"Yes, yes, I will be there!"

And feeling as if I would faint again, I fled the garden.

From Kate's Notebook.
Friday, August 12, 1803.

Trouble comes in clusters, and in my turmoil over finding Paul-Marc yesterday, and trying to appear my usual self around William, I do not need the disagreeable thing that has just happened. What have I done to bring all this upon us? Bill, the Ostler from the Fox Inn was working in our garden—I had asked him to help repair the stonework on the wall next to the road. I happened to look out the upstairs window and saw that he had invited a Soldier into the garden and was speaking to him.

Unbeknownst to me, William had also seen the Soldier in the

garden, and hating to see strangers on our property—for so we thought of the Cottage—had gone into the garden. I saw them conversing for a while, and the interchange between them becoming ever more heated, and then I heard William order the Soldier to leave.

"Shove Off!" cried the Soldier, with a rude gesture.

"What is your name, Sir?" demanded William.

"Trooper John Schofield of Captain Leathes' Royal Dragoons," he cried, "and you damned well better be prepared for trouble!"

"I said *Leave*," said William, raising his voice.

"I'll knock your Damned Eyes out first, you little Runt!" cried Schofield.

At this point I ran down the stairs and into the garden.

"Turn him out!" I cried. "Damn these Soldiers!"

William was in the process of doing just that. Though he is not tall, he is very strong from all these years of working the Press. He picked up the Soldier by his elbows and pushed him out the gate.

By this time the commotion was attracting the attention of the neighbours. Mr. Cosens, owner of the Mill at Felpham was passing, and his servant's wife, Mrs. Haynes, who lives next door to us, came out of the house with her daughter.

Schofield turned around, swearing and aiming a blow at William. William swore back, and dodging the fists, picked up the Soldier again by the elbows and frog-marched him, kicking and screaming, the fifty yards or so to the door of the Fox. I ran behind, and so did Mrs. Haynes and her daughter.

At the door of the Fox, Mr. and Mrs. Grinder came out, along with their daughter and another soldier, Trooper Cock, he was called. Mr. Grinder ordered the soldiers to go indoors. Mr. Hayley's gardener, John Hosier, came past just then and said to Cock, "Is your Comrade drunk?" They both swore and threatened us all, but eventually went inside. William and I have just returned home, quite agitated. "I hate Violence," said William. Thank goodness it is over.

Saturday, August 13.

Evidently the incident is not over. Mrs. Grinder has told us that Schofield and Cock went on yesterday to drink in the tap room for hours, and Schofield said that William had uttered seditious words, and that he would go to Chichester and charge him before a Justice of the Peace. He insisted that Bill the Ostler had heard the treasonous language and must go with him to be witness. When Bill refused, there was another violent scene. Mrs. Grinder said also that a man named Markson, who leaned heavily on a cane, sat quietly in the tap room listening to the whole thing. "What does it mean, to be charged with Sedition?" I asked William, troubled. "It is very serious, my dear," he said quietly. "Men have hanged for it."

Sunday, August 14.

I have seen Paul-Marc one last time.

The footpath to Bognor follows the Beach, where the wind blows fresh and the sky seemed endlessly blue. It was a day one would expect to be happy, but we were miserable.

Paul-Marc had cut his hair since the old days, and it curled around his ears like a boy's, though he would be thirty-five now. The back of his neck seemed so vulnerable. I stroked it, and he smiled. We were sitting on a rocky outcrop, looking at the sea.

Pity consumed me. I let him kiss my lips, my bosom. I remembered the smell of cloves about his person.

"Have you changed your mind?" he asked. "Will you come to London with me?"

I shook my head. I tried to explain, but he would not listen. Even when I told him of our latest problem about the Sedition charge, he did not seem to care. He became agitated.

"How can you abandon me, now that I have found you at last?"

"Please, Paul-Marc, can you not see that was another life?" I pleaded.

"You have been the one light in my dark life all these years, and now you would leave me?" he said, incredulous. He picked up a stone and threw it into the sea. I watched it splash and disappear.

"It cannot be," I said, "my place and my heart are with William now. And he is in trouble! You must accept this!"

Paul-Marc's boyishness disappeared.

"I can make your life miserable," he said. I knew he referred to my forgeries. "I will see that John Flaxman learns what you have done."

I was appalled.

"You cannot mean that! After all we have meant to each other? Love does not have to turn to Revenge. My dear, we can still love each other in Spirit—we can always be friends." I spoke the age-old words of the end of love.

"You will see," he said, "I will not let you forget me."

I was apprehensive. I stood up and prepared to leave.

"Please be my friend," I pleaded. "We will always be part of each other. I thought of you so often during all these years, as you have thought of me."

"No, I cannot be only your friend."

"Oh, Paul-Marc, my heart is breaking. You have been so dear to me. Can you not let me go in peace?"

He looked at me a long time, a resentful, desperate look.

"Just go," he said.

So I fled the rocks and the sea, and I hope, my past.

Monday, August 15.

We have just been informed that William will have to appear tomorrow in Chichester before a Bench of Justices to answer charges brought against him by Schofield. He called William a "Military Painter"—he'd probably mistaken that for Miniature Painter. The Soldier has declared William said that if Bonaparte should land in England, he, Blake, would side with him, and said, "Damn the King of England—his Soldiers are all bound for Slaves!" And Schofield swore that I said that I would fight for Bonaparte as long as I am able!

We are both terribly upset. William is taking a glass of brandy. I have taken laudanum for my terrible headache. I feel a little worm of fear inside me such as I have never felt before.

Tuesday, August 16.

William is writing a long letter to Mr. Butts about the events of the day, and I am writing here in my Notebook. It is a warm evening, so we do not have a fire. It has been a long day. We went to Chichester this morning, where William appeared before a Bench of Justices to answer the charges.

Schofield and his accomplice, John Cock, made the accusations, and William and Bill the Ostler denied them. The Clerk who wrote down the Accusation told us in private that the Justices are compelled by the Military to suffer a prosecution to be entered into. But they must know it is a Perjury! There is not one witness who heard William say anything he is accused of.

Mr. Hayley had kindly come along with us. He has been a pillar of strength to us both. I don't know what we would have done without him, for William was forced to find bail in the amount of £250 to ensure that he would be present at the Michaelmas Quarter Sessions at Petworth. Mr. Hayley put up £100, and kind Mr. Seagrave, our Printer from Chichester, lent us £50, and William and I had to pay the other £100. This is the sum of our entire savings at Felpham; it is so unfair.

To add to the tumult of my feelings, I caught sight of Paul-Marc on the street! There he stood, leaning on his cane, his dark eyes intent on my face. I looked away, sick at heart.

After it was all over, we went back to Turret House for dinner with Hayley. I am sorry for any irritable thought I ever had about him, and I am sure William feels the same. Hayley has also been very understanding about our desire to return to London. He appears to me now as a loving brother.

The fear which hovered around us like a mist expressed itself in different ways. I took to my bed from time to time, not wanting to get up in the morning at all. William did something interesting. He took a big glass goblet, we call it a Rummer, and engraved upon it with a hard tool the faint outline of an Angel. On the other side, he scratched the words:

> Thou Holder of Immoral Drink
> I Give Thee Purpose Now I Think.

And on the sturdy stem of the rummer he inscribed: Blake In Anguish Felpham August 1803.

All our Neighbours were very kind about expressing their Concern for us, and their sorrow that we were leaving the Village. They became afraid of speaking or even looking at Soldiers, and were appalled at the trouble and expense we had to endure to defend ourselves at this unfair Accusation.

We went back to London in the middle of September. I became very sick to my stomach on the journey, and on arrival at the house of James Blake, where we stayed for the first few weeks before we found lodgings in No. 17 South Molton Street, I went straight to bed.

Of course, my Illness had something to do with Paul-Marc and that whole situation, as well as the Sedition proceeding. I could not stop thinking of him and the sadness of parting from him in that way.

It seemed to me that we had scarcely got to London before William had to turn around and go back to Petworth for the Quarter Sessions on October fourth. He was away about four days, during which time I tried to take myself in hand and get up and walk about London. I found it buzzing with the alarm of War. Handbills were passed out on the street, urging us to "Seize the Musket, grasp the Lance . . . slay the Hell-born Sons of France!"

I heard young Mothers threaten naughty children, "Be Good or Boney will get you!" Napoleon Bonaparte was now First Consul of France and rumour had it he would be Emperor one day. London was preparing for Invasion, and the manufacture of Small Arms was undertaken in many workshops, some that used to cast copper plates for us.

Nevertheless, the Shops looked elegant to me, having been so long in the Village. I decided to buy a hat to cheer myself up, and found a lovely Turban with a big silk bow on one side. Hang the Expense! I thought.

I wore it to greet William on his return. He was full of grim news. He had appeared before several Justices, including John Sargent, a friend of Hayley's, and the Duke of Richmond, who seemed quite hostile, he said. There was also the Earl of Egremont, and John Peachey and William Brereton, men whose faces struck him as especially Accusing.

William had pleaded "Not Guilty" and was formally bound over to appear at the next Quarter Session in January. Our dear Hayley had at this time engaged for him the young lawyer, Samuel Rose.

Letter to William Hayley from William Blake.
October 7, 1803. London.

Dear Sir,

Your generous & tender solicitude about your devoted rebel makes it absolutely necessary that he should trouble you with an account of his safe arrival which will excuse his begging the favor of a few lines to inform him how you escaped the contagion of the Court of Justice—I fear that you have & must suffer more on my account than I shall ever be worth—Arrived safe in London—my wife in very poor health—still I resolve not to lose hope of seeing better days.

Art in London flourishes. Engravers in particular are wanted. Every Engraver turns away work that he cannot Execute from his superabundant Employment. Yet no one brings work to me. I am content that it shall be so as long as God pleases...

How is it possible that a Man almost 50 Years of Age who has not lost any of his life since he was five years old without incessant labour & study... how is it possible that such a one with ordinary common sense can be inferior to a boy of twenty who scarcely has taken or deigns to take a pencil in hand but who rides about the Parks or Saunters about the Playhouses... how is it possible that such a fop can be superior to the studious lover of Art can scarcely be imagined. Yet such is somewhat like my fate & such it is likely to remain. Yet I laugh & sing for if on Earth neglected I am in heaven a Prince among Princes & even on Earth beloved by the Good as a Good Man...

To me, this letter was like a Song one sings to keep up one's Spirits when everything goes wrong. William was in Truth terribly upset at the thought of a Trial. And he began to Doubt himself.

"Could I have said those things to Schofield and not remember?" he asked me one evening at supper.

I passed him some bread and cheese, and refilled his pewter mug of Porter.

"No, of course you did not say those words!" I maintained.

"But I have thought them, I confess to you." He took a big draught from his mug. He appeared Distracted.

"I could not bear to be found Guilty, Kate," he said. "I do not know what I would do."

He stared into the fire, which was slowly dying, and the room became cold. But William did not leave the table. He kept drinking the Porter and staring into the glowing coals.

"Damn the King! Damn all Tyrants!"

"William, calm yourself!"

"Napoleon will soon be Emperor of the French! *Vive Napoléon!*"

"William, for God's sake! Someone will hear you!"

He slumped into his chair again and hung his head in his hands.

"I am afraid," he said simply.

I put my arms around him and comforted him as best I could.

I was so worried about William's State of Mind that the next morning I called on John Flaxman, who had always before understood William's Nervous Fears. It took considerable Determination on my part to brave this visit. I subdued my personal fears and guilt for William's sake.

"Is it possible he is Guilty?" John asked, rather coldly.

We were standing in his Reception Room, which had several marble statues displayed around blue-painted walls. There were only three chairs in the room. I sat down on one, unbidden.

"This is a bad Affair," John continued. "I have heard William say Rash Words before this."

"He is Not Guilty!" I asserted firmly. "I know. I was there. If anyone said anything like that, it was probably me." I stood up defiantly.

John, always stooped, raised his head and looked squarely at me.

"Then you are fortunate not to be on Trial."

I could sense his Exasperation. He was a busy man, of course. He then assured me he would write Mr. Hayley and be sure that Samuel Rose was the very best Lawyer for William's case, and as for William, he would invite him to a Coffee House and try to cheer him up. I felt embarrassed that I had come to see him. William's old nickname for him, Steelyard the Lawgiver, was still apt.

Then Nancy joined us, and John politely took his leave.

Nancy, wearing a sprigged morning gown, looked fashionable as she always did, but I was more conscious than ever of my plain gown and old lace collar. This was the first time I had seen her since our return to London from Felpham, so I was taken aback at her unsmiling greeting.

"I am surprised to see you here, Kate," she said, "but since you have come, I presume it is because of the letter?"

"What letter?" I replied, suddenly overcome with foreboding.

"We have received a letter from a Printseller in Chichester—a Mr. Markson—asking John to authenticate a drawing for sale there. He said that Mrs. Blake had brought it in for sale."

"Oh . . . yes."

"It was not a Subject that John had drawn for many years. I wondered where you had obtained the picture."

"John must have given it to us before you went to Italy," I floundered.

"I see," said Nancy, "pray, be seated, Kate."

I did not want to sit down. I wanted to leave.

"You know, I think you are up to some mischief, Kate. Is it because William is in trouble? Are you selling his Collection?" Her green eyes looked at me sharply.

Half of me went weak with Relief. She did not suspect the picture itself.

"Yes." It seemed the easiest thing to say.

"Does William know?"

"No."

"I do not approve of what you are doing at all!" said Nancy sternly. "I believe it would be best if I told William."

Out of thin air I grasped an idea. Call it Intuition, or Imagination, but it came to me as a gift.

"If you tell William anything at all," I said calmly, "I really must tell John about your long Flirtation with William."

Nancy went pink to her hairline. We were soon chatting like a couple of schoolgirls, and that Crisis was over.

That afternoon, William sat by the fire, staring and staring. This was one of his worst Black Moods. In desperation, I sent for his sister Cathy to raise his spirits, but she only succeeded in depressing mine.

"William is quite Mad, sometimes," she said, matter-of-factly. "I should not be surprised if he did say those seditious things."

"But do you not understand why he is frightened?" I said. We had gone out on the street together, to confer. It was cold and foggy outside. The faint clop of horses hooves echoed through the mists.

"Because he could go to Prison, of course! And think of the shame it would bring to the Family."

"To you and James? You would worry about such a thing if William were to go to Prison or Worse? Oh, Cathy, go home . . . I do not want to talk to you further today!"

So she went home in a huff. I went back up the stairs to our rooms and poured William his afternoon drink of Porter, making sure to have some myself.

William with great effort roused himself from Melancholy and tried very hard to put a cheerful face on things during the weeks before his Trial in January. He had some work from Joseph Johnson, and even Henry Fuseli gave him some designs from Shakespeare illustrations to engrave. Now I could not shake the Melancholy which had taken over my days.

In cold December, I received a letter from Paul-Marc with an address in Spitalfields, secretly delivered to me by a little street urchin when I was in the vegetable market on Berwick Street.

Ma Chérie—may I not still address you so? I attempt one last time to turn your heart. My darling, I could not have survived without the memory of you to sustain me, and only the hope of loving you again allows me to live now. Do not reject me, or I will not answer for what I will do.

My whole body trembled as I finished the letter, and my mind was in turmoil. I had loved him once so much. He could still touch my heart. But William's trouble was so frightening now that it clarified my life. Nothing could persuade me away from my husband's side ever again.

I replied to Paul-Marc:

Blake, *Mrs. Blake* (c. 1805). Courtesy of Tate Gallery, London/Art Resource, New York

My dear, what has passed between us must remain a Memory. My poor William is in terrible trouble. The Trial is to be on January eleventh in Chichester. We are both worried and miserable. The thought that William could be Executed if he is found Guilty haunts our days. Please try to forgive me for what appears to you a Desertion. Part of my Heart will always be yours, but I am, forever, William Blake's wife.

19

In Which There Is A Trial

As I tell my story to Fred, it is important to me to be as truthful as possible. He has become so intrigued with William, so busy collecting documents and recollections of William's friends. He goes about speaking to Mr. Linnell and Mr. Butts, and he continues to sell drawings and prints for me. The Trial interests him mightily, so I have unearthed Cathy's letters, and I will tell him about my own personal trials.

At the beginning of January 1804, I knew that I could not accompany William to Chichester to attend his Trial for Sedition and Assault, set for January eleventh. I was so weak I could scarcely raise my head from my Pillow. I had lost all interest in eating. I burst into tears at unexpected times.

"How can you add to William's burdens like this?" Cathy scolded me, her grey eyes so like William's, stern. She had made numerous cups of herbal teas for me, to no avail.

This only made me weep again.

"Please, Cathy," I begged, "go with William to Chichester. Leave me here—young Mrs. Enoch downstairs can see to my needs."

"It is only Female Trouble, you can leave her for a few days," Cathy said to William, who had come into the bedroom. We only had two rooms in South Molton Street, and they were comfortable enough, but you could hear every word between them.

Poor William had no choice. It was *not* Female Trouble; I think it was Fear. A Guilty verdict could mean he would hang. But William was better off thinking it Female Trouble. I tried to put on a brave face the day he and Cathy left to catch the Coach for Chichester. I wept not at all, and told William I would pray for him. Somewhere in the months between August and January, I had stopped hating God. I just wanted Him to help us. I bargained in my Prayers: if God would let William be Not Guilty, I would be a good Christian for the rest of my life. I waved from the window as they disappeared down South Molton Street.

William had prepared a clear memorandum for Mr. Rose, showing plainly that Schofield was lying, that none of the people at the Stable Door of the Inn heard any of the words William was supposed to have said, and that the witness in the garden, Bill the Ostler, has said on Oath that no word of the remotest tendency to Sedition was uttered. And there was one thing we had found out about Schofield that might help cast doubt on his testimony. He had been a Sergeant, but had been demoted to Private because of Drunkenness.

But what if the Judge knew of William's past friendship with Tom Paine or of his work for Joseph Johnson, who had been to prison himself just for being a publisher of works supporting Parliamentary Reform? What if they knew of our friendship with Mary Wollstonecraft? Any of these things could prejudice the Court against William. Was it any wonder I retired to my bed, pulled the covers over my head and stared into the darkness?

What is this place? This shadowy dream-world where the trees grasp with gnarled fingers at my skirts as I pass? There is no Sun, nor Moon, nor Star, but rugged wintery rocks under foot. Yet I am propelled by I know not what Energy towards an empty field, in the midst of which stands a towering stone Church, and over the door is a Gothick window with two panes of glass and a circle at its peak, which seems to me like an Accusing Eye.

Inside, the huge space is cold and empty, the plaster is peeling from the walls, and at the end of the room, I see myself, seated at a Loom, weaving with silken thread. I saw to my horror that I was weaving female babies. One of the babies was clothed in fire and gems and gold. As I watched, she turned into a beautiful woman with golden hair. It was myself, only I had golden hair. I had always wanted golden hair. And I saw that she was embracing a man, and that man was William.

But then a strange thing happened. The beautiful woman got older and older, and as she did so, the man became younger and younger until finally she picked up the baby Boy. And then she did a terrible thing. She nailed him down upon a rock, and she bound his head with iron thorns, and pierced his hands and feet, and thrived upon his cries.

As I watched, she magically grew young again as he grew older, and he was young and handsome, and she a beautiful Virgin. Now he broke his manacles and bound her down, and had his way with her. What kind of strange dance of the Sexes was this?

The scene changed again and the Church became a Courtroom. Everyone was there, William, Mary, Henry Fuseli, Mr. Hayley, even Paul-Marc. Why were they at William's Trial? They were all looking at me. Mary appeared to be the Judge, for she wore a wig. Then I realized that I was not wearing any clothes. I was overcome with Guilt and Shame. Mary pounded on the table with her gavel. The blows echoed in my head, in my very bones. The room closed in on me, the knocks became louder and louder . . .

Knock! It was my own door. Where was I? I woke with dread in my heart. But it was only kind young Mrs. Enoch from downstairs come to see how I fared now that William had gone to his Trial. I wept in relief, for the Dream was over, but I pondered it a long time.

Letter to Mrs. Catherine Blake.
Wednesday, January 11, 1804. 4 P.M.
17 South Molton Street, London.

Dear Kate,

William has asked me to send you this account of his Trial, the main part of which has just ended. We are awaiting the Verdict, and my poor brother is too agitated to write, but he knows you are eagerly awaiting word of us, and I will prepare this letter so that once the Verdict comes, we can post it off immediately. I know, Sister, that we have had our differences in the past—I have felt that you kept William too much to yourself, and that you kept me from Paul-Marc—but this Trouble must unite us. We must help each other, especially if the verdict goes against us.

I write this letter on a small table at the back of this cold and gloomy Guildhall in Chichester. The stone walls are damp, even though they have hung draperies over some parts of them. This used to be an old Priory, and one can see that there were graceful Gothick windows at the end where the Judge is sitting, but they have been boarded up, which adds to the gloom. The ceiling is high and rises to a becoming Arch above us.

The Judge is the Duke of Richmond, who—Mr. Rose told me—is also the Field Marshall for the Troops around Chichester. Mr. Rose is not happy that the Duke is our Judge. Both he and Mr. Hayley are afraid he is bitterly prejudiced against William.

Incidentally, poor Mr. Hayley had an accident a few days ago which almost prevented him appearing as William's character witness! He was galloping his new horse, which stumbled, and Mr. Hayley pitched forward to strike his head on a very large flint in the road. If it had not been for a new hat that he had been persuaded to wear that very morning, he could have been killed. So he wears a bandage on his brow, and he moves even more stiffly than usual with his cane. He said that living or dying he was going to make his appearance at the trial of his friend Blake. He did speak very well of William. But I will write things here as they happened.

The twelve men of the Jury trooped in. Then the Judge, very stern in his red robes and wig took his place on a raised platform. A Clerk of the Court then read the charge against William, who was sitting with Lawyer Rose at the side of the platform, across from the Jury. I cannot remember every word, but it was awful.

He said something like: On the twelfth day of August in the Year of our Lord one thousand eight hundred and three war was carrying on between the persons exercising the powers of government in France and our Lord the King and that William Blake late of the Parish of Felpham in the County of Sussex being a wicked Seditious and evil disposed person and greatly disaffected to our said Lord the King and wickedly and seditiously intending to bring the King into great hatred contempt and scandal ... said William Blake did maliciously unlawfully wickedly and seditiously did pronounce utter and declare the English Words: "The English know within themselves that Buonaparte (meaning the Chief Consul of the French Republic) could take possession of England in an Hour's time and then it would be put to every Englishman's choice for to either fight for the French or to have his throat cut. I think that I am as strong a Man as most and it shall be throat cut for throat cut and the strongest Man will be the Conqueror ... Damn the King and Country and all his Subjects! All you Soldiers are sold for slaves!"

And then on the charge of Assault on Schofield: that William Blake ... in and upon one John Schofield in the Peace of God and of our Lord The King, then and there being, did make an Assault and him the said John Schofield, did beat, wound and ill treat so that his life was greatly despaired of, and other Wrongs there did to the Great Damage of the said John Schofield and against the Peace of our Lord the King, his Crown and Dignity.

Well, I cannot remember it all, but you can imagine how terrible it sounded.

The Prosecutor, in his black robe and wig is a heavy man with a deep voice. He made an opening speech in which he talked about how "atrocious" and "malignant" were the charges attributed to William. Those were his words. He said that no justification or extenuation of the charge could possibly be attempted by the Defence ... And so on.

Then the Prosecutor called his Witnesses.

First Private Schofield took the stand. As you know, he is a blond man of sturdy build and a belligerent expression. He is wearing his Soldier's uniform with its red coat and brass buttons all polished. He removed his hat in the witness box and said that he was in the Blakes' garden only to tell the Ostler that he was ordered to march to Chichester and could not help with the digging he had promised because he had no time to spare. He said that William came out, and with no provocation said all those treasonable things.

Mr. Rose then stood up to cross-examine Schofield. I thought Rose looked a little pale and tired, but he attacked Schofield with energy. He picked on some of the more unintelligible sentences.

"What meaning did you understand for the words you say Mr. Blake uttered, *it shall be throat cut for throat cut?*"

"That he would fight," said Schofield.

"That he would fight the French or have his throat cut by the French?"

"Yes...No...I am not sure," muttered Schofield.

"Were these words addressed to you at that time?" asked Rose.

"Yes."

"And who else was in the garden then?"

"Mrs. Blake and the Ostler."

"Where was Mrs. Blake standing?"

"Behind me."

"Is it not possible that these words, if indeed they were uttered at all, could have been addressed to Mrs. Blake?"

Schofield was confused.

"I suppose so."

"You suppose that Mr. Blake was not speaking to you at all."

"No, no, of course he was speaking to me."

But Schofield was rattled. With that success Mr. Rose finished his cross-examination.

The second Witness for the Prosecution was Private Cock. He is a shifty looking piece of work if I ever saw one.

"Will you tell the Court what you saw and heard," said the Prosecutor.

"I was at work in the Stable, Sir, and I heard a great noise, and I saw Mr. Blake and John Schofield outside the Stable door—collaring each other, ye know, and Mrs. Grinder was in the middle, separating them, and Blake says, 'damn the King, damn the country. You soldiers are all slaves.'"

At this point a cry rang out in the court which froze us all in our seats.

"False!"

It was William. His eyes were flashing. His voice was full of conviction.

"Outbursts will not be tolerated!" boomed the Judge.

But William had impressed us all.

When Rose cross-examined Cock, he made much of the conflicting testimony regarding where the words were supposed to have been spoken...Schofield said in the Garden, but Cock said at the Stable door.

And then it was time for Counsellor Rose to address the Jury and call the Witnesses for the Defence. To me he looked paler than ever, but he cleared his throat and began strongly.

He said he would never defend anyone who would be guilty of

such a terrible transgression: My task is to shew that my client is not guilty of the words imputed to him... We stand here not merely in form, but in sincerity and truth to declare that we are not guilty. I am instructed to say that Mr. Blake is as loyal a subject as any man in this court: that he feels as much indignation at the idea of exposing to contempt or injury the sacred person of his sovereign as any man...

Rose coughed a little and then continued. He described William as an artist and engraver, brought to Felpham by Mr. Hayley, whose reputation in the countryside was unimpeachable. He mentioned how art has the ability to secure the bosom from the influence of discordant passions... if any men are likely to be exempt from angry passions it is such an one as Mr. Blake.

Now Kate, at that point I thought to myself he had better not go on long in that vein, for I know full well William has expressed plenty of angry passions in his time. Rose moved on to point out the shady reputation of Schofield, and then to reiterate the conflicting stories of the witnesses during their cross-examination, and to state that he would be calling Mrs. Grinder, Bill the Ostler, and Mrs. Haynes your next door neighbour, who would all testify that none of them heard any such words being said. I will call these witnesses and you shall hear their account. You will then agree with me they totally overthrow the testimony of these Soldiers.

And then a terrible thing happened. Poor Counsellor Rose was overtaken by a terrible fit of Coughing. He staggered somewhat and collapsed. He seems to have a Fever, but he refuses to leave the Court till he knows the Verdict.

But this is what happened next.

The Assistant Counsellor to Mr. Rose called the Witnesses. There was Bill the Ostler, of course, who testified he heard not a word of sedition. Mr. Cosens, owner of the Mill, who was passing by, also heard nothing. And the best one was Mrs. Haynes, the Miller's wife, your neighbour, who noted sensibly that when two people quarrel, they are always at pains to explain to bystanders just what they were quarrelling about, and that Schofield had not said one word about sedition on the day in question.

But I think Mr. Hayley's glowing testimonial of William has had a great effect on the Jury. The Judge, the Duke of Richmond, seems very put out about it. Hayley even called William a Genius, as well as an Honourable Man and Eminent Artist.

And just now the Jury is returning!

Oh, Kate, I am so excited I can hardly write. They have found William NOT GUILTY! The Court is erupting in Applause! Everyone is Cheering! The Courtroom is in Uproar! The Judge is banging his gavel for Order! William has just embraced me, and is being embraced by Mr. Hayley. Oh, thank God for this Day!

I will send this off immediately by Post Chaise to London and will write more later.

Your Devoted Sister,
CATHY BLAKE

Letter to Mrs. Catherine Blake.
Thursday, January 12, 1804. Late at night.

Dear Sister Kate,

I must now tell you of the events which occurred after the delivery of the Happy Verdict, which saved William from a terrible fate.

Poor young Counsellor Rose was very ill, but went home to bed happy at the success of his case. As far as I know, he has a bad fever and cold.

As the Courtroom cleared, Mr. Hayley went up to the Judge, and said, "I congratulate you for having the gratification of seeing an honest man honourably delivered from an infamous persecution."

Richmond replied grumpily, "I know nothing of him." Not very gracious.

Well, though the hour was late, we were all invited to Miss Harriett Poole's house in Lavant for supper, Paulina, as they call her. It is a grand house, don't you think? I was driven up her fine circular driveway in a little cart, while both William and Mr. Hayley were on horseback. Have you noticed that Mr. Hayley is never without his umbrella, even on horseback, and that he always uses military spurs? No wonder he fell off his horse!

We were served a fine supper of cold chicken and ham, and small meat pies, washed down with lots of ale and wine. Everyone was very merry, making toasts to William, and the Ladies (that included me!) and King and Country of course. Miss Poole had been ill with Shivering Fits, and could not attend the Trial, but was well enough to have the party, and very solicitous she was to us all.

"There are Angels at our table," said William, drinking down his wine at one gulp.

Paulina giggled. Mr. Hayley smiled indulgently. I looked for the Angels, but I have never been able to see William's Angels, unlike you.

"Pray, drink more wine," said Paulina, and glasses were filled all around.

"Angels are happier than Men because they are not always Prying after Good and Evil in one another!" William declaimed. And we all agreed with him, and drank toasts to Angels for much of the rest of the evening.

We expect to return to London the day after tomorrow. William is writing you also, so you will have this news the day before we return.

Your Devoted Sister,
CATHY B.

P.S. Kate, there is something I must tell you. I left out an incident that happened at the Trial, but my Conscience will not let me conceal it.

In the Courtoom, I saw a tall man I thought I had seen before. Suddenly I recognized him! How could it be? He was our Paul-Marc! He, who we had grieved for as dead! Can you believe this?

I followed him out of the Court, after it was all over, and William was acquitted.

Oh, Kate, his story is so sad—wait till you hear it! He did not die in France, as we believed. He escaped the Terror in Paris—he has been with Napoleon in Egypt! He is ill and bitter—I am not exactly sure why he is quite so cynical—but we must befriend him again. He said he would like to see me in London, where he is soon to settle. He has been living in Chichester, evidently, and so heard of the Trial.

I have Herbs that will cure his recurring Fever and Chills. As soon as we return to London, I am going to help Paul-Marc get better.

$\mathscr{P}art\ \mathscr{F}our$

LONDON 1804

Blake, *Europe*, Plate 11, Copy E (1794). Lessing J Rosenwald Collection, Library of Congress. Copyright © 2003
the William Blake Archive. Used with permission

20

In Which We Return To London and Inspiration

My joy at receiving these letters was not unmixed. As soon as it really dawned upon me that my William was free of this terrible cloud, I began to feel much better. I shook off my Sloth and cleaned our two rooms from top to bottom, washed all the china plates, and polished the copper kettle. While I worked, I tried not to think of Paul-Marc and Cathy.

I caught myself musing upon all this frantic activity. In every marriage, there is one who plays the Martyr, I thought. That is the one who slaves away to please the other, who tries to cater to every whim, and then resents it, becomes Irritable, and ever so often does something destructive to lash out. I saw that in our marriage, that one was me. I used to be shrewish and rail against William, but in recent years I had become more subtle. Encouraging Mr. Hayley's friendship, just when his Patronage was chafing William so badly, for instance.

Even my Illness, preventing me from attending the Trial, was a way of punishing William. I was not there to sustain him. Surely I had not become ill on purpose! But the effect was the same, was it not?

Lost in these thoughts, I attempted to tidy William's work table.

He had written many works at Felpham, some without titles, some Poetry, some Prose. There was a neatly written stack of pages I had not noticed before. They seemed to be fair copies of Ballads I knew he had written. But there was a long one that was new to me—it was titled "The Mental Traveller." I read it, growing more and more troubled.

It began:

I traveld thro' a Land of Men
A Land of Men & Women too
And heard & saw such dreadful things
As cold Earth wanderers never knew . . .

And it went on about the birth of a baby Boy, who was given to an old woman who nailed him down upon a rock and caught his shrieks in "Cups of gold," and tortured him, cutting his heart out. A wisp of memory crossed the corners of my mind as I read:

Her fingers number every Nerve
Just as a Miser counts his gold
She lives upon his shrieks and cries
And she grows young as he grows old

Till he becomes a bleeding youth
And she becomes a Virgin bright
Then he rends up his Manacles
And binds her down for his delight

He plants himself in all her Nerves
Just as a Husbandman his mould
And She becomes his dwelling place
And Garden fruitful seventyfold . . .

My God, it was my Dream! Our minds, as usual, were attuned. But in the waking world, the poem told me something of William's mind, rather than my own. It was still there, that resentment of Marriage, that *ambivalence*—because the female lover did become his dwelling place.

But then an odd thing happens. He becomes a kind old man who feeds the Beggars and Travellers who pass his door, till he is cast out by a fiery Female born from his own hearth. Could this be what happens to a man's feminine side if it is denied? It turns to a brilliant force which drives him out of himself?

In the poem, the Old Man has to find another Maiden to rejuvenate him. But the cycle of love and pursuit goes on *"Till he becomes a wayward Babe, And she a weeping Woman old."* And this Babe is horrible:

> But when they find the frowning Babe
> Terror strikes thro the region wide
> They cry the Babe the Babe is Born
> And flee away on Every side
>
> For who dare touch the frowning form
> His arm is witherd to its root
> Lions Boars Wolves all howling flee
> And every Tree does shed its fruit
>
> And none can touch that frowning form
> Except it be a Woman Old
> She nails him down upon the Rock
> And all is done as I have told.

This poem appalled me. It was a terrible view of the relationship between Man and Woman.

I noted another poem carefully copied out in neat script, "Auguries of Innocence." It began:

> To See a World in a Grain of Sand
> And Heaven in a Wild Flower
> Hold Infinity in the palm of your hand
> And Eternity in an hour

I had not realized I was holding my breath till I sighed. Here, at least, was the William I loved. This poem was in short rhyming lines, full of wisdom and feeling and brilliance:

> A Robin Red breast in a Cage
> Puts all heaven in a Rage
> A dove house filld with doves & Pigeons
> Shudders Hell thro all its regions . . .

It was a long poem, about animals and people and ideas, written with wit:

> If the Sun & Moon should doubt
> Theyd immediately go out.

And there was the old flash of political criticism:

> The Whore & Gambler by the State
> Licencd build that Nations Fate
> The Harlots Cry from Street to Street
> Shall Weave Old Englands winding Sheet.

The verses ended with four lines that gave me hope that William and I might overcome our difficulties, and forgive each other as Human Beings:

> God Appears & God is Light
> To Those poor Souls who dwell in Night
> But does a Human Form Display
> To those who Dwell in Realms of Day.

I vowed to be a better wife to William when he returned.

From Kate's Notebook.
January 14, 1804.

William came home this morning in a flurry of excitement and affection, and immediately dashed off to see John Flaxman on some business for Hayley, and this afternoon he is going to call on Joseph Johnson. Now he is writing to Hayley, warning him never to mount a Trooper's horse again. He heard from an old Soldier on the Coach that they are schooled in so many tricks of starting and stopping short that they are dangerous even to an experienced rider! William told me that Hayley paid Samuel Rose a handsome fee for his Defence, but poor Rose is very sick. We are so indebted to both of them, but especially Hayley.

My feelings are so confused regarding Hayley . . . I will not know how to behave when next I see him. I regret what passed between us—what if I have hurt his feelings now that I am so much cooler toward him? Does he even know that my feelings toward him have changed? William is assuredly feeling great brotherly affection and gratitude to him, and that was how I felt toward him when I took leave of him in October. But did I mistake his words?

"Goodbye, Mistress Blake," he had said, looking intently at me with his fine grey eyes set under those familiar arched brows, "let us always remember what has passed between us with Joy."

From Kate's Notebook.
January 16.

Cathy has come calling shortly after her return from Chichester. She was wearing a new bonnet with a feather. I could tell she was bursting to tell me news of Paul-Marc, but I carefully avoided giving her any chance to discuss the subject beyond the merest platitudes. I simply do not want to know where or how he is. I strongly suspected he was the Mr. Markson who had written to the Flaxmans. Now he is going to befriend Cathy! It is intolerable! I feel so betrayed and sick at heart. I can only avoid seeing both of them.

Mr. Hayley paid a quick visit to London in February, and came to see us. He climbed the narrow stairs to our rooms, leaning awkwardly on his cane. When William went to fetch some ale from the King's Arms on the corner, we were left alone.

"William wrote to me that you had been near the Gate of Death, until he returned," Hayley said to me. "I had to come to be sure that you are well."

"I improved almost as soon as he came back," I said. "Poor William came down with a dreadful cold for a week."

There was an uncomfortable pause.

"Mr. Hayley," I began courteously, "I must thank you for all you have done for us. I know you have paid Mr. Rose, lent us money, commissioned work for William . . . I do not know how to—"

"Hush, Kate," he interrupted. "You need not thank me. Don't you know that I did it for you? Surely you know that I—"

Now it was I who interrupted him. I placed my fingers on his lips.

"Please, sir, say no more."

He took my hand and kissed it, as if we were being formally introduced.

"Friendship, then?" he smiled.

"Of course," I smiled. I moved to put glasses on the table just as William returned with the ale.

One last favour Mr. Hayley did for me was to tell of a new cure for Rheumatism. I had suffered from pains in the knees and legs since Felpham, but now Mr. Birch's Electrical Magic, as William called it, was all the rage. Mr. Hayley sent me to Mr. John Birch, who had written an *Essay on the Medical Application of Electricity* and I do not know what he did, but the combination of his Lotion of Calamine and Electric shocks to the knees quite cured me of pain for several months.

William believed also in the power of Magnetic Healing, and took me to visit Richard Cosway, the Painter and Magician, known to us in our Swedenborgian days on Poland Street. Mr. Cosway now lived nearby, across Oxford Street in Stratford Place.

He was a well-known Mesmerist, to say nothing of being the most fashionable Miniature Painter in London. His vivacious wife Maria was also a skilful artist. What more could anyone desire?

And the house was magnificent! It was decorated elaborately

with mirrors and chandeliers, and beautiful bronzes and ceramic figures.

"Please observe my Watch, Mrs. Blake," said Richard Cosway, his piercing blue eyes locking into mine. He dangled a gold watch on a chain in front of my nose. I felt my mind leaving my body. I hated the Sensation.

"No!" I jerked myself back.

"But, Kate," William said, "you must surrender your Will and accept Instruction."

"No, never," I said. "Please forgive me, Mr. Cosway, but I cannot do it."

"Well, well," he said, "there's no harm done, I am sure. Some people are not good subjects for hypnotism."

He turned his attention to William.

"And how is the engraving progressing?" he asked. Patronizingly, I thought.

I was more than Annoyed. I knew William's talent was equal to Cosway's. Both had seen Visions, yet no-one called Cosway Mad. I could not help but compare our condition in life to theirs: their Riches and our Poverty, their Fame and our Obscurity.

William often seemed content to believe that he was Known in Eternity, that Material Success was not worth the Ground beneath his Feet, but when I was looking for a Guinea or two to buy salt, flour and meat, I could have done with a little worldly prosperity.

In March of 1804 I again became Nervous and Sleepless.

"I know you are still upset because we've learned that Paul-Marc Philipon is alive," William said to me out of the blue, as I sat staring into space, paint brush in hand.

We had been working on a new order for *Songs of Innocence and of Experience*, and I was trying out fresh colour combinations with rose and purple madder for figures in the designs.

I did not know how to answer. This was a subject I had not raised on my own, though we had exclaimed over it together when William first returned. But Cathy was always dropping in with bits of news.

"I am glad he is not Dead," I said carefully, "but I do not feel that he wants to see us. He prefers Cathy."

I tried to paint a stroke or two, but my hand began to tremble.

"I understand him," said William, placing his hand on mine. "He suffered terrible experiences we can only Imagine. He is not as he was. He wishes to begin again."

"So you would befriend him again?"

"Of course! He is Human like ourselves. And he is tortured and alone. It is good that Cathy can care for him."

Cathy was working as a Healer and Midwife in North London. She was not living with Paul-Marc, but she was visiting him every day, preparing meals for him, and keeping him company. He was wasting away before her very eyes, she said.

"I think Cathy is in love with him." I dropped my paintbrush.

William looked at me intently.

"You were close to him once," he said quietly, retrieving the brush, "so you may feel some Jealousy now that Cathy is his friend and you are not. I think you should see him and make your Peace."

I did my best to make Peace with Paul-Marc, but he would not make peace with me. He lay wan and feverish on a bed in a cold room cheered only by a few daffodils Cathy placed in a blue bowl. He would not speak to me, but his eyes burned into mine. Then he turned his face away.

"Is he going to get well?" I asked Cathy in dismay, once we were out of the room.

Cathy had never been good-looking, but she had become hand-some as she grew older and now she had a confident air. Her abundant brown hair was neatly arranged. I might have liked her if she had not reminded me so much of her Mother.

"It is in God's hands, of course," she said, "but I do not think so. Each time he gets the Fever, he weakens."

I began to cry. She brushed away her tears, too.

"Do not come again, please," she said, "it only disturbs him. Let me have him now. It is my turn."

How much had Paul-Marc told her about himself and me? I never knew.

I left them alone, there in the bleak North of London. I never saw Paul-Marc alive again.

· · ·

Early in October that year, William and I entered the first of eight light-filled Rooms, and saw something wonderful. We were visiting a new Gallery which had opened when we were in Felpham.

"Count Joseph Truchsess lost his fortune as a result of the French Revolution, and has brought his huge collection of Old Master paintings to London, hoping to sell them to the British Government," said William. Count Truchsess had, at his own expense, opened a gallery opposite Portland Place near the New Road.

We had never seen so many Paintings in one place before! They glowed from the walls, hung three deep, room after room. Used to seeing such pictures only in black and white engravings, I was overwhelmed.

There was the *Madonna and Child*, by Dürer, and *The Woman Taken in Adultery* by Guilio Romano—both made my heart jump.

"Look at this!" exclaimed William over a triptych. It was by the School of Michel Angelo, showing the Virgin's birth and death. "And there is a *Last Judgment!*"

I was especially attracted to austere pictures by artists of the North, with names I had never heard before, like Quentin Matsys and Jan Mabuse. There was a *Virgin and Child* by Martin Schongauer and a *Christ Crucified* by Lucas Cranach. William loved these Northern paintings with their clarity of line and form and their Biblical subject matter.

There were eight paintings by Rembrandt. They were mysterious and shadowy. I was drawn to them, but William was troubled.

"I do not care for these paintings," he said. "They look as if they were in a dark cavern, whether morning or night."

"Look at this!" I exclaimed, indicating a painting by Rubens, the *Conversion of St. Paul*. I knew that William had been contemplating his own design on this subject.

"It is almost too much, Kate!" he said. "I am so Inspired!"

And the wonderful thing was this. When we came home, still full of the beautiful images we had seen, William had a Vision.

It happened that I had left the room to fetch myself a shawl, for it had grown chilly. When I came back, I saw him, rapt. Around him was such an Aura, such light, that I was afraid to move or speak.

Yet I sensed that he was engaged in a struggle. He stood upright, legs firmly planted as if he were about to do battle.

Then I saw it. The Grey Presence once again. The drum-beat of my heart sounded in my ears as before. What was this thing that haunted us? Did it have anything to do with me?

"Who are you?" I cried aloud.

It was William who answered, softly.

"He is my Spectre. Now I know him. He is my dark self."

The Shadow loomed over us.

"He wants you," I whispered, "I feel it!"

Then I became angry. Had I laboured all my life to be vanquished by this?

"You will not have him!" I willed my thoughts toward the Spectrous Shadow.

"Take Me! I will stand for him!"

At that very moment, William shouted to the Spectre, "I Embrace thee as a Brother! I see thou art myself!"

He collapsed to the floor, sobbing. I ran to his side.

The dreadful thing disappeared, and the room flooded with light.

William sat up and looked at me with awe and love.

Holding my face in his hands, he said, "What a Wife I have in you."

And then he embraced me as if we were newly wed.

From a Letter to William Hayley from William Blake.
October 23, 1804.

...O Glory! And O Delight! I have entirely reduced that spectrous Fiend to his station, whose annoyance has been the ruin of my labours for the last past twenty years of my life. He is the enemy of conjugal love...I was a slave bound in a mill among beasts and devils; these beasts and devils are now, together with myself, become children of light and liberty, and my feet and my wife's feet are free from fetters...

...Suddenly, on the day after visiting the Truchsessian Gallery of pictures, I was again enlightened with the light I enjoyed in my youth, and which has for exactly twenty years been closed from me as by a door and by window shutters...He is become my servant who domineered over me, he is even as a brother who was my enemy. Dear Sir, excuse my enthusiasm or rather madness, for I am really drunk with intellectual vision whenever I take a pencil or graver into my hand, even as I used to be in my youth, and as I have not been for twenty very dark, but very profitable years. I thank God that I courageously pursued my course through darkness...

From Kate's Notebook.
Tuesday, November 6, 1804.

There was a drawing of William's that used to hang in his Mother's house, of a nude young man with outstretched arms, seeming to Dance. I always loved it. Then William made a Colour Print of it about eight years ago, when I knew by then that Dancing in William's Art was always ambivalent; it was always associated with the Fallen, material world. He preferred Calm and Stillness.

Today I saw that William had reworked that Dancing design again, making it into an Engraving. Now the young man is older and more muscled, and his arms are still open to embrace the world in a gesture that reminds me of Christ on the Cross, and his face is serious. He stands on a Worm of Mortality—I know these Meanings by now! The Bat of Ignorance flies away in the distance. Under the picture, William has written: Albion rose from where he labourd at the Mill with Slaves / Giving himself for the Nations he danc'd the dance of Eternal Death.

Now I know better what happened to William the night of the Spectrous Shadow, and what he meant when he told Hayley he was "a slave bound in a mill," like Samson in the Bible. William, like his hero Albion, accepted his Mortality, and rose from where he labour'd, a new Man.

I wonder if I can do the same.

"This is a dangerous time for us," said Sister Violet regretfully, as she welcomed me back into the group. Once again I was Sister Rose.

It was a few months after we returned to London, when I attended a meeting of the Wise Women with my Sister Sarah. Sadly, the group was smaller than before, Sister Marguerite having died of Fever, and Sister Iris, who had piped an air so beautifully for us once before, had been arrested for infanticide. This was one of the dangers of the work

Blake, *Glad Day*. Courtesy of the Huntington Library, Art Collections and Botanical Gardens, San Marino, California

Blake, *The Dance of Albion (Glad Day)* c. 1803/1810, engraving (Bindman 400). Courtesy of National Gallery of Art, Washington, Rosenwald Collection

of a Midwife, if a baby died and the parents mistrusted her. The little circle of women continued to support each other and to bring babies into the world, despite the movement to have male doctors in attendance at Childbirth.

Yet there was another reason that a shadow had been cast over the group. A new Statute had lately passed in Parliament, which made it punishable by Death to give Potions which would end a pregnancy. I thought fleetingly of Cathy, working on her own. Ah, well.

"We need more than ever the Spiritual Sustenance of the Mother," said Sister Violet, as we took our places in the Circle. The whitewashed room was dimly lit by candles, which caused shadows to flicker on the walls.

"Sister Gentian, please prepare the Pipe."

Sarah rose, and from the folds of her skirt removed a long clay pipe, which she placed before us on the table. Then from her sleeve she withdrew a small packet of fragrant leaves. With these, she packed the Pipe, and then, lighting it with a taper lit from a candle, she took in three deep breaths. I secretly wondered if it could be Devil's Trumpet.

As the Pipe was passed around the group, a heavy smell hung in the air. It was not unpleasant. When my turn came, I inhaled the smoke rather uncertainly, then with more pleasure. I felt a Calmness wash over me, such as I had experienced only with Laudanum.

"Come, lie down here," instructed Sister Violet. I became aware that the others, Sarah and Sister Hyacinth, and Sister Lavender, had already made themselves comfortable on cushions spread about the floor. I took my place, and allowed the incense and candlelight to fill my five Senses. I travelled inward to a place that was mine alone.

And I saw in a Vision the most beautiful man I had ever beheld, the naked form of a God, whose loins were smooth and golden, and from whence sprang a Shaft as if made of Light. And I knew I wanted him for the father of my Child, a child I had never had, and the fact that I was past Childbearing never occurred to me. He seemed a mixture of William and Paul-Marc, and familiar as the Voices in my head. In my dream, I was young again, and he favoured me. Our union was a commingling from head to foot, a melting into each other.

Suddenly there appeared a black Shadow, a malevolent Spirit, the mirror image of my Lover. I was horrified, but at the same time, I wanted him. I knew he was also Mammon, for he offered me a golden necklace. I wanted it! As I struggled with my feelings, the two Forms were locked in combat.

Then I seemed to hear William's voice in my head . . . "he is become my servant who domineered over me, he is even as a brother who was my enemy."

I looked with compassion on the struggling figures who I knew were my own selves.

And I forgave myself for the Envy which had been my besetting Sin all my life.

From Kate's Notebook, n.d.

He who plays with History plays with Fire. William did not write that, but he should have. I played with History by pretending to be John Flaxman, and it very nearly brought disaster upon me. I could have lost William had he ever found out. He might have forgiven me, but I would have lost his Respect. Somehow I have never felt the same Guilt about the few pornographic drawings I did in the manner of Henry Fuseli. I reason that any man who enjoyed those pictures deserves to be deceived. Henry was always "Borrowing" ideas from William, come to think of it. And has not William copied images from others? Trying to work out the niceties of these problems is hard for me . . . but God allowed me not to be Discovered, so I think I am Forgiven.

William was adding the finishing touches to the engraving of a large copper plate. He worked intently with his burin, revolving the plate with his left hand, making deliberate marks. I saw that it was a Title Page. The design was curious. At the bottom lay a beautiful naked woman with long curly hair and butterfly-like wings along her whole body. On each side and along the top were other winged women, one seemed to be weeping. In the centre of the page, in large flowing script, was its title, *Jerusalem*, and under that in equally large letters, *The Emanation of the Giant Albion*. At the bottom of the page, in small letters, was the date, *1804 Printed by W. Blake Sth Molton St.*

I saw, too, that at his side was a smaller plate, another Title Page.

This one showed the back view of a naked man, gesturing towards billowing clouds, his arm breaking through the letters of the name *Milton*, so that down one side, under the *T-O-N* were the words, *a Poem in 2 Books*, and on the opposite side, *The Author & Printer W Blake 1804*. And at the bottom of the page, under Milton's feet, were the words: *To Justify the Ways of God to Men.*

"What is going on?" I asked. "Are you ready to engrave *Milton* already? And what is *Jerusalem?*"

William looked at me with a pleased expression.

"No, I am not ready to engrave *Milton* yet," he said, "but I think it is almost finished. I see the end in sight. And *Jerusalem*, ah, that is a huge work in my mind. I do not know when it will be done, except for one or two sections which I have ready to print. But you see, I have put the year *1804* on both plates, because now my Inspiration has returned."

We had a long talk that night. We looked back twenty years to 1784, which marked the beginning of the firm Parker and Blake, and William's entry into the world of Commerce. It seemed to him the beginning of a Dark Time, since when he had to labour as an Engraver to earn our daily bread, and put aside any hope of a Patron who might send him to Italy to study Art. And we talked of our Marriage, and its good and bad times. He confessed to me his anger at my Jealousies, and I to him my Resentment of his talent and how I sometimes felt like a slave to it. I confessed my Envy of the superior abilities of so many of his friends, especially Mary and Elizabeth. I said that I was truly grieved that I had ever doubted his visions. I told him how sorry I was that we never had children. He said that he was sorry, too, but I must not blame myself, that I had always been the wife he wanted. So we forgave each other.

There is a Plate in *Milton* which William designed to show how the Divine Vision returned to him. It is a full page Plate inscribed WILLIAM. Here William illustrated himself, naked and bending back in receptivity as Milton's spirit comes toward him as a starry comet to enter his foot. He did a mirror image of this design, named ROBERT, to show that Robert's spirit had never left him.

Blake, *Jerusalem*, Title Page. Courtesy of Yale Center for British Art, Paul Mellon Collection

And then, too, he engraved a Plate showing our cottage at Felpham, and above it an Angel hovering, who was Milton's feminine self, called Ololon in the poem. Her union with Milton signified Milton's redemption, and William's also and the new marriage that William and I had achieved.

Part Five

London 1830–1831

Blake, *Jerusalem*, Plate 57. Courtesy of Yale Center for British Art, Paul Mellon Collection

21

In Which Mr. Tatham Behaves Most Strangely

From Kate's Notebook.
Monday, January 4, 1830. Lisson Grove.

*I*n my continuing conversations with Frederick Tatham about my life with William, I suppose that I am extraordinarily defensive when talking about our residence in London when we returned from the three years in Felpham.

We lived in South Molton Street for eighteen years. It wasn't so bad. It was one floor up, and I always kept our rooms clean and tidy, in spite of William's engraving things around everywhere. Of course, there was neither garden nor tree, not like our Cottage. There was no help for it.

I would say, Mr. Blake, the money's gone, and he would say, Oh, damn the money! To put it bluntly, we were poor. In my heart, I raged against Obscurity and Neglect.

There had been that nasty business with the publisher Robert Cromek over book illustrations for Blair's *Grave*, designs which William invented but which Cromek had given to someone else to engrave. Then there had been a terrible falling out with Stothard, because William maintained Stothard had stolen his idea for a painting of Chaucer's *Canterbury Pilgrims*. This picture now hangs on the wall of my room. Cromek had somehow been involved, too, for we thought Cromek had suggested the idea to Stothard while knowing that William planned to execute a work on the subject.

William showed his Canterbury Pilgrim picture at our big Exhibition and Sale in 1809. Or rather, we had hoped it would be a sale. We worked very hard for it. The Exhibition was held in James Blake's haberdashery shop and residence in Broad Street, where the sixteen pictures filled several rooms. We worked for days, making frames, and painting the walls, deciding where to put which picture.

One picture, *The Ancient Britons*, was huge—it was fourteen feet long by ten feet high. Some people thought that this was the best picture that William ever made, with naked figures as large as life. It represented the last battle of King Arthur with Roman soldiers, when all the Britons were overwhelmed by brutal arms, except for the most Beautiful, the most Strong, and the most Ugly, as William said. They stood for three General classes of men. This painting was commissioned by a Mr. Pughe in Wales, who eventually took it away to his estate.

The other pictures were not so big, but I thought they were impressive. Several were Biblical in theme: *Satan Calling Up His Legions, The Body of Abel Found by Adam and Eve, Soldiers Casting Lots for Christ's Garment*. William always had an eye for the dramatic moment.

We charged 1s. as the price of admission. William wrote a Descriptive Catalogue for his Exhibition, bound in blue-grey wrappers. It expressed all his ideas about Art. For this we charged 2s 6d. Mr. Crabb Robinson, the journalist, bought four copies!

We had such hopes for this Exhibition. It was to reestablish William in the Art World of London. That did not happen.

Hardly anyone came to see the pictures. No one understood the Descriptive Catalogue. The only review was by Robert Hunt of the *Examiner*.

He wrote of the "ebullitions of a distempered brain" and called William "an unfortunate lunatic, whose personal inoffensiveness secures him from confinement." He called the Catalogue "a farrago of nonsense, unintelligibleness, and egregious vanity, the wild effusions of a distempered brain."

After this horrible experience, William and I retreated from the public for ten years. We took engraving commissions, and William made illustrations for John Milton's poetry. It was not till 1818 that he began again to make copies of his Illustrated Books.

In those dark years, William seemed to quarrel with everyone, even Flaxman. Today I showed Frederick the Notebook in which William had written angry epigrams about many of his friends. He had written about Flaxman and Stothard:

I found them blind and taught them how to see
And now they know neither themselves nor me.

And about Cromek:

A Petty sneaking Knave I knew
O Mr. Cr—how do ye do.

Frederick recognized in Blake's Notebook the manuscripts and working pages of many early poems and ballads, and many sketches of designs he had seen finished in the *Gates of Paradise*. All around these sketches were written long prose passages of a treatise about Art. And then there were the epigrams.

Frederick read aloud:

Of H's birth this was the happy lot
His Mother on his Father him begot.

"Who is H?" he asked me, while I was busily dusting the books and pictures in the sitting room where we had been talking. I was embarrassed.

"That would be Mr. Hayley," I said. "William turned against him during those hard years in London, though we had been very grateful to him at first."

"Yes, I can see that," said Frederick, who had just caught sight of the lines:

On H—y's Friendship

> When H—y find out what you cannot do
> That is the very thing he'll set you to
> If you break not your Neck tis not his fault
> But pecks of poison are not pecks of salt
> And when he could not act upon my wife
> Hired a villain to bereave my Life.

"What could he have meant by that?" he asked, shocked.

"William sometimes got upset thinking about the Trial," I said, "and he used to wonder if Hayley had sent Schofield to trick him."

"What has become of Mr. Hayley? I have not heard much of him in these years."

"We heard about ten years ago that he died," I said. "I grieved for him. But do you know, he married again before that, in 1809, I believe. He was sixty-four, and married a much younger woman of twenty-eight. It never works, those December-May marriages."

"Why, what happened?"

"Mrs. Flaxman told me that Mrs. Hayley left her husband after three years. And he was very hurt. And you know, there was a curious story going around that he had manacled his wife to an elm tree in his garden. But I do not believe that at all."

Frederick put down the Notebook. I laid it aside, and reminded myself to send a message to young Samuel Palmer, one of the group of Frederick's friends, the Ancients, the youngest of the lot, who had been especially fond of William. I have a plan for the Notebook.

I brought Frederick another manuscript to examine. The Title Page had been called *Vala, A Dream of Nine Nights* but that had been crossed out, and written over it the words *The Four Zoas*, and underneath, *The Torments of Love and Jealousy in the Death and Judgement of Albion the Ancient Man.* As we turned the pages, Frederick saw sketches of many lovely female nudes, and erotic illustrations of all

kinds. For the second time in half an hour, he was shocked, yet fascinated. I could tell.

"Did Mr. Blake ever engrave this poem?" he asked cautiously.

"No, never. He abandoned it when he started *Jerusalem*. But he
used a lot of the material in *Milton* and *Jerusalem*. You see, it is all
about the Fall, and then the history of being Human, and then about
the Apocalypse. William invented a System to explain the Human
Condition. Most of it is there. Albion is his name for the Eternal
Man who stands for us all."

"Indeed," said Frederick.

I took the manuscript and carefully put it away, wrapped in a silk
scarf. I sensed the ambivalence of Frederick's response. Knowing his
streak of prudery, I thought better of letting him see any more of the
drawings.

From Kate's Notebook.
February 10, 1830.

Frederick has confided in me in both tears and elation. I do not know
what to make of him. I fear he is sorely lacking in judgement, but I am
touched that he is now as frank with me as I have been with him.

Yesterday, on his way home from a Prayer Meeting, he saw a young
woman, frail, and impossibly fair. Her brows and lashes were pale as
her hair. She was shabbily dressed, but of good carriage. It took some
moments before Frederick realized that she was a woman of the
street. By that time, his eyes had met hers.

She smiled. He looked away, passing her by. Then he looked back.
She leaned against a lamppost, and in the darkening evening light, her
hair was like a luminous halo under her bonnet, which was crowned
with a ridiculous feather. He thought she looked hungry.

He paused and turned back, driven by an impulse he could not
control.

"Have you eaten?" he said. The words came scratching out of his
throat.

"I'll 'ave a bite with ye, sir," she said, taking his arm. Frederick
walked with her into another world. There he had a dream, which he
described to me.

Frederick moved between worlds. Below, he could see Earth, a blue planet. Above, a white light, and a mysterious figure guiding him. He wanted to reach the light more than anything he had ever desired before, but something was slowing his progress. To his horror, he saw hands clutching at his garments. The hands pulled him into a field full of people, to whom he tried to speak, but his mouth was dry, and no words would come. He knew he had to speak to all these people, he had something important to say, but he could not utter a word. The scene changed before him, and he was in a smokey room hung with dark velvet draperies, somewhere he recognized he had gone with the girl. He woke. He was lying on a bed, fully clothed.

The girl was beside him, asleep, her ridiculous hat beside her. Frederick was appalled. The opium had a smell both sweet and acrid. He was amazed at himself, repulsed, yet strangely elated. He knew what he must do. He had to save the girl. He would take her home to Maria and me.

Maria is hysterical.

"Here? In this house? This creature? Frederick, are you mad?" she cried.

"It is our duty as Christians! We must feed and clothe her, and give her work," he said.

"But have you no consideration for me, your wife? Have I no choice in this matter? Is this not my home too?"

The girl was in earshot. She was in my kitchen, while I conferred with the Tathams. Her name is Jenny Boggs. That is all she will say. She is beautiful in a pale, fragile way. I soon saw that she had not the slightest idea of what was going on around her.

"Mrs. Blake, what shall I do?" Maria was wringing her hands. "What will people think?"

"People will think you are kind, Mrs. Tatham. You will help this poor, sick girl till she is well. I will teach her needlework," I said.

"I already know 'ow to sew," said Jenny, suddenly raising her head from the kitchen table.

"Then I will teach you how to cook!" I said.

Maria is incapable of making decisions, and Frederick is adamant that the girl will stay, so I found her a bed in the attic, and bade her sleep till morning.

William's lines echo in my head: The Harlot's cry from Street to Street/Shall weave Old England's winding sheet.

Friday, February 12.

I have taken control of the Jenny situation because Maria is so distraught.

"Never you mind, my dear," I told her, "I will turn Jenny into my helper and you need not bother about her getting in your way."

"I never want to lay eyes on her!" said Maria, her dark eyes welling with tears.

I put my arms around her.

"I will fix it, my dear," I said.

Nevertheless, Jenny is not so malleable. At first, I could tell she thought it a lark to be in a gentleman's house and given three good meals a day. Soon she became bored, and on top of that, complained of Headache. Privately, I thought a little Opium would have cured it. I could sometimes divert her by speaking about William and his visions. She liked to hear about them, since she herself had vivid dreams.

This morning we were in our blue-tiled kitchen making a cake. I had just showed her how to measure the flour into the little scale with brass weights.

"Tell me something about William," said Jenny, as she dumped the flour into a big yellow mixing bowl. "Tell me about one of his visions."

"Well, once he saw a Fairy Funeral," I said, choosing one I thought appropriate for a young girl. "It happened when we lived in Sussex. William was walking alone in the garden. He said there was a great stillness among the branches and flowers, and more than common sweetness in the air. He heard a low and pleasant sound, and did not know where it came from. But then he saw the broad leaf of a flower move, and underneath he saw a procession of creatures the size and colour of green and grey grasshoppers, bearing a body laid out on a rose leaf, which they buried with songs, and then disappeared!"

"Do you think he took Opium?" asked Jenny with interest.

I did not answer directly.

"I have seen such things myself!" I said.

"And didn't nobody think you was mad?"

That old refrain. I broke some eggs into the mixing bowl and gave a spoon to Jenny.

"Stir this," I said, "and yes, many people thought we were mad. There was one awful man named Robert Hunt, who wrote over twenty years ago about William's Art Exhibition at James Blake's house. And then, of course, when people heard of the drawings of the Visionary Heads that William made for Mr. Varley, they thought William lived in a Madhouse!"

"Oh, who were the people he drew?"

I added some raisins to the mixing bowl.

"Well, they were all dead," I remarked. "There was Richard the Lion-Hearted, and Edward the Third, and the Spirit of Voltaire."

"I don't know them," said Jenny.

"There was the Ghost of a Flea, and the Man Who Built the Pyramids," I went on, "and many, many more. William talked to them all as he was drawing them." The Portraits had often looked to me a little bit like William himself, with strong faces and glowing eyes.

"But yer husband spoke to them all?"

"Oh, yes. They were definitely there. That is why it hurt to be called Mad. But William always said that Posterity would be the judge of his work."

"What's Posterity?" asked Jenny, stirring the cake slowly.

"Future people," I told her. "And do you know, it is only three years since William died, and there is already going to be an essay about him this year by Mr. Cunningham in a book called *Lives of the Most Eminent British Painters*. Most eminent! Our Mr. Tatham is also going to write a biography, and I have been telling him all about our life. So you see, what some people call Madness is really talent misunderstood. People do not understand Artists!"

March 12.

Jenny is paler than ever and listless. Frederick asked me what to do.

"I like the girl," I told him, "but I think you should let her go. She is used to her freedom, and you cannot keep her in a cage. She may come to a bad end, but it will be her own choice. I think she will run away, in any case."

He insisted on taking her to one last Prayer Meeting. He asked me to go along. I dressed Jenny plainly in a brown dress the Tathams had given her, put a black straw hat on her fair hair, and off we went.

As usual, the meeting was held in a private home, as Edward Irving is in trouble with the London Presbytery. They have issued four charges of heresy against him for insisting in a written tract that Jesus could resist temptation because the Holy Spirit dwelt in him, otherwise He was a man like any other. Sounded like something William would say to me. But the religious establishment argued that Jesus was Divine. No, maintained Irving—Jesus was human. He even once referred to Christ's human nature as "that sinful substance," horrifying an Anglican clergyman who happened to be visiting!

Nevertheless, Irving is conducting private Prayer Meetings and people are filling with the Spirit and speaking in tongues. Yet he always insists on order. There are only two periods in the meeting when it is allowed.

This time we entered the home of a prosperous Scottish merchant in Great Marlborough Street. Mr. Irving, tall and commanding, greeted us cordially. The early morning sunlight filtered into the room through shuttered windows, illuminating about twenty-five people, sitting silently.

We started by singing a hymn. Frederick sang loudly, and Jenny not at all. Then Irving stood up and raised his hands high above his head. A man began reading from Isaiah: "Cry aloud, spare not, lift up thy voice like a trumpet, and shew my people their transgressions, and the house of Jacob their sins."

This was followed by Irving speaking quietly about sin and repentance and forgiveness. And then he said, "Now let the Lord do as seemeth Him fit among the people."

The room was completely still. I could hear Jenny breathing beside me. I noticed that her breath seemed to be more agitated by the minute, and glancing sideways, I saw her breast heave and her shoulders shudder. Then a shriek issued from her lips, and suddenly a torrent of words came forth, short and unintelligible—syllables that were English and not English, but rhythmical—*hey amei hassan alla do* . . .

Jenny spoke this way for two or three minutes! The room listened in rapt attention, till, lapsing into normal English she cried, "Oh I repent, I repent!"

Then she fainted into Frederick's arms, while another voice in the room took up her refrain. We revived Jenny with smelling salts, and she sat exhausted till the end of the meeting, when Irving rose and said it was visible that the Spirit of the Lord was actively at work. He asked a Blessing and praised God for the opening of another mouth.

I saw that Frederick was so elated he could hardly speak. He was sure Jenny was Saved! He had accomplished his mission.

We walked home in the bright sunshine, Jenny alternately weeping and laughing. I divined that Frederick then and there imagined what his future calling might be—a finder of lost souls.

Monday, March 18.

After all the excitement of the last few days, Jenny has gone back to her old neighbourhood to work in a Bakery and help look after children in the Presbyterian Church Sunday school. I sent her away with a kiss and good wishes—who knows what her fate may be? Maria is relieved she is gone.

Frederick wants to resume work on his biography of William.

22

In Which My Story Both Ends and Begins

From Kate's Notebook.
Tuesday, April 2, 1830.

"When did you move from South Molton Street?" Frederick asked me this morning, as he was going over his notes. He motioned me to sit in a chair near him.

"It was after William finished *Jerusalem*," I said, arranging my skirts neatly. "Yes, it was about 1821, when our Landlord sold the house, and we went to live in my sister Sarah's house in No. 3 Fountain Court near the Strand. That is where you met us, is it not? A plain brick house with three storeys. We had two rooms up one flight of stairs."

It was a small, peaceful space, with one room used as a sitting room, where William's colourful temperas and water colours hung on the walls, and a table and chair or two stood about for visitors. There was one painting in that room, *The Body of Abel Found By Adam and Eve*, which William had shown at the Exhibition in 1809, but it had not found a buyer, so there it hung.

In the other room, all living took place. There was a small fireplace in one corner, and opposite, a large window with a valance and drapery from which one could catch a narrow glimpse of the Thames, "like a bar of gold," William had said.

The bed was placed so William and I could see the view, and by the window was William's long work table, and a cupboard which held inks, papers, and engraving tools and supplies. I remember the piles of books on the floor, and on the table, portfolios of drawings. On the wall was a print of Dürer's *Melencholia*. This room was also used as my kitchen, and over the coal fire there always hung a kettle with water ready for tea.

This was the room where Frederick and his friends, The Ancients, all artists, came to visit William. They sat at his feet and listened to him speak about Art and Life. They called our rooms The House of the Interpreter. These young men made William so happy. They made up for the years of neglect. William had regained his serenity working on *Jerusalem*, and now people were drawn to him as never before.

"I recall one day Henry Fuseli came to see us in Fountain Court," I told Fred. "William was having his dinner. It was only a piece of cold mutton. 'Ah by God!' said Henry, 'this is the reason you can do as you like. Now I can't do this!' I suppose there were some advantages to our simple life! I do miss Henry now that he is gone. He died two years before William, you know, and so did John Flaxman, just one year before."

I brushed a tear from my eye.

"William was not at all well that year. He had shivering fits and stomach pains almost every month. It kept him from walking out very much with Mr. Linnell, but it did not keep him from his work, of course."

"It is sad for you to grow old and lose your husband and friends," said Frederick.

"But I am so lucky to have you and Maria," I said, taking his hand in mine.

Frederick smiled.

"You know, I always take comfort in the print Mr. Blake gave me," he said, "the wonderful God leaning down from the clouds to create the world with his compasses."

The Ancient of Days. That is the print William coloured on his deathbed for young Fred. William sat bolstered up on his pillows, his shivering fits mercifully gone for the moment, while he worked on the picture, shading the clouds carefully with his brush. William always had a strange relationship with that picture. At first he thought of that God as a Tyrant, but now he accepted Him as part of himself. Lovingly, he added a few last strokes of colour. Then at last he threw the picture aside triumphantly, and exclaimed, "There, that will do! I cannot mend it. I hope Mr. Tatham will like it." And then he looked at me, who had stood by watching hour after hour.

"Stay, Kate!" he cried, "keep just as you are—I will draw your portrait—for you have ever been an angel to me."

And he quickly drew a wonderful likeness of me. Then he sang, joyously, a truly celestial song. He said we would never be parted, that he would be with me always. I kissed him and brought him a bowl of soup, but he refused all nourishment, and fell peacefully asleep.

But it was a sleep that never ended, for I could not wake him again. I listened to his breathing through the night, heavy and laboured. I prayed for him to go peacefully into that other realm. At length, I realized that his sweet spirit was indeed gone from his mortal flesh. I wept.

It was August twelfth, 1827. We buried him the day before our Forty-fifth Wedding Anniversary.

From Kate's Notebook.
Monday, April 12, 1830.

Thinking about old friends with Mr. Tatham the other day reminded me of the rich life I have had, not rich in material things, of course, but rich in Experience. I suppose if I have learned one lesson, it is the lines that William added to the *Gates of Paradise:*

> Mutual Forgiveness of each Vice
> Such are the Gates of Paradise.

We really lived by that in those last years, when the world neglected us. All we had was our regard for each other. And the work, of course. There was always Mr. Butts or Mr. Linnell to commission something, the *Job*, the *Dante*, the *Paradise Lost* designs. Thank God for them, for keeping bread on our table. William was never taken up by the fashionable world. Obscurity was our garment.

Yet the outside world would occasionally visit us.

"Haff you seen this!" said Henry Fuseli one April afternoon in 1818, placing a slim novel in my hands. The title read *Frankenstein*.

"Do you know who wrote that?" Henry went on, "It is by Mary Wollstonecraft's daughter, by God! Little Mary Godwin. She ran away with the poet Shelley!"

So the girl that Mary bore before she died had grown with a mind of her own, and become an Author, like her mother. And what a strange, compelling book it was. Dr. Frankenstein's creation, the monster, excited my Sympathies. What if he had been beautiful, instead of hideous? Then everyone would have loved him, and his story would have been different. Instead he was the Shadow self of his creator. Shadow selves bring danger, as William and I well knew. Strange that such a young girl should know it, too.

Tuesday, June 22, 1830.

Sometimes I think back to all the places we have lived: our first rooms in Green Street, our house on Poland Street, our Shop, and then our lovely Hercules Buildings where we did such good work. How Promising life seemed then! But William was somehow a prisoner of his own Mind; he wanted to be a Commercial success, but the Visions kept distracting him. That and Sexual Desire . . . and Politics, of course.

It wasn't me . . . was I not the good wife—most of the time? My crimes were secret, after all. In the end, they did harm only to me.

The Felpham Cottage was pretty—but so damp and cold. I think of it with a mixture of pleasure and pain. Back to London and South Molton Street for almost twenty years of hard work, no money, and Visions! At the end, we were in those two little rooms at Sarah's house, where the young men came to pay homage to us, and we could see the sun shine on the river.

Ah, but the *Job* designs have a special place in my heart, for they seem to tell the story of our Life: like William, Job has Visions of God and Satan, and Troubles and Despair. Then there comes Enlightenment, when Job and his wife recognize the true face of God in the

Blake, *Job*, Plate 6 (c. 1805). By permission of the Houghton
Library, Harvard University

Whirlwind. At the end, there is Harmony for both Job and his wife, and children.

I loved especially the water colours of the *Job* story that William designed originally for Mr. Butts. Mr. Linnell in later years ordered a set for himself, so William re-drew them with a few alterations. I like best the delicate washes of colour of the Butts set—of course, I did them myself, that's why!

It was Mr. Linnell's idea six years ago to have them engraved, and so William made a set of small pencil studies, and by 1825 he had engraved twenty-two plates. Mr. Linnell paid for the copper, and agreed to give us a hundred pounds in advance. I always wondered if that was a fair price, for there were one hundred fifty sets printed, and surely more than thirty sets were sold—though that is all I was told about.

These days, I thank God for young Frederick and Maria. I do love them and care so much for their well-being. They are like the children I never had. I will never forget that Frederick hurried to William's deathbed all the way from Oxford, though he was ill himself, and he only nineteen then.

Frederick tries so hard to be a good man and artist. I see something of William's Fervour in him, but, I fear, not his talent, though Fred made a wonderful double portrait of William, showing him in both Youth and Age. (I like it much better than that formal oil portrait of William that Thomas Phillips painted. He made William look like a Gentleman!)

There is something dangerous about Frederick's piety: it is not forgiving. He has not the love of the human form divine that William had. I see a cloud come over his face when he looks at *Vala*. Yet I believe he has a good heart, if he can only overcome his prudery. William could have helped there.

From Kate's Notebook.
August 28, 1830.

"Samuel Palmer has come to see you, Mrs. Blake," announced Frederick earlier today.

Palmer came to me and embraced me warmly. I thought he looked

Blake, *Job*, Plate 21 (c. 1805). By permission of the Houghton Library, Harvard University

just like the young Christ, with his long curly hair and sensitive face. He wore a short beard.

"How kind of you to send for me, Madam," said Palmer. "I think so often of those blessed days when we conversed with you and Mr. Blake in that enchanted room in Fountain Court."

I had dressed in my best black muslin dress with white lace collar for the visit. My hair, no longer black, but not white either, was pinned up with an ivory comb.

I had a carefully wrapped parcel on the table nearby.

"Do you remember when Mr. Linnell introduced you to William? He asked, do you work with fear and trembling? And you replied, yes indeed, and he said, then you'll do."

"And I remember when I first came to Fountain Court, and the copper plate of the first *Job* design was lying on the table where he had been working on it. How lovely it looked by the lamplight, strained through the tissue paper."

"Were those designs your favourite works?" asked Frederick, who had hovered nearby, rather curious about the reason for Palmer's invitation.

"No, my favourite designs are those enchanting woodcuts for *Virgil*, commissioned by Dr. Thornton," said Palmer. "Who can resist those little dells and nooks, those miniature glimpses of Paradise?"

"They always reminded me of Felpham," I said, "especially the one with the apple tree."

"Do you remember what you said to me once?" said Palmer to me. "You said, 'I have very little of Mr. Blake's company; he is always in Paradise.'"

I laughed. Then I remembered my reason for asking Palmer to visit.

"There is something I want you to have," I said to him, taking the parcel from the table. "It is William's *Notebook*. I know you and your brother William are interested in curious books, and I know my William loved you."

Palmer was overcome. Tears came to his eyes.

"I do not know what to say . . . I . . . ." he stammered.

Frederick was completely put out, I think. He has proprietary feelings about all William's possessions since I told him he is to inherit everything from me.

"You are a fortunate man, indeed," he said to Palmer. "See you look after it!"

Palmer kissed the book reverently.

"It shall be kept safe for ages to come," he promised.

I was satisfied.

From Kate's Notebook.
September 18, 1830.

Today I had a visit from John Linnell. I have never been fond of him, even though he was William's dearest friend and kept us going with commissions like the *Job* and Dante designs. William used to spend so much time with him and his children in Hampstead! They all loved him, especially little Mary Ann who sang at the pianoforte. Ah, well.

I do not forget that Mr. Linnell advanced me the money for William's funeral and made all the arrangements for me—the Shroud, the elm Coffin, the Hearse and Coach and Pair, the Atten-dants. He gave me a position as housekeeper at his studio in Cirencester Place, but I did not get along with him. I do not like tak-ing orders. After eight months, I moved to a little room in Charlton Street on Fitzroy Square, which I still keep and visit from time to time, for some of my furniture is stored there. But I found it too lonely to live there all the time. So I moved here to the Tathams, and here I stay.

There is something so annoying about Mr. Linnell's attitude to me. I am old enough to be his mother, yet he treats me as if I were a child—and a not too bright one at that.

He is concerned about money for the Dante designs. He says he paid William in advance for one hundred and two drawings and seven copper plates, all of which are in his keeping. He maintains he is owed almost £300 in the event any are sold. But I have been informed by Frederick that Linnell has made tracings of these designs! That would certainly devalue the drawings for any other buyer. I tried to explain my point of view, but he could not be persuaded. He said he would not discuss the subject more, unless someone comes along who wants to purchase the designs.

As he bade me goodbye, I suddenly could not abide the ill-feeling between us. He had been William's good friend and patron. We had both loved William.

John Linnell, *William Blake at Hampstead*. Courtesy of Fitzwilliam Museum, Cambridge.

"Mr. Linnell, in William's memory, I cannot let these arguments stand in the way of our friendship, after all these years," I said, offering my hand. Impulsively, I went on.

"I want to give you something of William's."

I picked up the manuscript of *Vala*, so worn with use, and sewn together by my own fingers, which lay on a side table where Frederick had left it.

Surprised, Linnell took it in his two hands, and bowed. Then he did the most unusual thing. He quoted to me lines of William's:

"Awake! Awake! Jerusalem! O lovely Emanation of Albion . . . For lo! The Night of Death is past and Eternal Day Appears upon our Hills."

So I have forgiven Mr. Linnell, in spite of Frederick's indignation.

I was given a Vision last night, a Vision of my own end, though I know not when it will be. Yet I know I will die in the arms of Maria Tatham. I saw the scene clearly, every detail in outline as if it were engraved.

Maria held me in her arms as a daughter would comfort an ailing Mother, while dear Frederick held my hand. I told them that they were to inherit all my things and William's works. I have already told them that in real life, but in my Vision, I saw something strange and troubling.

It was as if I were looking through flames, and Frederick was on the other side, reading William's manuscripts and flinging into the fire many of them—*The Book of Moonlight*, *The Song of Cathedron*, *Lucifer: A Drama*, and *The Garment of Pity*. He was chanting: "Shameful! Shameful! Inspired by Satan!" And yet another manuscript, written in William's best copperplate hand, would burn.

I saw that William was standing beside me, but he was not alarmed, though I was weeping.

"Do not Fret," he said, "I have written enough for Posterity. Those works are known in Eternity. Poor Frederick will never understand. He will seek all his life and never find. He thinks my Energy was inspired by Satan, but it is he who worships the wrong God. Come, Kate, let us go."

I turned toward him, and he took my hand. Together we went into the Future, leaving the flames burning brightly behind us.

Letter to Mr. John Linnell from Frederick Tatham.
17 Charlton Street.
Fitzroy Square.
Tuesday, Oct. 18, 1831.

Dear Sir,

I have the unpleasant duty of informing you of the death of Mrs. Blake, who passed from death to life this morning, at ½ past 7—After bitter pains, lasting 24 hours, she faded away as the whisper of a breeze.

Mrs. Tatham & myself have been with her during her suffering & have had the happiness of beholding the departure of a saint for the rest promised to those who die in the Lord. That we all may thus be transferred from wretchedness to joy, from pain to bliss

Is Sir
The sincere desire of yr
obliged Servant
Frederick Tatham

After a night of painful anxiety & watching I write this hardly knowing whether to rejoice or tremble.

Biographical Notes

William Blake (1757–1827) is one of England's great religious poets and artists. He was an engraver by trade, and printed and coloured his own works, including the well-known *Songs of Innocence and of Experience*. He saw visions and his friends seemed to take that for granted, though some called him mad because his long prophetic poems, such as *Jerusalem*, are so difficult. He was devoted to his wife, though there is some evidence in his poetry that there was conflict in the early years. I have taken liberties with this.

Catherine (Kate) Blake (1762–1831), the poet's wife, married William when she was twenty and he twenty-five, and was devoted to him all her life; they never had children. He taught her to colour his works, and she became also a skilful printer. They descended into extreme poverty before he died, but he had a loyal group of young followers at the end, one of whom sold Blake's Notebook twenty years later to Michael Rossetti, brother of the poet Dante Gabriel Rossetti, who edited Blake's collected works for nineteenth century readers. Catherine became housekeeper to Frederick Tatham after Blake died, and lived free from want from the sale of his paintings. She died in her seventieth year and was buried near her husband in Bunhill Fields, which today is a gravesite near the Barbican in London. A cenotaph commemorates both of them.

Elizabeth Billington (1768–1818) was famous in her day as a singer and retains an important place in musical history. She made her debut at Covent Garden at the age of ten, first as a prodigy of the harpsichord. She began to take singing lessons from James Billington, whom she married in 1783 and from there her career developed. Her first appearance at Covent Garden as a singer was Rosetta in *Love in a Village,* and was hugely successful. She lived in Italy after 1794, returning to Covent Garden and Drury Lane in 1801 to an immense salary. Her portrait was painted by Sir Joshua Reynolds and exhibited in 1790 at the Royal Academy. There is no record that she ever met the Blakes, though they did live on the same street.

Thomas Butts (1757–1845), minor civil servant, was Blake's devoted patron and friend. Gilchrist, Blake's biographer, told the story of Thomas Butts' visit to the Blakes, finding them acting Adam and Eve in the garden, while reciting *Paradise Lost.* Many of Blake's friends did not believe the story. Butts generously commissioned scores of designs from the Bible, watercolour suites of *Paradise Lost, Comus,* and much more. He also bought some of Blake's illuminated books. His wife Betsy ran a boarding school for girls at their home, where Blake may have taught. Catherine and William were close friends and constant visitors at the Butts' home.

John Flaxman (1755–1826) was a famous Neoclassic sculptor in his day, and widely known in Europe for his outline drawings of classical subjects. He and Blake were friends from student days. Flaxman worked for Wedgewood, who sent him to Italy, 1787–1794. When he returned, he devoted himself to monuments. He became a member of the Royal Academy in 1800 and Professor of Sculpture in 1810.

Henry Fuseli (1741–1825), writer and artist, was born in Switzerland. He came to England in 1764, when he met Joseph Johnson. He worked as a journalist and translator before studying art in Italy. Returning to England, he became immediately famous in 1782 for his erotic painting *The Nightmare.* He was an eccentric man, bisexual, a great swearer, and a good friend of Blake, whom he much admired. He was the same age as Johnson, that is, about twenty years older than Mary Wollstonecraft, who wanted to set up a *ménage a trois* with him and his wife. He retreated into respectability in later years and became a professor of the Royal Academy.

William Hayley (1745–1820), born in Chichester, was one of the best known writers of his day, being a poet, playwright and biographer. His best biography was his *Life of Cowper* (1803), the poet whom he had befriended. He also patronized Flaxman, and was closely associated with Romney. He befriended Blake, and wishing to help, invited him and his wife to Felpham, where he tried to turn Blake into a conventional Miniature Painter and engraver of Hayley's own verses. He was a generous and good-hearted man, whose well-meaning patronage eventually drove the Blakes back to London.

Edward Irving (1792–1834), Scottish Clergyman and charismatic pioneer, became a phenomenal success as a preacher in London at the Caledonian Chapel. He was a friend of the Carlyles, who were dismayed when he allowed speaking in tongues at his prayer meetings, and in 1830 he was convicted of heresy by the London presbytery, and finally deposed in 1833. Many of his congregation went with him and founded the Catholic Apostolic Church, commonly known as Irvingites. Irving died of consumption in 1834. Pentecostalism generally traces its roots back to him.

Joseph Johnson (1738–1809), bookseller and publisher, knew all the progressive thinkers of his day and provided a place to meet at his Tuesday three o'clock dinners. He became the official distributor of the literature of the Unitarians, and so was at the center of reforming and radical ideas. He encouraged Mary Wollstonecraft and became her friend and patron.

John Linnell (1792–1882), patron of Blake, was a painter and engraver. He seems to have recorded every paper that crossed his desk, so that his collection of journals, letters, and account books has become a valuable archive.

Frederick Tatham (1805–1878), son of Blake's friend, C. H. Tatham, was one of the Ancients, young artists who esteemed Blake in his later years. Tatham and his wife supported Catherine Blake as housekeeper after William's death, and from her inherited all Blake's effects. In the following years, he printed copies of the Illuminated Books from Blake's copper plates and held sales of Blake's works. It is said that he burned many of Blake's manuscripts and designs, because having become a zealous Irvingite and itinerant preacher, he thought that Satan had inspired Blake. Tatham, c. 1832, wrote a *Life of Blake*, which may be found in G. E. Bentley Jr.'s *Blake Records*.

Mary Wollstonecraft (1759–97), feminist, was author of *A Vindication of the Rights of Woman* (1792), for which she became famous in Europe. She had a well-known affair with Henry Fuseli, and an illegitimate daughter by Gilbert Imlay, before marrying William Godwin in 1797. She died five months later of childbed fever, shortly after giving birth to another daughter, Mary, who grew up to marry the poet Percy Shelley and write *Frankenstein*. Blake illustrated Mary Wollstonecraft's early book, *Original Stories For Children* (1789), and they were thought to meet at Joseph Johnson's Tuesday dinners in St. Paul's Churchyard. There is no proof Mary ever had a flirtation with Blake, though scholars agree that his *Visions of the Daughters of Albion* was inspired by her.

$\mathscr{A}uthor's \; \mathcal{N}ote$

When I was writing *Blake and the Language of Art* (McGill-Queens; Alan Sutton, 1984) in the years when I was a university professor, I often used to wonder what it must have been like to be Catherine Blake, the wife of such a singular man. That question stayed with me a long time, and sparked this story, which is a tapestry of fact and fiction, though I have tried to remain true to history and the biographies of people the Blakes knew.

While not much is known about Kate, a great deal is known about her William: all his Letters, Poems, and Notebook entries in the story are authentic, and are taken with permission from David V. Erdman's edition of Blake's works, *The Complete Poetry and Prose of William Blake* (University of California Press, 1982). Other documents about Blake included here, such as Frederick Tatham's letters, are found in G. E. Bentley Jr.'s indispensable compilations: *Blake Records* (Oxford: Clarendon, 1969) and *Blake Records Supplement* (1988).

I am also indebted to Blake's first published biography, Alexander Gilchrist's *The Life of William Blake* (Macmillan, 1880), the recent evocative biography by Peter Ackroyd, *Blake* (Sinclair Stevenson, 1995), and Joseph Viscomi's *Blake and the Idea of the Book* (Princeton,

1993). Although my novel was written before I read G. E. Bentley Jr.'s magisterial *The Stranger from Paradise: A Biography of William Blake* (Yale 2001), it enabled me to check on revision many details and the accuracy of family names of Bouchers and Blakes, though much about the Bouchers is invention.

Mary Wollstonecraft's first letter from France is authentic, though it was not sent to the Blakes. Other of her letters are imagined or a pastiche of some she had written. My main sources here are Claire Tomalin's admirable biography, *The Life and Death of Mary Woll-stonecraft* (Weidenfeld & Nicolson, 1974 and Penguin, 1992) and William Godwin's *Memoirs of the Author of a Vindication of the Rights of Woman* (Richard Holmes, ed., Penguin, 1987).

All of Kate's Notebook and Poems are imagined, as is the character Paul-Marc and the situations involving him. I have often capitalized nouns in Kate's story to suggest the atmosphere of eighteenth-century language. Kate really painted *Agnes* (from the novel *The Monk*, by Matthew Gregory Lewis in 1796), a watercolour she gave to Mrs. Thomas Butts in 1800. The picture is now in the Fitzwilliam Museum, Cambridge.

My special thanks:

To Fred Candelaria, friend and mentor from the beginning, and to Carol May Mahoney, who listened and read with unerring judgment. To Sally Stiles and Ian Slater for getting me started. To Alev Lytle Croutier, my first editor. To early and continuing reader, long-time colleague and friend, Eric Rump. To my dear friend, Myrna Cameron Elliott, who saw immediately what I intended to write and forgave what she did not approve. To Barbara McDaniel for meticulous advice on style, and to other members of my writing group: Tessa McGuinness, Tami and Michael Skog, and Dave Thomson, whose sensitive responses and great desserts add such pleasure to the writing life. To G. E. Bentley Jr., whose scholarship made this story possible, and whose friendship has long been valued. To Kelly McKinnon, Gwyn and Joan James, Eileen Spencer, Nelson Hilton, Carolyn Warner, and Judith Wardle, for friendship, advice and support. To Dr. M. Trembath and my daughter, Renée Warner, for midwifery advice. To the editors of *Blake/An Illustrated Quarterly*, Morris Eaves and Morton D. Paley, and managing editor Sarah Jones, for running an excerpt from the book on their Web site for several months. To my wonderful agent, Charlotte Gusay, and her team in Los Angeles, particularly Melissa Herr for an outstanding critique. To my perceptive editor, Diane Reverand. To my husband, John Pelham Warner, who has been my steadfast friend all my adult life. This book is dedicated to him, and to the memory of my brother, Donald E. Jabour.

And I especially salute the spirits of those remarkable men and women who lived two hundred years ago, and allowed me to give them imaginary existence in these pages.

Janet Warner
Aldergrove, British Columbia
July 2003